THE BARBARIAN KING

BOOK THREE

THE BARBARIAN KING

The Adventures of Cassandra Rho

PHILLIP MARTIN

Published 2024

Printed in the United States of America

ISBN: 979-8-9873344-8-5 (Hardcover)
ISBN: 979-8-9873344-6-1 (Paperback)
ISBN: 979-8-9873344-7-8 (eBook)

Cover design by Daniela Ivanova
Map art by Shaun Carroll
Edited by Fabled Planet
Design and layout by Teddi Black Design

For information, address:
Phillip Martin
Phillip@cassandra-rho.com
www.cassandra-rho.com

Books in The Adventures of Cassandra Rho Series:

A Witch Is Born
The Quest For Zolmex
The Barbarian King
The Awakening (coming soon)

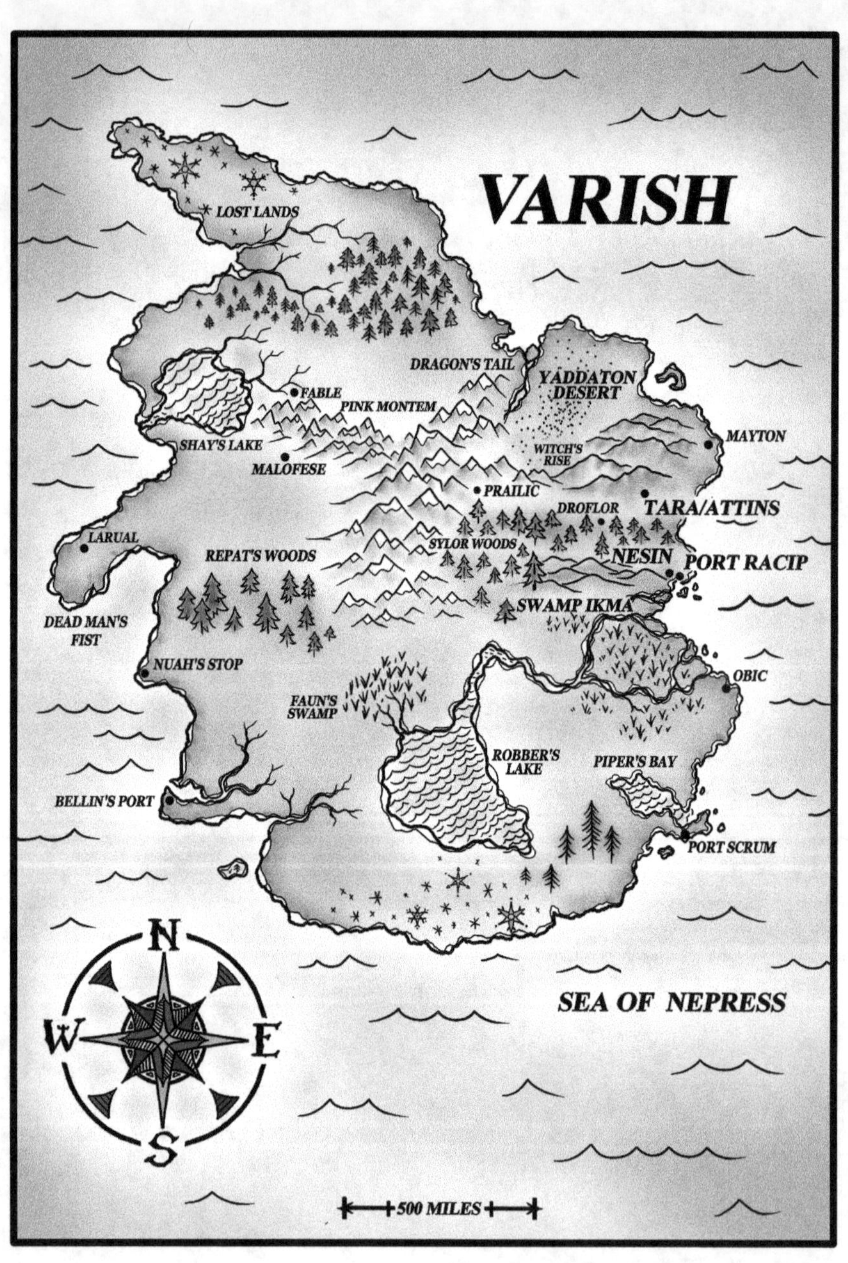

VARISH
LOST LANDS
DRAGON'S TAIL
YADDATON DESERT
FABLE
PINK MONTEM
SHAY'S LAKE
MAYTON
WITCH'S RISE
MALOFESE
PRAILIC
DROFLOR
TARA/ATTINS
LARUAL
REPAT'S WOODS
SYLOR WOODS
NESIN
PORT RACIP
DEAD MAN'S FIST
SWAMP IKMA
NUAH'S STOP
OBIC
FAUN'S SWAMP
ROBBER'S LAKE
PIPER'S BAY
BELLIN'S PORT
PORT SCRUM
SEA OF NEPRESS
N
W   E
S
500 MILES

CONTENTS

PROLOGUE

T HE CAROFEXIAN PRIEST, PRESIN, MADE HIS WAY THROUGH THE bright ice castle he and his fellow priests called home. Located in the icy world of Glacies, the palace, known as Iciale, was one of the more prominent structures the carofex had built. Glacies was home to many magical creatures, including snow dragons and ice creatures that could freeze humans in the blink of an eye. However, carofex, although similar in appearance, were not human and could not only live among the ice creatures but could control the ice just as easily.

Old by carofex standards, the priest walked briskly through the frozen halls, ignoring the other carofex that greeted him. His white robe hung with icicles, making him sound like a walking chandelier as he approached the part of the palace in which the high priest, Clade, resided. His news could not wait, and he needed to inform his master of the most wonderful information he had discovered. News that would change his position in the castle. If his lead was correct, Clade would finally offer him a room on the top floor of Iciale, the one reserved for the most distinguished priests.

Two ice creatures moved to intercept him as he made his way to the giant steel doors that led to the top floor of Iciale. The creatures, known as dibolicies, or more frequently referred to as ice demons, were powerful indeed. That they were locked into servitude to the carofex only confirmed the power of the human-like race. Presin did not confront the creatures because even with his enormous control over ice, it was doubtful that he could defeat *one* of the ice demons in a battle, much less two of them.

He stopped and held his arms out to his sides as was customary, and the creatures approached. They were nearly eight feet tall, made entirely of ice, and almost transparent. Their red, beady eyes were the only thing that did not blend in with the icy walls, and alerted others to their presence. Shards of razor-sharp icicles lined their arms, which they used to hug their opponents and impale them during battle. Their strength was unmatched by most creatures in the world of ice, earning them much respect, especially by the carofex, who bound them to servitude only on rare occasions. But there walked Presin between the two of them and through the massive steel doors that opened into the most fantastic part of the palace.

Soon he found himself in Clade's chambers. The high priest dismissed the dibolicies, who bowed slightly and retook their positions guarding the portal. Clade's sitting room was magnificent, decorated with many treasures secured from his conquests. One shelf contained items, from magical helms, armor, and various weapons to horns and other instruments that looked priceless to Presin's old eyes.

"Please sit," Clade offered, with a hand outstretched to a chair made of ice that seemed molded to the floor.

Presin sat and waited as the high priest fixed a beverage from the bar across the room. Clade wore a much fancier robe with many intricately etched symbols. Most of those symbols were related to the carofex goddess, Censah. Others offered the high priest various protections from magical and physical attacks. Clade appeared unprotected, but those aware of his status knew that to be an illusion. It had been nearly a year since Presin had visited the room, and much had changed, including the owner. He now seemed more powerful.

"So, why have you come to me, Presin?" Clade asked, handing him an icy beverage and breaking his thought.

"Pardon the sudden interruption, but I have come with exciting news," Presin explained, taking his frosty mug and gulping down the alcohol within.

Clade sat opposite his visitor and similarly drank from his mug.

"I have been studying the carofex of the human world," Presin continued.

"Yes, not so strange, considering I asked you to keep an eye on the monastery there," Clade answered, seeming annoyed.

"There is activity in the monastery; the fools once again have awakened a freld," Presin explained, on the verge of jumping from his seat.

"The freld named Menji?" Clade asked, referring to the creature of fire that the fire carofex called an ally.

"The same."

"They summon him occasionally; what is so interesting this time?" Clade prodded, seeming to lose patience and possibly his complete attention.

"Nothing, except my spy there has learned of movement in Novafontera," Presin said with a wide smile.

"Novafontera? The rotting city?"

"Yes, and as my spy followed the carofex from Mecca-Loraine, he was sidetracked by emanations from the city. So, he investigated and found the calling—" Presin tried to explain.

"Show me your spy at once!" the high priest interrupted, sitting straight in his chair and tossing his mug to the floor.

Presin could not hide a smile as Clade began assembling the information. He reluctantly reached into his pocket and found his spy, pulling it out gently and displaying it in his uplifted palm. The creature, a creation of pure ice mixed with a dose of priestly magic, rose slowly in Presin's palm. It stood no more than three inches tall and was perfectly human-like, except for the wings that sprouted from its back. It had taken Presin three months of prayer and thousands in gold invested in rare materials to assemble the tiny spy. The creature was see-through, like the dibolicies. It looked to Presin, immediately sending a telepathic link.

I am ready to serve, it imparted to Presin, its master.

"An ice spirit?" Clade asked.

"Yes, Clade, a creation from our lady Censah."

"As well as a piece of your spirit, correct?" Clade asked with a smirk.

"Yes, of course," Presin replied, the smile melting from his face.

It had taken him a very long time to create the little spy, and in doing so, it had cost him a small fortune and a piece of his essence. Making an ice spirit was no small feat, especially for a priest of Presin's standing. Clade meant to destroy it, Presin reasoned. Doing so could lead to the artifact

Clade sought and, in turn, a promotion in the castle to a lifestyle desirable by any reasonable carofex. Presin would make that sacrifice.

"Master Clade, he found the sword—"

Clade held up a hand to cut him off. "No, do not tell me. I will see it for myself."

"Yes, master," Presin said, lowering his head and raising his hand toward the high priest, offering him his most divine creation.

The tiny ice sprite turned to look toward the high priest, not understanding what was taking place. "Do not be afraid, little one; you have served your master well. Now let me see what you have seen," Clade whispered.

He took the little sprite, pinching its tiny wings between his thumb and forefinger. It panicked at first, but Presin sent soothing telepathic messages not to be afraid, even though it was about to be destroyed. He looked up when he heard the sprite's squeals of fear just in time to see Clade slip it in his mouth. The tiny creature pleaded for help, but Presin just sat there as Clade rolled it around his tongue, melting it, and eventually killing it. By savoring the sprite's essence, he would see images of what it had seen in the human world.

He looked at the lesser priest, his eyes still wide, then opened his mouth and released an icy breath, showering his floor with the remnants of the sprite.

"A great and powerful demon has invaded Novafontera." Clade spoke calmly.

"Yes, mighty indeed."

"And this filth has stirred something in the castle's bowels?"

"Yes, master, the sword," Presin answered, the smile returning to his face, the pain of losing his sprite fading.

"Iustia," Clade whispered.

"Yes, the lost Sword of Justice carried by the paladins of the New Order over six hundred years ago!" Presin answered excitedly.

A large smile found its way to Clade's lips, which was unusual for the high priest. If they could obtain the lost sword and add it to the growing collection of artifacts in Iciale, his reputation would precede him. He would become the most potent carofex in the world of ice.

Clade turned to Presin and said, "Retrieve it."

Presin fell back into the icy chair and blanched at the thought. "Master, I cannot. I dare not travel to the human world."

"Is it still winter there?" Clade asked, ignoring the man's groveling.

"No, late autumn, but close. There is snow on the ground."

"So, you can travel there?"

"Yes, but—"

"Not you, fool!" Clade said, standing over the sniveling priest.

"Then who?" Presin asked, now very confused.

"Have you forgotten your charge so easily?"

Presin thought for a moment before realizing to whom he was referring. He had left the girl at a young age in the bowels of Iciale. How long had it been, ten, maybe fifteen years ago? He had lost track of her and cared even less.

"The ugly one?" he asked.

"Yes, the half-human who you left to rot away in the dungeons," Clade responded, taking his seat once more and folding his hands in front of him.

"I don't know if she is even alive. How could she accomplish this task, master?" Presin asked in confusion.

"Fool, I have kept an eye on her; she is more valuable than you know."

The proclamation startled Presin, and he fell back in his chair again. Master Clade had been watching over his charge, the ugly half-human, half-carofex his sister had birthed.

"I am confused, master. How can the girl help?"

"She is skilled with a sword, more than any carofex I have witnessed. If you can get her there and reach the sword, she can use its power to slay the demon."

"What if she fails?"

Clade smiled and sat up in his chair. "That is your problem. See that she does not."

Presin swallowed hard and nodded slowly. Clade escorted him out with assurances that he would obtain station in the highest level of Iciale upon successfully retrieving the sword. The possibilities of what the future held dangled in front of him like a carrot, and his first order of business would be to visit his ugly niece and determine how the half-breed could benefit them in the quest. He slept little that night.

Early the following day, Presin found himself at the entrance of the bowels of Iciale, having a heated discussion with the gatekeeper. "I told you already, her name is Sasha De'Formen; she is my niece," he repeated to the obtuse man.

The gatekeeper studied his book again, shaking his head. "I have no record of such a person imprisoned here. So, what was her crime?"

"Fool! She committed no crime. She is hideous, an abomination to our grand palace. I locked her away when she was but a child so that we would not have to look upon her," Presin explained.

"Wait, did you say she is ugly?"

"Hideous," Presin insisted, hoping that the imbecile recognized who Sasha was.

"Does she wear a mask of ice and fight with the gladiators of the dungeons?"

The words stunned Presin and he creased his brow; he had heard nothing of his niece being a gladiator. And as ingenious an idea as an ice mask sounded, he was not responsible. But, on the other hand, if the guard was correct and she was a gladiator, perhaps Sasha would be qualified to retrieve the lost sword.

"Priest?" the gatekeeper asked after several moments of silence.

"Yes, that is her, my niece."

"Very well; she is at the bottom cell level. Just ask any of the guards there." The gatekeeper signaled the guards to open the door.

Immediately, the smell assaulted him. Presin put a hand to his face, covering his nose and mouth as he stepped through the portal. Two guards met him there as the door closed behind him.

They noticed his discomfort and shared a smile. "Don't worry; it only gets worse the farther down you go," one of them said.

"What is that foul smell?" Presin asked, not recalling the odor being a part of the place when last he had been there.

"Mostly sewer," one answered.

"Yeah, mixed with the stench of the vile creatures imprisoned here," the other added.

Presin nodded and stood there gazing down the passage that sloped downward in front of him. There was no light there, and one guard handed him a lantern. The walls appeared made of stone instead of ice as the upper levels. He stood there for a long while, until one of the guards asked, "Would you like a dibolicie escort?"

"What? No, of course not; I am a priest of Censah and require no escort," Presin informed the arrogant guardsman.

In truth, he would have taken one, not knowing what awaited him. However, he was Presin, priest of Iciale, powerful and unafraid. So he advanced, leaving the fools behind him. But unfortunately, they were correct concerning one issue: the stench grew stronger and stronger the further he traveled. He walked for some time, passing intersections with more guards and doors and asking directions to the lowest level.

Eventually, he arrived, but not before nausea had taken hold in response to the stench. Had his niece lived down there the last dozen or so years? The other priests wanted to murder Sasha when she was born. He had saved her by putting her down there at the age of five, but would anyone call this a life? Either way, he had allowed her to live, even if it was miserable.

A guard escorted him down the final stretch. The uneven stone floor was hazardous enough, but metal bars lined the sides of the passage, forming cells filled with various creatures and criminals. The place repulsed him, so he was relieved when they finally reached Sasha's cell. The guard banged on the cell door and called into the darkness, "Ugly One, you have a visitor."

There was no response, and Presin stepped back, feeling the danger from within that dark cell.

"Don't make me open this door; I will see that you have no playtime for the next month of moons. Now show yourself, Ugly One," the guard said.

At first, nothing happened, and the silence was palpable. Then, as the guard lost his patience and reached for his keys, a slender female figure entered the light offered by Presin's lantern. She walked to the bars, standing close to them so Presin could see her. A helmet of pure ice covered her face, save for her eyes and mouth. She was quite pitiful in appearance, but that didn't seem to affect the guardsman.

"That's a good girl. I'll leave you two alone. When finished, Priest, walk back to my station, and I will open the gate for you," the guard instructed, then walked away, leaving Presin alone with his niece.

Presin just stood there, looking over the young woman before him. Indeed, too much time had passed, and the little girl he had left there all those years ago was no longer a girl. Thankfully, the ice helmet covered her face, and he could only vaguely make out her ugly features through the thick ice. Her eyes and mouth were visible, but they did not reveal the grotesqueness of her features. It became apparent how such a mask would benefit those who had to tolerate her presence.

"What?" she asked softly, breaking him of his thoughts.

"Sasha? Is it truly you?"

"Sasha? There is no one here by that name. My name is Ugly One," she answered, gently laying her ice-covered face against the bars.

"No, woman, remember when you were but a child? I brought you here to live."

"My uncle left me here long, long ago."

"Yes, I am your uncle. I am the one who left you," Presin said excitedly, stepping closer to the bars.

"Uncle?"

"Yes."

She turned away from him, revealing the back of the ice mask so that he could see it encased her entire head. "I have no uncle," she whispered.

"Not true, Sasha. I have returned to commission your release. I am here to set you free!" he exclaimed, holding his arms grandly.

Sasha remained motionless and silent.

"Sasha, did you not hear me? I, Presin, your uncle, am giving you a chance at freedom."

"I heard you," she said softly. "Why do you wish my release after all these years, Uncle?"

She slowly turned back around, her ice mask rubbing against the bars, making an uncomfortable scraping sound. Presin looked on disgustedly—the tiny woman appeared like a broken wretch. How could she be the grand warrior at which Clade hinted?

A question came to him suddenly. "Who makes you wear the mask?"

"Why do you care?"

"To be honest, I don't. However, I would like to know who has done this to you so that I may properly punish or congratulate that person as I see fit," Presin answered, his lips curling into a smirk.

Sasha just glared at him for a moment and finally sighed. "An evil man, just like you."

The arrogant smile slowly left his lips, replaced with a stare at the defiant, bold young woman. "You are making a serious misjudgment with your actions, Sasha. Remember, I am your only hope of ever leaving this filthy place. Unless, of course, you wish to remain here."

He stepped up closer to the bars and put his face near hers so that he could whisper. "I have no love for you, dear niece, so humor me, or I will walk away, and you can call this sewer your home for the rest of your days. Is that what you want?"

Sasha looked at him, her lips quivering and her hands wringing the bars of her cell. Tears welled in her large, blue, human-like eyes. Eventually, she lowered her gaze to the floor and slowly shook her head.

"Good, then tell me who ordered this most wonderful mask," he taunted, daring to rub the back of it as her head remained lowered.

"A man named Clade."

The weight of that answer indicated Clade knew much more about this woman than Presin did. Suddenly, she grabbed his hand tightly and pleaded with him. "Please, Uncle, let me out of here. I'll do anything!"

He pulled his hand from her grasp and wiped it on his priestly robe in disgust. "Never touch me again. Do you understand? I'll have to burn my robes now!"

"Yes, Uncle," she whispered, again lowering her gaze.

"Good. If you are so eager to leave this place, you must perform one task for me. There is a sword of great importance to Iciale—"

"Iciale?"

"Yes, this very palace you live in," he explained, holding his arms out wide.

They looked slowly at their surroundings, and Presin quickly dropped his arms. "Well, not here, but above the dungeon level. It is a remarkable place."

"If you say so."

"Do not back-talk me, girl. If I say it is so, then it truly is," he yelled louder than he intended. When several creatures in nearby cells answered his words with snarls and yelps, he drew closer to his niece again. "I need you to retrieve a sword, and in doing so, you will escalate the standing of our family."

"Standing?" she asked skeptically.

He grew tired of the game. He wanted to leave the stench of the dungeon, and the sooner the better. Her cooperation would make that a reality.

"Listen closely, Sasha, for I will ask you only once. I need you to travel to the world of the humans and retrieve the sword known as Iustia. If you bring it back, I promise your release from here," he lied, having no such power. Adding to his empty promise, he said, "Also, I can free your mother if you succeed."

The mention of her mother had Sasha perking up. "She is alive?" she asked excitedly.

"Of course," he lied.

Sasha's mother had experienced a most painful death shortly after Sasha was born. Not even Presin could stop the execution of his sister for whoring with a human.

"Yes, I will do it!" Sasha answered. "When do I start?"

The arrogant smirk came across his face again, and he whispered, "Patience, my niece. I will send for you tomorrow and fill you in on all the beautiful details."

Presin left soon after, wanting nothing more than to be far away from her and the stinking dungeon. His ugly niece now faced a dangerous mission that Presin knew would probably result in her death. On the other hand, if Clade's views concerning her fighting prowess were accurate, she might be able to pull it off. But either way, the hideous girl would need to die. If the mission didn't kill her, Presin would see to it afterward. After all, he could not suffer a blood relative such as Sasha to live once he was a high priest of Iciale.

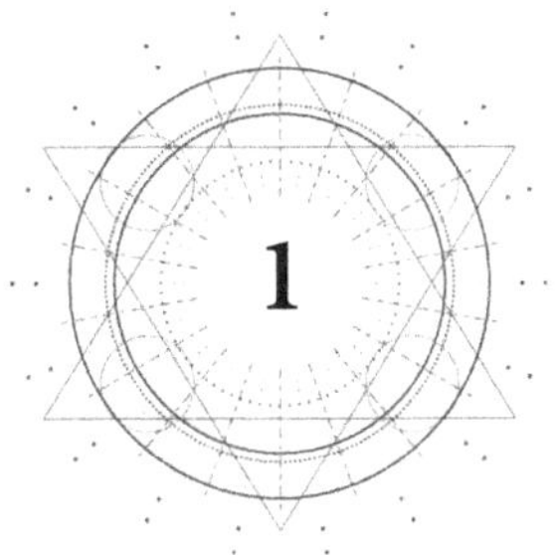

SLEIGHT OF FLAME

LYNNA WALKED BRISKLY FROM HER SMALL APARTMENT ON THE south side of Pelesea, the peaceful harbor city that Kringus and Penelope Brahmore ruled. It was late autumn, and although the temperature had warmed the last few days, she still felt the cold bite of the evening breeze under the new dress her mother had made for her. The young girl was on her way to her uncle's home, who lived just a few blocks away. Although she was only fifteen, her parents allowed her to walk the short distance to her uncle's house because crimes were minimal in Pelesea. In addition, her uncle had become ill in recent weeks, and she helped him each night, fixing him dinner and cleaning his home. Her mother allowed her to do so only after completing her school work. Therefore, it was late and already dark when she left the house.

She felt perfectly safe walking alone in Pelesea. She had walked the streets the last ten years, traveling six blocks from the tiny apartment where she and her parents lived to school and back. Pelesea was one of the safest cities known to exist, with the king and queen striving to keep all civilians safe and poverty-free. Granted, Lynna and her folks lived in the city's poorest part, but even that was usually safe and crime-free. In her excitement to reach her uncle's home, she didn't notice the predator in the nearby alley observing her.

Boz watched the girl walk swiftly past the alleyway. He had monitored her for the last few weeks and decided she would be the centerpiece of his diabolical plans. Of course, he didn't want to harm the girl; she and her family appeared to be upstanding citizens. But he was not there to find good people; he was there to find Cassandra Rho. And although Lynna was nearly five years younger than Cassandra, her body frame matched Cassandra's and, therefore, was a necessary tool for his plans.

Lord Ronnis D'Breeth had hired him to find Cassandra and bring her back to Mecca-Loraine. Boz was born in that small town, calling the Brotherhood of Fire Monastery his home. He was a carofex, a race that could control the element of fire. His brotherhood was attuned to it, and he could control flames as easily as he could kill someone with his bare hands. His monastery was the only one in that part of the world, and it had gained a grand reputation. People were not only intimidated by the carofex that dwelled in Mecca-Loraine but were also suspicious of them. Boz liked it that way; it made his line of work more manageable.

Others frequently hired his brothers as mercenaries or to find and retrieve people who wished to remain unfound. So, when the wealthy and desperate, such as Lord Ronnis, came calling, the carofex eagerly answered. Boz had made his way to Pelesea, hidden safely in plain sight of King Kringus, whom he met and befriended in Oldorburg, Cassandra's home town. Kringus and his men had been under attack, and Boz had conveniently shown up to assist in the conflict, using it to get close to Kringus. Boz had fought alongside the king, ensuring his victory. Naturally, Kringus had invited him to travel back to Pelesea after Boz explained his monastery was studying the Rho girls, Cassandra and Kessi. Since Cassandra was in Pelesea, Kringus had offered for Boz to travel with him and his men to repay his work in Oldorburg.

Boz had played the part perfectly, gaining the king's complete trust, and now as his plan came to fruition, he sighed. Perhaps the tasks were too menial for him, for they had become easy of late. Nevertheless, he shook the troubling thoughts from his head and focused on the task at hand. He had never failed a mission and was not about to start with this one.

On the other side of the great city, near the castle itself, were the massive docks of Pelesea. Nearly forty priestesses of the goddess Sinnis boarded a large cargo ship, unpacked, and settled in for the long journey across the ocean to the volatile lands of Varish. Led by the stunningly beautiful young priestess, Alleah Mansuell, they prepared the empty hull to be their home for the foreseeable future. Their purpose: to investigate the tragedy that had befallen the tiny village of Tara. Alleah feared that Gorl, the opposing god to Sinnis, was behind the raid that had killed all inhabitants of that place, save for one. Greyson Kavince was that survivor, and he had escaped with his life to Pelesea a few months earlier. Now, he prepared to travel with the contingent of priestesses back to his old home to dig up the memories of a past life. The attacks on Tara had left his friends and family murdered. Alleah hoped that Greyson would provide a plethora of information after exploring the ruined village.

Binta Mulay stood on the dock with Greyson after Alleah and the other priestesses had boarded the ship. The deckhands scurried around the couple, preparing the boat for sail. She looked into Greyson's eyes one last time before he set sail. He was her most fantastic lover, and they had been inseparable the last few months since they had met. She loved him dearly and knew he loved her just as intensely. She dreaded the trip he was about to take—the void of losing Cassandra Rho was still fresh. Cassandra, her best friend and love interest, had been imprisoned by the king for treason nearly a month earlier. Since then, Binta had struggled to find happiness, knowing that Greyson was intent on leaving her to travel to Tara. The day she had feared had finally come, and she didn't know if she could see it through. All she had was Greyson, and he was sailing far away.

Binta had met Greyson at about the same time she started falling romantically for Cassandra. She hadn't intended to be involved with the young man; she had focused her thoughts on Cassandra at the time, but Greyson was charming, attractive, and confident. She soon discovered he was also an excellent lover. He had exploited their newfound relationship, letting his lust for Cassandra get the best of him. Once he found out Binta had feelings for Cassandra, he desired a strange sexual relationship that entailed the three of them. Binta had been a willing participant if it did not harm Cassandra. After Cassandra discovered the ill-advised charm spell Greyson had cast on her, she rejected him in no uncertain terms. And so, the strange romantic relationship the three shared was on hold. Furthermore, Cassandra was being held prisoner by the king, with no visitors allowed, which made the potential tryst seem a very distant memory.

Binta had not seen or heard from her friend since her imprisonment. Her joy at having Cassandra in her life and the intrigue Greyson offered by wanting to include her in their sexual affairs had made her blood boil and had given deep meaning to her life. The possibilities had Binta tingling with excitement. But Greyson's foolish charm spell had stopped that, and Cassandra's treasonous threats toward the king had landed her in jail. The world had quickly changed over the last month, and Binta did not like it.

The ship's deckhands pulled up the boarding planks, leaving one for Greyson, a sign that his goodbye had ended. Binta looked one last time into his eyes, her own filling with tears. Her heart raced; she did not want him to leave. Now was the wrong time for him to go, and she tried not to make him feel guilty. He had a duty to his god, Plath, and to all the priestesses of Sinnis currently waiting for him on the large ship. Most importantly, he needed to make the trip for his peace, to say goodbye to his dead friends so he could let go of his past. She understood and supported him, but that didn't make the goodbye any easier.

"I wish you were not going," Binta said honestly.

"Yes, me too, my love. I wish you were going with me, but do not fret, for I shall return in short order," Greyson assured her.

"It has been three weeks since they jailed Cassandra. Once you leave, I shall be truly alone," Binta answered, wiping the tear off her cheek as she struggled to remain strong.

"You will be fine, my love," Greyson reassured her. "Grow the temple in my absence, and fully give yourself to Plath."

"Dear priest, it is time," one of the deckhands said from behind him, waiting to pull the last plank.

Greyson nodded to him and turned back to Binta. He kissed her forehead and hugged her tight. "Do not fear for Cassandra, and indeed not for me. Plath protects me. I feel that upon my return, the three of us shall share a bed as once was our plan."

Binta looked up to meet his gaze, feeling that all-too-familiar pang of lust with the thought of sleeping with Cassandra. Given the circumstances, the feeling was fleeting and soon replaced by the fear of being alone. She was fragile, and it broke her heart to say goodbye. And yet, as the deckhand had said, it was time. Greyson hugged her tightly once more, then turned and boarded the ship. He stayed at the rail, smiling confidently, and she returned that smile the best she could. But, on the inside, she was dying.

Binta kept her gaze on the dock as the massive chain pulled the anchor from the water. She had attended one semester at Victoria's School of Magic and had learned little. Now she was an acolyte of Plath, a god she barely knew. As she lifted her head to watch Greyson leave, Binta understood that she loved Greyson and Cassandra equally. She needed them both but had neither.

She felt a great emptiness; she felt alone. She had been a loner most of her life, but she had fallen in love after meeting Cassandra and sharing that first special kiss with her just months earlier. She truly loved them both and desperately needed them now. Greyson had insisted that she quit Victoria's school and become a priestess of Plath. She reluctantly agreed and now had no plans to attend the spring semester when Victoria's school opened again. Instead, she would live at the temple and continue building the church Greyson had begun in his short time in Pelesea. Her heart was not in it, but it was Greyson's wish, and she loved him, so she would see it through.

"Binta?" Greyson's words interrupted her thoughts.

She watched him lean over the rail and wave as the ship began to leave the docks. "I will return, I promise!" he yelled.

The boat was taking Greyson away and the rest of her broken heart with it. She did not cry until he was out of sight. Instead, she stood stubbornly on the dock and waved. Then, once she could no longer see him, she turned and made her way to the temple, sobbing the entire way.

Matilda had paid Malikai handsomely to teleport her to Pelesea. She had urgent business in the city, fearing that the great demoness, Vasheba, was set on murdering Cassandra Rho. If that happened, Matilda's dreams of world conquest would end. She had to reach Pelesea quickly and had paid Malikai to send her there. The price was high and the same fee as always—two days full of sex.

She usually did not mind paying; he was an excellent lover. However, her task was more urgent than usual, and the delay had her more than a little anxious. Still, the stubborn wizard had insisted on payment in full before performing the powerful teleportation spell, and Matilda had no choice but to comply. Finally, he cast his magic, and soon after, he and Matilda found themselves in a small room of a nondescript inn on Pelesea's south side. They arranged for Malikai to stay in the city until Matilda found her prey, instead of returning to his home in the Yaddaton Desert. Once found, the old wizard promised to teleport her and Cassandra directly to Nesin, Matilda's fortified cavern home on the other side of the world. But, of course, that came with a price, one she had to pay in advance.

Malikai's room, which Matilda learned he had purchased for such occasions, was in Poppy's Inn, and he had purchased it from the owner years ago, making an offer the man couldn't refuse. Now it would serve as Matilda's headquarters in her quest to find Cassandra. He explained that he owned the room and had similar rooms in most large cities in which to teleport safely to. The room was unremarkable, and Matilda surmised the cost was low for the wizard. That didn't deter him from demanding his payment for remaining in Pelesea.

Soon she found herself bent over the bed, Malikai behind her, collecting his payment. Matilda was tired and eager to find Cassandra, but sex with Malikai was not unpleasant, so she closed her eyes and enjoyed the moment until he pulled her hair back hard, lifting her head from the pillow. There in front of her was the mirror that Malikai had created for such an occasion. She tried to recall if the mirror was there when they had arrived. She did not remember Malikai setting it up, but there it was, just a few feet from her face. She was ashamed at what she saw, her head pulled back and Malikai smiling. She did not like giving that power to him, and the mirror only worsened it.

"Call to him," Malikai demanded. Matilda could only respond with a low moan as he quickened his pace.

"Call to him," the old wizard repeated.

Matilda looked into the mirror and admired her lover's reflection. He was old for a human, with a long grey beard, and she estimated he was at least twice her age. Yet his physique was that of a young man. His rock-hard abs were visible in the mirror, just below the tip of his pointed beard. She greedily consumed his perfect body with her eyes while he used her. He smirked and nodded to the mirror. She stared at her reflection, an expression of pure ecstasy plastered across her face. Strands of her sweaty hair that were not tangled in his fist hung down her face and bounced to the rhythm of their lovemaking.

"Call," he said once more.

"Cerus," she finally called to her husband, too wrapped up in the throes of lovemaking to resist her lover's demands.

The mirror began to shift as a fog swallowed her reflection, leaving a swirling grey mist in its wake.

"Again," Malikai demanded, smacking her hard on the backside.

"Cerus!" she yelled then, her body betraying her.

The mirror fogged more before eventually clearing and showing her a new image. She no longer saw her reflection. Instead, it was replaced with the view of her quarters in Nesin, where the twin to the mirror stood. An empty chair sat in front of the mirror in a private part of her room. Cerus, her jealous and most dangerous husband, came into view shortly after, answering the mirror's call and sitting in the chair—a frown on his face and a look just short of rage formed there. Matilda could see his neck muscles flex at the disturbing scene, yet he said nothing. She knew he was a very jealous man but he also liked watching. That took her another step toward pure ecstasy.

"Tell him to whom your perfect body belongs," Malikai coaxed loudly enough for Cerus to hear.

"You," she whispered.

"Louder!" the wizard commanded.

"You!" she said, loud enough for Cerus to stir in his chair.

"Tell your fool husband the truth," Malikai demanded, smacking her backside hard enough to leave a handprint.

"My body belongs to Malikai, Cerus!" she screamed, nearing a climax.

"Who is the greatest lover you have ever known?" the old wizard asked, prodding her on, enjoying the humiliation Cerus endured.

"Greyson Kavince!" she screamed without thinking.

Her night with Greyson came flooding back to her then, and she remembered the intense lovemaking they had shared. Matilda was twice his age and yet, they had shared a night full of passionate sex; a night she would never forget. She had not planned on screaming out the young man's name. She knew what Malikai wanted and Cerus secretly wanted to hear. But to scream out Greyson's name caught her off guard. She could tell by her husband's reaction that it had also surprised him, and now his anger came to the forefront as she fell into the throes of an orgasm.

Cerus approached the mirror as if he might punch it, watching his wife give herself to the wizard he hated. Malikai dismissed the image with a wave and focused again on the task of pleasing Matilda. Once finished, he collapsed on the bed with her, breathing hard and very satisfied.

"Greyson Kavince?" he asked, folding his arms behind his head.

"A most excellent lover," she whispered, lost in thought.

After a brief silence, he finally responded, "A surprise choice, I assure you, but it still was enough to cause your pathetic husband discomfort."

"He will kill you for this," she whispered in all seriousness. "He hates this game you play, and Greyson is still a sore subject for his ego to endure."

"You are the one who mentioned this Greyson fellow."

"Yes, and it was unscripted, I assure you."

"So, he is your greatest lover?"

"Honestly, Malikai?" she asked, not wanting to wound his ego.

"Of course."

"He was," she said with a nod. "Cerus killed him, just like he will kill you."

"He will try, and at the end of that brief battle, I will add his great spear to my collection of magical trinkets, and you, my lover, will be a widow."

Matilda did not doubt his words, but her thoughts switched to Cassandra as she recovered from their lovemaking. There was work to do and little time to do it. She had delayed too long in the dull room, pleasing Malikai. As he dozed off, she rose and began to dress. It was time to go to work.

As the sun sank into the ocean that night, two powerful wizards arrived at Franklin Ruben's large manor, where he and his daughter, Cass, lived. Lady Victoria, head of the school of magic, and Baxter Von Glord, her close friend and one of the school's instructors, were shown in by a servant and waited patiently for Mr. Ruben. They had arrived to check on Cass, who was deathly ill, having been magically cursed while traveling on an ill-advised expedition with Cassandra, Greyson, and Binta a month earlier. Although Cass's life hung in the balance, and she was a current student at the school, Baxter could not stop thinking of his one true love, Cassandra Rho.

He had saved Cassandra from certain death twice now and had fallen madly in love with the young woman, although she was half his age. He had kissed her to break the tension between her and the king a few weeks earlier. His heart spurred the kiss, unscripted and natural. And since then, he had thought of little else. His thoughts betrayed him often when in the company of Victoria. She knew him better than anyone, so as they sat in Franklin's small greeting room, he focused on Cassandra and the life they would share once she was released from jail.

He would need to find a way to help her control her temper and stay out of trouble with the king. She was young and temperamental, and his age and wisdom would help her adjust. But first, she would need to be released, no easy task given the severity of her actions. He dwelled on the events of a few weeks ago with Kringus, and he knew Cassandra would be dead already if he had not stepped in. He had listened to his heart, and the kiss had been a natural reaction. As Cassandra's anger had boiled over with Kringus's failure to find her family, Baxter knew what a dangerous path she was taking. The only way to stop her that day was to kiss her, so he had.

Victoria clearing her throat broke his contemplations and snapped him back into reality. Soon he felt the familiar flush on his cheeks.

"We are here to see to Cass's needs, Baxter. I ask that you focus."

"Kringus refused my request for a meeting again this morning," Baxter complained, ignoring her words.

"He will not see you, Baxter. You are not impartial, and he does not want you to influence his decision concerning Cassandra's punishment."

"You could gain a meeting with him; you are part of the New Order, and he will see you if you request it."

"Baxter, we have been through this. I will not use my station to trick

Kringus into meeting with you. It would be best if you forgot Cassandra Rho; she is no longer a student at the school and is no longer our concern. Your focus currently should be on Cass Ruben only."

"I am in love with her." Baxter spoke softly, staring intently to measure her reaction.

"Oh, Baxter," Victoria said, sitting back in her chair with a sigh and shaking her head. "We have been through this before. It is inappropriate."

"No longer. She is not a student, so I see no problem with our love," Baxter argued.

"It is more inappropriate now than ever before. She threatened the king and now finds herself jailed. You should not be involved with a criminal."

"I will not let anything happen to her. I love her, Victoria."

"Love," Victoria said, and she shook her head once again. "The girl is volatile. You do not know if your feelings for her are reciprocal."

"It does not matter; I would die for her."

"Careful, my old friend, you may get your wish. Cassandra Rho is—" Victoria stopped suddenly as the servant returned.

"Lord Ruben instructed me to take you to Cass's room, where he awaits you," the servant said.

Victoria nodded grimly, and they followed the man through the large manor. Although he spoke nothing else of her, Cassandra remained at the forefront of Baxter's thoughts. He was worried for Cassandra because her life hung in the balance. Could he sit back and allow harm to come to her if Kringus decided it was warranted? Baxter knew what he would do if he found himself in that situation. Then he and Cassandra would both be outlaws. He was startled from his contemplations when they reached Cass's room. The sight that greeted them, as well as the smell, had him off balance.

Cass was a beautiful young woman, and Baxter remembered her as a vibrant and healthy girl. But unfortunately, her beautiful olive-colored skin was a sickening pasty white, and her lengthy, black hair matted to her sweaty face. She was shirtless and her bed filled with ice to try to break her fever. Her father had covered her breasts with a scarf gently draped across them, allowing Victoria and Baxter to easily access the mortal wound underneath her left breast. A bandage covered it, but blood and pus oozed around the edges and through the white cloth. Cass's breathing was labored and raspy, and both wizards knew immediately that the smell was the stench of rotting flesh. The girl was rotting away.

"The priests just left for the night. They placed the bandage only moments before you arrived," Franklin said, sitting in a chair next to the bed, stroking his daughter's hair.

Neither wizard could believe that the bandage was fresh, and they understood that the girl was beyond them. Her father looked as if he hadn't slept in a week, and that probably wasn't far from the truth. Baxter felt guilty about the amount of attention he had given Cassandra over the last few weeks while Cass was slowly dying. Seeing her made him realize how selfish he had been.

"What do the priests say about her prognosis?" Victoria asked, coming closer to examine Cass.

"The same thing they said a week ago. She is cursed, and the wound is beyond their healing."

"And you have summoned us to help in what way?" Victoria asked.

"Lady Victoria, I need you to dispel this magic that is killing her," Franklin answered, nearing tears. He grabbed his daughter's hand and stroked her knuckles lovingly. "She is weak; she is fading. I need your help."

"May I?" Victoria asked, pointing toward the wound.

"Please," Franklin answered, kissing Cass's hand.

Victoria gently pulled away the covering and gasped at the sight. The wound was deep, and the surrounding flesh was blackened with rot. Pus and blood constantly oozed from it. She looked back to Baxter, who met her gaze and slowly shook his head.

"Can you not help her?" Franklin asked, standing up with tears rolling down his cheeks.

"This is magic we cannot begin to understand. What happened to those who ventured into the mysterious cave is unexplainable," Victoria said, referring to the magical cave into which Cass had followed Cassandra.

"Do not fail me, Lady Victoria! I cannot lose her!" The large man was desperate and fell to his knees, grabbing Victoria's hand. "I cannot lose her as I lost her mother," he said more calmly, bowing his head and sobbing.

Victoria patted his back and let him hold her hand for comfort. She looked once more Baxter's way, and he could only shake his head, no answers evident.

"Let me go back to my tower and research this. The only hope is to find a scroll in my collection that may cancel this magical disease," Victoria said, trying to reassure the man.

Baxter gave her a curious look, knowing they had nothing to compete with the curse that had befallen the girl. But then he noticed that Victoria's eyes had changed. Instead of their bright blue, they had become cold and black, her pupils expanding to eliminate all the white. Baxter's jaw hung open, having seen the transformation before and knowing what was to come next. They needed to leave immediately.

Victoria pulled her hand away gently as Franklin held his head in his hands, sobbing uncontrollably. Baxter took her place next to him, patting his back and offering comfort as Victoria slowly backed away, the changes already taking effect on her body.

Baxter mouthed, *Go!* to her.

She covered her head with her cloak to hide her new features, especially the freshly sprouted horns on her forehead. Finally, she turned and fled the manor. Baxter could hear her rushing down the steps and a gasp from what he assumed was a servant. He needed to get back to her quickly, but looking at Cass's distraught father, he had a feeling it wouldn't be anytime soon.

As Victoria desperately made her way back to the tower before her morphing features betrayed her, Boz sat atop one of the many buildings on the south side of Pelesea. It was dark, with cold air rolling in from the ocean. It was a perfect night for what he had planned. Thus far, Boz had gained the king's trust, and if things went according to schedule, that trust would stay intact after his diabolical act. They would hail him as a hero instead of the criminal he indeed was. He intently watched the door for Lynna to exit her uncle's home. He expected her appearance at any moment, and his window of opportunity was slim. He had planned the attack for two weeks, and it was now that he intended to strike.

Once the door opened and the girl said her goodbyes, she quickly started home. She hugged her arms tight, trying to fight the chill of the autumn night air. She walked briskly with her head down and never noticed the dark figure of Boz drop silently behind her from the roof. It was dark, and nobody was about, and the carofex timed his arrival perfectly to grab Lynna from behind, cover her mouth, and pull her into the alley he had occupied earlier.

He kept her tight against him and pinned her arms to her side with only one of his. He maneuvered his other hand that covered her mouth so that it also covered her nose, cutting off her air supply. Her muffled screams carried little on the night wind that howled between the buildings. She struggled against him, but he was a carofex, physically perfect and robust. The girl had no chance to break his grip.

She bit his hand and freed one arm to scratch deep gouges in his forearm before he could restrain her again. He grimaced and willed away the pain that flared in his palm and waited patiently as the young girl slowly lost consciousness. Once her body went limp, he released his grip and caught her in one fluid motion before she hit the ground. He looked around to make sure no one saw. Then, satisfied that he was undiscovered, he carried Lynna to a nearby empty warehouse and quickly took her inside. He gently laid her down in a dark corner away from any windows, then produced several stones from his pocket. They were not ordinary but red firestones he had taken from the monastery.

He rubbed the firestones together in his hands and felt their warmth immediately. He looked around one last time to ensure no prying eyes were upon him, then called forth the magic of those stones. They grew hotter in his hands, so hot that a typical human's flesh would have melted from their bones. Not so for a carofex like Boz—the fire was his friend. The flames finally erupted from the stones, swirling in a blaze of yellow and orange, and still he felt no pain from the heat. He controlled the rocks just enough to open the small gate. There was no need to garner any unwanted attention. As soon as the flame reached six feet in height, he reached out to the world of fire and called forth his servant.

"My friend, it is time," he whispered into the flames.

The flames swirled and changed hues, from yellow to blue to orange to dark red, finally settling on an intense white. The heat from the fire was so strong now that he could slightly feel its bite, and Lynna moaned softly. A red, clawed hand reached slowly from the extra-dimensional fire and grabbed the girl's leg. Menji, the freld, a creature from the world of fire, answered to Boz and served him willingly. The demon-like creature was pleased to help cause such deception in the world of humans and gladly answered Boz's call.

Boz encouraged the creature. "Excellent. Take Cassandra to the designated meeting place, and I will be there in three weeks."

"Yes, my master," came the submissive response in a deep, grating voice.

Boz temporarily called forth more flames, widening the gate. It lasted only a moment, and the girl gained consciousness before the freld dragged her through. Boz knew the fire would consume her, so he quickly touched her forehead, bestowing a protective ward from fire temporarily upon her. One that would keep her from being roasted alive as his ally took her. She screamed briefly before the creature pulled her through, and Boz dismissed the flames. The ward would last just long enough for the freld to take her to Cassandra's cell. She would be dead shortly after.

He gained his feet and looked around to ensure there were no witnesses. Confident there were none, he left the old warehouse and began his journey to the jailhouse, located far on the city's northern side. He had just enough time if he hurried. He quickly moved from shadow to shadow, ensuring no one noticed him. The streets were empty, but he could take no chances. So far, the plan was working perfectly.

Cassandra sat in her cell in a meditative position, legs crossed in front of her and hands held out, palms up. Her eyes were closed, and her lips silently mouthed a prayer to her goddess, Gella. Of course, she had no idea it was early morning and most of Pelesea was asleep. Sitting in a windowless cell for so long will do that to a person, and she had lost track of time long ago. King Kringus was evidently struggling with his decision on what exactly her punishment should be. She found that very insulting since his delay in traveling to Oldorburg had directly led to her mother's death. Cassandra was not a criminal but was simply brave enough to voice Kringus;s failure. She wished Baxter had not stopped her that day by kissing her. Cassandra would probably have died, but her vengeance against the king would have prevailed. She knew she could have killed the king if Baxter had not interfered.

Her thoughts remained on her family: Sera, her mother, and Kessi, her twin sister. Both were now dead, her mother for sure, as Cassandra had viewed her cold, lifeless body. Kessi was missing, but Cassandra only assumed the worst for her. She also thought of Binta and Greyson and why they had not visited her. She believed the king forbade it as part of her punishment. Cassandra inquired of the guards almost daily when they brought her meals, the only time she saw another person.

The guards ignored her questions concerning the lack of visitors. She knew they were not allowed to give her any information. The lack of knowledge and the monotony of waiting was why she found herself praying in the early morning hours, finding the strength to attempt an escape. She had decided that the next meal delivered would provide the perfect opportunity for her attempt. After that, she would be free of the god-forsaken cell, or she would be dead. Either way, she would spend no more time in the lonely place.

She prayed and simultaneously allowed the mystical symbols to float around her mind, mixing with her call to Gella. She asked for the blessing from her goddess to carry out her escape, but she would undoubtedly need her magic to make it possible. Few knew she could cast spells and manipulate magic around her without using a spellbook or components. Their ignorance would guarantee her success. Ronnis D'Breeth had found out the hard way when she nearly killed him, and she planned to educate the next guard at her cell similarly. A simple jail cell could not contain her. She had stayed put, being a good prisoner and trying to sort out her feelings and long-term plans. No longer. The king's delay in releasing her had insulted Cassandra and made most of those decisions for her. It was time to act.

With her eyes closed and deep in prayer, she didn't notice the change in the lantern's flame down the hall. It was the only light source in the area, and it flickered and flared and quickly doubled in size, consuming the lantern. Cassandra's prayer was finally disturbed when the lantern fell from the wall and crashed to the floor. She opened her eyes with a jump and saw the hallway engulfed in flames!

Tyrus, a young guard of Pelesea, had been on duty that night, and when he heard the crash of the lantern, he was immediately alerted and prepared for anything unusual. After all, Cassandra was a fledgling witch, and that did not sit well with him. He rose to unlock the steel door that led to the prisoner cells and Cassandra. Before Tyrus even reached the door, he felt the immense heat emanating from it, and by the time he arrived, the door had already turned red. He could not get close to it, much less open it.

"Cassandra Rho!" he yelled toward the door. "Can you hear me?"

There was no response, and he stood frozen, not understanding if it was a magic trick the woman was using on him or if the place was on fire. Finally, when Cassandra began to scream, he sprang to action. It sounded as if she were being burned alive, and there was little doubt that was precisely what was happening. He ran out of the jail and rang the emergency bell attached to the corner of the building. Two nearby guards came rushing as a third hurried away to call reinforcements. They soon formed a bucket brigade from the jail to the docks and hurriedly passed the buckets of water. Unfortunately, most of the building was in flames by then, and Cassandra Rho's dying screams echoed through the streets.

"Do not hold out much hope, Mr. Ruben, for Cass's wound is grievous. I suspect Lady Victoria will find little that will help," Baxter said to Cass's father, who stared at his daughter, unblinking and unresponsive as if his world were crashing down around him.

Baxter had spent the last few hours at Cass's bedside, trying to comfort Franklin. The man had sobbed openly for quite some time, and Baxter felt that was his way of finally giving up, of recognizing he was going to lose his daughter. Baxter's mind drifted back to Victoria. She would be in her tower now, the transformation complete. He knew why the physical change overtook her, and he needed to be there for her. He had waited patiently with Mr. Ruben because it was the right thing to do, but it was time for him to leave.

He took one last, sad look over Cass, knowing that it would be the last time he would see her alive. She was young, not more than eighteen or nineteen, and had her whole life before her. He was genuinely saddened by her imminent death, especially seeing how it had affected her distraught father. He said goodbye, but Mr. Ruben hardly heard him and remained catatonic. He didn't want to leave the man, but he knew that if Victoria could find a way to save the girl, she would need his help. Also, she would be an emotional mess right now because of the involuntary transformation her body was undergoing. He had to go to her.

Baxter exited the manor and headed toward Victoria's tower. He vaguely noticed the faint smell of burning wood hanging in the air as his thoughts rested on Cass and Victoria. Then, a contingent of four guards rushed by, which gained his attention at the early hour. He turned to see them running toward the docks. There he noticed the chaos as it looked like a water brigade had formed, mixed with guards and a handful of city folk. Smoke hung thick in the air that way, and the brightness of a large fire danced on the ground. The various buildings hid the fire from view, but he knew it was in the general direction of the jail. And Cassandra! His heart skipped a beat.

Another set of guards came rushing his way, and he tried to stop one of them with a raised hand. "What is happening?" he asked.

The man did not stop entirely and backpedaled toward the docks, not having the time to chat. "The jailhouse is on fire!" he said. "Can you assist, good wizard?"

Baxter didn't answer, already spellcasting as soon as the words had left the man's mouth. The guard half-nodded, then turned and ran on. It was difficult for Baxter to concentrate on casting the spell, his mind thinking of Cassandra, his one true love. He could not let her die, so he summoned the magic he had used a month earlier to save her from the caves. He formed a tear in space, stretched the portal as far as he could toward the jail, and stepped through. The other side of his door took him to within a block of the burning structure, and his heart dropped immediately. The entire building was burning when he arrived, and the heat it produced had defeated the water brigade. He needed to do something quickly, so he ran toward the fire, casting one of his most potent spells as he did.

Cassandra knew something was amiss. She rose from her meditative pose and shielded her eyes from the flames, which continued to grow brighter. Cassandra could not sense magic in the area but knew it was not a natural fire, whatever the source. She watched in horror as the flames spread like water along the floor, some approaching her cell, but most of them climbing the door that separated her from the guardsmen. She understood then that her escape route was no longer an option.

She backed as far as she could into her cell as the slow-moving wave of fire crept toward her. The cell began filling with smoke, stinging her eyes, and the heat quickly overwhelmed her as wafts of smoke rose from her gown. She watched in horror as the fire started to take shape once it was in her cell. First, it became a pillar at least seven feet tall; then, it changed its hue to a bright white.

Her mind raced, thinking of some spell she could prepare. She had repeatedly tried to recreate Baxter's rift-door spell since they jailed her. It would allow her to move from one location to another, and it was the very one he had saved her life with at the mountain cave. She would have been free many weeks ago if she could have figured it out, but it was too complex to cast without some training. No spell she had available could help her; anything short of Baxter's door would be useless. And so, she watched and waited.

The pillar slowly opened, and a large, red-skinned creature stepped through. She imagined the creature that stood before her had to be a demon as its appearance was very similar to the pictures she had seen while researching the New Order back at Victoria's school. It stood seven feet tall, with two large horns sprouting from the top of its head and a barbed tail dancing behind it. It had a large mouth of fangs and clawed hands and feet. She did not understand why a creature such as the demon had invaded her cell. Her confusion only mounted when it dragged a screaming girl from the portal behind it.

She appeared to be no more than fourteen or fifteen, but Cassandra could not tell. She had no hair, all burned away by the fire, and her skin bubbled from the heat. She was melting from the intense fire. Cassandra tried to reach her as the demon tossed the poor girl to the floor. However, Cassandra could not bear the heat enough to do so and watched as the girl writhed in pain.

She tried to remain calm while patting out a flame on her gown that had jumped up on her shoulder. She backed herself to the far corner of the cell and silently called upon Gella to help her and the mysterious girl screaming on the floor. She closed her eyes and looked inward to her very soul. She felt peace immediately and somehow understood that Gella was with her. She was not a priestess, but she had pledged her life to Gella after her expulsion from Victoria's school. She had felt the goddess working within her those few weeks at the temple, but Gella's spirit filled her now—the goddess offered her power to combat her new foe.

She opened her eyes as a wave of soothing magic washed over her. It felt like Gella placed an invisible ward against the fire on her. As far as she knew, that was precisely what had just happened. Even her gown cooled at once, seemingly protected as well. At that moment, the demon-like creature seemed occupied with the cell door, so she ran to the girl. She reached her just as her screams subsided. She was horrified that the girl still struggled to move, but her eyes had burned away, and her lips bubbled. She tried to scream and speak, sensing Cassandra was with her. Cassandra looked on in horror and held the girl's hand as she passed into death. Cassandra said a quick prayer for the girl as she stilled.

The sound of the cell door clanging to the floor broke her concentration. She looked up and could only guess that the beast had knocked it from its hinges, giving a hint of its great strength. The door lay in the hallway, bent nearly in half. The creature turned and strode quickly toward her. She stood to face the nemesis and summoned a couple of energy spheres in her hands. They crackled with power, and she hoped they would at least affect the beast as she tossed them at it.

One hit it squarely in the face while the other slammed into its chest. It reminded Cassandra of how she had attacked Ronnis D'Breeth and nearly killed him with the same magic many months ago. Her skills were more powerful now, and a smile found its way to her face, knowing the spell had to hurt the thing badly. However, that smile was short-lived when it shook off the attack and looked at her with evil red eyes. She prepared to attack it again, but it pounced before she could summon the energy, and it was too fast for her to register the movement. It was almost as if it had flown the few remaining feet to close upon her. It grabbed her roughly by the throat and lifted her off the floor, bringing her face to face with it.

"What are you?" Cassandra asked, trying to pry open the powerful grip and kicking her feet in the air.

It smiled and touched a long, crooked finger to her forehead gently. She expected it to be an attack, but a wave of cooling energy washed over her. It was like Gella's protection but much more powerful. Now, she could feel none of the heat, as if she were immune to it. However, that did not keep the gathering smoke from stinging her eyes and sending her into a coughing fit.

The creature turned toward the extra-dimensional flame in the middle of the cell. She struggled to free herself, understanding that the thing was probably taking her to hell. She saw the motionless girl lying on the floor, her skin continuing to bubble and smoke, and she knew she could not let the creature take her through the flames. She would rather die in the cell than go through that gate.

She summoned the magic again and brought her hands forth to blast it in the face. She wanted to strike its eyes, a little trick she had learned from Greyson Kavince on their unsuccessful adventure a month prior. Unfortunately, the thing sensed her intent before she completed her spell, and its large hand slapped her hard across the face. She lost consciousness for just a moment, and in doing so, lost her thought process to summon the magical energy. She was vaguely aware that the creature walked through the portal, taking her with it. Before the demon dragged her through, her last thought was that she hoped Gella would still answer her call on the other side.

Boz had arrived at the burning building just before Baxter, cutting a path through the small gathering of people witnessing the spectacle. He played the part of a surprised passerby and gawked at the horrific sight. He did not hear Lynna's screams and understood his timing was perfect. Most likely, the young girl was dead. If not, she would be before he could save her. He began to strip.

Once naked, he rushed past the stunned guards, who struggled to get near the inferno. As a carofex, he was immune to most fires, magical or natural. However, the flames were straight from the land of fire, and he felt their bite. Not like Lynna had, of course, for the fire would consume any average human within moments. Instead, the flames felt slightly uncomfortable to him, with an occasional minor burn if he delved too deeply into them. He came to the door that led to the cells and could tell its integrity had weakened. The fire had made the metal extremely hot and would have melted the skin of anyone touching it. It merely felt a little warm to Boz. He focused his energy on a double punch, sending both fists hard into the door. It buckled but stubbornly held. He struck it twice more before it finally blasted from the hinges and fell away. Soon after, he found Lynna's corpse.

Boz exited the burning building with the husk of a corpse in his arms. He played the part perfectly, staggering and coughing as he appeared to struggle with the effort. He had allowed the fire to burn him slightly to make the impossible rescue more believable, his skin reddened in several places. When he was far enough away from the biting flames, he collapsed and willed his body to shut down, a talent only a carofex could achieve. To those witnessing him, it appeared he was unconscious.

Baxter had reached the jail about the same time his powerful spell was ready to cast. He released two large cones of ice from the palms of his hands and into the fire, which created a loud hiss and an abundance of steam. The gathered people stepped back as the scalding cloud licked at them. Baxter focused on the cells in the back of the jail where he suspected Cassandra to be. The icy substance melted as it touched the flames and produced ample water, which rained down upon the fire, slowly winning the battle. He could not tell for sure, but as he released his spell, he thought he witnessed a naked man run inside the burning building.

"Impossible," he whispered to himself.

He ignored the strange vision, assuming it was his mind playing a trick on him. Instead, he focused on battling the red-hot blaze with his conjured ice. A few moments later, a man carrying a badly burned person exited the still-burning jailhouse. He vaguely recognized the man as the carofex who had traveled to Pelesea with Kringus. The carofex was naked, and Baxter understood then that what he witnessed moments earlier was not an illusion; the carofex had run into the burning building. He had heard rumors from the elven brothers, Von and Lenore, that the man had a strange affinity for fire. Although the carofex's skin blistered in several spots and was a bright red, he was not nearly as injured as the woman he carried, the woman who Baxter knew without a doubt had to be Cassandra.

Baxter's heart broke and his magic faded, the ice slowly losing its force and eventually stopping altogether. He dropped his hands to his sides, no longer concerned with the fire.

Once the carofex had carried the corpse far enough from the burning building, he fell to his knees and gently placed the burned body, Cassandra's body, on the road before falling to the ground and losing consciousness. A few guards ran over to assist the man, who was burned but not severely. He was not injured badly for someone who had just run into an inferno. The guards gently rolled him over and covered his naked body. The carofex was in a semi-conscious state, moaning softly with the movement.

"Is he alive?" one guard asked.

"Yes, but we need to get him to the temple," the other reasoned.

They quickly gathered him up gently and carried him to a nearby wagon. Soon, it was moving toward the temple, taking the courageous young man to the priests for healing.

Baxter barely registered the action, his focus on the lifeless body of his beloved Cassandra. He eventually found the courage to move, and he staggered toward her, not taking his eyes off her badly burned and lifeless form. No one approached her, and he assumed that was for two reasons: one, they knew she was already dead; and two, she was a criminal in their eyes. Not to him; in his eyes, she was the one love that he had ever known. As he examined her still form, Baxter felt like he was in a dream. His heart ached at the sight of her. The burns were so bad, he couldn't even tell it was indeed her. Her skin was blackened and hung loosely from her bones. He put a hand on her charred face and just held it there.

She was hot, but he refused to remove his hand. It was his way of saying goodbye. She was gone, and he knew it, and that reality weighed on him as if a giant were pressing him down into the ground. He lost track of time, and his eyes welled with tears. He had failed her. Before their romance could even begin, this tragedy took her from him. Lying before him was a shell of empty promises, a future that now would take a different path. He wanted to die and didn't even realize a few guards were speaking to him until they moved to pick her up.

"Good wizard, we need to get her to the temple," one said quietly.

Baxter nodded but could not pull his gaze from the dead body of his love. He slowly removed his hand, and the guards moved to take her. Baxter didn't watch them go; he stared at the bare ground beside him where Cassandra had lain just a moment earlier. He might have stayed there for eternity if not for the horrific scream that broke him from his trance.

He turned to see a young woman who had just arrived being comforted by a few priests. The woman could not stand and knelt on the road, sobbing hysterically. He slowly rose and watched the unreal scene before him. It took him a few moments to realize that the young woman was Binta Mulay, a former student at the school and Cassandra's close friend. He knew she was close to Cassandra, and he felt her pain. If anyone could feel what he felt, it would be her. He moved to Binta and embraced her. She fell into his arms, crying hysterically. She repeated one thing over and over, and those words struck him like a bolt of lightning, and finally, he released his grief, tears flowing as he joined Binta in her despair.

Her words echoed in his head. *She's gone! She's gone! She's gone, Instructor Baxter, she's gone!*

He held her tight and listened to her heartbreaking words. He did not know how long he stayed with her, but he walked her back to the temple once they had played out their grief. Binta was so distraught that she leaned heavily on him and could barely stay upright. It took all his strength to keep her from toppling over. He looked back at the jail one last time to see the guards and city folk standing around it, watching it burn to the ground. It was gone, just like Cassandra.

The sun was high in the sky before Baxter left the temple the next day. He had tried to comfort Binta during the night. In truth, Baxter had needed her just as much as she had needed him. He had waited with her until she had cried herself to sleep. Once he was sure she was sleeping soundly, he reluctantly visited the temple morgue to confirm Cassandra had expired. It broke his heart to do so, but he viewed her remains one last time and said a tearful goodbye. He left the place with a broken heart.

He didn't remember walking to the tower that morning and only vaguely remembered Victoria's condition. When he arrived at her tower, he took a deep breath to steady himself, shook away his grief, and entered the hidden door, which only he and Victoria knew the location of. Once inside, he dispelled the many wards and golems and went to the top of the stairs. He saw no sign of Victoria there, and the doors stretching down the impossibly long corridor looked the same.

"Victoria, are you here?" he asked, his voice carrying down the long hallway and echoing for quite a while.

A door to the right opened, and he heard Victoria's voice call out, "I am here, Baxter."

He quickly went to the room and found Victoria standing in front of a full-length mirror, studying her features. Her transformation was complete now, including long sharp fingernails, large leathery bat-like wings, and a set of fangs to accompany her tiny horns and dark eyes. She smiled at the mirror, exposing her long canines, then quickly shut her mouth, smiling without showing her teeth. She spread her wings wide, engulfing a large part of the room. When she saw Baxter in the reflection, she quickly folded the wings and rushed to him, embracing him in a tight hug.

"I am sorry to hear of Cassandra," she whispered in his ear.

"You know of her passing?"

"Yes, I just found out this morning by an errand boy from the king. How tragic. I am so sorry." She pulled away and studied his face, obviously seeing the pain, then embraced him tightly once more.

"Why did this happen, Victoria?" he asked with a quiver in his voice.

"I have no answers, my friend, no more than how we can save Cass. Ultimately, it feels like all four people who ventured into the mountain are now cursed. It is almost as if the magic of the mountain didn't let them go and is destroying them one by one."

Baxter nodded, agreeing with her rationalization, then slowly moved to a plush chair and plopped down. He didn't realize until that very moment how exhausted he was. He considered Victoria's comments. Cassandra was dead, as hard as it was for him to believe that, and Cass would soon follow. Binta, now heartbroken, was in a very dark place, and he suspected her future would not be a happy one. Greyson had sailed out of the city with Alleah, possibly cursing that mission as well. Was the dark cloud from the mountain going to follow him and destroy all the priestesses on the ship? Baxter let out a loud sigh and shook his head in frustration. How could this tragedy play out right before him? He felt helpless to stop it.

"I have nothing to offer to heal Cass," Victoria said, breaking his dark thoughts.

Baxter looked up and nodded, understanding that the girl was too far gone for any help the wizards could provide. He stared at Victoria as she unfolded her wings again and bared her teeth in the mirror. She took a finger and touched the tip of one of those sharp canines and snapped it back immediately, shaking the pain away.

"Your father?" Baxter asked.

Victoria looked at him in the mirror with her dark eyes, looking more like a demon than a human, but her eyes were kind, and her beauty was still breathtaking. He had seen her true appearance several times before and thought the look was becoming. However, he knew she was very secretive about her true identity, especially since she felt that the folks of Pelesea would reject her if they knew the truth.

"Yes, my father has returned. There is no other explanation," Victoria said, finally leaving the mirror and sitting at her desk with a huff.

"Why has he returned?"

Victoria shrugged and said, "To ruin my life, I imagine."

That elicited a small chuckle from Baxter, and Victoria followed suit. Their joy was short-lived as the weight of recent events stifled their mirth.

"You look beautiful, you know?" Baxter said, breaking the silence.

"You say that every time this happens."

"That is because it is true."

Victoria shook her head and unfolded her wings. "Look at these things, Baxter. No one finds this attractive, except perhaps a demon."

"They look lovely!" came a faceless voice that resounded through the room.

Both wizards sat up and looked around, understanding they were not alone. Soon they saw the source of that mysterious voice as Victoria's father became visible in a chair near Baxter.

"Father!" Victoria shouted in surprise.

"My lovely daughter, hug me," her father said, standing up and opening his arms.

Victoria hesitantly came over and gave him a half hug. Baxter watched intently, not trusting the man in the least. He looked like an ordinary wizard with a pointy hat and long grey beard. Baxter knew better, though; he knew the truth about this particular wizard.

"You remember Baxter?" Victoria said, breaking the hug and holding an arm out to her friend.

"Bastard," Malikai said with a nod.

"Baxter," the younger wizard corrected.

"Of course," Malikai responded, then paid him no more heed. "This is how you speak of me when you think I cannot hear? You think that I will ruin your life?"

Victoria turned and took her seat behind her desk once more. "First, dear father, you were spying on me in my tower, and secondly, you stripped my disguise while I was in full display of strangers. If someone had recognized the change, it would have started a panic within the city."

"Well, firstly, your tower should not allow such intrusions. If it does, perhaps you are less powerful than you think. Secondly, you look more beautiful in your natural form. Bastard said so himself, so why hide it?"

"Baxter," Baxter corrected again, but Malikai ignored him this time.

"I am hideous," she answered, giving Baxter a hateful look. "Besides, the king and queen would not approve."

"Then they are not your friends," her father reasoned, walking across the room and fixing himself a drink from her bar. "Now, have a drink to calm yourself."

"No, Father, I am not interested in drinking right now."

Malikai nodded and downed his glass in one gulp. "Yes, of course you're not interested, but this is the perfect time with all the bad luck befalling your students. I heard you expelled several and now one is dying?"

Baxter nodded slightly but did not have the energy to argue with the brazen wizard. Instead, his thoughts wandered back to Cassandra. He reflected on the one kiss they had shared and how special it had been to him. Victoria's insensitive father had no idea what true love was; he had no idea how it felt to be heartbroken.

"Tell me of the student who is dying," Malikai said, drawing Baxter's attention again.

"No," Victoria answered. "We are not doing that."

"Suit yourself, but you know I can save her," her father stated, pouring another glass and downing it in a gulp.

"What is he talking about?" Baxter asked, sitting up at the flicker of hope.

"Nothing, it is not an option," Victoria answered.

"You haven't told him, have you?" Malikai asked, his eyes widening with the realization.

"Told me what?" Baxter asked.

Victoria just sighed, shook her head in frustration, and crossed her arms over her chest. Baxter looked back to Malikai for an answer, and the old wizard wore a significant smile.

"Very well, I will educate you," Malikai said. "Victoria is not my biological daughter."

"That explains a lot," Baxter said with a snort. When he noticed Malikai's stern look, his smile faded immediately.

"As I was saying, I found her on death's bed, and if not for me, she would no longer be of this world."

Baxter's mouth hung open, and he glanced at Victoria, who stared back at him, still hugging herself. He thought she looked like a pouting child, but he also understood that the truth was probably uncomfortable for her to hear.

"So, I saved her," the old wizard said and poured himself another glass.

"How? Are you a healer?" Baxter asked in confusion.

"Of course not, fool. I am a demon, as you should be able to surmise," Malikai said, holding his arm out toward his daughter.

"But you just said she is not your biological daughter."

"No, but my blood pumps through her veins now. Demon blood can heal anyone," the old wizard said.

"It also brings out the worst in those who have evil traits. Giving Cass demon blood could turn her into a monster," Victoria piped in.

"But it will save her," Malikai added.

"She could end up like you, Victoria," Baxter said.

"Exactly," Malikai agreed.

"You haven't seen the others, Baxter. They are evil and are a plague to the world," Victoria argued.

"Now, Victoria, you have always been jealous of your siblings because they are a little more rambunctious. They mean no harm, and usually, their antics are not life-threatening. So why not add to our happy family? Give the girl a chance to live," Malikai said.

"Yes, Victoria, you must give Cass a chance at life," Baxter pleaded.

Malikai downed another glass and smiled at his daughter, who looked at Baxter in frustration and said, "Shut up, Bastard."

Matilda left the tavern at Poppy's Inn earlier that morning, having stayed there all night, and climbed the stairs to the higher floors leading to her room. She had hoped for leads concerning Cassandra Rho, having lingered in the common area of the place, but the busy tavern was a dead end. Time was against her, and Matilda panicked at the thought of the mighty Vasheba taking her prize. The demoness had teased her that she was coming to Pelesea to murder the sacrificial lamb Matilda desperately sought. She had wasted plenty of time "paying" Malikai, and now she had spent all night chasing ghosts.

No one had mentioned Cassandra throughout the night as Matilda made her way around the busy place, listening for any clue that might guide her to her prize. Poppy's contained a popular tavern for the people living on the city's south side. Being close to the southern docks brought a steady stream of sailors who were quick to spend their coin on drink and tell their tales of adventure on the high seas. However, none of those tales involved Cassandra Rho. There had been no mention of Cassandra or where the brat might even be within the city. Worse, Matilda had no idea what the girl looked like and wouldn't even recognize her if she came face to face with her.

Dejected, she returned to her room to sleep for a bit and maybe even ask Malikai's assistance to locate Cassandra magically. She hardly noticed the black smoke drifting up far away at the northern part of the city, where the fire in the jailhouse was finally subsiding.

Cassandra awakened with a start to see the open sky above her. The stars twinkled on a clear, crisp autumn night. The scene was remarkable for her as she had not been outdoors since her arrest, and the cool breeze felt good on her skin. Her jumbled thoughts recalled the "demon" abducting her from the jail cell. She sat up suddenly and looked around. She was alone, aside from a roaring fire that she lay next to, which had melted the nearby snow, revealing a ring of dead grass where she sat. Surprisingly, her hands and feet were not bound, so she slowly stood.

Her surroundings did not seem like hell from the stories she had read. It was peaceful and serene, unlike the hot, despairing place she had expected. Plus, there were no demons or tortured souls. The site was outside somewhere in a forest, and she struggled to understand what the demon-like creature had in mind for her. It didn't want her dead because it warded her from the fire, and it could have killed her with its brute strength when it had the chance. Nor did it hold her prisoner, because she was not bound. She searched her foggy memory of the jailhouse fire to find answers to the puzzle.

She noticed the smoke from the fire seemed to waft around her quite a bit as she stood. It didn't seem to get into her eyes or throat but bunched around her torso and legs. She understood this fire was probably not just a typical campfire used for warmth. Sure enough, as she backed away from it, the smoke seemed to tighten, and she realized it looped around her ankles and wrists, to her horror. She pulled on it, but its hold was as strong as steel.

The more she pulled, the tighter the smoke became around her limbs. As she suspected, the fire was not an average blaze: it was her new jailer. Finally, she sat back down with a frustrated grunt, and the smoke lessened its grip as she relaxed. She looked around, expecting the creature to be somewhere near, but nothing seemed about in the surrounding woods. She examined the terrain to see if she recognized where she might be, but the forest looked unremarkable. She sat there for a long time before hearing popping sounds from the fire. The flames became brighter and more intense and grew in height a moment later.

She sat back as far as the smoke bindings would allow, shielding her eyes from the intense brightness. Soon the flames parted, and the demon-like creature stepped through. Cassandra tried to be brave and not show the creature exactly how terrified she was of it, but she knew she wasn't doing a good job. It smiled and dropped a few pieces of dried meat from its clawed hands onto the grass. It reached within the flames to bring forth a wooden barrel and placed it next to the still-smoking meat. The barrel had a tap on it, and she assumed there was something to drink inside. The creature turned to go back into the flames, but Cassandra could not let it go; she needed to know what was in store for her.

"Who are you?" she yelled out before it stepped into the fire.

It slowly turned and smiled evilly at her. She questioned her judgment in speaking to the creature, as it appeared it might just attack her and shred her to pieces. Finally, after a few awkward moments, it turned back and stepped through the flames. The fire shrank to average size, and she was alone again.

It took her many moments to try the tap at the bottom of the barrel. Then, to her delight, water poured out onto the grass. It was warm, but she knew it would cool as she rolled it the best she could away from the fire. Soon she was eating and drinking, and the food was excellent.

After her meal, she looked around with a sigh and made herself comfortable. She had no idea where she was or what was to come, but she would have to accept her fate for now. She would need answers, though, and battling that horror was not something she was looking forward to. A shiver ran down her spine at the thought of it. She got as comfortable in the grass as possible and drifted off to sleep, frightened but happy to be out of her cell.

"You still haven't told me why you have come to Pelesea," Victoria said as Malikai and Baxter prepared to visit Cass.

"Business brings me back. Why do you ask?"

"Well, I do not like you dispelling my disguise whenever you come near."

"You still insist on wearing a mask when your true self is so much more," Malikai said, shaking his head.

"This is not my true self, and you know it!" Victoria spat back.

"It is now, my dear. No matter what you were before, you are now a half-demon and would do well to embrace your heritage."

"Please release your hold on my appearance," Victoria pleaded.

Malikai stood there with a disappointed look on his face. Eventually, he turned with a shake of his head to leave the tower. "Come along," he bade Baxter.

Baxter just stared at Victoria, whose demonic traits were still visible. She looked at him blankly and said, "This will be Cass's fate."

He continued staring at her for a moment and replied, "You are beautiful, Victoria, as Cass will certainly be."

"No, Baxter, you do not understand; the process will bring all the bad stuff to the forefront. She may become a monster after the procedure. Is that what you want?"

Baxter stared hard at his friend, and thoughts of Cassandra filled his head. "No, but I just lost Cassandra. I'm not losing another one to the curse of the mountain when I can do something about it."

He turned to leave her room to catch up with Malikai, but he hesitated in the doorway. Victoria sat hard in her chair and stared into space. Her demonic features began to retract. She jumped up and looked in the mirror, watching them disappear.

She smiled and whispered, "Thank you, Father."

Satisfied, Baxter smiled and hurried on his way.

Matilda sat up straight in her bed, her heart racing. "Malikai?" she whispered, looking around the empty room.

The afternoon sun showed through the partially opened curtains. She had come back to the inn to find Malikai gone and endured a restless sleep where she dreamed of Vasheba devouring Cassandra. She needed to find the girl quickly, but how? She rose from the bed and dressed, not knowing what her next step would be. She needed Malikai's powerful spells, but she knew not when or if he would return to their small room. She decided then to make her presence known in the city and ask for an audience with the king and queen. She would tell the royal couple that she was a distant relative from Oldorburg, and sought to reunite Cassandra with her sister.

It was as good a plan as any, as something inside her pushed her to urgency. Vasheba was about; she knew she needed to act quickly. If the king harbored the Rho girl, that would bring her out of hiding.

She left the room and made her way into the main square of the city's southern side. The streets were bustling, and the shops were open for business. The sun began to sink, meaning the unnaturally warm day would soon grow cold. She had many steps ahead of her if she intended to reach the palace at the northern gate.

After a few blocks, she noticed a couple of city guards and thought to ask them the best way to relay the request to the king. So, she put on her most innocent face and approached them.

"Good evening, gentlemen," she said with a smile.

They turned in unison, and both wore sad expressions. "My lady. May we help you?" one of them asked.

She stopped and looked each in the face, surprised that both seemed dejected. "I need to get a message to the king. I have urgent news that will interest him. I was hoping one of you could help me with that or tell me the fastest way to reach him?"

They glared slightly, then the same one spoke again. "You may take your request to the palace gate and leave it with the guards there."

"But don't expect a fast response," the other added.

"Oh, and why is that?"

"Because of the tragedy that occurred last night, dear lady."

"What tragedy?" Matilda asked.

"The city jail burned to the ground overnight."

Matilda's mind raced. She knew that demons preferred fire as a means of attack. Had Vasheba been in the city looking for Cassandra last night? If so, had she found her? Her heart raced, thinking of the possibilities.

"Ma'am?" one of the guards said, and it was evident by the way they were looking at her it was not the first time they had addressed her.

"Are you in trouble?" the other guard asked, his interest piqued.

"No, nothing like that. How did the jail burn down?" she asked anxiously.

"No one is sure. We suspect the prisoner was trying to escape and cast a spell that backfired on her."

"Her?"

"Yes, there was one prisoner jailed there when it occurred. Unfortunately, she died in the blaze. She was an odd girl with strange powers."

"Yeah, rumors say she was a witch," the other added.

Matilda's thoughts spiraled out of control. Somehow, before she even heard the name, she knew it was Cassandra. Vasheba had killed the girl just as the demoness had promised. It took Matilda a long while to summon the courage to ask, "Who was the prisoner?"

"A young woman named Cassandra Rho."

The words hit Matilda like a ton of stones, and her knees nearly buckled. There it was, her failure splayed out in front of her. She had released the demoness into the world, and that act had ruined the Great Summoning.

She had failed, and there would be no world domination now. Her dreams were over.

She didn't realize it for a while, but the guards were beside her then, one holding her up, which was the only thing that kept her from falling to the ground.

"Are you sick?" one asked.

"No, I am fine," she lied.

They helped her sit on the top step of a nearby mercantile. After staying with her for a bit and Matilda convincing them she was fine, they took their leave. She sat on that step until well after the store had closed and the moon was high in the sky. Finally, the small priestess pulled herself to her feet, still in shock from the news of Cassandra's death, and wandered away to find a dark place to pray. She needed to appease Marnelphion in whatever way he required. She had failed him, and her life was now forfeit.

2

DEMON BLOOD

HE SERVANT RECOGNIZED BAXTER AND ALLOWED HIM AND
Malikai to enter, understanding that if the wizards had a way to
save Cass, there was no time to ask Franklin to grant them entrance.
So they hurried up the stairs, Baxter leading the way. When they arrived
at Cass's door, Baxter knocked slightly but opened it immediately instead
of waiting for a response. Inside, they found Franklin Ruben still by his
daughter's side. Cass's breathing was shallow and infrequent now as she
was very close to passing.

"You have a way to save her?" Franklin asked, standing up excitedly.

He looked as near death as his daughter, his complexion pale and his
eyes sunken with dark rings under them.

"Yes, well, maybe," Baxter stammered. "This is Malikai, and he has a
possible means of saving your daughter," he continued, extending a hand
toward Malikai.

"Yes, please, good wizard, I am wealthy and will pay you anything!"
Franklin pleaded with the older wizard.

"The girl stinks of rot. She may be past saving," Malikai said, removing
the bandage and examining the pus-filled wound.

"Please, you must help her. I will pay whatever price you ask."

Baxter watched intently, knowing Malikai's price would be steep and probably nefarious. Malikai only smiled at the desperate man and turned back toward Cass, removing the scarf covering her breasts and throwing it in the corner. Franklin took a step toward the scarf as if to protect his daughter's nakedness but thought better of it, understanding that Cass's life hung in the balance.

"We will discuss the fee arrangement once I save her. But, for now, you must understand that what I am about to do will change your daughter forever. She will not be the same girl she was before her illness, but she will be full of life."

"What kind of spell do you intend—" Franklin began before Malikai raised a hand to stop him.

"Do you understand that every second you waste brings your daughter closer to death?" the old wizard reminded him.

Franklin looked past the wizard and at his daughter's prone form. She no longer coughed, which meant she was suffocating from the infection. She had little time.

He eagerly nodded. "Yes, please begin your spell, I beg you."

"Get out," was all that Malikai said.

"What? I want to be here. Cass is my daughter."

"You are too emotional. You will get in my way, and that will be most unfortunate. Leave so that I may begin," Malikai insisted.

Franklin was about to argue some more before a gentle voice behind him had him spinning toward the door. "Mr. Ruben, please come with me. This wizard's techniques are unusual, and you will not tolerate them if you witness them," Lady Victoria said, having rushed over after her transformation.

"What is this about?" the confused father asked.

"It is about trust, Mr. Ruben. Do you trust us? You called on us, and this is the only way we know to save her," Victoria explained.

After briefly studying Victoria's smiling face, he nodded and took her hand, following her out of the room. Baxter made eye contact with Victoria as Franklin mumbled hysterically about paying any price. Victoria gave Baxter a tired smile, which he returned. He shut and locked the door and turned to Malikai, who was already undressing.

Binta's dream was perfect and filled her heart with joy and love. In it, she was once again in Cassandra's dorm room. They had been studying that night, but their conversation had become a personal issue. Binta had confronted her about the rumors circulating in the school that Cassandra was sleeping with Baxter. Soon after, they shared their first kiss. It was amazing then and just as wonderful in the dream. She awakened and quickly realized the sad reality that Cassandra was gone. She tried desperately to go back to sleep and recapture that perfect dream, but it was not to be.

She summoned the strength to sit up in bed and look around. She recalled the events of the night before and remembered how the commotion of the other priests had awakened her sometime early in the morning. She received no straight answer when she asked the priests rushing about what alarmed them, most of them panicking. She eventually decided to follow them out to investigate. Shortly after, she had found the source of their worries—the jail was burning. She had reached the site just as the strange man had exited the building carrying a lifeless form. She knew immediately that it had to be Cassandra, but she would not believe it until she witnessed the corpse. The sight was worse than anything she could imagine, and the smell only doubled the horror. She knew right away that her friend had passed.

Now, in hindsight, she wished she had just stayed in bed. She would never forget the sight of the carofex emerging from the burning jail with Cassandra's burned body. Her heart broke once more at the thought, and she cried again, unable to control the deep shudders of grief that grasped her tightly.

After crying a long while and attempting to come to terms with the deep pain of a world without Cassandra, she collected herself, washed her face, and gathered her courage. She would visit the morgue and say goodbye to her best friend. She took a deep breath and left her room, vaguely remembering Instructor Baxter helping her home the previous night and tucking her into bed. She would need to remember to thank him later. He loved Cassandra probably as much as Binta did, and his grief over her death was natural. She would need to rely on him over the next few weeks to survive the tragedy. He was unaware of Binta and Cassandra's budding relationship, and she would not tell him of it because that would probably hurt him further.

Ultimately, she hoped they could support each other and help navigate the tragedy. Her head was in a fog as she made her way to the morgue, and she could smell the stench of burned flesh before entering the room.

Several priests were there and allowed her to visit Cassandra in private. She learned they would hold a small service for her in two days. She thanked them, and they left her with Cassandra's corpse so she could say goodbye to her friend. Cassandra's body lay on a large block of ice, and a thick cloth covered her. With an unsteady hand, she peeled down the fabric far enough to view her charred body.

Cassandra's face was mainly just a skull with a bit of blackened flesh clinging to it. Binta broke down immediately and hugged the corpse, ignoring the awful smell. Her tears flowed freely and dropped upon Cassandra's face. She thought it a strange scene, as if her tiny tears were attempting to relieve her friend of the burns she had suffered. Binta couldn't imagine what kind of suffering Cassandra had endured. Her heart broke again as she slowly covered her friend's corpse and left the morgue.

She felt like the world's weight was on her shoulders. Cassandra was gone, and she would never hold her in her arms again, and Greyson was sailing halfway around the world. She intended to leave the morgue and visit the ruins of the jailhouse. Binta needed to find answers as to why this tragedy had occurred. She changed her mind as she considered the monumental task and the energy she would have to summon to see it through. Instead, she returned to her room in the temple of Plath and climbed back into bed. She would try to recapture the dream of Cassandra's kiss. Nothing else mattered at that moment; everything else could wait.

The guards led Sasha out of the dungeon area with her hands and legs chained. Once out of the main door segregating the dungeon area from the rest of Iciale, she immediately shielded her eyes against the light shining through the glass windows and reflecting against the icy walls. The guards were not sympathetic to her predicament and shoved her forward. When it was clear she could not see well, they each roughly grabbed an arm and led her to the top level of the magnificent palace.

The guards escorted her to Clade's room to stand in the middle of it. One of them kicked the back of her legs hard enough to make her fall roughly to her knees. It took her a moment to register the pain and the action that caused it. She immediately began calculating her revenge for such treatment. She had grown up in the sewers and learned to fight down there to survive. She could fight better than anyone she had come across, and Sasha knew she could outwit and outfight the two buffoons who stood on either side of her. If her temporary blindness had not hindered her so much, she would have gladly enlightened them on how dangerous she was, shackled or not. Instead, the young warrior steadied herself and took a deep breath. Revenge was not her goal right then, but she would measure the situation and not resist the urge to counterstrike if an opportunity presented itself.

Her thoughts were interrupted by the sound of a man's voice she knew, an evil man who had visited her frequently in the sewers the last few years—Clade. "Well, now, Sasha, I am honored to have you in my home," he greeted her.

She could tell a second person was with him and assumed it was her uncle. The great white light still blurred her vision. One of the guards pushed her hard in the back and she fell from a kneeling position and almost landed on her face. She managed to move her shackled hands in front of her, breaking the fall, but smacked her hands hard on the icy floor as a result.

"Answer the Lord of Iciale, Ugly One," one of them barked.

Again, her mind calculated the location of the fool's sword. The guard would already be dead if she had her vision and were not bound in chains. The other idiot guard would soon follow. She steadied her thoughts again, telling herself she was at a significant disadvantage. If she had her eyesight, she would take out at least three of them before death found her. That would be a fantastic way to end her life. However, she could not take that chance under the current circumstances.

"My lord," she whispered.

"What is wrong with her?" Clade asked the guards.

"She cannot see, my lord."

Sasha heard a derisive snort from one of the evil men, and one of them walked to her and placed a hand on her head, feeling the ice helmet as he walked slowly around her. She wasn't sure which one it was until Clade spoke. She had faced many dangerous and deadly opponents in the sewers, but none compared to the evil of Clade. He frightened her.

"You see, Presin, she has been trained at my discretion and understands that her life belongs to me now. So, while you left her down there to rot, I have given her a purpose."

"To find the sword," Sasha answered, knowing what the man wanted to hear.

He stopped walking. "You see, she is a strong warrior and smart. That will allow her to complete her quest for Iustia." He bent low to whisper in her ear, "And I will greatly reward you, my dear, if you bring back that most treasured artifact to me."

Sasha tried to focus her eyes but could only see a bright light that made her head throb. She slowly acknowledged the evil priest with a nod and bowed her head humbly.

"Good, my servant; you will not fail me. The time has come for me to remove this mask so you may mingle among the ugly humans. Would you like that?" Clade asked.

"Yes, my lord."

Clade's hand began to melt the icy mask.

"Do you think it wise, my lord?" Presin stammered.

"To remove the mask?

"Yes," Presin answered nervously, the ice falling off his niece in chunks to shatter on the floor.

"How else will she blend in with the human world? Do you want her to stand out and have the humans immediately notice her?"

Presin gulped nervously and slowly shook his head. "No, of course not," he whispered.

Soon the ice casing was gone, and Sasha's long blond hair spilled out around her shoulders, most of it still encased in ice rods. Presin covered his mouth at the sight of her but did not make a sound. Clade raised her chin with his finger to fully see her ugliness. Even the guards took a step back when he did.

The old priest only shook his head and whispered, "You will fit in nicely with the humans, ugly woman, do not doubt. Are you ready to make me proud and gain your freedom?"

"Yes," Sasha whispered, trying to get used to the mask's weight no longer burdening her neck.

"Good. It is time," Clade responded, nodding to one of the guards and taking several steps back.

The guard produced a key and began to unshackle her feet. So many thoughts flew through Sasha's mind at that point. She had the opportunity to kill the guards. She could do it with little difficulty, blinded or not. Did she want to stand against two priests without her vision? It was tempting, so tempting. However, the promise of being set free into the human world intrigued her enough to stay her hand. After the shackles fell free, the guards grabbed her arms and helped her stand.

"And now, my ugly warrior, go to the land of humans and find the city of Novafontera. It will not be far from the portal from which you will step," Clade instructed, keeping a healthy distance.

Presin took several paces away from her as well. Clade cast a spell, and a rift formed beside Sasha. They could see a world beyond the portal and hear a roaring waterfall. Clade had created the gate in the water of a great fall.

After casting the spell, Clade continued, "Go through the gate and know that you may return to the waterfall when the task is complete. I will then reopen the gate for you to step through once more. Do not return without Iustia, understand?"

"Yes, my lord," Sasha answered, raising a blind hand toward the rift to feel the cool mist there.

"Through the gate, you will find a sword, shield, and suit of armor, ready to battle the demon that guards Iustia. Remember your training and fight smart. The blade is somewhere in the cursed city of Novafontera, understand?"

"Yes, my lord."

"Good. Wear this medallion so that I may track you and know when you have returned to the waterfall," Clade said, producing a silver necklace with an icy-blue stone in the setting.

He approached the girl and placed it over her head. Although she could not see, she sensed his movement and bowed her head so that he could put it around her neck.

He whispered in her ear, "And if you try to escape and decide to start a new life with the humans, do not doubt that I will send the dibolicies to retrieve you. Do you understand this, Ugly One?"

Sasha turned to him; she was still unable to make out any details but could vaguely see a blurred outline of the man. She nodded and inched toward the rift. Before she could step through, Presin added, "And don't forget your mother, Sasha. Your success means you will reunite with her and begin life anew once you return."

She nodded in the direction of his voice and walked through.

Clade closed the rift behind her and dismissed the guards.

Once the two priests were alone, Clade asked, "Her mother? We killed that idiot years ago."

"Yes, but my niece does not know this."

Clade clasped him on the shoulder and gave a great belly laugh. "You will make a fine high priest living on the top floor of Iciale!"

Presin smiled at the thought and began to laugh as well. However, it was short-lived as Clade's visage became serious, and he added, "If she succeeds, that is."

Presin's smile melted away, just as Sasha's mask had done moments before. He swallowed hard and looked back to where the gate had stood. Now, there was nothing. All he could do was wait. The life of luxury that he so desperately desired now hinged on the success of his ugly and meager niece.

Sasha exited the waterfall, and the light was even more intense. Her blindness barely registered, though, for the cooling water had refreshed her, unlike anything she had ever experienced. The water continued to roar behind her and splash her. It was as if the filth of her life were washing away. She couldn't help but giggle like a small child at the joy her heart now felt. Even if only a tiny reprieve, she was out of the clutches of her uncle.

She wanted to dive in and continue this dream come true, but she told herself that would be unwise. So instead, she found the water's edge and, to her delight, discovered snow for the first time. She sat at the shore for a long while, her blind eyes closed and playing in the snow. She kept her feet soaking in the icy water, which felt lukewarm to her carofex senses. She even ate some of the snow, finding it delightful. She enjoyed her first few hours in the human world and forgot about her responsibilities as a happy child at play might. She was free for a brief time and for the first time in her life.

Later, as her vision began to return and the blinding light dimmed, blurry images began to take shape slowly, and she discovered the promised equipment. She ran her hands over the sword and could tell it was of the highest quality; the blade was razor-sharp and well-maintained. She entertained the idea of donning the armor and weapon, but a smile formed on her face instead, and she went back to the water and played. She felt truly alive in the human world and would enjoy it until her vision returned. Then she would begin her quest.

Cassandra sat cross-legged in front of the continuously burning fire. She had tried to kick at the logs that gave the fire its life in the hopes of dashing it, only to find no logs. Nothing was burning, yet the flame had continued for several days now. She was always alone with the fire and noted that no wildlife, whether docile or aggressive, approached her or the fire. The wild predators of the region seemed to know not to get involved in her dilemma. The demonic creature came and went, occasionally delivering food and water. She tried prying information from it each time it appeared, but it refused to speak to her. So, she sat and sat and sat some more. The days dragged by, and she found her new prison almost as bad as the jail of Pelesea.

She meditated on the issue, trying to recall the wise words of Cedric, her brief mentor before his death. Her father, the lich-god Kane, had sent him to help find her birthright. What a fool's errand that had been for her, and she hoped that Binta had fully recovered from whatever wounds she had endured during that ill-fated journey. She recalled the disappointing end of that quest, finding a scroll with cryptic words inscribed instead of Zolmex, her mighty birthright.

She shook her head and whispered, "Notel X," the meaningless words she had found there.

The flames shuddered and hissed, startling her from her thoughts. She looked around, expecting to see the red-skinned demon, but found nothing. Had her words made the flames react? Was it a hint from her father that she could escape the smokey binds? Who was her father, anyway? Some creature named Kane? A lich-god of some sort? According to Cedric, that was precisely the case.

"How lucky am I?" she spat, hoping her father could hear her.

Perhaps one day, she would get to tell him what she thought of him. But, for now, she needed to find a way out of her current predicament. She collected herself and managed to go deeper into her trance. She slowly opened her eyes once she had found a comfortable and relaxing place in her mind. Instead of seeing just the fire, she saw the fire for what it was—magic! She saw the arcane shapes floating in the fire and swirling along with the smokey cords that held her. They were far more advanced than she could control but were familiar, nonetheless. Given enough time, she felt confident she could dispel it. Since time was all she had, she took a deep breath and began dissecting the magical fire.

Baxter finished tying off the rope that bound Cass's left hand to her headboard. The poor girl barely breathed, and he saw no need for the binds. However, Malikai had ordered him to bind both hands and legs to the head and footboards, and the dying girl was now spread-eagled in her bed, struggling harder than ever to breathe. And still Malikai sat in the chair her father had occupied constantly over the last few weeks. His eyes were closed, and he wore only his large pointy hat and muttered what Baxter imagined was a spell. It looked to him as if Cass had only moments to live, and Malikai showed no signs of urgency.

"Malikai, she is dying," Baxter said, stepping toward the strange wizard.

Cass succumbed to a coughing fit at that moment, and Baxter went to her quickly, trying to comfort her somehow, understanding that her death was imminent. She coughed up blood and phlegm, spewing it all over her chin and neck. He turned to Malikai to gain the old wizard's attention and realized Malikai was upon him. With a strong hand, the wizard pushed him out of the way. Baxter watched in amazement as Malikai moved past him to lean over the dying girl. His appearance made Baxter take a few steps back. The wizard had changed, and he looked like Victoria, but his demonic features were more pronounced. His eyes were solid black like Victoria's, but his skin was dark red, and his muscles bulged. Also, his horns were much more significant than Victoria's. She had small stubs protruding from her forehead, whereas Malikai had large, curling, ram-like horns.

He held his pointy hat upside down, pulled a handful of a sand-like substance from it, and poured it directly on Cass's wound. The girl jumped to life momentarily as her body reacted to the strange sand. Her eyes opened wide for the first time in days, and she sat up in bed, pulling her binds tightly for just a moment. The reaction was brief, and soon she fell back into an unconscious state. Malikai packed more of the strange component into her wound, and Baxter watched in amazement as her body seemed to absorb it. Cass thrashed as Malikai held her down, letting her body take in the hellish substance.

After her fit, the wizard-turned-demon released her and stood once more. Malikai rummaged in the hat and pulled forth a vial filled with a white, milky substance. He handed it to Baxter, who took it gingerly and held it to his face, studying the contents. Next, Malikai produced a second vial, filled with a black, tar-like substance, and a small hollow horn, and thrust those into his hands as well. Baxter stood there, dumbfounded, as the wizard tossed his hat to the side and placed his hand on Cass's wound.

He silently spoke words in a language Baxter did not recognize, and lightning sparked from his fingertips, burning Cass's flesh and sealing the wound. The girl cried out several times but was still too far into the throes of death to fully understand what was happening to her. The smell of the procedure had Baxter nearly retching and just about dropping the items. He looked up to see Malikai's stern gaze, a silent warning to remain in control. Neither spoke a word, but the two understood each other, so communication was irrelevant. Baxter knew he played an essential role in saving Cass just by being there to hold the required items. That was important to him, and he meant to see it through. He had failed Cassandra; he would not fail Cass.

After a long time, Malikai finished with his powerful spell, which sealed Cass's wound, but her skin was red and badly burned. However, Baxter noticed her breathing was now less difficult. Cass remained unconscious, and he knew she was far from healed.

"Give me the horn," Malikai instructed, holding his hand toward Baxter while examining the freshly sealed wound.

Baxter handed it over, careful not to unstop the two vials he held. Malikai gently pried open Cass's mouth and inserted the horn, the small end first, leaving the large end sticking out. Baxter surmised that the wizard would use the horn to funnel the vials.

"No gag reflex; this is a good sign," Malikai smiled.

Baxter found the comment peculiar, especially given that Malikai was fully naked. To that point, Baxter was uncomfortable with the procedure, and the demon made him nervous. But after the comment, Baxter feared the demon's real intentions. He could not be part of that; he could not allow Malikai to harm Cass. His mind raced at the thought of confronting Malikai, not knowing what spells, if any, he possessed that could deal with the beast.

"The black vial," Malikai said, reaching for the small container in Baxter's hand.

Baxter handed it over quickly, and Malikai unstopped it and began to pour the sticky substance into the horn. It ran slowly, and Cass did not react to it as it drained into her throat. Baxter watched, expecting something horrible to happen, but the substance seemed soothing to the girl.

"What is that?" Baxter asked.

Malikai smiled and said, "You do not want to know, I assure you. Now, uncap that second vial and have it handy."

Baxter did just that, continuing to watch intently, expecting the worst as the final drops of the black liquid made their way down the horn and into her throat. She seemed to be at ease at that moment, which surprised Baxter and gave him some hope that they might be saving her. His thoughts drifted to unclean images of the young woman, and his eyes drifted to her perfect breasts. He knew he shouldn't, but he found her desirable, especially given her predicament of being bound to the bed. He liked the idea of having his way with her in her current state of helplessness.

He shook the naughty thoughts from his mind, not understanding their sudden intrusion. He blocked them out the best he could but couldn't resist them. His eyes slowly roamed her toned legs, ending with her crotch. He discovered many dirty ideas had come to him, and he desperately wanted the young woman. He felt himself losing control, ready to act on those desires.

He almost did before Malikai stopped him with a strong arm. "Easy, Bastard, let me take that from you before you do something you'll regret," he said, taking the vial of white liquid.

The filthy thoughts slipped away as soon as it was out of his grasp, and he was ashamed that he had nearly acted on them. There was no explanation as to what had happened, and at first, he thought it was a spell that Malikai had enacted. However, his eyes focused on the vial he had handed over, and he understood the strange liquid was the catalyst.

"What happened?" he asked, looking at the small container of milky fluid.

Malikai only smiled and said, "This is the milk from a nepalin."

"A nepalin?"

"Yes, a creature of hell. Nepalin are female demons with an insatiable sexual appetite. One drop of this milk could turn a normal human into a nymphomaniac," Malikai explained, then he took a sip from the vial.

Baxter registered the action and had a forethought of what the demon planned to do. But Malikai poured the remaining contents down Cass's throat before Baxter could react.

"Why did you do that?" Baxter asked.

"The milk also possesses extraordinary healing properties. So, Cass is safe now." Malikai nodded toward the young woman, who seemed to be breathing comfortably then. "There is only one thing left to do."

Malikai reached into his hat again, and Baxter went to Cass's side, amazed at how much better she looked. Her color seemed to improve immediately, and she had a peaceful look. He wondered if the demon could still save Cassandra. He shook the thought away, knowing it was too late for his beloved.

The sexual thoughts returned slightly as the young woman reacted to the milk. Cass moaned softly and attempted to close her legs to suppress her sexual desires. He could only imagine the milk's effect on her if the mere fumes had affected him so greatly.

"I need you on top of her," Malikai said.

"What?" Baxter asked in surprise. He saw the demon wizard holding a long serrated dagger. The blade looked wicked, and he didn't understand Malikai's intentions with the weapon.

"Hold her down, for she will thrash greatly with this last procedure," Malikai explained.

Baxter reluctantly did as he was told, nervous about why he needed to hold her down. He vaguely felt the cold water from the melting ice on her bed soak into his robe. He leaned heavily on her and waited for Malikai's next move.

Malikai brought the dagger to his forearm and cut a deep gash. The black demon blood poured from the wound, and Malikai held it over the horn funnel in Cass's mouth. Some dribbled onto her chin and face, mixing with her drying blood. Baxter still found the whole scene erotic and fought against the effects of the powerful milk.

Malikai let the blood flow for many moments before Cass reacted. Then, her eyes opened wide, and she let out a painful scream. She bucked violently as Malikai tried to hold her head steady, but more and more of his blood missed the funnel and poured on her face. Baxter tried to hang on, to keep her in place, but she seemed to grow stronger as the blood took effect. Eventually he lost the battle as she bucked him off, and he fell, hitting his head hard.

Dazed initially, it took him several moments to realize he was on the floor. When he returned to his knees and peered over the bed, Malikai stood, bandaging his arm with a smirk.

"It is done," he explained, nodding again to his patient.

Baxter looked over to Cass, whose eyes were open and black like Victoria's and Malikai's, the trace of demon blood reflected in those dark orbs. Malikai had removed the horn from her mouth, and she wore a seductive smile and bit her lower lip. She writhed in bed, still tightly tied but pulling against her binds.

"Cass, are you all right?" Baxter asked. She responded by running her tongue over her top lip seductively, licking at the coagulating blood there.

"She will survive and will be far improved over her previous self. Soon she will have the strength to break her binds. But, before then, I will collect my payment," Malikai said, climbing onto the bed and straddling her.

Baxter was at a loss, not knowing how to respond to that. Cass seemed more than willing to "pay" the fee, and it took many moments for Baxter to realize Malikai was waiting on him. Finally, he looked up to make eye contact with the demon.

"Well?" Malikai asked.

"Well, what?" Baxter responded, shaking his head.

"I am going to collect my payment from our now-vibrant young patient. Care to join?" Malikai asked, motioning with a hand to Cass writhing underneath him.

Baxter considered it for a moment, having difficulty defeating the effects of the demon milk. He eventually shook his head slowly, unable to find his words.

"What then, Baxter? Do you prefer to watch?"

"What? No!"

Baxter found his feet finally and made his way toward the door. He struggled with the idea of joining the perverted act but just as eagerly wrestled with the idea of throwing Malikai out of the room and away from the helpless girl. But unfortunately, Malikai was a potent wizard and a demon, which did not bode well for his chances.

"I know what you are thinking, and it would be unwise, Baxter. Mind your own business and comfort her father. Her payment will not take long."

Baxter stood frozen at the door's threshold, wanting to strike against the demon but not knowing if his powerful magic could harm him. He struggled with the decision for many moments, and ultimately, Malikai's stare boring a hole through him, and Cass beckoning with her gaze, led him to shut the door and leave.

Baxter found Victoria, Cass's father, and several servants waiting nervously in a sitting room. Franklin jumped up at his arrival and asked excitedly, "How is she?"

"She will survive," Baxter answered. Victoria gave him an accusing look. He knew she was correct; Cass should have been allowed to die. Somehow, what she had become seemed a much worse alternative to the beleaguered wizard.

"I heard her cry out. She had not made a sound for several days, and the scream seemed strong. May I see her?" Franklin asked.

Still locking stares with Victoria, Baxter could only shake his head slowly.

"Why? You said she would live," Franklin persisted.

Baxter finally found the strength to turn toward the man and said softly, "The process is not complete. Soon, you will see your daughter."

Just then, Cass's screams echoed through the house. Franklin looked at the ceiling in the direction of the sounds, not realizing they were screams of passion from his reborn daughter.

A smile found its way onto Franklin's face, and he said, "She sounds healed! She sounds strong!"

He hugged Baxter first, squeezing the surprised man, then going to Victoria and finally his servants, embracing them all with joy. "Thank you!" he said to Victoria and Baxter once his celebration played out.

Victoria just fixed her gaze on Baxter, who didn't say a word.

Two days later, Boz awakened to find himself in the temple of Gella, the sound of a strong autumn wind rattling the lone window to his room. He quickly recalled the events that led him there and understood it was time to leave Pelesea and collect his prize. He sat slowly in the bed and refocused his mind to evaluate the damage to his body. He closed his eyes and flexed his muscles slowly, letting the burned skin stretch slightly. The pain was minimal, and he knew he would quickly heal. He had allowed the fire to burn him just enough to make his rescue attempt seem genuine. Burns would not linger on his body, for he was a carofex of fire.

"You are awake," came a female voice from the door.

Boz opened his eyes to see a middle-aged woman there dressed in priestly robes that matched the decorations in his room. He surmised her to be the priestess in charge of him.

"You don't look too bad at all. I am Maina, and you are in the temple of Gella. Welcome, dear carofex," the woman said, making her way to his bed.

"The girl. Is she alive?" Boz asked, feigning interest in Cassandra.

With a solemn look, she shook her head and said, "No, she did not make it, but that does not make your efforts any less heroic. The king and queen have asked me to notify them once you awaken. They want to thank you for your actions."

"I need no affirmation for my deeds; I simply did what I could."

She smiled at him and replied, "Spoken like a true hero. I knew Cassandra, and even though she offended the king, she was a good person. She was just greatly misunderstood."

Boz paid little attention to the priestess's words. He closed his eyes once more and willed away what little pain remained in his slightly burned skin. He felt her hand on his arm, and his first instinct was to reach out and throttle her for touching him. Of all the things he disliked, touching was the first on his list. He fought back the urge and slowly opened his eyes to see her smiling at him.

"Thank you for your efforts, Boz. I will send a messenger for the king and then look at your wounds. At first glance, you look fine and should suffer no long-term effects."

"I am a carofex of fire and, therefore, will recover."

"Again, spoken like a true hero."

"I must leave and inform my brothers and sisters of Cassandra's passing," Boz said.

"I understand, and I will assure the king that you are well enough to travel if that is what you desire."

A few hours later, Boz found himself in the castle grounds. The king and queen had been alerted to his desire to leave, and they arranged to have him come to the castle beforehand. He gladly obliged, wanting to avoid any bad will with the royal couple by refusing the request. As soon as he arrived, the guards led him to the stables, and the stablemaster informed Boz that he had strict instructions from the king to provide the carofex with a strong horse and supplies for his trip. As Boz waited patiently for the stable workers to prepare the giant white steed, the king and queen arrived to see him off.

The elven brothers, Von and Lenore, accompanied them. Boz knew the elves, having traveled with them from Oldorburg. They were excellent archers, and the carofex had witnessed that firsthand. However, he had not seen King Kringus for several weeks and had not had a chance to see the royal couple in their official garb during his stay in the great city. Now, the king wore his crown and looked more official, wearing clothing far fancier than anything Boz had seen before. The queen, who the carofex had only seen briefly, wore her crown and a beautiful green dress.

The dress perfectly accented the queen's long red hair and unusually green eyes. She was also elven, her pointed ears sticking out of her long hair. He had heard rumors that she was related to Von and Lenore. However, the most striking thing about Queen Penelope to him was that she wore a sword on her hip. He made a mental note not to underestimate her if they crossed paths in the future.

"Boz, my friend, I am glad you have recovered from your injuries. Are you sure you must leave us?" Kringus greeted him, extending his hand, which Boz grasped in a firm shake.

The strength of the king's shake always impressed the carofex, and this time was no exception. Kringus was a barrel-chested warrior of many battles. His neck and chest, scarred from the fires of a dragon, were his badge of honor, but his high-collared shirt covered most of them now.

"I must be going. I must report to the monastery the death of Cassandra

Rho," Boz lied. He noticed the queen looking him over suspiciously, although she wore a smile. He understood immediately that she did not trust him, but he did not understand why. So, he elected not to acknowledge her stare that bored through him.

"I will not argue with you, but know you are an ally to Pelesea. Your actions are legendary, and you are considered a friend. So, you are always welcome here," Kringus said.

A stableboy brought the horse with packs of foodstuffs and other supplies and handed the reins to Kringus.

"Please accept this gift, Boz, from Penelope and me as a token of our appreciation," the king offered.

Boz nodded and took the reins. "I accept your gift. As a friend."

Boz clasped hands with Kringus once more and with Von and Lenore. He gave Penelope a slight bow, then mounted his horse. Before he could spur the horse on, Penelope asked, "There is a funeral tomorrow for Cassandra. Will you not attend?"

Boz matched stares with her, his face showing no emotion. They shared a moment then, a silent and awkward stare-down that Kringus surely noticed. After a few uncomfortable moments, Boz finally shook his head and said, "No, dear queen, my task was to monitor Cassandra. However, now that she has passed, I must report the sad event."

Boz nodded to Kringus and the elven cousins and slightly glanced at Penelope before spurring his horse on. The horse had taken only a few strides when Penelope stepped forward and asked, "One more question, good carofex."

Boz pulled the horse to a stop and turned, still stone-faced. They locked stares once more. After a few moments, Penelope asked, "How did you get to the burning jail so quickly if you were lodging near the city's far south side?"

"Carofex are naturally nocturnal, dear lady. I walked your streets most nights I was here."

"From the south side? That seems extreme to me."

They shared another moment, invisible daggers flying until Kringus came and draped an arm around Penelope's shoulder. "Your deeds are not in doubt, my friend; the queen is always curious concerning tragedies that strike our grand city. Safe travels."

Boz nodded to Kringus again and did not make eye contact with Penelope as he spurred the horse.

Once Boz was outside the castle gates, Kringus asked his beautiful wife, "What was that about?"

"He is lying," she replied, keeping her eyes locked on the carofex.

"His actions have been honorable, my love. Why do you doubt him?"

She gave him a look he had seen occasionally over the years when she knew something he did not. Then, finally, she replied, "It is obvious. You should not trust him, dear."

She turned and headed back to the castle, and Kringus looked to Von and Lenore for answers. The two elves glanced at each other and just shrugged. The three turned back to regard the retreating queen, each equally confused by the confrontation.

"You have been gone for days," Matilda told Malikai as he entered their room.

"We are not here on the same business," he replied.

"I need to return home soon, and I need you to take me," she responded glumly.

"Why are you so down? Have you not found your prey?"

Matilda looked at him desperately and shook her head. "I have failed; Cassandra has expired."

"Expired?" Malikai asked, fixing himself a drink.

"Yes, most likely the work of Vasheba. The jail burned with her in it just three nights ago."

"There was a fire?"

"You are not aware of this fact? Where have you been exactly?"

Malikai downed his drink in one gulp, then removed his hat, tossing it onto a chair. Next, he removed his shirt and threw it atop the hat. "What is this I hear in your voice, Matilda? Is that jealousy?"

"Don't be ridiculous, and don't think I am paying you anything else. We are square."

"Contrary, my dear, your useless husband is due a show, so you will not only pay dearly for that trip home, but we *will* use the mirror. Unless, of course, you would enjoy a long, lonely boat journey across the sea."

Matilda swallowed hard as he approached, knowing good and well she could not and would not resist his advances. She needed intimacy now, and maybe she *was* slightly jealous. She made no move to stop him as he slowly unbuttoned her shirt.

Maltor, the barbarian king, stood at the bow of his warship, studying the sky. The storm was coming fast and would most likely hit when they landed. That was what the barbarians intended. It would be a good raid, and if his scouts were correct, the booty would be plentiful. The expedition's sole purpose was to collect and enslave women for the carnal pleasures of his hearty warriors. Maltor and his tribe hailed from the desert lands on the harsh continent known as Varish, nearly two thousand miles across the vast ocean. His war party had almost sailed the distance, and his men grew more excited as the hours passed.

He wore his heavy camel-skin coat, which protected him little from the cold wind blowing off the ocean waters. He stroked his black beard, knocking some of the ice forming there onto the deck, and blew into his hands to warm them a little against the bite. His second in command, Jozerah, joined him as they discussed the coming raid. Both warriors had seen countless battles and were imposing figures to anyone witnessing them, each standing nearly seven feet tall. An army of barbarian warriors, equally as impressive, filled the ships' hulls. There were five ships, so the raiding party consisted of two hundred and fifty hearty fighters.

One among them was different in stature—a lone female allowed to travel with the band. Vixa oversaw training the new slaves in combat and was there to study the new captives to determine whether any were indeed trainable. However, she was female and, therefore, a second-rate warrior, never genuinely respected by the men of the tribe.

Vixa approached the two barbarian leaders, her red, unkempt hair flying about her in the strong wind. She stood six feet tall, much shorter than the male warriors of the tribe, but she was tall and muscular for the typical female under Maltor's rule and knew how to use her weapons. She excelled in combat and could wield two hand axes simultaneously during battle. Yet, as impressive as that was, Maltor failed to recognize her as a warrior or an equal. He allowed her to train the newly enslaved women because he felt she could handle that, but nothing more.

As she approached, the two barbarian warriors stopped their discussion and turned to regard her. She wore a wool blanket to protect against the cold, wrapping it around her shoulders. Even under the blanket, Maltor could see her shivering. The barbarians lived under the burning sun of the Yaddaton Desert, so the cold greatly affected them all. Even though Maltor and Jozerah were equally cold, they did not dare shiver in front of the lesser female.

Maltor pointed toward the hull. "Go back down where you belong, woman. It is too cold for you here."

Jozerah laughed, which only made the young female warrior bristle. Vixa was quick to anger anyway and did not particularly like Jozerah. She stormed up to him and threw her blanket to the deck. "Do you want me to show you why I belong here, Jozerah?" she asked, her hands on her axe handles.

"Do not embarrass yourself, wench. You remember what happened last time?"

"You cheated!" she screamed in his face.

In response, Jozerah flipped open his coat and began to withdraw his massive sword, but Maltor put a firm hand on his arm to stay it.

He turned to Vixa and said, "As much as I would like to watch your defeat again at the hands of a true warrior, we have no time for this. Why have you disturbed us, woman?"

"I want to lead the third boat," she said, focusing her ire on Maltor.

"Bolin's boat? You are not qualified."

"I am more qualified than Bolin!" she screamed, drawing the attention of the nearby deckhands.

The barbarian deckhands had witnessed the scene many times before, so they knew the king's orders before he even gave them. Even though they were not true warriors of the barbarian tribe, they were strong and prominent in stature. With a quick nod from Maltor, they grabbed Vixa from behind, holding her arms firmly so the volatile woman could not use her deadly hand axes.

"No!" she screamed, understanding the consequences of her actions. "Release me!" she said, struggling against the two barbarians.

"You are not a warrior, so get it out of your head, wench," Maltor said, making her struggle more. "Take her to my chamber and restrain her."

She screamed and kicked the entire way, and to her credit, she nearly broke free of the hold, kicking one man in the knee and biting the other's arm. She received several well-placed punches for her efforts, and the men eventually subdued her. They took her below deck, and Maltor and Jozerah returned to the ship's rail.

"She is a wild cat," Jozerah said with a laugh.

"Yes, the perfect thing before a raid," Maltor agreed.

Both shared a laugh at the woman's expense. It would be a good night for Maltor, a good omen for a perfect raid.

Unbeknownst to the barbarians, a ship sailed nearby on their port side. Although they did not spot the boat, the occupants, which consisted of Greyson Kavince and the troop of Sinnis priestesses, was well aware of the five warships that passed dangerously close to them. Alleah peered through the spyglass on that distant ship and observed the caravan passing perpendicularly to their current course. Greyson and a group of priestesses stood with her anxiously. Finally, Alleah handed the glass back to the captain, a beautiful woman named Jessica, who was a just and reasonable person, having sailed many times from Pelesea's port. Her interest in Alleah's mission and even the plight of the passing ships was sincere.

"You are correct; they fly no banner," Alleah said. "What do you think that means?"

"It is unusual for sure. It is common practice to fly one in these waters," the captain answered. "Anyone not doing so is either a pirate, a stranger to the waters, or generally up to no good."

"They look like battleships to me. Do you think they are warriors of Gorl?" Tesa, one of the higher-ranking priestesses, asked her.

Jessica looked through the glass again, but Greyson spoke up before she could answer. "No," he stated.

They all turned to regard him. He stood at the ship's rail, facing the fleet of unidentified ships.

"What do you know, Greyson?" Alleah asked, walking to him excitedly.

When she reached him, she saw that his eyes were closed as if in meditation, and she noticed that very little of his frosty breath was escaping his mouth. It was apparent he was deep in prayer.

She waited for him to open his eyes. "Greyson?"

His expression was relaxed and confident. "It is not who you seek, Plath has assured me. Those are not warriors of Gorl."

"They are not pirates; their ships are too big and slow for that. They are warships and formidable. I guess they are hostile to any boats in the area," Jessica reasoned.

Greyson shrugged. "Plath has not given me the insight to identify the crew or the cause of the ships. I only know they are not of Gorl."

"No matter who or what they are, my ship is ill-equipped to deal with five large warships," Jessica explained.

"Perhaps we should turn around and warn Pelesea," Alleah said.

"You will lose precious time, and the ships are not heading that way. Pelesea could do little to interfere with whatever is about to transpire," the captain argued.

They sat and watched as the ships grew smaller on the horizon. Eventually, Jessica added, "It is your call, Alleah; this is your mission. I will do whatever you suggest."

Alleah looked to Greyson for comfort, who said, "There is little we can do, but we are with you no matter your decision."

The gathered priestesses agreed and confirmed their pledge to follow the beautiful priestess of Sinnis.

After pondering and discussing it briefly, Alleah said, "We will continue, and once we reach Varish, we will inquire about the ships. Perhaps we will garner information from the people there."

"Yes, we are headed to Port Racip, which has a plethora of information. That is as good a plan as any," Jessica agreed.

Their course remained unchanged, and the ships were soon out of sight, Alleah deciding not to investigate the strange appearance of warships in the peaceful waters. Maltor's army sailed out of sight and out of mind. The priestesses of Sinnis continued their course, not understanding the death and destruction the passengers of those warships would soon cause.

3

ᛏRANSITIONS

ASS WATCHED CASSANDRA'S FUNERAL FROM A DISTANCE, LEAN-
ing against a random mausoleum housing some important person
she did not care to know. The funeral was held on the temple grounds
in one of the large cemeteries, and no one noticed Cass. She looked on as
a female priest said a few words. Cass yawned and stretched her arms, not
the least bit interested in what was being said. She was too far away to make
out the words, anyway.

The cold wind cut through her thin clothes like a knife and she loved
the feeling! She was alive after defeating death thanks to her new surrogate
father, Malikai. She welcomed the wind; it reminded her she wasn't dead.

The sound of someone crying brought her out of her daydream and
she saw Instructor Baxter comforting Cassandra's little girlfriend, Binta.
A smile spread across Cass's face as she recalled starting a rumor in the
school that Cassandra had slept with Baxter to get better grades. Soon
after, it was apparent that Cassandra and Binta were the ones she needed
to spread rumors about. And so, she had.

Not many people attended the funeral. King Kringus and Queen Penelope,
along with their entourage and guards, were there. Baxter and Binta huddled

together, Binta obviously very shaken. The queen's two elven cousins who always seemed to be about were there, as were a handful of priests and some people Cass didn't recognize. The turnout was small, especially given the fact that Cassandra had been jailed by Kringus a month earlier.

"I wish I could have seen that," Cass whispered to herself.

She had a good laugh at the thought, but then she noticed another couple arriving late and standing in the back of the gathering. She was surprised to see it was Malikai and he had a small woman with him. They kept their distance and her father seemed very uninterested. The woman seemed distraught, and Cass made a mental note to ask Malikai who she was later.

Cass absently ran her fingers over the blue stone in the medallion she wore. She had stolen it from Cedric's dying form and it was attuned with Cassandra's life force. The powerful item told her that Cassandra was not dead, and that she was close, near Oldorburg to the south.

"You're not fooling me, Cassandra. I will find you and make you pay for what you did to me."

Cass also recalled the promise she had made Cassandra as they battled in the cave during their adventure. She vowed to pay Binta a visit once she returned home, and she meant to keep that promise. Looking at the broken girl as she sobbed hysterically made Cass realize she was ripe for a visit. She watched a little longer as the gathering began to disperse, but her focus was on Binta. She smiled at the sad display of Baxter helping the distraught girl walk away, and many devious plans danced in her head at that moment.

Unaware of Cass's presence, Malikai and Matilda witnessed the burial of Matilda's dream of world domination. Malikai looked on with disinterest, but Matilda's disappointment at losing her prize was devastating. She had spent the last day paying Malikai for her trip home. Furthermore, he had made Cerus watch most of the sensual activity. Usually, she would have loved performing that way for her husband, and even though the sex was amazing, her thoughts dwelled only on her failure.

Now they stood in the cold, watching the scene play out. Once it was over and the small gathering began to disperse, Malikai turned to leave, but Matilda stopped him. "Wait, I want to visit the grave while it is fresh."

"Why?" the old wizard asked.

"I want to speak to her spirit if Marnelphion grants me the power to do so."

"To what gain?"

"Usually, when the goodly priests perform their ceremony to allow their dead to pass to the land of death, the spirit will linger for a bit. And, if it is here, I wish to speak to it."

Malikai, a demon who had seen many things in the bowels of hell, had not heard of any mortal having such powers. Of course, the more powerful demons could, but he had never heard of a human obtaining such an ability.

"How can you possibly perform such a powerful feat?" he asked.

"If Marnelphion hasn't abandoned me, he will allow me to discover the cause of her death. If it is Vasheba, as I fear, I will destroy her or die trying. My life is forfeit, and my sole objective is to pay back those responsible for taking it from me."

"I'm surprised you have that ability, much less the use of such a dark power in the middle of the day. Demonic powers function better under cover of darkness."

"Of course, but as I said, the spirit lingers temporarily, and I cannot wait until nightfall."

So, they waited in the cemetery until all others had left, then approached Cassandra's fresh grave. Malikai looked on as Matilda knelt and began to pray. She touched the new tombstone that Kringus had insisted on for the troubled woman. It was more extravagant than most stones, reflecting the king's genuine grief for Cassandra. As she began a prayer, Malikai noticed a familiar figure in the distance walking away. He watched intently and determined from the magnificent backside it was Cass Ruben. Before leaving the city, he would need to check in on his new daughter. The trip had been profitable for the demon as Mr. Ruben had lined his pockets with much gold. However, the "birth" of a new daughter was his most profound accomplishment during his stay. As Victoria had warned, Cass had a black heart now, which made the sex with her even more erotic. Cass had embraced her demon traits fully, unlike Victoria.

He did not focus on Matilda and the prayer she was in the middle of, but suddenly he felt dizzy, and his body tingled all over. A trickle of blood ran from his nose, and when he wiped it with his hand and looked dumbfound-edly at the blood, he felt his horns grow involuntarily. As they sprouted from his forehead and his canines began to elongate, he dropped to his knees, pain overwhelming him. He fought hard against the transformation and understood that only a mighty demon could force him to unwillingly reveal his proper form.

He managed to will the change away, relieving the immense pressure and pain in his head. No one seemed to notice his fit, so he tried to discern what exactly had happened. Matilda still had her hand on the tombstone, and her grip on it was so tight that her knuckles whitened. She remained deep in prayer with her eyes closed tight. Nothing short of the essence of Marnelphion would be strong enough to make him change shape. There was only one way a creature that powerful was remotely close, and that would be through Matilda. He looked on with a newfound respect for the tiny woman.

Matilda felt the vibration in the tombstone as soon as she touched it and knew that Marnelphion was with her. The energy that flowed through her arm nearly consumed her. She had never felt so powerful and held on tightly to the stone to avoid falling to the ground. She felt like her spirit was ripped from her body and placed in a swirling black fog. It reminded her of the moment she had reached the pit of Marnelphion back in Novafontera. It was an authentic out-of-body experience that made her feel very vulnerable. Her body remained at the gravesite, clinging to Cassandra's tombstone, but her spirit was elsewhere. She stumbled around, trying to find some footing in her strange new surroundings. She could not see or hear well, her senses dulled by the fog. There were weird noises around her, and thousands of muffled screams echoed in her head.

Occasionally, she could make out a single cry of "Mommy," but nothing else was discernible. The sound seemed to come from a child, and she followed it, not knowing what else to do. She lost track of time and knew not how long she had wandered. Finally, the cries became more apparent, and she could determine that the child was older, perhaps an adolescent and a female. It was Cassandra Rho, she knew; it had to be.

She followed the voice, and eventually, a shimmering image appeared in the swirling black fog. She was correct: it was a child, perhaps fifteen years old with blond hair and blue eyes. She looked terrified and confused, trying to make her way around just as Matilda had. She started walking away, and Matilda struggled to follow in the fog.

"Cassandra Rho?" Matilda managed to scream out to keep the child from wandering off. But, even screaming, her voice sounded dull and far away.

"Mommy?" was the girl's reply.

"No, I am a friend. Come to me."

The girl wandered back into view and was startled to see Matilda there. "Where am I?" she asked.

"You have died and will soon pass into the afterlife, Cassandra."

"Cassandra?" the girl asked, seeming more confused by that name than the fact she was dead.

"Yes, you are Cassandra Rho, and you died in a fire, remember?"

"Yes, I remember the fire," she answered, bringing her hands up to feel her face and touch her hair. "I am not Cassandra; my name is Lynna."

The words struck Matilda so hard that she almost lost the connection with the girl. Was it possible that Cassandra Rho was still alive? If so, how did she escape? She refocused her concentration on the girl. The black fog broke up as a bright light slowly became visible behind the child.

Lynna turned toward it and asked once more, "Mommy?"

"No!" Matilda screamed, but her voice sounded distant, and the girl seemed not to hear. She walked toward the light, and the connection broke. Matilda needed more answers and knew she would not find them if Lynna reached the light.

Matilda struggled to regain the hold. She needed to know what had happened to Cassandra. She needed to question the girl before the light took her to the afterlife. Who was she, and where was Cassandra? The image of the girl faded. The light began to hurt Matilda's eyes, and she closed them tight, losing sight of Lynna altogether.

Her attempt to keep contact with the spirit cost her dearly. The light began to draw her toward it as well. She struggled to retreat, to go back to where she had come from, but she could not resist the strength of its pull. The light hurt her, pierced her, and burned her. She did not belong in that light, which rejected her and ate at her very soul.

"Malikai!" she tried to scream, but her voice was no more than a whisper. She called the wizard's name several more times as the light sapped her strength and stretched her thin. Then, finally, she felt a firm hand on her shoulder, pulling her back just before the light completely consumed her.

It was easy to see that something was wrong with Matilda. Her entire body shook, and she clung tightly to the headstone. Her grip was so firm that her fingertips began to bleed around her nails. Malikai called her name, but she did not acknowledge him. Then she whispered his name in response.

"Matilda, can you hear me?" he asked, touching her shoulder.

She was bleeding from the nose and ears, so he pulled her off Cassandra's gravestone, and she collapsed in his arms. He looked around to ensure no one witnessed her collapse, then used his powerful magic to teleport them to his room and out of public view. He laid her on the bed and checked her heartbeat. She was alive but badly hurt by whatever demonic powers she had harnessed. He made sure she was comfortable and cleaned the blood from her face.

Malikai watched her sleep and did not leave her side for long. The demon was not part of her cause, but her display of power convinced him that her connection with her god was real. He felt the need to hunt, to maybe go to Cass and exploit her newfound lustfulness. His insatiable sex drive needed quenching. In the end, he stayed by Matilda's side that night. She didn't put up much of a fight.

Malikai purchased healing potions from a brew master a few doors down from the inn the following day. He administered those to Matilda, which seemed to help her raspy breathing. However, she remained unconscious and showed no signs of awakening from the near-death event. He did not want to involve the goodly priests, so Malikai knew her only hope lay with the demon-blood treatment. He knew she would make an excellent half-demon. Unfortunately, it was too soon after "healing" Cass, and he would have to wait a few days before trying the procedure on Matilda.

As it was, she was comatose, and he was restless. He cared for Matilda and hoped she survived the ordeal, but he would not wait in the small room with her until she recovered or died. He figured she was safe in the room and no one would bother her. He would check on her in a few days and perform the demon-blood ritual if she was still breathing and unresponsive. So, he left her alone; there was still a lot to do before he left the city.

Sasha had been in the human world for three days but had not moved far from the waterfall. She had found a pack full of food with her armor and sword, some of the best she had ever eaten. Life in the sewers did not provide ample opportunities to eat well, so Sasha took advantage. She stayed behind the falls during the day, venturing out occasionally so her eyes could adjust to the blinding light. She could see well, but the brightness hurt her, and she couldn't bear it long. And so she spent most of the day sleeping and eating the delicious food Clade had supplied. Apples were her favorite, though she did not know the name of the strange fruit.

She knew she couldn't stay there long because the food would not last. Therefore, she planned to proceed with the mission as soon as possible. In the meantime, she would conserve food and practice with her sword behind the falls. The blade was more balanced than any of the crude weapons she had used in the sewers of Iciale. She loved the blade and soon mastered it. The hardest part was trying to adjust her balance without her ice mask. Her head felt light as a feather during her practice routine with the sword. Her confidence grew, as did her coordination without the icy helmet weighing her down. In those three days, she found her balance and became proficient with the beautiful sword. Without the mask, she became a better fighter.

She enjoyed the evenings when the sun began to set. She would then venture out from the falls to explore the neighboring woods. Her vision was nearly perfect at dusk, without the ball of fire in the sky to blind her. She had never seen a river, her favorite part of the landscape. She loved immersing herself in the refreshing water and spent many hours there each night. She also loved the snow, which had begun falling a day earlier, although the reflecting sun from the snow-covered ground stung her eyes. The constantly blowing wind was invigorating, and she quickly fell in love with the human world.

As time passed and days slipped by, her thoughts became troubled. She did not want to go on the mission set before her, but she would do it if it meant freedom for her mother. She desired that more than anything, knowing the new world she slowly discovered would be a fantastic place to start life anew with her mother. She could not remember her, but she wanted to meet her, hold her, love her, and, more importantly, be loved by her. Those ideas danced cheerfully in her head, but she also knew without a doubt that neither Clade nor Presin would allow that.

A few miles north of the falls, a ranger known by the moniker Daro, Keeper of the Woods, had finally arrived home. He had spent the last few weeks in Pelesea, and although he enjoyed being near his friends in the grand city, he missed his little cottage in the woods. He had been gone far too long for his liking but was home at last. After settling in and unpacking, he plopped down in his favorite rocker and sipped some home-brewed root beer.

"Home at last," he said with a smile.

The New Order, a group of skilled individuals sworn to uphold the laws of the neighboring cities and communities, had ordered him back home to watch over the city of Novafontera. Daro was a member of that distinguished organization and was ready to return to his woods to watch over the cursed city. It was the second time he had inherited overseeing the dead city in recent months, and the first time ended with him skirmishing a trio of vampires that had crawled forth from the vile place. He would rest briefly, then roam his woods to see if he could find traces of more undead. He would need to prepare wards if they invaded his woods again. It was good to be home, and he felt comfortable in his little cottage. Feeling the fatigue of his trek home, he dozed off in his chair and dreamed of vampires.

Binta went about her nightly chores in the temple of Plath to keep busy and her mind off the tragedy of losing Cassandra. She missed Greyson sorely and needed him but vowed to stay strong and in control. In truth, she was an emotional mess, and it took everything she had to remain active. It was a constant battle to fight off the depression and the despairing thoughts. She was alone, and although that was familiar to her, the loss of Cassandra was too much for her to endure.

The priests of the other temple factions had visited her regularly since the tragedy, and so when there was a knock at the temple door, she assumed it was another well-visit from a priest or priestess offering food. She did not desire company, but it did lift her spirits a bit to speak with someone.

It was with great disappointment and shock that when she opened the door, she found not a priest with comfort food, but a middle-aged woman with a sick baby. She explained to the hysterical woman that she was not yet a priestess of Plath and could not heal her child. Binta asked a temple page to retrieve an actual priest and was relieved when Eldrick came and rescued her from the excitable woman.

After they left, Binta sat down in one of the pews and felt the world's weight on her shoulders. She needed to lock the temple doors; she could not keep them open as badly as she felt, emotionally. She just wanted to crawl into bed and die. She knew Greyson would be disappointed, but she didn't care. She had also neglected her prayers and her studies of the scrolls of Plath. What he didn't know wouldn't hurt him. She loved Greyson, but he would understand if he returned, which was not something she was sure of. Life had no meaning for her at that terrible time, and studying Plath was the furthest thing from her mind.

With a resigned sigh, she summoned the strength to rise and lock the temple doors. Before she reached them, the heavy doors opened swiftly, startling Binta and nearly catching her in their swing, and another woman entered. At first, Binta thought it to be another civilian looking for healing or charity, and she was about to tell the person she could not help them. But what she saw stopped her before she found her voice. The woman wore a cloak with a hood that hid her face, but the rest of her clothing left little to the imagination. Her attire made no practical sense for that time of year, with the cold winds blowing outside and the snow cascading in the air. She wore a short red dress a few inches above her knees and black knee-high boots.

As Binta took in the sight of the odd woman, she finally said, "I am sorry, I am closing the temple for the evening. I apologize—"

"Hello, Binta," Cass said, lowering her hood to reveal her smiling face.

"Cass?" Binta said, taking a step back in surprise.

Something about Cass seemed different, and Binta could not place it at first. But as she studied her nemesis, she realized it was the girl's rosy glow that was different. She looked perfectly healthy, but the last Binta had heard, the girl was near death. Also, she seemed to have an aura of confidence, even more so than her usual arrogant self. Cass was always confident, annoyingly so, but now seemed somehow even more sure of herself. Whatever the source of Cass's new strength, Binta found that it excited and frightened her simultaneously.

Cass entered without another word and shut and locked the doors behind her. She then sat in one of the pews, almost seductively, Binta noticed, crossing her legs slowly as she did. Her short skirt rode high up her thighs, revealing a long, perfect leg. Binta truly hated Cass and did not feel like humoring the woman, but the seductive display had her speechless.

"Why are you here?" she finally managed to ask.

"Why, Binta, are you not glad to see me?"

"I am never glad to see you, Cass, but I am surprised. I thought you were sick."

"I was. Indeed, the rumors are true. I would not have survived without the priests' miraculous healing."

There was a moment of silence, Binta's foggy mind trying to determine why Cass was there and what was so different about her. Binta's heart beat a little faster, but she did not know if it was from just being in the presence of the hateful girl or something else.

"I have come to give my condolences. After all, now that we are adventuring companions, I feel a sense of duty to check on you."

Binta bristled at the comments. She did not consider Cass a friend or an adventuring companion. If Cass was there to discuss Cassandra, a person she openly hated, Binta could not allow it. In addition to Cass's rocky history with Cassandra, the nasty girl had slept with Greyson during the so-called adventure and had openly admitted it. That was enough for Binta to want to pull every hair out of Cass's head. And why was she dressed that way and in her temple? Perhaps she was there to see Greyson? Would she be arrogant enough to walk right in and seduce him wearing her trampy clothes? A million thoughts raced through Binta's head, yet she hadn't the nerve to address any of them. Was she afraid of Cass? Indeed not. Something was amiss, but instead of dragging Cass out of the temple and clawing her eyes, Binta sat there and did nothing.

Cass looked at her with a strange smile, and Binta tried to stay strong.

Cass's gaze was piercing, as if the vile woman looked straight into her soul and knew all her secrets—her pain of missing Greyson, her overwhelming grief of losing Cassandra, and even the fact she didn't want to be a priest of Plath. She subconsciously took another step back, still not understanding the reason for the visit and suddenly feeling intimidated.

"Why have you really come?" Binta asked.

"As I told you, to pay my condolences, of course," Cass said, her visage becoming very serious.

"For Cassandra?"

"Yes, your girlfriend."

"You hated her, Cass."

"True, we had our differences, but that doesn't matter now, does it?" Cass asked, recrossing her legs.

Binta only nodded and meekly replied, "I guess not."

"I am here to take care of you now that you have no lovers," Cass purred.

How she said it, taking complete control of the conversation so arrogantly, caught Binta off guard. Did the wretched woman dare say that Binta was lonely or that she had no lovers? What was she trying to do? Binta's anger was great at that moment, but a pang of excitement in her stomach kept her from lashing out immediately.

"What do you know of it?" Binta spat, hiding her excitement.

"I know all of it."

Binta was stunned and had no response for the bold woman. She hated her and everything she had done to Cassandra and her. The continued arrogance was the most grating thing, and it took all of Binta's willpower not to throw herself at Cass. Instead, she found herself intrigued by what the despicable woman might know.

"What exactly are you getting at, Cass?"

"I slept with Greyson on our adventure while you cuddled with Cassandra. You remember that, don't you?" Cass teased.

Binta stared at her coldly, but again something kept her from ripping into her.

"You knew at the time, and more importantly, you liked it, didn't you?" Cass continued, standing and slowly advancing.

Binta inadvertently took another step back, and a smile formed on Cass's face. Cass continued her approach, and Binta seemed to shrink as she did.

Binta's heart raced, and a renewed sexual excitement washed over her. She didn't know what Cass wanted with her, but she knew she wouldn't like it. Yet, for some reason, that excited her immensely. Cass stood before her, and although they were similar in stature, Binta felt small and insignificant.

"You have sexual needs, which include domination. You are submissive, aren't you?" Cass asked, running her fingers through Binta's hair.

Binta pulled her head back, smacking Cass's hand away. "Do not touch me," she said through clenched teeth.

"You should not be so defensive, Binta. I know your kind, and I surely know you. You want this and need this. You hate me, which makes pleasing me even more satisfying, does it not?"

Binta could not believe the words she was hearing and stood there with her mouth agape. Cass slowly leaned in to her ear and whispered, "Admit it. The thought excites you."

Binta froze, stunned at the hateful girl's words. After all the things Cass had done to her and Cassandra, from beating Cassandra in front of the other students to having the idiot Jabell break Binta's ribs. But there was so much more, such as blatantly sleeping with Greyson, as she had just admitted. And what had happened in the cave between Cass and Cassandra? Binta suspected Cass had tried to murder her dearest friend, yet Binta could not summon the energy to confront her. Did she want Cass to dominate her in some way? She did not understand the strange feelings jumbled in her mind.

"Well?" Cass asked, running her hands through Binta's hair once more.

"Yes," Binta whispered before she could stop herself. However, she found the strength to grab Cass's hand and forcefully remove it from her hair. "But you will not touch me again."

She was ashamed to whisper that word to a woman she hated, but her lustfulness overwhelmed any rational thought. Cass was correct, she was a submissive, especially to Greyson, but this was entirely different. Binta had been in control of her submissiveness in the past, but now Cass was exploiting it. Cass used that need for her evil intentions, whatever they might be. Binta felt as if the wicked woman were exposing her inner desires and making her act on them. She hated her for that, but more importantly, she slowly realized that she needed that right now. She knew then that she would have to be strong to resist Cass's advances. She thought of Cassandra, her true love, and the fact she would never get to hold her in her arms again, never kiss her lips again. And that was all she needed to stand her ground.

"Get out," Binta growled.

"You need this, Binta, do not be a fool."

"No, you need this for some nefarious purpose. I don't know what you are up to, but you are surely not welcome here. Now get out, and don't come back," Binta said between clenched teeth, pointing toward the door.

"Very well, have it your way. You know where to find me when you change your mind," Cass teased, pulling the hood of her cloak.

She began to walk toward the exit, but Binta's anger got the best of her, and she said, "That won't happen!"

Cass stopped and turned back toward her, the cloak hiding all her face except her smile. "Too late, Binta, you are already mine. You just haven't accepted it yet."

Her tone and the finality of her words had the hairs on Binta's neck standing on end and her loins tingling. She had no response and was relieved when Cass finally started away. When she exited the temple, Binta rushed behind her and shut and locked the doors. Binta pressed her back to one of the doors and listened to her heart pounding in her ears. Cass's perfume lingered, and she found it intoxicating.

What had just happened? She despised Cass, but something about her had Binta curious and excited. She remembered when Greyson had charmed Cassandra to have sex with him, which had almost worked. She wondered if Cass had been so bold as to try that. There was no other explanation for her arousal at the thought of being submissive to Cass's demands.

Her mind swirled. What did Cass know that she didn't? It all seemed so bizarre. However, Cass had lit a fire in the pit of Binta's stomach for better or worse. That night as she lay in bed, her thoughts lingered on the encounter. Binta hated Cass and would never serve as her submissive; that is what her mind told her. However, when she reached between her legs, she understood that her body told her something completely different.

Cassandra had been at the small campsite for at least seven nights. The magical fire continued to burn and kept her warm enough, and the snow, which fell freely, melted and evaporated before it hit the ground anywhere near the fire. The creature continued bringing her food and water once a day, caring for her needs. However, the evil thing still refused to communicate with her. She had grown attuned to the fire and had studied the mystical symbols enough to know when the creature was coming. The fire was almost like a living entity, directly communicating with the beast. The flames would alert it if predators came near or if Cassandra tried to escape. Although connected to the demon-like creature, it was not a part of the beast. Therefore, she had studied the fire and had unraveled its secrets.

Each day she called the ravens that were plentiful in the area, and each day, more and more seemed to answer that call. Now the trees were full of them, all awaiting her command. She could sense them more strongly than at any other time. She practiced her control over them as she waited for the inevitable next step the demon creature had in store for her. She was surprised at how well she could summon and control the birds. She still did not understand how she was doing it, but she was becoming proficient at it, nonetheless.

However, she still did not feel she could summon enough to overwhelm the creature, so Cassandra dismissed the birds when she sensed the beast coming through the fire. They immediately flew away but stayed close enough to heed her call if she needed them. They seemed to understand what she was doing as if they were reading her thoughts.

The flames grew intense, and the creature stepped through. It had the usual keg of water under its massive arm and a sack of food. It dropped the items and examined its prisoner. Then, confident that the smoke binds were still intact, it moved to step back through the gate. As it did, Cassandra smacked a rock into the back of its head. It stopped and turned a hateful look her way.

"Hey, ugly, talk to me. Why do you keep me alive?"

It growled but said nothing. It turned to leave once more, and again, Cassandra hit it with a rock. It turned back on her, its hands instantly engulfed in flames as if to strike at her. Just as Cassandra suspected, it struggled to maintain control and was obviously temperamental. Finally, it stopped, and the flames on its hands extinguished.

"Talk to me, or I will destroy you."

Its laugh was thick and guttural. Instead of speaking, it picked up her food and water and carried it back through the gate.

"Wait! What do you want with me? What are you?" she screamed after it, but it continued through, and the gate closed. Cassandra stomped in frustration and called again, "Who are you?"

Soon all that was left was the gentle fall of the snow. Cassandra sat down with a growl and realized how hungry she was. It would be quite a while before she would eat again. The frustrated girl took a deep breath, understanding that she had taken a significant risk in confronting the beast. She was just tired and scared, tired of being a prisoner and scared of the unknown. She had to do something, so she decided to battle the beast the best she could. The next visit, she would unleash her wrath upon it, and like how she felt in the bowels of Pelesea's jail, she would escape or die trying.

Ronnis D'Breeth had procured an abandoned watermill a few miles east of Mecca-Loraine with the help of his friend Barktuck Misol, the high priest of Meshlor. Barktuck bribed the old building owner, and now Ronnis had full access to the place for the next few months. He would spend that time exacting his revenge on Cassandra Rho. She had taken everything from him, and now he would return the favor. According to their arrangement, the carofex, Boz, would deliver his prize within the next two weeks. Ronnis had set up a nice torture chamber where Cassandra's screams would echo for months before he would dispose of her.

He had boarded up all exits, especially the broken windows, so she could not use witchcraft to summon the vile ravens. Ronnis had dealt with the nasty birds once before and would not endure their interference again. His hatred of the young woman fueled his drive to have Cassandra. He blamed her for the diminished quality of his life, taking Sera from him and taking away his looks. She would pay dearly once he had her in the millhouse.

Barktuck had provided him with an endless supply of various poisons. Being a high priest of Meshlor allowed Barktuck to produce dangerous liquids magically. Ronnis would use those to drug Cassandra and have his way with her. Bottles full of the stuff lined his shelves. He would use some poison to torture Cassandra, but most of it would sedate her. He wanted her to feel the many nightmares he had in store for her but not be able to defend herself. He had had her in that scenario before until Baxter had spoiled his fun. He foresaw no issues this time and expected to complete his task without interference once Boz delivered the prize.

Barktuck joined him for the initial firing of the newly refurbished stove. It seemed to work well, and Ronnis's torture room soon became nice and toasty. The two friends sat and watched the stove for a few moments, ensuring the refurbished equipment had no issues.

"The stove works nicely. It should keep you and your prey warm enough for all the games you have planned," Barktuck said with a chuckle.

"Yes, but warmth is not my main objective," Ronnis answered with a wicked smile.

Barktuck sat up in his chair, intrigued. "What exactly do you have planned, my friend?"

Ronnis had a crazed look in his eyes, which was obvious even through the porcelain mask he wore. Barktuck had gifted the cover to Ronnis after Cassandra had attacked him and, in truth, nearly killed him. Ronnis rarely wore it around Barktuck but always wore it in public places. Ronnis slowly removed the mask to show his scarred face. A gaping hole marred his right cheek, showing off the teeth that remained on that side. Cassandra's attack had created a hideous wound and knocked several teeth out that day. Ronnis turned his head so that Barktuck could better see the injury. Unfortunately, it was so ugly that it made the priest uncomfortable, and he had to look away.

Ronnis sat back in his chair and said, "I want her to know how this feels. I have many pleasurable events planned for that one."

Barktuck nodded and let it go at that.

Daro patrolled the forest with Grey, his companion wolf. His friend had come to him a few days earlier, and Daro knew right away that something had the wolf bothered. He had packed his gear and strapped on his swords to investigate the issue, and hiked several hours in a southwesterly direction from his cottage. He simply followed Grey and he knew he was close to the source because the wolf began pacing. Daro drew both blades and stepped into the shadows. "What do you hear, boy?" the ranger asked, trying to spot the source of the wolf's ire.

He didn't see anything from where he was and turned to regard his companion. The wolf was nowhere in sight, and Daro saw the tracks in the snow leading away. Daro sighed and shook his head at the sudden absence of his friend. The wolf did not shy from battle and was notorious for showing up after a skirmish had commenced. He knew in his heart that his friend would stay close and join any fight that Daro might find himself in. Then he heard the singing deeper in the woods, faint and unusual. The mysterious source sounded female and was thick with a strange accent. It seemed to be coming from the same direction as the Wolf's Crest Waterfall, for he could hear the low rumble of the falls as well.

He followed the song, finding it more comforting the closer he got. Judging by its tone, it did not seem an evil thing, whatever the source of the music. The snow was falling hard, and it was nearly dusk. It was unlikely to be human but just as unlikely to be a vampire since the sun still hung low in the sky. He decided that the faster he resolved the issue, the better, in the event the vampires had ventured forth once more from Novafontera.

When he finally found the source, it was a most curious sight. He peered through the thick branches of a white pine cluster, giving him plenty of cover but obscuring his vision significantly. The image had to be an illusion because it didn't make sense. It appeared to be a human female swimming in the waters. The temperature of that water had to be freezing—no average human could endure that without some magical protection. He was confident Grey was on the other side of the falls by now, ready to jump in if needed.

"Who are you?" he whispered, then tightened the grip on his blades and advanced past the pines. As the river came into view, the woman emerged from the water, shaking the ice crystals from her hair as she did. The smile on her face was genuine, and her expression was serene. He slowly lowered his weapons, wholly mesmerized as she emerged naked. He took in the sight but could not believe his eyes. She still sang, oblivious to his presence, and he continued to watch, his mouth agape in utter fascination. She was simply the most beautiful creature he had ever seen. Her eyes were crystal-blue, and her long blond hair hung in frozen clumps over her shoulders. Her body was physically perfect, and her face was that of a goddess. He stood frozen. His mind couldn't focus on anything other than the stunning creature before him.

As she completed her song, she stood and ran her hands through her hair, ice chunks falling around her. The blissful smile on her face remained, and Daro found himself stuck, unable to move or even react when she finally noticed him. His eyes were roaming her perfect figure when they finally met hers. She let out a small yelp of surprise, but instead of covering her body, she covered her face and stood perfectly still, her fingers open enough so she could still stare accusingly at the ranger.

Daro shook his head slowly and started to back up. He didn't know what to do, so he said, "No… it wasn't me."

He fell backward over a log, the crash knocking the wind out of him. He was very skilled on his feet and hadn't taken a tumble like that in many years, especially in his woods where he knew the terrain so well. He struggled to catch his breath and slipped several times in his haste to regain his footing. He finally stood and looked at her once more. She still stood naked with her hands over her beautiful face and screamed when he looked.

He said, "Nope," then turned and ran.

He did not stop until he reached his small cottage and comfortable chair. What had he just witnessed? Was there a true goddess in his woods? He jumped up and locked his door, breathing a sigh of relief. Then, as he thought about it, he understood that a locked door was no match for a goddess. So he slowly backed away from it, never taking his eyes off the handle. He eventually ran into his chair and took an involuntary seat. Not many times in his life had he become a bumbling fool, but this had been one of them.

"Is she dead?" Cass asked, observing Matilda's still form.

"No, but she may never awaken," Malikai said, drawing his drink.

"Is she your woman?"

"No, just a friend."

"What happened to her?"

"It doesn't concern you, my daughter. Why have you come?" Malikai asked.

Cass immediately lost interest in Matilda and walked up to her surrogate father. "I have discovered many desires in my rebirth," she said seductively, running a hand over his chest.

Malikai downed another gulp and said, "Explain."

"I have never felt more alive! I have so many ideas, so many things to accomplish. Although, I must confess that I have not slept in two days."

"This is not uncommon," Malikai said, chuckling as he poured another drink. "Many feel this excitement during their rebirth. It is the sheer power of the demon blood boiling inside of you. It makes you restless initially, but you will learn to control your impulses."

Matilda moaned and mumbled a few unintelligible words, tossing her head back and forth as if in a bad dream. Malikai went to her and shook her gently, calling to her, but she did not awaken. Soon the fit passed.

Cass stood over the bed with her hands on her hips. "You care for her, don't you?"

"She would not be in my bed if I did not."

"Is she like us?"

"You mean, does she have demonic blood?"

Cass nodded, wearing a smile.

"No, she is human," Malikai said.

Cass picked up Malikai's drink and downed it. "I have many plans, dear father. Perhaps when this one dies, you will be interested enough to hear them?" she said, waving a hand toward Matilda.

The look Malikai gave her confirmed that he had some feelings for the woman. Cass was smart enough to change the subject and said, "I must go. Perhaps you will find me when your friend has overcome her sickness."

"Perhaps," Malikai said with a nod.

Cass was in her room shortly after with two dresses on her bed. Both were from her wardrobe four years prior, when she was fifteen. Of course, they did not fit her now, but she had kept them because they were two of her favorites. One was red, and the other was green, and they were far too short to be worn by a fifteen-year-old, but she had worn them because of the attention they garnered from the boys at school. She had new plans for them and laid the collar and leash she had just purchased that morning next to them.

"For my new pet," she purred, thinking of giving Binta another visit that evening.

She had almost confessed her plans for Binta to Malikai, but he was too distracted by the sickly woman to help. She would take on that project herself. However, Cassandra was still alive, and Malikai could be of great assistance, possibly using his magic to find the little bitch. What fun she could have with Cassandra if she could get Binta to fall entirely under her control! The possibility of exploiting them both by using their love for each other sounded intriguing.

There was a knock on her door, followed by the monotone voice of the main servant, Kelm. "Miss Cass, dinner is served."

"I'm not hungry," she answered with an annoyed sigh.

"Your father insists, young lady. He has guests."

"What?"

"Please come down immediately, or your father will be most displeased."

Who would be visiting? The question intrigued her more than a little. "I'll be right there," she finally answered.

She left her presents for Binta lying on her bed and made her way down just moments later. As she entered the dining room, her mouth dropped open in surprise. There at the table sat Lady Victoria and Instructor Baxter. Her father was also there, with a happy look on his face. Food lined the table, but no one had started their meal yet.

"Cass, please join us," her father said, standing and motioning to the empty chair.

Cass slowly made her way to her chair, but she felt so uncomfortable in the presence of Victoria and Baxter that she could not make eye contact with either.

"She is as healthy as ever, just like I said!" Franklin exclaimed, pinching his daughter's cheek.

Cass just smiled and glanced at Victoria, who wore a fake smile, which seemed to be a common occurrence whenever she visited. They began their meal, and her father continued to make joyful comments about his daughter in between bites. Cass picked at her food and just tuned out the conversation. Her father was so happy that she was alive, and he told the guests that he owed them everything for their role in saving her. Cass locked stares with Victoria, and they held it there a very long time, Baxter watching intently. Her father, happy as a lark, had no idea what was happening before him.

"So, where is Malikai? I expected him to be here tonight," Franklin asked.

"He is busy and apologizes for not attending," Victoria said, covering for her volatile father.

"I bet he is saving another person, perhaps someone we even know?" Franklin said, his eyes widening at the thought.

Victoria and Baxter shared a knowing glance that did not go unnoticed by Cass. Her face grew red, and she stabbed at her fish steak. After a few moments, Cass looked up to see everyone was looking at her. She slowly turned to her father and shrugged. "What?"

"You are playing with your food and have hardly taken a bite. You must eat to recover your strength, young lady."

"I am fine, Father. I have never felt better," Cass replied, smiling evilly at Victoria.

"A few days ago, you were on your deathbed. I thought I had lost you. Now eat so that I know you are whole once more. I want you to maintain your health and never become that sick again."

Her father then leaned over, kissed her forehead, and smiled. Tears filled his eyes, but Cass, having played the game long enough, blurted out, "Why are you here?"

"Cass, your manners!" Franklin said in shock.

"It is an honest question, Father."

"I invited them here as a show of appreciation. Victoria and Baxter saved your life, along with that Malikai fellow."

"I also want to know if you will attend the school this spring. I have decided to reinstate you," Victoria added.

"That is wonderful news, Lady Victoria!" Franklin exclaimed, clapping his hands together.

"No," Cass stated flatly.

That stole Franklin's joy, and he stared at his daughter momentarily, unsure if he had heard her answer. "What? My daughter, this is a great opportunity for you to re-establish yourself as the top student in the school."

"I no longer need you," she answered, but to Victoria and not her father.

"Cass, mind your manners—" Franklin began before Victoria put up a hand to stop him.

"Your heroic actions and attempts at making peace with Cassandra and Binta made me change my mind. Now that you have escaped death, I thought I would offer you a new chance as a student," Victoria explained.

"Yes, she will be honored to attend in the spring, Lady Victoria," Franklin began.

"Shut up, Father!" Cass yelled, standing up.

Franklin looked at his daughter as if she were a ghost, as if the person standing before him was not honestly his daughter. But, of course, he had no idea how accurate that was.

"Perhaps we should leave," Baxter said as he and Victoria stood.

"Get out!" Cass yelled, struggling to control her demonic impulses.

"If you change your mind, you know where to find us," Victoria said as she and Baxter let themselves out.

"She will, Lady Victoria. She will change her mind!" Franklin yelled after them.

After they had left, he turned an angry stare at his daughter. "You have never acted like this. What has gotten into you?"

"Malikai, you fool… in more ways than one," Cass answered coldly.

"Go to your room right now, and be thankful I don't tan your hide, girl. Go up and think about how you have behaved tonight."

Cass stood with a smirk and made her way upstairs. She took her time only to annoy him, and he fumed as she slowly ascended the stairs. Before moving out of sight, she took a final glance back and saw her father wipe his brow nervously. She smiled.

Later that night, after her father was asleep, Cass dressed in the same skimpy outfit and knee-high boots she had worn a few nights prior while visiting Binta. By now, Binta would be putty in Cass's hands and worked up with anticipation. Tonight, Cass would take full advantage of that. She reached into her drawer, pulled out her newest purchase, a leather whip, and clipped it on her belt. Cass didn't know how to use the weapon yet, but that didn't matter. Just the sight of it would keep Binta in line.

She put the two dresses and the collar into a sack and headed for the door. She could hear her father snoring in his room down the hall, and the servants had retired to their quarters. She snuck out of the house without making a sound. She wore her hood up as she crossed the street and made her way the two blocks to the temple. Heavy but peaceful snow fell, and the city seemed to be tranquilized by it. She passed no one on the street, and when she entered the temple, few priests acknowledged her, much less approached her. Even in her tiny outfit, none seemed to notice anything unusual. Perhaps it was due to the recent tragedy at the jail, but she was unsure. She stopped and rubbed the scar under her left breast. Cassandra would pay soon enough for that scar, plus some. A smile crept across her face, and she went to the temple of Plath.

She opened the door as she had a few nights prior, but instead of finding Binta hard at work, the place seemed deserted. No candles burned, and the room was pitch black. She remembered a room off to the temple's right, probably Greyson's quarters. Binta was perhaps there, sound asleep. Cass felt her way along the pews until she found the door. She turned the knob and opened it only to find more darkness.

She could not see, and had the means to summon fire, but decided to wait, not wanting to display that power in front of her new pet so soon. Instead, she called out, "Binta, are you there?"

No answer came. Cass turned to grab a candle off the altar when she saw a figure standing at the pews. She dropped the sack and candle in surprise, and her heart raced, not because she was afraid, but because it excited her. Who could it be? She could not see anything but the silhouette, which was most intriguing.

A blue flame appeared in the person's hand and lit up the immediate area as much as a small lantern might. Now she could see the mysterious form for who it was—Instructor Baxter. The flame engulfed his hand, and she knew it to be a simple spell to provide light. The shadows danced across his face, making him appear angrier than he was.

"You will not harm Miss Mulay, Cass," Baxter warned.

"I am only here to visit. We have become close now that Cassandra is gone," Cass lied.

"Do not speak her name again," Baxter warned through clenched teeth.

"Am I in trouble, Instructor Baxter?" Cass asked innocently.

"Not yet, Cass. I want you to know I am watching you. I understand now that I should not have allowed Malikai to heal you, and I should have listened to Victoria."

"Lady Victoria did not want me to live?"

"No, that's not it. Victoria tried to save you, but Malikai was your only real hope. She warned me what you might become after he performed the ritual."

"And what have I become?" Cass asked, taking a step toward him.

"A monster, Cass. Even your father will see it in time and understand the error of having Malikai involved in your healing."

"You are bold, wizard. Do you dare challenge the glorious work of my new father?"

"No, what he did was nothing short of a miracle. However, I fear he wasted his effort on someone who was not deserving."

"How dare you play god with me," Cass growled, and she summoned a much brighter fire than Baxter's. It engulfed her whole hand in a bright, substantial orange flame, not in soothing blue light like Baxter's.

Baxter did not flinch and said, "I wanted to save you, Cass, because I felt guilty over not saving Cassandra. So, I did what I thought was right. Now I warn you once more, leave Binta alone. She has endured enough and is dealing with Cassandra's death, much like I am."

"You presume much," Cass spat.

"Do I? This very evening at the dinner table, I read your thoughts. I know what you had planned for her this evening."

Cass could only laugh, not only because she thought the situation funny, but because the nasty wizard had invaded her thoughts without her knowing it. She had underestimated him and would not do so again.

"Good night, Cass." Baxter turned to leave, extinguishing his flame, but turned after a couple of steps. "By the way, Victoria rescinds her invitation to reinstate you and feels you should leave with Malikai when he exits the city."

Cass just stared at him hatefully, without a response. Finally, Baxter turned and exited the temple, and Cass was left alone. She lowered her flaming hand slowly and willed the flame away, leaving her again in total darkness. Someone had interfered with her fun for the first time since her rebirth a few days earlier, and she did not appreciate it. She eventually made her way back home and crawled into bed. However, sleep did not come easily for the troubled young woman.

It had been nearly two weeks, and Cassandra was ready. She had mastered the magic that her smoke shackles were comprised of, and her command over the ravens had become impeccable. She was so attuned with them now that she knew they would attack when she commanded it, and it would be a vicious death for the fire creature. It had made her go without food for two days, and when it had finally delivered the goods, she had nearly killed it then and there. Her weakened state was the only thing that stopped her. She was ready to see it through this time. She sat in a meditative stance, cross-legged and eyes closed. It would be coming soon; she could feel it through the fire.

She focused on the birds, at least three hundred strong now, all in the trees above her. Not one made a sound, and the silence was palpable. The only sound evident was the gentle rustling of the leaves in the trees. She knew this was the calm before the storm. In short order, she would be free from the creature. She focused on her magic, sorting the symbols and preparing the battlefield.

Not so far away, Boz felt the disturbance keenly. His connection with the freld known as Menji, Cassandra's keeper, was more substantial than Cassandra's connection with the ravens. The creature delivered more food to their prisoner, but something was wrong with the gate. It was as if the magical fire had become poisoned, as if someone new now controlled it. But who?

Cassandra Rho was a witch, according to Ronnis, and so he reasoned that his prisoner had found a way to control the fire. He just hoped that Menji would not kill the girl; she was no good to him dead. Boz spurred on his horse even faster in the thick snow, although the steed struggled in the fresh powder. He was still a good week away from the rendezvous point; the carofex hoped he would find Cassandra in one piece when he arrived.

The creature stepped through the fire gate and didn't notice that it closed behind it. Cassandra sat meditating like usual, the smokey binds still holding her close to the fire. It dropped the food sack and began to move back toward the fire. Two stinging balls of energy slammed into its back. They did minor damage but stung it, agitating it. The creature spun around to confront its prisoner and instead found Cassandra standing away from the fire, the smoke binds gone, and her hands crackling with green energy.

It growled threateningly and took a step toward her. "Not so fast, ugly," Cassandra said. With a swipe of her hand, smoke billowed forth from the fire and wrapped the creature tightly about the chest, arms, and neck.

The shocked beast was pulled to its knees by the strength of those binds and could not disguise its look of surprise. It pulled hard at the smokey restraints it had created and controlled for the last few weeks. It was obviously not a dumb creature, but it had difficulty understanding why the smoke and fire would not answer its call. Then another sphere of magical energy struck it in the face. And that time, it hurt.

"Why have you kidnapped me?" Cassandra demanded, summoning another ball of energy in each hand.

The monster growled and strained to bring its bound hand up before her, snapping the bindings. It threw a gout of flame from its palm, aimed for Cassandra's face. She brought her hands up at the last second, smacking them together and using the two spheres of mystical energy to create a magical shield that deflected the flame. However, the force of the strike sent her flying back to land hard on the cold ground. When she recovered from the impact, the creature had broken the smoke binds and advanced on her. Cassandra tried to remain calm, but she did not know what to expect from the volatile beast. So, she went with her backup plan and reached out mentally to the ravens.

She could feel them, all of them. They swarmed down from above, converging on the monster that had held her prisoner for the last two weeks. But they were not quick enough. Cassandra snapped out of her meditation to feel the beast's hot hand around her throat. It hoisted her into the air, her legs kicking and her hands tugging at the vice-like grip. She couldn't breathe and couldn't possibly break the hold. It looked hatefully into her eyes, and she could see the blistered skin on its face from her attack. It held up a glowing palm that produced immense heat and brought it to her face, and she realized it would burn her similarly.

A raven flew into the side of its face, distracting it for a moment. Cassandra began to black out, stars forming in her vision. The thing swatted at several birds but did not relent its grasp. The ravens were swarming chaotically, and she understood that they had no direction due to her lack of concentration. She closed her eyes and refocused. She could feel them all around, but they were confused and disorganized. She soon had them working together and coordinating their attacks, and the demon creature dropped her to the ground.

She gasped for air and struggled to sit up in the snow. As she caught her breath and regained her senses, she saw the horror of what the birds could do. It was a hideous sight as the ravens bored its eyes out first and pecked and clawed at its skin. She eventually felt sorry for it as it let out a pitiful scream. Then, a few ravens flew into its mouth and attacked it from the inside, pecking out its cheeks. It killed many ravens in the process, but it mattered not; it was overwhelmed and soon dead. The birds flew back to the trees, leaving a bloody pulp of tissue where, just moments before, the creature had stood.

A pang of guilt washed over Cassandra, but then she remembered that just like the wolf all those years ago, this creature had meant to harm her. She had done what she could to survive and eliminated the threat. The fire died and became nothing, taking her heat and light source. That turn of events was something she had not considered. She was cold immediately as the winter wind cut through her thin acolyte gown.

Cassandra had no idea where she was or how close she was to any shelter. All she knew was that she wouldn't last long in the elements. The snow was still coming down with no end in sight, and she berated herself for not considering the harsh weather in her plans. But then, Cassandra noticed one lone raven in the snow at her feet, its beak covered in blood. She held her palm up, and it flew to her. She stared intently into its eyes and understood that it would die for her; all of them would, she knew.

"I need shelter. Can you find that for me?" she asked it.

The bird studied her for a few moments. It cocked its head back and forth as if trying to comprehend her words. She tried to develop a mental link with the creature, communicate with it, and relay what she needed. After a few moments, it cawed and flew away. Cassandra watched it fly into the night and disappear. With a shrug, she followed. She wasn't sure if the bird was leading her, but that direction seemed as good as any.

4

BROKEN SPIRITS

QUENTIN AND ELLA PEEBLES HAD NURSED ARRIN MALIK, THE captain of Pelesea's army, back to health, finally breaking the poison's hold over him. Kringus had left Arrin a month earlier at the small community called Farmer's Stop, which Quentin and Ella called home. Arrin, along with the cavaliers Erik and Marcus, had been too injured to travel home, so the king had made the difficult decision to leave them under the care of the farming couple. Kringus had vowed to send for them quickly, so the king had sent men to escort them back home as soon as possible.

The three men, nearly fully healed, were delighted to see the contingent of twenty Pelesea knights and three priests that entered Farmer's Stop on a cold winter night. They had come via the ship *Siren's Scourge* through the docks of Mecca-Loraine, located less than one hundred miles to the south. Old friends became reacquainted, and Quentin and Ella threw a grand celebration in their enormous barn for the men of Pelesea. The king had sent a small fortune in gold and foodstuffs to pay the farmers for their hospitality. And so, the celebration continued well into the night.

The following day, the men of Pelesea said their goodbyes to the couple, Arrin expressing his heartfelt thanks most of all.

"Dear Ella, I will remember you holding the cold cloth to my head on those nights I struggled with delirium. You are a wonderful woman," he said.

He approached Quentin, clasped hands, and said, "Your hospitality has earned you an ally in Pelesea and a friend in me. Understand that our gates are open if you or your community ever need anything."

Quentin smiled, his weathered face and firm handshake indicating he was no stranger to manual labor, a shared trait of the hearty people of Farmer's Stop. "The pleasure was all ours, my new friend. Besides, we have nothing else to do during the winter."

Arrin laughed, saying, "Also, the wagon and the two strong horses that pulled it from Mecca-Loraine are yours."

Quentin looked back to the barn and shook his head. "We couldn't possibly—"

"There is no arguing the point, sir; they are yours. Use them as you see fit, and understand the horses will work hard for you in the fields."

Quentin nodded and clasped hands with Arrin again, the king's generosity overwhelming him. Ella approached her husband, smiled, and grasped his hand tightly to keep him from falling over. Erik and Marcus took their turns saying their emotional goodbyes, and soon after, the men of Pelesea left Farmer's Stop to begin their journey home.

The snow still fell but did not deter them; their spirits were high. Each man rode a steed from Pelesea's stock, the empty hull of *Siren's Scourge* easily housing the magnificent horses during the trip. Arrin, Marcus, and Erik rode slowly in front, leading the knights through the thick snow.

"In this snow, it will take us thirty moons or more to reach Pelesea," Marcus said.

"At least we are healthy again and able to ride these most wonderful horses," Erik added, patting the neck of his strong mount.

"This is true, Erik; I am happy to be alive, and we owe the good folks of Farmer's Stop for this opportunity to travel home. Not just Quentin and Ella, but all the members of that small community," Arrin said. Both cavaliers nodded in agreement, each fondly remembering their treatment at the hands of the hospitable farmers.

Arrin summoned Benjamin with a wave of his hand. Benjamin was one of the cavaliers who had journeyed from Pelesea to bring them home. The man spurred on his mount to get it even with the three leaders of the troop.

As he made his way beside Arrin, he asked, "Yes, my lord?"

"My good friends here," Arrin said, motioning to Erik and Marcus," feel that it will take a month of moons to reach home. Do you agree with this?"

"No, sir, not if we are going to make the scheduled stops," Benjamin answered.

"Scheduled stops?" Erik asked.

"Please enlighten these good men of the king's wishes you told me about when you first arrived," Arrin said.

"Kringus requires us to stop at Oldorburg to check on the status of the small town."

"Yes!" Marcus yelled, punching a fist into the air.

"We hope that the young captain of the guard has been appointed sheriff and the town is no longer a cesspool of evil," Arrin reminded his excitable friend.

"Of course, Arrin, but my sword is ready to pay back those responsible for the deaths of our friends and allies if the opportunity arises," Marcus vowed.

"So, we head to Oldorburg, which, like Marcus, I look forward to revisiting. However, Benjamin, you said there were *stops* to make. Where else are our services required?" Erik asked.

"After we visit Oldorburg, we are to check in with Daro on the status of Novafontera," the young cavalier replied.

"However, Erik, before considering Novafontera, we will ensure Oldorburg has a solid foundation. We all know our first visit was a failure, and Kringus desires that fact resolved as quickly as possible. With our group, we can help eradicate any evil that remains there," Arrin explained.

"Of course, you know Marcus and I are ready to avenge our friends. We will travel to Novafontera once we are certain Oldorburg is under the rule of goodly people," Erik confirmed.

"We plan to stay for the winter," Arrin added, then watched for the reactions from Marcus and Erik.

"In Oldorburg?" Marcus asked immediately.

"If that is what it takes to make the town a safe place for its citizens," Arrin answered. "Otherwise, if Max has control of the town and is indeed the new sheriff, we will help solidify his hold there."

Marcus and Erik both nodded in agreement. Arrin smiled, eager to put their failures with the town behind them.

They said nothing as Benjamin fell back in line, and the troop slowly made their way through the deep snow. Their failure at Oldorburg was fresh on their minds, and each was mentally prepared for what they might find there. There would be another fight if the evil priests were still in control. This time they were well-equipped and better prepared. This time, if the people of Oldorburg needed them, they would not fail, by decree of King Kringus. They were only eight miles from the small town, so they steeled their resolve and trudged proudly through the snow toward their destination.

That night, Quentin and Ella sat in their cozy home, their cupboards and bellies full. Kringus's gift of foodstuffs was far too much for them to store, so they gave a little to every other family in Farmer's Stop. Each home in the small community now had plenty of food for the coming winter. However, the farming couple missed Arrin, Erik, and Marcus as soon as they left. The three young men were like sons to them, and they had enjoyed having them in their home. After dinner, they sat and watched the fire crackle in the fireplace, Quentin smoking his pipe and Ella knitting a shawl.

"It's tranquil," Ella said without looking up from her work.

"Yep," Quentin answered with a puff on his pipe.

That was the extent of the conversation because they knew what each was thinking. Nothing needed to be spoken between the old married couple. Quentin and Ella had been together for nearly fifty years, and they knew each other well, so the silence spoke volumes. Quentin finally resigned himself that it was time for bed. He stood and walked to the fire, stretching his back. He stabbed the logs with the poker and emptied his pipe in the fireplace.

Something crashed through the window. Startled, he rose and went to the window to find a small hole. "What in the name of great Phena did this?"

He looked around the immediate area of the room, trying to find the culprit, and was about to ask Ella a second time what had made the hole when he finally found the source. There, sitting in her favorite chair, was his wife and companion for most of his life, with a quivering arrow sticking out of her eye socket. The shawl was in her lap with her hands folded on top of it. She seemed peaceful, maybe even asleep, if not for the grisly murder weapon sticking from her eye.

"Ella?"

A blood-curdling scream from the neighboring home snapped him out of his fog. The scene before him was real: his wife, his best friend, was dead. He was thankful she had died instantly, but he was a hardy farmer, devout husband, and defender of his family—whoever had done this would pay.

"I'm sorry, Ella," he said, gently squeezing her lifeless hand. The tears came as he went to his room and retrieved his sword.

He returned to his wife shortly after, still strapping on his sword belt, when he finally saw the savages in the room. Three prominent men wearing strange animal skins stood around his dead wife. They had long hair and wore beards to match, snow matted to each. One had a bow and quiver and pulled the arrow out of Ella's eye socket, taking her eye with it with a sickening pop.

"Don't touch her!" Quentin screamed, and he drew his weapon, letting the belt and scabbard fall to the floor. He barely registered the screams of agony echoing through Farmer's Stop as he advanced on the one with the bow, his sword over his head, ready for a downward chop.

The intruder with the bow threw the broken arrow to the ground and smiled, beckoning Quentin to continue his attack. Quentin obliged, wanting nothing more than to avenge the death of his wonderful wife. The bowman never even moved and looked on with amusement. Before Quentin even got close enough to strike, one of the other killers drew a massive sword with the speed of a cat and stuck it into his side. He didn't feel the pain immediately, but the force of the strike stopped him in his tracks. He looked down and noticed the wound and the sword sticking from it as his weapon clanged to the floor.

Quentin fell to his knees, just a few strides away from the bowman, tears running freely down his cheeks. All three shared a laugh at his expense, and he stubbornly tried to reach for his fallen weapon. However, the man whose sword stuck from his side kicked the thin blade out of reach. He was an imposing figure who stood before Quentin, blocking his view of Ella and her killer. The man was massive in stature, muscles cording his naked arms. Quentin looked up at his attacker, who smiled briefly before pulling the sword free and decapitating the old farmer.

Quentin's head rolled and stopped near the fireplace as his lifeless body fell to the floor and began to pool blood. Maltor nodded to his men and sheathed his sword. The other two moved to search the place as the barbarian leader made his way to the door. He observed the carnage around him and was satisfied that the small community posed no real threat. The first strike of their raid would not yield many slaves, but it was an excellent way to warm up his men for the next strike. Other homes were burning as his men herded the livestock out of the barns.

He turned to his men and said, "Take anything of value, then burn the place down."

His men did just that, and within a few moments, they left Farmer's Stop to burn to the ground. Eighty of the nearly one hundred people who populated the place lay dead all around the community. The barbarians took the remaining few inhabitants, all women, as slaves. Maltor and his barbaric warriors had left their mark on the land.

Arrin and the men from Pelesea were hours from the carnage and too far away to witness the massive fire. However, Cassandra was not, and that fire saved her life. She was a few miles away when she first noticed it, wandering in the wilderness, nearly frozen already, having been freed from the freld only a few short hours before. The raven had led her to nothing that resembled a shelter, and her clothes and shoes were soaked. Her feet were close to being frostbitten, and she was near exhaustion, walking in the knee-high snow. Nevertheless, the fire was a beacon of salvation for her, so she hastily approached it.

When she entered the remains of the farming community, the fires were still burning strong; one, mainly, was especially hot. She thawed out her frozen extremities for a bit and gathered kindling and whatever she could find nearby to dry out beside her. She had to keep the fire going at all costs.

She knew something awful had happened there but could not investigate until she warmed up. Just surviving was her priority; she would deal with the rest of the mystery in the morning. She fought the bite of the cold while snuggling as close as she dared to the warmth. She considered how similar the situation was when she was in Kane's caves, trying to thaw from the frozen water. This feeling was the closest she had ever felt to being that cold. She focused on the heat and how nice it felt on her frozen extremities. She eventually drifted off to sleep.

Binta stood in front of the tiny apartment with a fake smile. She waited patiently for an answer to her knock. She was visiting people's homes, trying to gain interest in the church of Plath. Her heart wasn't in the effort, but she had to try. She had to do something to occupy her mind. If not, she might give up on everything or succumb to Cass's suggestions of servitude. As she thought of it, a bolt of intrigue shot through her stomach, so, when the door finally opened, she was caught off guard.

"Yes?" a middle-aged man asked, standing in the doorway.

It was cold outside, and the man wore little to protect him from the biting air. He shivered as he waited for her to respond, looking her up and down. Binta knew he was judging her. Could he somehow read her naughty thoughts? Had her expression betrayed her?

She stammered for a greeting. "Hello, good sir, I am Binta, an acolyte of the church of Plath. I—"

The door shut before she could say another word. She sighed and turned to face the main street of Pelesea. People rushed about, the cold wind biting them as they went about their business. They were eager to escape the cold, and she realized her hands were nearly frozen. How long had she been out in the weather doing this? Binta didn't know how long she had walked the great city's streets, but she was cold. And she was done. She had gained little interest in Plath that day, wandering from home to home, and she knew that she would achieve better results if she at least believed in the cause. However, she did not. She missed Greyson greatly. She needed him. She missed Cassandra even more, and that loneliness crept into her soul.

She began her trek back to the temple. Unfortunately, she was several blocks away, and the snow was deep, so it took her quite a while to get there. As she neared the docks, she passed the home of Franklin Ruben. The house was gigantic, reminding her of how spoiled and nasty Cass was. Binta hurried by the house, hoping not to garner the attention of anyone inside. She made the temple a little while later, stomped the snow from her boots, and hurried toward the section of the temple dedicated to Plath.

Since the church of Plath was new, the sanctuary and Greyson's quarters, which were now Binta's, were in the lower levels of the giant structure. It took her a while to reach it, and along the way she thought of a nice hot bath to warm her up. As she finally came to the sanctuary of Plath and brought her key forth to unlock the doors, she stopped in her tracks. The doors were not only unlocked but opened just a crack. No light showed from within, and she heard no sound. Her heart raced, and she envisioned Cass inside, wearing her short skirt and knee-high boots. That made her heart beat harder.

She gently lifted the small lantern kept by the double doors and used the accompanying flint and steel to light it. She slowly opened the door and let her lantern brighten the empty sanctuary. She could see no one, and nothing seemed out of place.

"Hello?" she asked.

There was no answer, so she went in and locked the doors behind her. She felt a little uneasy, knowing someone had entered the sanctuary in her absence. There could be no doubt that it was Cass, and she felt like running to Victoria's school and taking Baxter up on his offer of moving into the dorms until she felt safe. He had asked her to stay the night before, and she had been weak enough to accept. She had rested well, but she knew she had to carry on with Greyson's work. Sleeping in her old dorm room made no sense and was not the answer she needed. Baxter had been kind to her because he knew her pain; he cared for Cassandra as much as she did. He also understood Cass's intentions.

But he failed to understand that Binta was not totally against the idea of serving Cass. Sure, she hated the woman, and yes, she was afraid to be around her. However, that only excited her for some strange reason. Baxter didn't understand her immediate needs. She appreciated him and knew he served her best interests, but she needed to sort out the dark cloud that was Cass on her own.

"Cass?" she asked, louder now.

There was still no answer, so she went to Greyson's room and lit another lamp. Again, nothing seemed out of place, and she relaxed a bit. Perhaps she had forgotten to lock the doors when she had left. Either way, no one was there, and nothing was out of sorts. She took off her winter coat and shook the melted snow from her hair. She needed that bath more than ever, so she gathered her clothes, soap, and a towel and headed for the temple bathhouse.

As she made her way back to the sanctuary door, she finally found what was out of place. On the pew, the same one Cass had sat upon a few nights ago, was a pair of underwear. She dropped her bath supplies and just stared at them. They were tiny and see-through, and Binta imagined they could only belong to Cass. She looked around, expecting to see the nasty woman emerge from a dark corner, but all was silent. Finally, after an eternity, she found the courage to approach the pew. Images of Cass raced through her head, making her more than a little excited.

She gently picked the underwear up with both hands and held them in front of her. Cass's perfume assaulted her. She brought them to her nose and inhaled. Her heart pounded in her chest as she sucked in her scent once more, and the smell of sex mixed with the fragrance assaulted her senses. There was a sweetness to that scent, one that calmed her and aroused her simultaneously. She had never been with another woman before, and the thought of it had her heart racing. Waves of lust overwhelmed her, and she could no longer control herself; she quickly returned to her room. She undressed and fell to her bed, one hand holding the underwear to her nose and inhaling Cass's aroma while the other moved between her legs. She played, something she had not done since the night of her first kiss with Cassandra, and soon she lay spent and panting, one leg hanging off her bed.

Afterward, she hid the underwear under her pillow and headed to her bath. She was so sexually charged that she could hardly contain herself long enough to bathe. All she could think of was Cass and how badly she wanted to succumb to her innermost desires. Not once that night did her thoughts dwell on Cassandra or Greyson. She desperately welcomed that reprieve.

Cassandra awoke several times that night with the cold air biting her. She would frequently change positions so the fire could reach the parts that were cold, but she was far from comfortable. She knew during the ordeal of that first night that if she let the fire go out, she would die. Winter was setting in, and she had no shelter. Her rest was uneasy, and she often woke with a start, panicked at the thought of the fire extinguishing. She used those times to feed the fire and successfully kept it burning until morning. The snow had stopped, but the wind still blew strong. As she gathered kindling to keep the essential fire fueled, she witnessed the carnage that was formerly Farmer's Stop.

Several buildings smoldered, blowing smoke around the area and making it difficult for Cassandra to breathe. Blood covered the snowy ground, and bodies littered the snow. She found men, women, and even children strewn about, some missing their heads, which she would discover a few yards away. It repulsed her and made it hard to remain in the murder scene that was once a small village, but she needed the fire to live, so she stayed and hoped the killers of the many people lying about her were far away. She tried to ignore the decapitated bodies and focused on finding shelter, but no structures were left standing. The wind bit her as she foraged for kindling. She spent most of the morning doing so and collected quite a bit, laying it next to her fire to dry.

She figured that whatever or whoever caused the carnage was no longer there, or she would have encountered it during the night. So, she walked around the area, understanding, from the many snow-covered fields and the remains of large barn-like buildings still burning, that it was a farmers' community. She discovered no food stores, which she found odd. She reasoned that the food was either consumed by the fire or stolen by the murderer. She would not last long without food. She could melt snow for water, but no food would be a problem.

She discovered many tracks on the opposite side of the area from where her fire burned. She had no training in tracking or recognizing footprints, but they looked human, with livestock and at least two wagons. She presumed that these were the tracks of whoever orchestrated such a horrific attack. She found a road near the ruined community, giving her hope that someone could come by and find her. But strangely, the attackers had not used the road and instead traveled perpendicular to it, their tracks crossing it, then disappearing into the woods.

She returned to the fire and found an old bucket along the way. After filling it with snow and placing it near the fire to make water, she sat down and threw some wood into the hungry flames. She was in trouble, she knew. She was already hungry and ill-equipped for travel. Cassandra's only real hope was that someone would come along and find her, but who would be traveling in a snowstorm?

She sat and stoked the fire, afraid for her life. There were too many variables that all resulted in her death. If the fire burned out, or if the murderers returned, or someone with ill intentions traveling the road found her, or if wildlife decided to make her dinner, or if she simply didn't find any food, she was as good as dead. None of the options appealed to her, and she huddled closer to the warmth to formulate a plan.

By the day's end, all the other buildings were smoldering embers. The cold would soon extinguish them, and her lone fire would be her only hope of survival. Cassandra curled up as close as she could to it and dozed off several times. She tried to stay awake the best she could to maintain the fire and watch for potential travelers. On the rare occasions when Cassandra slept for more than a few hours, she would wake up with her back and feet numb as the freezing wind bit at them. And if not the cold, her growling stomach would wake her.

On her second day at Farmer's Stop, she investigated what remained of the many buildings, the fires all but dead. One wall of a tiny home remained partially standing, about four feet defiantly battling the wind. She cleared an area around it and gathered other remnants to build a rudimentary shelter. The debris provided some protection from the relentless wind, which she was thankful for. However, she needed her fire transported to her new spot. Cassandra dug out a small hole using a charred board and lined it with rocks, making a fire pit the best she could. She used her bucket to move some hot embers from the larger fire to the newly constructed firepit and soon had the fire burning heartily at her new protected location.

She watched the original fire slowly burn out. She wanted to keep both going, but she did not have enough wood to maintain them; she felt weak and needed to conserve her energy until she found sustenance, and so she resolved to keep the smaller fire well-fed and alive. She hoped someone would see her soon because she was unsure how long she could tolerate the harsh conditions.

The following days were miserable for Cassandra as she fought against the stubborn wind, the ice, and the snow that refused to stop falling. By the fifth day, she was desperate enough to scavenge for food again, searching the burned barns and homes to find a morsel. She found nothing. She entertained the idea of calling the ravens and killing a few to eat. But, in the end, she did not want to break their trust, even if it meant certain death for her. So, she succumbed to the fact that she might die in a ruined place with no name, located somewhere she did not recognize. She would die in a lonely grave surrounded by massacred bodies of people she didn't know.

"Perfect," she whispered.

As she drifted off to sleep on the fifth night, she finally remembered her holy symbol of Gella. The ordeal of defeating the demon and wandering alone in the snowstorm had distracted her from the one thing that could be her salvation—her goddess. She reached into her shirt, pulled out the medallion, and held it tightly with shaking hands.

She prayed to her goddess, asking for help. "Oh powerful Gella, I have failed you. In my desperation to survive, I have shunned you. I don't deserve you, but I remain your humble servant. Take me from this misery if it is your desire. But, if you deem it not my time, please lend me the power to survive this. I cannot take much more."

She fell asleep and rested peacefully for the first time in many nights. Cassandra's dreams were calm, and she felt closer to her goddess than she ever had. The feeling she had was like that morning in the Pelesea sanctuary when she first opened her heart to the goddess weeks earlier.

She awoke with a start and realized she was freezing. To her horror, the fire was nearly exhausted, and the sun was high in the morning sky. She added what little kindling and firewood she had at her disposal and managed to save the fire. Soon it was burning well, and she resupplied her depleted wood reserve. It took all her energy in her weakened state from lack of food. She decided to find food that day one way or another.

Suddenly, she recalled a powerful spell that Maina, the high priestess of Gella, had performed. On the morning of the autumn equinox, she had summoned food for the other disciples of the goddess. It was a creation of magic given to Maina by Gella. An idea came to Cassandra then. She was not a priestess of Gella, but she believed in the goddess and worshipped her. Perhaps Gella would grant her the power to create food using Cassandra's knowledge of arcane magic.

She sat next to the fire, closed her eyes, and began a prayer that she hoped would save her life. She had not trained as a priestess, but she had watched Maina and the others perform potent spells and tried to recall them. She felt a surge of power course within her, and she assumed it was the goddess giving her the strength and wisdom to create the powerful spell. She saw the symbols Maina had used that day months ago and knew them to be holy, not arcane. Still, she could see them, and she tried to sort them. Cassandra opened her eyes hours later, the fire again dangerously close to burning out. But she ignored it, too caught up in the power she felt inside her.

The energy of her goddess coursed through her arms, and power welled in her very being. She concentrated on the task and held her hands toward the ground before her. Green energy eventually flowed from her fingers and swirled around the grass, slowly forming a substantial mass. After a long while, Cassandra fell back, exhausted, the spell draining her of her last bit of energy. When she collected herself and viewed the results, there was a loaf of bread, some dried meat, and fresh fruit on the ground. Cassandra had asked Gella for help, and the goddess had delivered. She ate well that day and greedily, barely controlling herself to conserve some of it for the coming days. Cassandra did not know if she could perform the feat again, so she saved as much food as possible. She rightfully thanked Gella that night for saving her life.

It had been nearly two weeks since Cassandra had died in the horrible fire, and Binta found herself at her friend's gravesite. It was a cold morning, but the sun shone brightly, and the rays caught Cassandra's tombstone, making the newly etched lettering of her name glow for just a bit. That name would always shine in Binta's heart. Even though they had only known each other briefly, they had become soul mates. She would never get over Cassandra's death, especially how it happened, alone and in the grips of a raging inferno. She knelt and placed freshly purchased flowers at the base of the stone.

"I miss you. I love you," Binta whispered.

She stood then with tears in her eyes. Greyson would be far at sea, and it would be months before he returned to her, if he returned at all. She ran her hand over Cassandra's stone, knocking off the snow atop it. She resented Greyson then, yet she knew his course was just and good. He was thinking of others, while Binta was selfish. She needed him there; she was weak and afraid of falling for Cass's temptations. She had played with the underwear for days and completely neglected her duties to Plath. This was the first day she had been out since she had found them in the sanctuary. She feared Cass would eventually break her. The thought frightened her yet excited her all at the same time.

She had stayed strong thus far, with the help of Baxter, who seemed to be genuinely concerned for her. He was protecting her from Cass, keeping her away from the temple of Plath, but Binta wasn't sure how she would hold up if she saw Cass again. She felt weak and vulnerable. Being at Cassandra's grave helped her remember the harsh reality of her life and not focus on the stupid game Cass was playing. She would be fine and get through this, and soon enough, Greyson would be home. She would just stay far away from Cass until then.

She decided then that she would ask for her old dorm room back. She had resisted that idea at first but now thought better of it. Baxter said she could use it rent-free for a while if she desired. That way, Cass could not get into her head. The temple of Plath would be fine without her anyway, as she was not generating new followers. Luckily, the council of high priests had agreed that the church of Plath would owe no rent to the temple until Greyson returned. So, she would go to Baxter and, after his approval, collect her things and move back into the dorm. Perhaps she would go back to school the next semester and have a fresh start. The priesthood was not for her, but the thought of having a fresh start made her feel a little better.

"Goodbye, my friend, I will visit you as often as—" she began, before a voice from behind interrupted her.

"Hello, Binta."

Binta turned to find Cass behind her, and she stepped back with a small yelp. She nearly lost her footing and managed to keep her balance by steadying herself on Cassandra's tombstone. "Cass, where did you come from?"

"Why? Do I make you nervous, Binta?" Cass asked coyly.

"Of course not, Cass, I only—"

"Because you are acting nervous," Cass interrupted, advancing a step.

Binta sat fully on the tombstone and nearly toppled over it. Cass advanced another step and was now in Binta's personal space. Binta wanted to push her away, but she could not. That feeling of intimidation mixed with sexual excitement washed over her once more. Cass reached out to her and brushed the side of her face with the back of her hand. Binta recoiled, but Cass only smiled at her discomfort.

"You have something of mine, don't you?" Cass asked.

Binta knew what she was referring to, and a bolt of excitement charged through her loins at the reference to Cass's underwear. She did not respond but only stared into Cass's mesmerizing eyes.

"Your silence speaks volumes, my new slave."

"I am not your—"

"Bring them to my house tonight at midnight. I need them back."

"I—"

"Shh," Cass interrupted, placing a finger on Binta's lips.

Cass then walked away, leaving Binta sitting on Cassandra's tombstone, needing the support to keep her from falling over entirely. Binta wanted to tell the nasty woman that she had trespassed by entering Plath's temple and that she had thrown out the underwear, but that was not the case. Her mind raced, and her heart pounded at the thought of showing up at Cass's door with her underwear in hand. That wasn't the point, though, and Binta knew it. What did Cass have in mind for her?

She watched Cass walk away, still dressed in her tiny dress and knee-high boots. Again, something struck her as strange about the woman, and she felt the overwhelming desire to follow her. The only woman she had ever considered sleeping with had been Cassandra, but as she watched Cass's seductive walk, she became mesmerized.

She stood and even took a step that way when Cass turned and said, "Do not be late, or I will have to punish you, understand?"

Cass moved her cloak to the side, revealing a whip coiled neatly on her hip. The sight of it brought all of Binta's desires to the surface, and all she could do was meekly nod.

"Good," Cass said, then turned and continued her walk through the cemetery.

Binta watched until she was out of sight, then relaxed and breathed a little easier. Her heart raced in her chest, and she considered what was happening between her and Cass. Whatever it was, she wanted it then more than ever as her sexual desires overwhelmed her good sense. The thought of returning to her old dorm room was distant.

"Greyson, I need you," she whispered.

Binta collected herself and headed back to the temple. She rushed along, head down, deep in thought, so she was startled by Baxter's voice when he yelled out, "Binta!"

She stopped abruptly, only a few blocks from the temple, and turned to see Baxter catching up through the snow. The various wagons and carriages had packed it well on the main street, but navigating it was still tricky. She waited for him to reach her.

"Hello, young lady, how are you doing?" he greeted her with a smile.

She liked Instructor Baxter and appreciated him looking out for her and comforting her in her time of loss, but she had little time for a chat. She put on her best smile and said, "Fine, just heading back to the temple."

She could sense him studying her face and seeing through the lie. However, he just played along. "I haven't heard from you for a few days, so I wanted to ensure you are doing well."

"Yes, I have been out recruiting people to the temple. I'm just trying to stay very busy to keep my mind off things." A sudden flash of Cass's boots crossed her mind, and she swallowed hard.

"Any luck?" Baxter asked suspiciously, one eyebrow lifted.

"With what?"

Baxter looked at her like her hair was on fire but said nothing. Binta knew she wasn't fooling him but was thankful not to explain herself.

"Please continue, and I will walk you back to the temple," he suggested with an outstretched hand.

They began to walk, struggling through the knee-high snow. Neither spoke for a long while until Baxter finally blurted out, "You would tell me if Cass was bothering you, right?"

"Of course," Binta lied.

"You haven't seen her?"

"Not since that day she came to the temple," she lied again.

"Good, perhaps Cass has moved on to something else. However, Victoria wanted me to reiterate her offer for you to stay at the dorms. You may have your old room back and stay there until Greyson returns. That way, you will not be alone, and with the new semester starting in a few weeks, it would make it easier for me to check in on you."

"I appreciate the offer and welcome your well-visits, but it is unnecessary. I have work to do at the temple, which will keep my mind occupied," Binta said, ironically not wanting to accept the offer she had greatly considered just a short while ago.

They reached the temple doors, and Baxter gently touched her shoulder. She turned to regard him, and it looked as if he might cry as he said, "I have struggled with Cassandra's death the last few weeks, and I know it is equally hard on you. Having Victoria to talk to during that time is the only way I have kept my sanity. The offer to live in the dorms is open, and we will save your room. Please reconsider; I think talking occasionally will help us both."

It took all of Binta's strength not to break down and cry. Baxter now offered her what she needed, yet she refused it, thoughts of Cass fluttering in her head. Her strange, perverted sexual desires were overriding her judgment. However, bending to Cass's will was the proper way to keep her mind off Cassandra. She missed her dear friend but did not want to discuss her death. Still, it took all her willpower to refuse the offer, and soon after, Baxter said goodbye and started toward the school.

She watched him go, using all her self-control not to run after him and let him take care of her. She managed to hold her ground and, with a sigh, entered the temple. Her thoughts dwelled on Cass. She had much to do before midnight; most importantly, she needed a bath and wanted to apply her makeup. She wanted to look nice for whatever Cass had in mind for her.

It had taken Boz nearly a week after Menji died to reach the site of his murder. The place where he stood was supposed to be the rendezvous point from where Boz would take Cassandra the rest of the way to Mecca-Loraine. But now, the fire that had held Cassandra captive had long since been extinguished. And his friend and ally lay dead at his feet. Not much remained of the freld after a week of the vultures picking his bones. But the remains of other, smaller creatures littered the area, which appeared to be birds. He reasoned Cassandra had summoned them to attack Menji; he was familiar with her power over ravens. Boz studied the area and found no trace of Cassandra. So, she had escaped, but was she still alive in the harsh weather?

After extensively searching the area, he found what had to be a trail of broken snow. Unfortunately, Boz was no tracker, and the snow and wind had covered most of the evidence, but it was the only thing leading from the fire pit, and it had to be Cassandra's tracks. They just appeared as uneven lumps under the snow, which was as deep as two feet in some areas. He led his horse along the same path, which would lead him to either Cassandra or her frozen body. She had a six-day lead on him, and if she had run into trouble, she would undoubtedly be dead by now.

The going was slow, and he lost the trail several times due to the strong wind that had blown it away or covered it in snow over the last few days. It was so bad in some spots that the brown grass showed through the snow. Luckily, he always found the trail once more and continued his chase. At one point, it cut sharply to the west and appeared to head somewhere close to Farmer's Stop. If she had made her way there and survived the trip, he wouldn't have much longer to travel in the infernal cold. Farmer's Stop could not be more than a few miles away.

If Arrin and the others were still there, it would give Boz's character credibility since he had traveled with Kringus when they had departed Farmer's Stop, leaving Arrin and two others behind. He would offer to take Cassandra to Mecca-Loraine, and would need to lie to convince her to go with him. Boz did not want to use force because Ronnis D'Breeth and Mecca-Loraine were still about one hundred miles to the south. To provoke Cassandra's wrath and an attack from those wicked birds was something he did not desire. It would be much easier to leave Farmer's Stop together as allies. He would need to convince her that Mecca-Loraine was her new destination; he would need to lie.

Cassandra lay beside the fire, simply trying to survive the night. Unless the weather was nasty in the morning, she would travel the road and hope to come across a town or other place where she could find shelter. Cassandra hoped a warm bed might be just a few miles away. But, on the other hand, she also risked the possibility of finding nothing but barren hills of snow. She wished she knew where she was so she could make a more educated estimate of her chances. The demon creature had deposited her in a nondescript wooded area, and she could be anywhere in the world.

She could not keep sitting by the small fire in her ineffective shelter, hoping for someone to find her. No one had traveled the road, and she would wait no longer. She had found some cheesecloth in a partially burned barn and had made a coat out of it. She used scissors she found in the rubble to cut the cloth and a rope as a belt to hold it. She had also wrapped her feet tightly with the fabric, and she felt more comfortable now than she had since she had arrived. She would say goodbye to her fire and the small community in the morning.

Before sunrise, a hand was on her shoulder and shaking her. She awoke with a scream and sat up quickly, her hand glowing with a greenish light of magical energy. Her first instinct was to unleash the magical sphere on the new arrival, but she crawled away backward instead and gained her feet as quickly as she could. The man wore a heavy coat and was bundled well against the harsh wind. The idea that this man was one of the original attackers returning to the crime scene crossed her mind.

"Who are you? Speak up!" she ordered.

The man stood slowly, his hands raised. His head was hooded, and she could not see much of his face. The fire flickered on his strong chin.

"I mean no harm," he said in a disarming, monotone voice.

"Why are you here? From where did you come?"

"I am a weary traveler and have come for a night's rest and to gain shelter from the cold. These ruins are what remain of Farmer's Stop, correct?" the man asked, his arms outstretched.

"I don't know the name of this place, but I can tell you everyone here is dead."

The man dropped his hands and said, "I have no weapons; I mean no harm."

Cassandra did not see any weapons on his belt, but that didn't mean he didn't have any hidden beneath the oversized coat.

"How did you get here?" she asked suspiciously, her other hand forming a ball of glowing green energy to match the first.

"My horse," he said, pointing behind him.

Cassandra looked over his shoulder to see a large horse tied to the remains of a destroyed building. She measured his actions, and he seemed safe. His story made sense, but Cassandra did not want to trust him. She remained ready to strike, her energy burning powerfully in each hand.

He finally said something that put her at ease. "I have food and extra clothing in my saddlebags. You must be cold?"

Cassandra looked at her makeshift attire and thought she must look ridiculous to the man. Perhaps Gella had sent him to rescue her, like how the goddess's spell had saved her life. Was this man Gella's way of keeping her from a cruel death?

"I am Boz, a member of the Brotherhood of Fire Monastery of Mecca-Loraine," the man said, presenting a hand to shake.

Cassandra did not take the offered hand, and the green energy spheres still crackled in her palms. She felt safe with the energy ready and at her disposal. The man withdrew his hand and smiled. He then waved a hand over the fire, which grew warm and bright. Cassandra took a step back.

"Do not be alarmed; I have synergy with the fire," he said, staring into the small blaze as if in a trance. "I can start a fire, control it, and even extinguish it with but a thought."

As he spoke, he waved his hand dangerously close to the flames, and the fire responded, jumping to lick his palms or changing hues. For a moment, Cassandra considered how the change in the fire, its increased warmth and erratic dancing, reminded her of the demon-like creature's fire. She focused on the flames, looking for the arcane symbols that the previous fire was comprised of. If Cassandra saw them, she would unleash her magic on the man. Her vision blurred as she sought the symbols she expected to find within the flames. She called to them, coaxing them out, but none answered. There was no magic to the fire.

She blinked and noticed the stranger was standing and looking at her, puzzled. She sighed, dismissed the globes of energy, and offered her hand. "I am Cassandra Rho."

There was a hint of recognition in his eyes when she told him her name as if he knew her. The man was mysterious, and she did not trust him. Yet, he could help her, and she would be a fool if she declined it. He shook her hand and smiled warmly.

Boz led her to the horse and produced food and a large blanket. He helped her back to her small shelter, and the two sat there waiting for the sun to rise. Cassandra ate hungrily and felt warm for the first time since escaping the fire creature. The blanket was warm, the food was delicious, and the fire seemed friendlier with Boz manipulating it. She began to trust the man so much that she didn't even notice that the food was very similar to what they had fed her in the jail at Pelesea.

Boz didn't say much as they waited for dawn, but she learned that he was on his way to Mecca-Loraine and would take her if she wanted to tag along. He guessed they could reach it in less than three days by horse, weather permitting. For the first time since arriving at the ruined community, she hoped to survive.

The travel was difficult due to the excess snow the horse had to navigate. It took them closer to four days to arrive due to several snowdrifts they had to circumvent. The going was slow, and the pair spoke little. Cassandra huddled close to Boz, wrapped in her blanket as they traveled.

Binta nervously walked up the mansion's steps to Cass's home. No lights were on inside, and she almost turned around and left. The reality of the moment weighed on her heavily. Was she about to go through with this? Why? There was no reason to. She wanted to return to the dorms and accept Baxter's offer. She would be safe there, and she would be happier than staying at the temple. Yet, she stood before Cass's door with the vile woman's underwear in her pocket. She had bathed and fixed herself up, hoping to impress Cass, but she knew deep down inside she should not be there. She delayed, not knowing what to do next. She stood on the steps for many moments, contemplating her next move.

Suddenly, the door cracked open, and a figure appeared at the threshold. It was too dark for Binta to see, but the mystery person had to be Cass, as Binta noticed those amazing knee-high boots that seemed to glisten in the moonlight. Binta couldn't speak as her voice caught in her throat. Finally, the moment she so desperately needed had arrived.

"Did you bring them?" came Cass's voice from the doorway, confirming that it was indeed her.

"Yes," Binta managed to reply, her voice barely audible.

"Come in, and be quiet," Cass instructed, grabbing her by the arm and pulling her in.

Cass locked the door and turned to Binta. "My father and the servants are asleep; I want to keep it that way, do you understand?"

"Yes," Binta whispered.

Cass grabbed her by the shoulder, and Binta was surprised at the strength she found in that grasp. Cass led her through the dark hallways with little light available. They climbed the massive staircase, still entirely in the dark. Binta let Cass guide her because she could see little. The house smelled of perfume and cinnamon, and the silence was deafening. Binta felt uncomfortable and regretted coming almost immediately after entering. Cass eventually ushered her into a room and locked the door quietly behind her. She then made her way to the dresser and lit a small lamp. Light flooded the room, and the sight took Binta's breath.

Cass's room was more extensive than the entire house where Binta had grown up. Large fluffy pillows and blankets filled the enormous bed, making it appear very inviting. Expensive paintings hung on the walls, and many stuffed animals lined a set of shelves. The furniture looked very expensive, and the large wardrobe hinted at Cass's massive clothing collection. Binta was speechless and just stood there, taking in the scene.

"I knew you would come," Cass said, breaking Binta's trance.

Binta finally focused on the scantily dressed girl, and she became lost in the vision. Cass wore a short dress under her cloak. Her hair was clean and put up, and it occurred to Binta then that Cass had probably bathed in preparation for their meeting just as Binta had. Binta felt like the woman towered over her, and simply being in Cass's room made Binta feel like she was in the den of a predator.

"Well?" Cass asked, taking a step closer.

"It's magnificent," Binta responded, her eyes roaming the room again.

"Not the room, Binta, my underwear," Cass said with an outstretched hand.

Binta could feel her cheeks turning red, and she reached into her pocket to produce the garment. She shyly handed them over. Cass took them and stepped closer, making Binta take a step back.

"I forgot to wash these before dropping them into your possession. But I bet you know that already, don't you?" Cass teased, walking around her, with her boots clicking on the wooden floor. "I bet you were naughty with them, alone in that big temple without your lovers, weren't you?" Cass continued.

"Don't be ridiculous," Binta whispered.

"Humph," Cass said with a smirk, then walked over and pulled something out of the top drawer of her dresser. She walked confidently back to Binta, smiling evilly. Again, Binta felt frozen in place, and her heart nearly pounded out of her chest. Cass stood before her once more and put her hands on her hips. Binta knew that her underwear as well as the item from the drawer were in one of Cass's hands, but she could not identify the item. She felt compelled to look at the floor, embarrassed but excited for what might happen next.

"You are here of your own free will, standing in my room," Cass said, taking a finger and lifting Binta's chin to meet her gaze. Binta felt weak under her stern visage and wanted to look away. She could not.

"I came to return your—"

"You came to be my slave," Cass interrupted.

Binta shook her head in disagreement, but Cass grabbed her around the throat. Again, the grip was powerful, almost steel-like. Binta tried to remove her hand but couldn't hope to pry it from her throat. She did not understand the newfound strength Cass displayed. She surmised that it must be from the effects of a powerful spell.

"Don't touch me. You may not touch me unless I desire it," Cass said threateningly. Binta released her hand immediately, and Cass dragged her roughly to the bed and sat her down on it. She then threw the underwear and what appeared to be a collar down next to her as she released her hold on her throat.

Cass did tower over her then, and she stood too close for Binta to be comfortable. Her face was level with Cass's midriff, and she suddenly wanted to kiss her there. She barely managed to control that impulse and instead looked down at her feet again. Cass grabbed a fistful of her hair and turned her face to meet her gaze.

"Oww!" Binta screamed, but she did not dare touch Cass, knowing that was not allowed.

"You are now my slave and will do exactly as I say, right?"

Cass's face was near hers, like the prelude to the night Binta kissed Cassandra. However, this was different, this was wrong, and Binta hated

Cass thoroughly at that moment. Cass had known Binta would come to her, that she had taken liberties with her underwear, and that she would do whatever Cass demanded. Somehow Cass could read her as quickly as if reading a book. The worst part was Binta hated her more than anyone she knew. That somehow made her want to please Cass more. She nodded as much as she could with Cass's firm grasp of her hair.

"Good girl," Cass said, releasing the hold of her hair. "Now, open your mouth."

Binta did as she was told and held her mouth open, knowing better than to break eye contact with her tormentor. Finally, Cass took the underwear from the bed, took a small vial of a white, milky liquid, and poured some on the garment. The faint scent of the substance had Binta swooning, and her juices flowed. She had never felt so sexually charged, and when Cass stuffed the underwear in Binta's mouth, she readily accepted it.

"Now, you keep that in there until I take it out, do you understand?"

Binta heard Cass's words but could not hope to respond. Her entire body seemed to contract when the white liquid touched her tongue. She moaned with pleasure and squeezed her legs together in a failed attempt to fight her mounting arousal. She sucked what she could from the delicate fabric, wanting the liquid, desiring its effect on her. She briefly became unaware of her surroundings as the liquid invaded her body, fluttering her heart and scrambling her thoughts.

Cass smacked her across the cheek. The hit was so vicious, it nearly knocked Binta off the bed. Binta sat back up, her eyes watering, and made eye contact again. The world came back into view as her breathing and heartbeat slowed back to normal. She saw Cass towering over her, an angry look on her face.

"You will answer me when I speak to you, and you will address me as mistress, do you understand?" Cass asked.

Binta could only focus on the liquid as the effects coursed through her body. She had never felt so aroused, and she would gladly have sex with anyone at that moment. She needed that release, desired it more than air for her lungs or water for her throat. She tingled all over and wanted to sexually please Cass. She hoped that would be the following command from her mistress.

And there it was, Binta was a servant to her most hated enemy as she mumbled the words, "Yes, mistress," through the underwear.

She would now be indebted to the evil girl for as long as Cass desired. The pledge made Binta's loins ache, and she squeezed her legs together again to ease the mounting tension.

"Good. Now put this on, and never take it off. It is a symbol of my ownership of you. You now belong to me, and your body is my property. Understand?" Cass asked, handing her the collar.

"Yes, mistress," Binta said, her voice muffled as her tongue entwined with the fabric in her mouth. She secretly sucked the remaining liquid from the underwear as she put the collar around her neck and fastened it.

"Anytime you do not do as I tell you, I will punish you by using my little friend here, do you understand?" Cass asked, moving her cloak again so Binta could see the coiled whip on her belt.

Binta's eyes widened at the sight of the scourge, and she quickly nodded and said, "Yes, mistress."

"Get undressed; I want to test your obedience," Cass demanded, returning to her top drawer.

Binta stood and removed her small jacket, then her blouse, exposing her breasts. Her nipples were hard, and not from the room's temperature. She felt dizzy with lust; the liquid drug from the underwear made her feel warm, and Cass's perfume was intoxicating. She needed sexual release, just as an alcoholic desperately needed a drink.

She unbuttoned her pants and shimmied out of them when Cass turned and said, "Leave your underwear on. Understand?"

Binta nodded once more and mumbled, "Yes, mistress."

She watched Cass approach her, drinking in every bit of the girl—her beautiful face, her short dress, tall boots, and the bit of skin visible between the two. Most importantly, Cass's smell was arousing. She desired to please Cass more than ever.

"Open your mouth," Cass demanded, and Binta complied. Next, Cass took the panties out, tossed them on the floor, and produced the small vial again. The milky liquid still filled most of it, and Binta's eyes widened at the sight. She wondered what would happen if she drank even another drop. Could she survive that? Would too much stimulation kill her? She didn't care, she wanted it, and if Cass desired to give it to her, she would drink it all like a good slave.

"Tilt your head back and drink all of this," Cass said as she raised the vial above Binta's head.

"Yes, mistress," Binta said eagerly, tilting her head back and opening her mouth wide, her tongue waiting for the next wave of ecstasy.

Before Cass could pour the strange substance down her throat, a male voice came from the other side of the room: "No, my daughter!"

The sudden intrusion startled them, and they turned in unison to see an old wizard materialize from nowhere. He had a long grey beard and a pointy hat, like the typical wizards of old.

"Father, why have you come?" Cass asked disappointedly.

Binta knew the strange man was not Cass's father, having seen Mr. Ruben several times over the last few months. However, she had never seen this wizard before.

"You dare to steal from me?" he scolded Cass.

"She is my new pet; I wanted to break her fully," Cass said, ignoring the accusation.

"One drop of this could make her a servant to her filthiest desires. She is fully under your control already, and you do not need to administer the demon milk," he said, taking the small vial from Cass and screwing the lid back on.

He then stuffed it in a small pouch as he began to drink in Binta's near-nakedness. Binta did not cover herself. She wanted him to see her, and more importantly, she wanted the older man to have his way with her. She had never felt so free with her body, and lustful thoughts danced in her head.

"How much did you give her?" the wizard asked as he observed Binta's openness.

"Hardly any," Cass said like a child scolded by a parent. "Only a little through my underwear she was eager to keep in her mouth."

The wizard bent and retrieved the garment, the trigger to Binta's current predicament. He sniffed them, smiled at Binta, and tucked them into another pouch in his robe.

"You are lucky; humans usually die if they have direct contact with the milk and do not ingest demon blood to offset the effects."

He took Binta by the chin. His grip was firm and much more substantial than Binta expected. He let a finger slip into her mouth, and she instinctively sucked on it.

He smiled and said, "It is a miracle that she lives, and I am curious to see how much control you have over her. The effects of the milk, mixed with your natural pheromones, should have her very obedient to your desires."

To Binta's disappointment, he removed his finger from her mouth and added, "Permanently would be my guess."

A wide smile appeared on Cass's face as she grabbed a small chain and attached it to Binta's collar.

"I want to test your theory," Cass said, holding her pet's leash.

She turned to the wizard and added, "Besides, I only borrowed the one vial while you kept that corpse company."

"Matilda is none of your concern. She will snap out of it soon, or I will leave her to rot. Either way, my patience grows thin, so she will soon no longer be a problem."

Cass just shrugged as she climbed into her bed, sitting against the headboard and motioning Binta to sit near her feet at the end of the bed. Binta complied and knelt by Cass's feet. She could feel the strange wizard's eyes on her and licked her lips in anticipation. She welcomed his touch as he gently tugged on her nose ring and issued an approving growl. It was the milk! What did the old wizard call it? Demon milk? She knew it was wreaking havoc on her sexual desires and stirring up the naughty thoughts that swarmed her mind. She wished Cass had given her more of the liquid so she could sink further into the ecstasy she now floated in. She wanted to serve Cass, and being on the bed with her made her heart race. What was Cass planning for her? Binta chewed her lower lip while studying the high leather boots before her.

"I should punish you for your reckless regard for my possessions!" he said.

"So, spank me later. Right now, let us enjoy my pet," Cass replied with a shrug.

After a few moments of silence, the old wizard finally said, "Very well, carry on as if I were not here."

He then undressed, tossing his hat in a chair and pulling his old robe over his head. Binta looked away, her heart racing again and her body tingling in anticipation. She knew it was the work of the milk, but she didn't care.

"Do you like my boots, slave?" Cass asked, pulling slightly on the leash.

"Yes, mistress," Binta said honestly and anxiously.

"Good, because I want you to lick them clean," Cass continued, jerking the chain hard so Binta fell on all fours. "Do not touch them with anything but your tongue."

Binta obliged, licking the boots from ankle to knee, cleaning them with one long stroke of her tongue each time. She loved the feel of the leather on her tongue and how degrading the act was. She was eager, perhaps too much so, and licked every inch of the long boots, panting like a wild animal as she did. She had to lie almost flat on the bed to perform the demeaning task, but Cass made sure to add to her humiliation.

"Offer yourself to Malikai so he may use your body as he desires," her mistress commanded.

Binta gasped at the rude command but knew better than to disobey. She desired what would come, so she gladly did precisely as told. She knew she was giving the old wizard an eyeful, even wearing her thin underwear, which left little to the imagination. She stuck her bottom out wantonly, hoping he would take her. The act drove her to lick Cass's boots with renewed vigor.

When Binta's saliva covered most of the boots, making them shine in the lamplight, Cass increased her demands. "Now the bottoms."

Binta looked to Cass as if questioning the command, and the delay cost her a slap across the face as Cass quickly sat up and struck her. Binta saw stars as the swing was more potent than she would expect from a girl Cass's size. It took her just a moment to recover and fight back the tears, and she quickly went to the dirty sole and started licking. The humiliating act had her loins aching for attention. She knew the wizard was behind her, ravaging her with his eyes. She licked furiously, anxious for the following command.

"Did I ever tell you about how Cassandra cleaned my boots in the caves?" Cass purred.

Binta slowed her licking at the mention of her friend's name but knew better than to stop. As far as she could tell, if she denied any of Cass's commands, the woman would hit her, and she was confident the old wizard would not interfere. However, the mention of Cassandra's name nearly broke her from the lustful spell the milk had on her. The rational thoughts buried in the back of her mind screamed at her. Cass was a bad person and an enemy. Why was she agreeing to any of the acts Cass was demanding?

She stopped briefly to pick at the dirt on her tongue, and the degrading act turned her thoughts back to the sexual buildup between her legs.

"Cassandra was at my mercy and licked them like a whore, just like you are doing."

This story was Binta's first hearing about events between Cassandra and Cass in the caves after they were separated. She did not doubt Cass's words and understood that there were probably many degrading things Cass had done to her friend. The thought of them had Binta even more aroused. She knew it was wrong but could not stop; her body betrayed her. She licked harder and squeezed her legs together in a failed attempt to suppress her aching loins. Cass pulled the leash again, interrupting her and making her crawl up the bed a little. Cass parted her legs, so Binta found herself between them. She looked up, and seeing another woman exposed that close made her bite her lip and squeeze her legs together again, stifling the sexual charge there.

She often had dreams of being in that same position, but with Cassandra, where the feelings of love mixed with the lustful thoughts. She never dreamed she would be this close to pleasing another woman, especially one of Cass's caliber.

"Lick my thighs, slave," Cass demanded.

Binta went to work, licking and kissing her mistress's thighs. She took turns kissing one, then the next, and then licked back to Cass's knees. She had never been with a woman before but could smell Cass's scent, and her lust for the woman was boiling over. Cass slowly pulled the leash, making Binta inch closer to her. Binta was ready to please Cass, her arousal overriding any logical thoughts, but just before she reached her goal, Cass grabbed a handful of her hair and pulled her head up. Binta made eye contact with her new mistress and awaited her command.

"Keep your gaze here as you pleasure me," Cass said, pointing to her eyes. "And do your job correctly, or I will severely punish you. Do you understand me, slave?"

"Yes, mistress," Binta said.

Cass released her hair, and Binta sank back to eye level with Cass's sex. She made sure not to break eye contact with her mistress. Instead, Binta inched forward, ready to please her. At the same time, she felt the wizard behind her pulling her underwear to the side, exposing her entirely, and she arched her back to give him better access. Cass put her hand on the back of Binta's head and pushed her forward, and for the first time, Binta tasted another woman. She loved it, and she tried her best to please Cass. She was in uncharted territory, but her lustful desires had her working hard. She performed acts on Cass that she enjoyed being done to herself, things she had saved for Cassandra. Cass moaned and Binta worked harder, watching her mistress close her eyes and slightly open her mouth. She was obviously enjoying Binta's work.

Soon after, Binta felt the old wizard take her. He was not gentle and did not waste any time thrusting fully into her. Binta moaned loudly, her screams muffled as Cass held her head tight against her. Binta was lost in her lust-filled daze, the milk and the servitude adding to the pleasure that the old man provided. Malikai was somehow just as significant as Greyson, and she could not control herself after such a buildup. Cass again muffled her cries, but Binta somehow maintained eye contact through her first orgasm, and Cass soon followed.

Afterward, Cass released her and moved off the bed, letting Malikai have his way with her. Binta felt the part of a streetwalker, a complete and obedient whore as Malikai brought her to climax repeatedly. The wizard had the stamina of a much younger man, and it took a long while before his lust finally played out. Binta collapsed on the bed, completely exhausted, but not Malikai, who stood and approached Cass. Binta turned on her back and saw them together, looking at her, whispering and smiling. She couldn't believe she had finally participated in a tryst with two other people, the goal she and Greyson had dreamed of with Cassandra. However, the reality was, Binta had been used by two evil people instead of giving in to her honest desires to be with Cassandra and Greyson. She suddenly felt sick. She wished she were far away from Cass and safe in her dorm bed. She was humiliated.

Cass walked over to her and grabbed the leash, roughly pulling Binta off the bed. She fell to the floor and banged both knees, the pain making her grimace.

"You sleep there, slave," Cass said.

"I will leave; I do not want to be a burden," Binta said, hoping to regain control now that the awful act was over.

Cass pulled her hair back, and Binta winced but did not scream. She looked Cass in the eye as she towered over her.

"You will do exactly as I say, slave. And right now, I say for you to lie on the floor and sleep."

"Yes, mistress," Binta whispered.

Cass released her, and Binta lay prone on the floor, not wanting to anger the volatile woman. Shortly after, Cass and Malikai began their lovemaking on the bed as Binta curled up into a ball. She missed Cassandra and Greyson and felt a world of guilt for being there. Binta silently cried herself to sleep as Malikai and Cass carried on their lewd acts for most of the night. Her rest was frequently interrupted by Cass's screams of pleasure. Also, wearing only her thin underwear kept Binta cold and unable to sleep soundly. Cass entirely broke her spirit that awful and humiliating night as she slept like a dog on the hard floor, trying to forget the appalling acts she had performed.

The following day, Binta rose as the early morning sun found its way through the window. She was relieved to find Cass and Malikai intertwined but asleep. She remembered the previous night and wanted to escape the horrible room. She was humiliated for what she had done. She briefly recalled Cass referring to the old wizard as her father, but she did not dare linger to reflect on such a perverted topic. Instead, she unfastened the chain from her collar and tiptoed across the room to gather her clothes and make a hasty exit. She did not bother to dress; she would do that once outside Cass's room.

When she turned, she found Malikai standing at the door, completely naked. She gasped and hugged her clothing tightly against her. For the first time, she could appreciate the size of her lover from the previous night. He was just as significant as Greyson, whose endowment far exceeded any lover she had previously taken. This man was unnaturally large, and not just his manhood. His chiseled features also gained her attention. His muscled arms and torso were that of a very young man, and if it weren't for the grey pointy beard, she would never believe the body belonged to an older person.

"Going somewhere?" he teased.

Binta stepped back, then glanced to the bed to see Cass awake and wearing a lewd smile. She flung the covers off to reveal her naked body. Binta swallowed hard, and that familiar lustful feeling washed over her. However, she felt more in control of her desires now that the milk had run its course. Cass beckoned Binta with a crooked finger. Perhaps not. Her heart raced, and her mouth became dry.

Malikai was beside her then and took the clothes from her grasp, but she never lost eye contact with Cass. She went to the bed, and her mistress handed her the leash. She took it and refastened it to her collar. She knew what Cass expected from her, so she gave Cass the other end of the small chain and took the same position as the night before, face down on the covers and her backside in the air. She felt the part of a wanton whore at that moment, and she loved it!

Cass pulled on the leash, bringing Binta toward her. After a night of sex with Malikai, the smell of sex and sweat was strong. It made Binta writhe excitedly, especially when Malikai pulled her underwear down to her knees. The scene played out exactly as the previous night, with Binta pleasuring Cass and Malikai taking her from behind. The sex was just as incredible, and Binta could not help but fall into the role of plaything for the two warped individuals.

Cass stuffed Binta's clothes in a sack under her bed when they finished with her hours later. "You will no longer need these," she explained. Then she went to her chest of drawers and pulled a tiny red dress from it. "Put this on," Cass demanded.

"Yes, mistress," Binta said, and she put the small garment on. It barely covered her butt and seemed to be made for a child. She pulled at it, but it would not reach beyond her underwear.

"You look perfect, my slave," Cass purred as she ran her fingers through Binta's hair. She then grabbed two fistfuls of hair and pulled her head back, making Binta grimace in pain. "Were you going to leave without permission this morning?"

Binta didn't answer because she didn't want Cass to strike her again. She could not look away as Cass had a firm grip on her hair. Finally, she whispered, "Yes, mistress."

"You are no longer allowed to think for yourself, do you understand? You and your body belong to me, and you will never try leaving my side again, correct?" Cass asked, tightening her grip on Binta's hair.

"Yes, mistress," Binta answered with increasing discomfort.

"Malikai will take you to your room now, and you will stay there until I say otherwise, understand?"

"Yes, mistress."

"Good."

Cass gave the leash to Malikai, and he smiled knowingly and said, "This may tickle."

Before Binta could ask what he meant, he grabbed her arm and muttered a few words. Binta felt pulled through space as she and Malikai teleported to a small room. When the world finished spinning and came back into focus, she could make out her unremarkable surroundings. It was mainly unfurnished, with just a bed, a nightstand and a lamp decorating the place. One small dirty window let in the morning light. After Binta recovered from the teleportation, Malikai unhooked the chain from her collar.

"This will be your room for the foreseeable future," he said with a wicked smile.

"I've changed my mind, Malikai; I wish to return to the temple," Binta pleaded.

"There is no turning back. You have accepted Cass as your mistress, and your mistress she shall remain. You no longer have free will, but carnal pleasures will abound more than you can imagine. Just be glad you did not consume more demon milk, or you would be dead. As it is, you are only hopelessly obedient to her. You are genuinely her property now and should resign yourself to that fact.

"So, you are to stay here and await her call. I have no idea what she has in store for you, but I can imagine it will be very pleasurable for you both. And let me make this abundantly clear: if you provoke her or refuse to follow her commands, she will hurt you badly, possibly kill you. So, sit here and think about that and understand you are now a sex slave to Cass. Nothing else matters but that."

He patted her behind and left the room. When the door shut behind him, she could hear the wood warping in the jamb and knew he had magically sealed it. After a few moments, she tried the door, and sure enough, it would not budge. So finally, with a sigh, she sat on her bed.

"What have I done? Oh, Greyson, please come back to me soon. I need you," she whispered.

Her thoughts eventually betrayed her, and she fondly recalled her three-somes with Cass and Malikai. She felt truly out of control and understood the sweet milk had much to do with it. She regretted ever going to Cass, but she could do nothing to change the past.

Nearly four days after leaving the ruins of Farmer's Stop, Cassandra and Boz crested a hill to find the walls of Mecca-Loraine only a few miles away. They were closer to the ocean now, and the wind was colder, but Cassandra remained warm. Although the two had little conversation during the trip, they shared body heat, especially at night. Boz owned a large bedroll, thanks to Kringus, and he and Cassandra both fit in it. The arrangement was very personal and intimate, but Cassandra welcomed the warmth after sleeping nearly a week outside near a small fire. She sat behind him on the giant horse, wrapping her arms around his waist and peering over his shoulder as the town came into view. Mecca-Loraine was much larger than Oldorburg but not nearly as impressive as Pelesea.

"Mecca-Loraine, my home, and our destination," Boz explained.

He spurred his horse, and soon they were at the northern gate. The portcullis remained lowered, giving Cassandra the impression that the inhabitants were not welcoming. As they neared, the activity atop the wall became agitated, as men began to bark orders and prepare to defend their town. They reminded Cassandra of ants atop an anthill, running this way and that, but each one perfectly performing its function. Still, Boz did not change his pace or even lower his hood to be recognized. She could not make out the words of the men operating the portcullis, but they finally acted as if they recognized him and hastily opened the gate before they were within a few hundred yards of the town.

"Quite a welcome," Cassandra whispered as they passed through the gate, the guards nodding nervously.

The portcullis lowered behind them, and the gatekeepers watched them as they moved onto the main street. Cassandra noted the town was quite beautifully laid out, with the business section occupying the northern half and the civilian homes and strongholds littering the hill on the southern side of the town. Separating the two was a vast bay lined with docks and boats. The sun was setting over the ocean, cascading orange and red rays equally along the sky and the bay. Although the temperature was quite cold, the view was breathtaking.

"My home," Boz said, pointing to a structure on a hill in the town's eastern part.

It appeared to Cassandra to be a giant lump of unfinished clay with almost no beauty or imagination in its appearance. The structure contained few windows, the design was dull, and the smooth walls climbed at least ten stories into the red sky. It just did not compare to the architecture of Pelesea.

"Nice," was the only polite thing she could say.

They rode toward the structure as lanterns appeared in the few windows, perhaps unseen servants lighting them as the sun disappeared. There were few people out in the cold at the late hour, and the horse had no snow to contend with, the streets long since cleared of the stubborn stuff. The slight howl of the wind blowing off the bay waters and the clomping of the horse's hooves were the only sounds.

She expected him to head straight for the ugly building, but instead, he kept on the cobblestone road, which would eventually bend around the bay, and lead to the homes on the town's south side.

The action surprised Cassandra, so she asked, "Are you not going home?"

"No," was the curt response.

She waited for him to elaborate, and when he did not, she pried further. "So, where are we going?"

"To the villa of Meshlor, a structure of no small feat on the south side of the town."

"Why?"

"There is someone there I can leave you with who will see to your needs," Boz explained.

"Leave me with?" Cassandra asked, understanding then that Boz wanted to be done with her.

She didn't care much for his company, but he was the only person she knew in Mecca-Loraine. She did not expect to be in the town long and would quickly find passage back to Pelesea. But she had no coin, food, or connections, all things that Boz could supply.

"Yes, I must return to my monastery and my brothers."

"Monastery, that explains a lot," Cassandra said with a snort.

"How do you mean?"

"Nothing," Cassandra said, covering her mouth to suppress a laugh. The strange man's dry personality and business-only attitude fit perfectly with what she thought a monk would be like.

The two said nothing more as the road branched into many blocks of business buildings after passing the entryway to the monastery. Eventually, the buildings thinned, and the road continued to a small patch of land between the eastern wall and the bay's edge. There, the road accessed the many docks. They continued past the docked ships and advanced toward the rows of homes lining the hills. By the time they reached the large structure that was the villa of Meshlor, it was nightfall, the fiery red sun and all its beauty long gone.

A stable boy grabbed the horse's reins, and Boz said, "Please move my horse inside for a bit. I will not be gone long."

He helped Cassandra off the steed.

"Wait, you are just dropping me off and heading back out?" Cassandra asked.

"I must be getting back. My friend will take care of you. He has food and shelter and owes me a favor. You may stay a few days; then, he will help you reach your next step in your travels."

"You seem confident he will agree with those demands."

"Of course; we are good friends, and he is a man of his word."

"But he doesn't even know you are coming," Cassandra said.

Boz looked at her and shrugged. "He will help; I am confident."

Cassandra did not ask more from the man who had saved her from certain death. She owed him her life and would not plead with him to stay; he had done enough.

Something in her mind nagged at her, though; something seemed too convenient. How had Boz even found her in the harsh weather unless he was intently looking for someone? Why was he so confident that his friend would help her and that he would retrieve his horse in a matter of minutes? These things seemed almost planned, yet how could she question her good fortune? She let it go as an acolyte appeared and showed them in.

"A temple?" Cassandra asked when the young man had run off to inform the residents they had arrived.

"No, living quarters for priests of a certain faction. The temples lie on the business side of the bay," Boz explained with a wave of his hand.

Cassandra tried to process that information; again, something nagged at the back of her mind. Something about the place seemed wrong, yet it felt lovely being indoors and away from the biting wind. She had lived in the elements since killing the fire creature ten days ago. Although the place felt wrong to her, it was nice to thaw out for once.

Another man soon arrived, recognizing Boz. She wondered if the man was a priest because he wore a symbol around his neck in the shape of a broken halo on the end of a silver chain. She had seen the sign before, but she could not place it. She also felt that Meshlor was a god she had stumbled across but couldn't recall where. She assumed it was at the temple in Pelesea, but she wasn't confident.

She watched as Boz and the man spoke quietly. She could not hear them, but something in the back of her mind kept screaming at her that she should flee, that something was amiss. Boz had given her no reason not to believe him, but Cassandra had never trusted anyone, and so she grew suspicious. She stood and was about to approach when the two men turned toward her, Boz's face expressionless as usual and the other man smiling.

"Our time together has ended, Miss Rho," Boz said with a bow. "This is Jack, one of the priests that resides here. He will see to your needs."

The other man waved politely.

"Will I see you again?" Cassandra asked, trying to pry more information from her rescuer.

Boz just stared at her for a long moment before nodding. "Yes, please come to the monastery before you leave, and we shall exchange goodbyes. If you decide to stay, you can visit me at the monastery anytime."

Cassandra extended a hand and said, "Thank you, Boz. I will not leave without saying goodbye."

He shook her hand, nodded, and left; his face still expressionless. She watched him go, trying to figure out the recent turn of events. She jumped when a hand gently touched her shoulder. She turned to see Jack standing close.

"Sorry, young lady, I did not mean to startle you," he said with a slight bow.

"It is not your fault; it has been a rough few months, and I am just on edge," Cassandra said with a slight curtsey.

"I understand, and we are here to serve you under the direction of Boz the carofex," Jack explained with a bow.

"A carofex?"

"Yes, the monastery is the home to the carofex, Boz, and his kind."

"What is a carofex?"

Jack laughed heartily and said, "You don't know much about Mecca-Loraine, do you? We will fill you in over your dinner."

"Dinner?" Cassandra asked, her stomach growling at the mention of food.

"Yes, we will feed you and give you a room for a week until you get on your feet. But first, we are drawing you a hot bath. Steph will be in shortly to show you the way."

"So, the church of Meshlor owes Boz such a great favor as to provide for me without question?"

"Of course, Miss Rho; all inhabitants of this place owe the carofex, and the church of Meshlor is no exception. They provide us with protection, and we pay them back as they require it," Jack said.

That made sense to Cassandra. Of course, the folks of the town would trade goods for protection. That would explain the reaction of the gate-keepers when they passed the north gate. It would also be reasonable that he was traveling alone in a snowstorm if he was such a hearty warrior. She didn't understand what a carofex was, but she felt better. That feeling only grew when a young teenage girl came in and introduced herself as Steph. She wore an acolyte robe, like the one the boy had worn when they had first arrived.

"Steph will show you to your bath, and as you wash the road from your bones, I shall see to your dinner and a room," Jack said, leaving the way he had come.

"Follow me," Steph said with a smile, and she headed for a door at the side of the room.

Cassandra sighed and let her suspicions melt away. She would take a long bath and relax a little; she was paranoid. Who could blame her, after all? After being arrested, then kidnapped, how could she believe anything nice could be happening to her? She followed Steph to the bath area. Shortly after, she found herself in a comfortably warm room with a large pool of water. Several porcelain tubs sat around the pool, and many shelves with towels, soaps, and other bath supplies lined the walls. No one was in the bathhouse except Steph and Cassandra.

"The priests have magically heated stones inserted in the pool, which keep the water at a very warm temperature," Steph explained as she filled one of the tubs with buckets of water from the larger body of water.

"You are an acolyte?" Cassandra asked.

"Yes, like you," Steph answered.

"What?"

"Your robes, they are acolyte robes as well, correct?"

Cassandra remembered the worn and tattered robes Maina had given her at the jail. They were soiled and ripped in several places but had endured the ordeal, a testament to the strength of Gella. "Yes, I am an acolyte of the goddess Gella," Cassandra confidently answered.

"Gella? Never heard of her," Steph said honestly, never taking her eyes off her work.

Cassandra was about to explain who Gella was when Steph laid down her bucket and blew a strand of hair from her face. "Well, acolyte, please remove your robe, and I will see it cleaned."

"Remove my clothes?"

"Yes, you cannot bathe with your clothes on," Steph said, and she went to one of the shelves and grabbed several towels, soap, and some unidentified bottles. "Besides, we are the only ones here."

The tub looked inviting, so Cassandra removed her dirty clothes and put them on the floor. She felt uncomfortable standing there unclothed, so she quickly stepped into the tub. The water was pleasantly warm, and she sat in it with a relaxed sigh. She lay her head back on the porcelain and rested her arms on the tub's sides. She closed her eyes and let the warm water take hold.

She heard the water splash slightly and opened her eyes with a start to find Steph kneeling by the tub with a dripping washcloth and a bar of soap. "It is customary for me to wash you as our guest, unless you prefer to do so yourself," Steph explained.

"Uh, that is fine, I think," Cassandra replied hesitantly, her hands instinctively covering her private parts.

"Sit up then, and I'll start with your back," Steph said.

Cassandra did and was surprised to find that she was slightly off balance with the simple act of sitting up. She nearly fell over sideways but caught herself before hitting her head on the porcelain. "Sorry, I must be wearier than I thought," she told the young girl.

"No problem. Give me just a moment, and you may lie back down," Steph replied, seemingly unconcerned with her tipsiness.

Steph scrubbed her back while Cassandra tried to gather her thoughts. She felt like she would drift off to sleep at any moment. She was tired from her travels, but a deep weariness had quickly come over her, and without warning. Was it her body's way of healing after such a long ordeal in the elements? The warm water was so relaxing, and she welcomed it. It had been so long since she had rested fully. She peered into the water and lost herself in the warmth and the unusual aroma of the soap Steph was using. Before she knew it, she was lying back, resting her head again, and Steph was bathing her front. She no longer tried covering up as her arms hung limply in the water.

"It's Meshlor, you know," Steph said with a smile.

"Mesh—lor?" Cassandra said, trying to formulate the words in her fuzzy mind.

"That's right, Meshlor. A substance from the most wonderful god laces the heating stones which paralyzes your muscles," Steph explained excitedly, her eyes growing as wide as her smile.

"Para—" Cassandra mumbled.

"Yes, it paralyzes your muscles. But, if you are worthy of Meshlor's attention, you have immunity. And this soap is made with a tranquilizer that will put those of weak faith to sleep. It is quite a powerful combination," Steph explained, holding the bar of soap under Cassandra's nose.

The scent was intoxicating, and as Cassandra breathed in the fumes, her eyes rolled into the back of her head, and she slipped under the water. She could not move; none of her muscles answered her call. Cassandra panicked. She could see Steph's blurry image kneeling beside the tub. The young acolyte seemed to be watching. Was she going to let her drown? Cassandra tried to scream but could not even do that. Her lungs ached for air; she could not hold her breath for much longer. Eventually, the faded image of Steph moved, and at first, Cassandra thought the girl had left. However, she felt her tugging her a few moments later. Steph pulled her out of the water so her head rested on the back of the tub once more. Cassandra coughed up some water and tried unsuccessfully to speak as Steph moved her arms to drape over the tub's sides.

"You must be careful, because Meshlor does not think you are worthy. I will help you stay above the waterline only because Barktuck demands it."

Steph leaned over and grabbed Cassandra by the hair, her visage turning dark as she gritted her teeth and frowned hatefully at Cassandra. "You know what I would typically do to a pathetic wretch like you, don't you?"

Cassandra could not hope to answer and could barely lift her eyes to meet the angry girl's intense stare. The name Barktuck sounded familiar, but her foggy mind could not process why. Cassandra knew she was in trouble and at the girl's mercy. Eventually, the grimacing stopped, and Steph began to laugh.

"Of course, you don't; you are a pathetic acolyte of Gella. But we must wash your hair now to be nice and clean before Barktuck retrieves you. And we will use lots of this wonderful soap," she exclaimed, lathering her hands, then running them deeply through Cassandra's hair. Cassandra remembered little after that as she drifted in and out of consciousness. The sweet call of sleep was too powerful for her to resist.

A distant and dull pain echoed through Cassandra's mind. She let it fade away and allowed herself to fall into her peaceful rest once more. However, the pain returned, and this time was followed by a sound, a muffled voice. She tried to tune in to that sound, to focus on it, but it faded away once more. It returned quickly, and was intense. Her eyes fluttered open to find she was sitting in a chair. She was vaguely aware of her nakedness, her wet hair hanging around her shoulders. She could not hold her head up and looked at her lap as blood dripped from somewhere. Was it her blood? She could not be sure.

"There she is," came that condescending male voice she had chased through the fog.

A firm hand pulled her head back by the hair, and she could now see an older man standing behind her chair, shaking the sting from his hand where he had slapped her. She would have fallen from her seat if a second man wasn't kneeling beside her, holding her up. She ran her tongue over her cut lip and understood the source of the blood. Cassandra tried to recall how she got there, sitting naked in a chair with several men around her in a strange room. She remembered a bath, but none of the men.

The man behind her leaned over to whisper, "Welcome back, Cassandra Rho; we have been expecting you. Now behold your new master."

The man's breath stank of alcohol, and his grip tightened on her hair as he spoke. She could feel his hatred for her as much as she could hear it. His face was familiar but seemed like it was from a long-ago dream. All she knew was that his feelings for her were intense. Another figure appeared in front of her, a man wearing fancy clothing and a cape to accentuate them. He wore makeup, white as chalk, and he scared her.

"She doesn't seem very respectful, my lord," the man behind her teased.

The man with the makeup stared at her, saying not a word, but his strange eyes spoke volumes. It appeared as if he would pounce on her and could barely control himself from doing so. Cassandra tried to shake away the cobwebs to remember who the men were. She vaguely noticed that the man kneeling beside her chair was now manipulating her arms and hands, but she could not look down with the older man's tight grip on her hair. Cassandra then realized the man before her wore a porcelain mask, not makeup, which unnerved her even more. Still, she did not know who could be behind it.

He slowly approached, the clicking of his heels echoing on the stone floor. Cassandra took a moment to look around the best she could. It was a small room with stone walls, and she could hear running water nearby and a fire. Of course, she could see neither, but she was confident she did not recognize this room.

"Intertwine the rope through her fingers as well," the masked man said.

"As you wish," the man working on her arms replied.

The masked man knelt before her and slowly removed the mask to reveal Ronnis D'Breeth! Her mind cleared quickly as she recognized the torn face and could feel the evil and hate emanating from it. Was she in Oldorburg? She did not think so, but she could remember little since her arrival at the temple of Meshlor. She focused on the symbols that she knew floated all around them. But unfortunately, due to the lingering effects of her stupor, she could not see them and, therefore, could not manipulate them to form a spell. Ronnis just stared at her; the man who had ruined her life and killed her family was within her grasp, and she focused hard on channeling that anger to awaken from the drugs they had given her.

At that moment, she recalled the face of the man behind her—Barktuck, the priest from Oldorburg! He was responsible for poisoning her, drugging her, and giving her to Ronnis all those months ago. The reality of who those two were sunk in, and her heart began to pound in her chest. She was in trouble, with little hope of someone finding her. She couldn't even count on Boz returning. Then, as her mind cleared a little more, she realized that Boz had been the one to deliver her to Ronnis. She understood that her doubts about the strange man now made sense. She was in trouble, and she was very much alone.

Suddenly, Ronnis grabbed her by the throat and squeezed with his gloved hand. He brought his face to hers as Barktuck released his hold on her hair. "I now have you in the exact condition you were in when that meddling wizard stole you from me. And now, I will finish what I started."

The gleam in his eye left little doubt that he had gone mad with anger. He was the villain, so how could he be angry with her? She had done nothing except defend herself and her family. How was she to blame? She was more frightened than she had ever been.

"Baxter does not know you are here, and your stupid birds can't get through these walls in time to save you. This time, I will finish what I started."

Cassandra could only look at him with her eyes wide. His grip around her neck tightened, and she could feel her oxygen cut off. She surmised he would have killed her then if the rope guy had not spoken up.

"Finished," he said, standing.

Ronnis released her, and she slumped in her chair, gasping for breath. Barktuck pulled her up by her hair into a standing position. She grimaced in pain, and as the feeling slowly returned to her extremities, she realized her hands were immobile. She looked down to see them tied together with a thin rope at the wrists. The twine ran through her fingers, spreading them wide and immobile.

"Take her to the table and tie her down," Ronnis said, standing to watch.

The rope man guided her to a stone table in the center of the room. Cassandra could see a stove; the smell and sound of a fire came from within it. Shelves full of vials lined one wall. She imagined that they could only be poisons of Meshlor.

The man pushed her roughly onto her stomach, and she banged her chin on the hard surface as she fell face first on the table. The stone was not as cold as she expected, and she assumed it was due to its proximity to the hot stove. The man manipulated her and repositioned her several times under Ronnis's direction. When finished, her arms were straight before her. A thick rope was tied around her waist, looping under the table to keep her immobile. That position left her standing but bent at the waist and lying face down on the table. The rope man then tied more rope to her bound wrists and looped it through a hook in the ceiling. He tested it several times, pulling it to make her raise slightly off the table with her arms stretched painfully over her head, then lowering it so she was flat against the table again. Once Ronnis was satisfied, the man tied her ankles to the table legs.

Once done, she had little-to-no mobility, her legs were slightly spread, and her bare butt was on display. She could feel more and more of her movement coming back to her as the drugs wore off, and she realized then how restricting the ropes were, especially with her fingers. Her mind was coming back slowly, and soon, she could cast her spells. She would kill Ronnis, even if it meant her death. She was confident she could do so, even with the tight binds to her hands, but she needed more time to shake the grogginess.

Ronnis had the man pull hard on the ropes, making her rise off the table and exposing her breasts. She grimaced as the pull on her arms was excruciating. She did not dare make a sound, not wanting Ronnis or Barktuck to gain the pleasure of her misery. However, it was evident on her face because Ronnis smiled evilly at her discomfort. She expected him to do awful things to her, and she needed to regain her senses to prevent it. He slowly withdrew a strange sword from his hip and held it under her throat. If the ropes broke or the strength of the man holding the rope gave out, the blade would impale her through her neck. The weapon was black as night and glistened in the flickering light. She swallowed hard as Ronnis ran the tip gently over her skin.

"I have many bad things planned for you, Cassandra. I will carve a hole in your face, beat, cut, and torture you. In the end, you will beg for death," he teased, continuing to run the blade over her throat. "I have paid much to have you here, so I will not kill you immediately. No, our time together will last for years, I imagine. But do not doubt I *will* kill you eventually."

"You are mad," Cassandra managed to say.

He quickly withdrew the blade and grabbed her throat once more. The pressure hurt her neck and bent her backward even more, making her groan a little with the tension in her back. Again, the blade came back into view, but with the sword's grip facing her. It was shaped like a snake eating its tail with rubies comprising the eyes. He said nothing and eventually released his grip so she could breathe once more. He motioned for the rope handler to lower her, and the pressure on her aching back and arms relented. She rested on the table, catching her breath. She watched as Ronnis opened the stove door and placed the sword partially into it, hilt first. Then, curiously, he left it there and came back to her.

"I have paid a lot of gems for you, and I will get my money's worth. We will begin our fun tomorrow, but I expect you to understand our arrangement tonight. Yes, I expect you to fight at first, but that will eventually fade as you realize you are helpless. I want you broken, Cassandra Rho, and tonight we will take the first step to achieve that."

She said nothing but knew she had to get out of there. Ronnis's hate of her had him on the brink of madness. His anger was taking his revenge to a whole new level of evil. She watched as he obtained a sizeable smithing glove from the shelving and then donned it to withdraw the blade from the stove. The snake head was red-hot, and the little ruby eyes seemed to glow, mocking her with what would come next. He walked over to her and menacingly waved the weapon in front of her face. Her eyes widened, and she tried to move away from the smoldering snake head. However, the ropes left her nearly immobile; she could do nothing. Finally, he walked down to her backside. She was helpless in her current position; even turning her head to follow him was difficult.

"Yes, I have paid a lot for your little ass, Cassandra. So naturally, I feel compelled to mark my property," Ronnis teased.

Cassandra could feel the heat from the sword near her exposed hip, and she tried to move without success. "Please, Ronnis, do not do this!" she screamed, understanding what the crazed man had in mind.

She looked behind her the best she could to see him standing there, arrogantly holding the smoking sword hilt just inches from her. He smiled and said, "Yes, I believe we will get along just fine, Cassandra Rho."

He pressed the hilt against her skin, and the pain was more intense than anything she had ever felt. He held it there for a long while, placing a firm hand on her backside to keep her from moving, not that she could move much anyway. He burned her, branding her with his awful weapon. The pain had her nearly passing out, and the sickening stench of burning flesh filled her nostrils. Ronnis laughed at her struggles and enjoyed her shrieks of pain. He had become a monster. Finally, after what seemed like an eternity, he pulled the blade away and admired his work. Cassandra cried as she tried unsuccessfully to deal with the immense pain.

"Think about this tonight, Cassandra. Consider that you are my property, and tomorrow morning I will take what is most precious of yours. Tomorrow, I will abuse your body and break you further. You are mine now and wear my mark. Sleep well, little witch."

Cassandra could only cry in response. She vaguely heard the laughter that Ronnis and Barktuck shared with the third man who had bound her. They left her there all alone to deal with the tremendous pain. Once they were gone, she struggled with her binds, her arms already aching and her fingers stretched wide by the rope. She tried to shake the fog from her mind, the drugs still having an effect. However, the potent concoction in her system and the horrific pain in her burned hip prevented her from adequately forming any spells. Even if she could summon magic, such as her globes of energy, she could not correctly direct them into the ropes with her hands bound so. She finally gave up and cried herself to sleep. It was the most miserable night of her life.

5

RESCUED?

ARRIN AND THE TROOP FROM PELESEA ARRIVED AT OLDORBURG days before Cassandra and Boz had reached Mecca-Loraine. They had found the guard's young captain, Max, in complete control of the small town. He had eradicated the faction of Meshlor shortly after Kringus and his men had left a few months earlier. Soon after that, he became sheriff. Arrin and the others were prepared for war when they arrived but were pleasantly surprised by the turn of events. Arrin found himself in Max's home with his wife and a small child, the little girl a spitting image of her mother. The cavaliers Marcus and Erik joined them as Max prepared dinner. The home was small for a sheriff but was cozy, and the family seemed content.

"We are pleased to find you in control of Oldorburg, Max," Arrin said as they ate.

"And I am just as happy to find you are alive, Arrin of Pelesea."

"I admit that I have not healed fully yet, but I grow stronger daily," Arrin answered.

"The poisons of Meshlor are not easily defeated," Max said somberly.

"We found barrels of the toxic substance in the temple. The goodly priests helped us locate them and dispose of them."

"You are certain all evil priests were destroyed or arrested?" Erik asked.

"We attacked right after your king left, just as he instructed. As a result, we were able to overwhelm them all," Max began.

His daughter Sade became restless, smacking her hands on the table and letting out a small yelp. "She is getting sleepy, Max. I will take her and get her ready for bed while you and our guests finish your discussion," Tanna, Max's wife, said.

"Thank you, my dear," Max answered with a smile. Once they were in the other room, Max continued, "The priests of Meshlor were mad, every one of them. Instead of surrendering when our victory was imminent, they cut their throats. They preferred death over being captured."

Arrin shared a troubled glance with Erik and Marcus, gaining a better understanding of the fanatical priests of Meshlor. "So, you arrested none of them?" Arrin asked.

"No, they died fighting or took their own lives before we could capture them. We wished to arrest at least a few to interrogate them. But unfortunately, it was not to be. I would have been lenient and attempted to reform them."

"Well, you did the right thing, removing them from power. We have come to support your cause and are happy that you have things under control," Arrin said.

Max smiled weakly at the comment and nodded. "I appreciate the gesture and know Oldorburg is forever in debt to Pelesea. I am glad you approve of our new governorship."

"You seem troubled, Sheriff; what weighs on your mind?" Arrin asked, recognizing Max's discomfort.

"Their leader escaped."

"Are you sure of this?" Arrin asked, sharing a concerned look with Erik and Marcus.

"Yes. I feel that he fled the town and is no longer a danger to us. However, I believe him to be very powerful and quite dangerous."

"Any idea where he may have gone?" Marcus asked.

"No, he could be anywhere by now. I feel responsible for him being out in the world, roaming free and spreading his vile religion. However, I have not the resources to chase the crazed fanatic."

"You have done well, Max, despite the failure to destroy the head of the priests. Do you know his name?" Arrin said.

"Yes, Barktuck Misol. During the battle, he killed Buster Agnew, the merchant guild's leader, and I feel he is responsible for injuring you, good knight, and killing your magnificent horse," Max said to Erik.

Erik winced at the memory of the battle. He had charged his warhorse into the fighting, but just before arriving, vines with razor-sharp thorns had sprouted from the ground in front him. He could not avoid the perverted field of cutting vines, the thorns slicing easily through his armor just as they did into his horse's flanks. Erik had barely survived the vicious attack, the wounds and the memory still paining him. Marcus patted his shoulder, and the two shared a knowing look. After all, it was a costly battle, but one that the cavaliers of Pelesea had won.

"But you are certain he is no longer in Oldorburg?" Arrin asked.

"Yes, quite certain."

"Then you have done your job to protect your people. Perhaps Kringus can spare some men to help find this Barktuck fellow once the snows have melted," Arrin offered.

"Yes, that would be most generous of your king. Whatever support Oldorburg can offer in the search, I'll gladly make it happen."

After that, the four men ate without speaking, letting the words sink in. Soon Tanna rejoined them, Sade fast asleep in her crib. The food was good and the company friendly. After dinner, as the three men from Pelesea were about to head back to the inn where they had secured their rooms, Max said, "There is one more thing you should know."

"Do tell, good sheriff," Arrin said.

"Please let Kringus know that Ronnis D'Breeth also escaped that night. After securing the temple, my men and I went to the orphanage to question him, but he was gone. So, my gut tells me that he and Barktuck escaped together."

"Interesting. I will tell Kringus when we arrive home. However, that may be a while," Arrin answered.

"Oh?" Max asked.

"If it is not an inconvenience to you, Kringus has asked that we stay here for the remaining winter to learn more about the priests of Meshlor."

"It would be an honor to have such distinguished guests in our town. I will see to it that we discount your room and board," Max offered.

"That is unnecessary, my new friend," Arrin said with an upraised hand. "We have brought plenty of coins and will pay the cost to stay. Also, since we are here for the next few months, perhaps you can show us around the orphanage and the temple. It would be good for me to gain an understanding of this Ronnis fellow as well."

Max agreed, and the men from Pelesea bid him and Tanna a good night and returned to the inn. They felt good about the new sheriff and decided that the town seemed more at peace now than it had been a few months earlier. The way Arrin saw it, Pelesea and Oldorburg could well be allies by the end of winter's grasp.

Malikai spent time with Binta during those first few days she called the tiny room home. She soon discovered she was in an inn somewhere in Pelesea, but the old wizard would not elaborate. He took her to a bathhouse and ensured she was clean, making the bath a daily routine. A young woman assisted her in cleaning her tiny outfit, the short red dress Cass had given her. He replaced her underwear with a more transparent pair, calling them a gift from Cass. Malikai also delivered strong perfume and told her to keep it handy for the nights she was working. Of course, Binta had no idea what that meant, but again, Malikai refused to elaborate. He delivered meals to her and checked on her at least once daily. The view from her window showed she was three or four stories above a busy part of the city, but one she did not recognize. Her life quickly became one of routine and monotony.

When the wizard appeared on the third day, Binta asked, "So, where is Cass?"

He laid the small tray of food on her bed and said, "You miss her that much?"

"Of course not; I think it strange that you are the only one who seems to be taking care of me. I am Cass's slave but did not agree to be a prisoner. I want to leave this room, Malikai; what you do to me isn't right."

The anger that flashed across his face reminded her that she knew little of him, and that he was probably capable of anything. He walked over to where she stood next to the window, and she backed away until she felt her nearly naked butt hit the corner of the room. He closed the space between them, and she lost her nerve and looked at her feet.

"You think you have a choice in the matter? Do you think you willingly serve Cass now? If so, you are sadly mistaken, little girl."

He reached up and put a finger under her chin, lifting her head and drawing her gaze toward his own. She tried to back up even further, feeling his touch's power, but could no longer move. This man, her newest lover, was a mystery to her, and he frightened her very much. He smiled at her discomfort, and she wilted.

"You are an excellent submissive, and Cass will have fun with you. I only wish that I could remain a part of it."

"You are wrong; I am in control of this. I can stop it at any time," Binta argued.

He laughed and replied, "You vowed to serve Cass and donned the collar. As far as my wild daughter is concerned, you have signed a contract in blood." He released her chin and walked to the window, gazing at the street. "And, besides, there is nothing for you in Pelesea besides the role you now serve. Your friends and lovers are long gone, as well as your self-esteem."

"I have my temple, and I have Greyson."

"What, that lucky young man sailing around the world with a ship full of exotic and beautiful women? You will be nothing to him by the time he returns." Malikai turned back toward her and said, "You know I speak the truth. You belong here now, and if you do what Cass tells you to do and she finds you useful, you may live a long and happy life."

Those words fell heavily on her, and she sat on the bed next to the tray of food. Malikai was right, she knew. Even if Greyson returned, Cass would make sure he never found her. She would probably take him as a lover to spite Binta. Nevertheless, Binta found the forced sex exhilarating, and servicing Cass was as satisfying as it was humiliating. She could live with all of that, but she wanted the dream of Cassandra and Greyson. That possibility seemed a lifetime ago. She knew Malikai spoke the truth; there was no turning back.

Malikai made his way to the door and went as far as putting his hand on the knob when Binta spoke. "Wait, are you leaving already?"

He turned with a smile. "Why, do you require more from me?"

She glanced at the tray of food and shook her head. Then, she stood and made her way to stand before him once more. "Of course not. I appreciate the food, but I wish your visits were longer. I get lonely in here all day by myself."

"I do not have time to babysit Cass's new pet."

"You are the only one who seems to care. I thought maybe—"

"You thought what?" Malikai interrupted, taking his hand off the door and stepping toward her.

Binta could not answer because she had nothing to say. She wanted company. He was not a nice person, but neither had he mistreated her. He was the only source of company she had; if he left, she would be alone for a long time before he returned to bring her food or take her to the bath-house. But he wasn't her choice as a companion or a friend; she just hated the small and lonely room she now called home.

"Do not misunderstand, girly; I do not care for you. To me, you are simply a good time. I am taking care of you while Cass plans the coming days. Do you understand?"

Binta nodded and nearly broke down in tears. But instead, she kept her gaze on the floor, unable to look at the hateful man with any dignity.

"Good," he said, then she watched his feet turn and walk out the door.

With a lonely sigh, she sat on the bed and stared blankly at the wall. Soon after, out of boredom, she ate the food Malikai had left and wondered what Cass had planned for her. A chill ran down Binta's spine at the thought of the many possibilities.

Maltor and Jozerah, his good friend and second in charge, watched as the fancy wagon dropped off two men at a strange structure. It had a giant wheel on the side that was partially submerged in a river, which intrigued the barbarians. Maltor was suspicious of the wagon at first, but the men and the unusual structure they entered piqued his interest. Their barbaric raids of the countryside had been very successful: their boats were stuffed with treasure, livestock, and human slaves. Mecca-Loraine was their last stop and most prominent target. Once they saw no weakness in the great wall surrounding the place, Maltor called off the attack. Shortly after, the strange wagon had made its way out of the gate, suspiciously unguarded. Maltor had already sent the rest of the horde back to the ships, ready to depart for home. However, he, Jozerah, and Vixa had remained behind to claim one last prize—and Maltor decided then the fancy wagon would do.

The three savage warriors were in a cluster of trees as the unsuspecting driver began the short trip back to the gates of the town. Vixa looked to Maltor, and he nodded for her to proceed. She smiled and took her position. Soon after, when the wagon was close enough, a missile smacked the driver in the chest. He sat there awkwardly before falling off the seat and into the snow. The wagon slowed and eventually stopped, the horses no longer interested in pulling the load without a driver to coax them. Maltor and Jozerah watched as Vixa slipped out of the trees and retrieved her axe from the dead driver's chest. She then waved to Maltor with the axe and jumped into the empty carriage to ensure no one was inside. By the time Maltor and Jozerah reached her, she had finished her inspection.

"No passengers or coin on board," she explained with a shrug.

"The horses could prove useful, though," Jozerah added.

Maltor nodded. "If they are here when we return, we will take them. What about him?" he asked, pointing toward the dead driver.

They approached the dead man, and Vixa rummaged through his pockets, finding his purse. Jozerah grabbed it from her, and when Vixa tensed at his sudden action, they shared a brief stare-down. Maltor stepped between them, giving his friend a slight smile, and took the purse from him. He poured the coins into his hand and tossed the bag into the snow.

"Shall we return to the ships?" Jozerah asked.

Maltor stared at the building the men had entered and shook his head. "One more kill before we return home and away from this devil-snow."

The other two followed his gaze and nodded. The trio quickly and quietly approached the small building.

Cassandra awakened to joyous laughter, familiar enough that she knew who was entering the building before they had even appeared. The fire had nearly died out, and the small room was freezing. Cassandra's arms ached, and her ankles throbbed from being tied to the table. Worst of all was the pain in her right hip, where Ronnis had branded her the night before. She remembered spilling candle wax on her finger as a child and her mother, Unis, filling a small glass with cool water and sticking Cassandra's finger in it. The pain left her finger instantaneously, but only as long as she kept it submerged in the water. She dreamed of lowering herself into a cold body of water and how that water would not only dull the pain but eliminate it. The intensity in her hip had lessened as the night went on, but the lack of relief was maddening.

Finally, she heard a key in the door, which soon creaked open. She did not look back because she already knew who was there. She could hear the two men enter, stomp the snow off their boots, then remove their coats. Footsteps came toward her, and the two grew eerily silent. Peripherally, she could see that one man was on each side of her. She kept her face down on the table, feigning sleep. She felt vulnerable and understood she was in for a long, grueling day. She also understood that she could do little to stop the two evil men and their vile intentions.

"Have you ever seen a more inviting sight?" Ronnis asked.

"I have to say no, my friend," Barktuck answered.

"It's a shame the fire has almost burned out; she is shivering," Ronnis added, removing his gloves and placing an ice-cold hand on Cassandra's lower back.

She jumped at the touch and screamed in surprise. Her whole body seemed to tense, making her stiff joints pain her more, and the agony in her hip flared back to life. She rose to her elbows, grimacing in pain. Ronnis finally lifted his hand, and both men shared a laugh. Cassandra relaxed and lay her face on the cool stone top of the table. She watched as Ronnis and Barktuck fed the fire, then shared a drink. Cassandra was hungry and very thirsty, but she would not give either the satisfaction of asking them for food or water. She lay there and awaited the inevitable.

She was exposed to the horrible men but could do little about it. Both circled her with their drinks in hand, occasionally taking a sip and making lewd comments. She felt she was in the ocean surrounded by two sharks. The temperature did begin to rise, but the warmth was of little comfort to her. Instead, the inevitable rape she was about to endure held her attention. She tried to think of a way out of the predicament and tried desperately to move her fingers, but the small rope lacing them kept them immobile. Her mind was clearer than the previous night, and she could see the arcane symbols floating around her. She needed a way to coax them into a spell and manipulate them, but the magical characters were difficult to control without using her hands, especially her fingers.

Ronnis took the rope that bound her wrists in his hands and pulled it, making Cassandra lift off the table a bit, and her arms ached in protest. Ronnis pulled it even further, exposing her naked breasts, and she moaned from the dull pain in her arms and back. He looked her over and smiled lewdly. He wrapped the rope's end around the hook on the wall so she remained in the painful position. He walked back over to her and removed the mask. She looked away, not giving him the pleasure of seeing her reaction. He grabbed a handful of her hair and pulled her gaze toward him so she could see his wounded cheek.

"Now, you listen to me, you little witch. I have waited a long time for this, and you and I are going to agree on a few things before the fun begins."

He let his free hand roam over her breasts, pinching her nipples hard. Cassandra grimaced but refused to make a sound; she would not give him the pleasure. His attack became more forceful until she finally cried out. He smiled wickedly as her tear-filled gaze fell upon a familiar pendant, hanging from a chain around his neck, that a similar foe had worn.

Ronnis noticed her staring at his valuable necklace and said, "Oh, you've seen one of these before, haven't you? So, you know your magic is useless against me, don't you? Even if you free your wicked little fingers from the restraining rope, your spells will not affect me."

Cassandra recalled her time in the cave with Cass when the woman attacked her. Cassandra had taken a plunge into magically freezing water, and Cass had attempted to drown her. However, Cassandra had summoned the incredible magical energy found in the water and forced it into her necklace, one like Ronnis's. The subsequent explosion had torn a hole in the nasty woman's chest, and Cassandra had survived. She would do the same if she could get a hold of Ronnis's necklace. She smiled at the thought of it.

Ronnis smacked her hard across the face, dazing her and disheveling her blond hair so it hung in her eyes. She hoped it hid the tears that now flowed freely.

"Why are you smiling, Miss Rho? Do you not understand your doom?" Ronnis yelled, his bloodshot eyes bulging in their sockets.

He moved her hair from her face and squeezed her head with both hands. "Understand, Cassandra; I mean to cause you significant physical and mental pain. I will reacquaint you with the Black Adder if you dare interfere with my plans. You remember my sword, the one that branded you, so you'll wear my mark for the rest of your days?"

Cassandra stared hatefully at him as he continued to put more pressure on her head. She grimaced once again but refused to answer. Cassandra would not cooperate any more than she had to. She had prayed the previous night, asking Gella for the strength to escape the predicament. If the goddess refused to go that far, she asked for the power to make the torture as difficult for him as possible. If Gella allowed her to free herself, she was confident she could kill Ronnis quickly. She had grown powerful since the last time she was in his presence. And the loss of her mother and her sister fueled her anger. The pain in her head grew as Ronnis continued to apply pressure. He pressed so hard that his arms began to shake. Cassandra closed her eyes and focused, determined not to answer or scream out.

Finally, Barktuck intervened. "You don't want to kill her yet, my friend. Enjoy her before you terminate her, remember?"

Ronnis released her and nodded. Cassandra shook her head, the only means she had to disperse the pain. She watched as the older priest made his way to the shelf containing the various bottles of poisons. He perused the shelves until he found what he sought, taking one of the smaller flasks.

"I assume you'd like to start with a tranquilizer?" Barktuck asked.

"No, that won't be necessary," Ronnis replied with a shake. "I want her completely aware of what I do to her today. I wish her to feel it when I take her."

Ronnis leaned down, so he was whispering in Cassandra's ear. "And, if you strike out at either of us as we ravage your body, my weapon will exact a swift and severe punishment, whether a hole in your cheek or a missing digit. Perhaps I'll take a finger, an ear, or even an eyeball. Fight back, resist in any way, and you'll find the answer."

Cassandra again refused to answer. Finally, Barktuck came back to stand beside her evil tormentor with an equally stupid smile on his face. Ronnis slowly drew his weapon and pointed the tip at Cassandra's throat. She swallowed hard, the thought of that evil blade against her making her more nervous.

"I think we have an understanding, Barktuck. She is stubborn but not stupid; she will do as I say. Now get undressed."

"Me?" Barktuck asked.

"Sure, if you would like to enjoy the fruits of our captive," Ronnis explained, untying the rope from the wall and gently letting Cassandra fall back to the table.

The pain in her back and arms subsided, finally released from the awkward angle, and she breathed heavily. She heard Barktuck's priestly robes fall to the floor. She knew what he would do and needed to find a way out of it, and the time had come for her to break free or suffer rape at the hands of the two evil men. She considered the idea of using her magic against the priest. Her hands and fingers were compromised, but she could still try a spell. If they did not drug her again, she could fight back. She raised her head slightly to see Barktuck naked from the waist up. He noticed her cold stare and lost some of his bravado.

"What if she tries something?" Barktuck asked, stopping his undressing.

"She won't. We have an understanding, don't we, Cassandra?"

Cassandra did not answer Ronnis but held her cold gaze on Barktuck. She could send forth her magic and, at the very least, disable the old priest. However, Ronnis had that awful weapon and would strike back at her. If she thought he would kill her, it might be worth the chance, but he wouldn't. Ronnis had made clear his plans to torture her; she knew her rape was inevitable. Of course, if Ronnis thought the ropes restricted her from spellcasting, she held a slight advantage. He would drug her so she could not form her spells if she were to give away that advantage now. Cassandra decided then that she would take their torture this day and endure the raping that was sure to come. She would survive it, and she would kill Ronnis for it. Eventually, they would become sloppy with their routine, and Cassandra would kill them when they least expected it. For now, she had no choice but to submit.

"Yes," she whispered.

"Are we clear of the consequences, you evil little witch?" Ronnis asked, waving the black blade of his sword in front of her face.

"Yes," Cassandra answered again.

A smile crept across Ronnis's face, and he rose and said, "There, you see, she will cooperate. Enjoy her mouth as I take her from behind."

Then Ronnis was gone, moving behind her, leaving the priest smiling at her. He began undressing once more and soon was naked in front of her. Her mind flashed back to the only naked man she had ever witnessed. She remembered how Greyson looked as he walked past her that day, not knowing she was peeping. She thought he was much larger than Barktuck and not nearly as wrinkly. She had to suppress a smile, despite her predicament.

"Now, little witch, it is time for your penance. Just behave like a good little whore and Meshlor may forgive you yet. Otherwise, your time here will be most unpleasant. Understand?" Barktuck asked.

She nodded, and his smile grew. He adjusted the rope slightly, pulling her arms painfully over her head so her head was level with his crotch. He grabbed a handful of her hair and brought his manhood up to her face. She only stared at him hatefully.

A sharp smack to her behind had her yelping with surprise and her branded hip screaming in pain. She fought the pain in her hip as Ronnis said, "Open your mouth, Cassandra. Today you begin paying me back for all the grief you have caused me."

She thought of her mother then and of Kessi. Tears welled in her eyes as she slowly opened her mouth, obediently awaiting the filth that was Barktuck Misol.

"That's a good girl," she heard Ronnis say as his fingers began to poke and rub where no man had ever touched.

She closed her eyes and awaited the inevitable. But, instead, there was a sudden thump at the door that startled all three of them. Barktuck released her hair and took a few steps back, and Ronnis's probing fingers retracted.

"Who could that be, Barktuck?" Ronnis asked.

The priest only shrugged and began pulling on his pants. Ronnis made his way to the door, mumbling curse words. Cassandra was facing away from the door, and with her arms stretched slightly above her head, she could not hope to turn and see who had come. A brief feeling of hope flashed through her mind as she imagined Boz coming to her rescue. However, she quickly dismissed the feeling as she understood that the villain was responsible for her predicament. Barktuck roughly put a hand over her mouth so she could not call out.

"Who is there?" Ronnis demanded.

Another thump on the door was the only answer he received. Ronnis unsheathed his weapon and unlocked the door. "Who dares disturb—" he began, but he quickly lost his voice. Cassandra heard a commotion and saw peripherally what looked to be a hand axe flying into the corner of the room.

She heard shuffling from several people behind her and saw Barktuck's eyes widen just before another axe struck him on the forehead with a sickening crack. Cassandra watched the man as his filthy hand slowly fell from her mouth and he crumpled to the ground. Someone had entered the room, and they were either there to help her, or she was in considerably more trouble than she had been moments before.

She heard multiple footsteps but did not dare move. If the group had come to rescue her or had pure intentions, they would have spoken by now. And they would have freed her from her binds and covered her nakedness. Instead, she fell into her trance, calming herself and preparing for whatever new foe awaited her. She saw the arcane symbols that floated around her, the characters she could proficiently manipulate into deadly magic. She was ready for whatever had come, or so she thought.

A woman stepped into her field of vision, and it was a sight she did not expect. The woman was muscular and tall with wild red hair and skin that seemed too leathery and tanned as if she had been in the sun far too long. She wore a filthy animal skin, caked with what appeared to be dried blood. She was pretty, but her wild, unwashed hair detracted from her beauty. Then the smell of body odor assaulted Cassandra's senses, and she knew that the woman was uncivilized and most likely unruly. After all, she had just murdered Barktuck and possibly Ronnis. What would stop her from burying her axe in Cassandra's scalp?

Cassandra swallowed hard as the savage woman bent and retrieved her murderous axe from Barktuck's head. The sickening sound reminded Cassandra of thick mud sucking at boots after a hard rain. Two much bigger brutes came to stand beside the woman. The two men looked as savage as the strange female warrior and smelled equally bad. They all stared at her, and one of the men had a vulgar expression that she was pretty tired of seeing.

"A prize from the gods, Maltor," the smaller of the two men, the one with the lustful expression, said, pointing to Cassandra.

The one named Maltor looked over to the man with a stern gaze and said, "No."

"But we should enjoy our spoils, don't you think?"

"No, Jozerah, not this time," Maltor said as he bent to study Cassandra's face.

He felt her hair as if he were evaluating a piece of cloth, pinching and rolling it with his fingers. His breath was more potent and more intense than his body odor. Cassandra jerked her hair from his grasp and whispered, "Gross."

At first, the large man named Maltor, who seemed to be the leader, smiled, showing his yellowed teeth. "Spirit, I like that," he said so only she could hear.

"A sexual feast is before us; should we not eat?" Jozerah asked, walking behind Cassandra and running a hand over her buttocks. Cassandra closed her eyes and tried to tolerate the touching, but the practice of every man doing that had her patience running very thin.

"No!" Maltor commanded, rising to stare hard at Jozerah.

"As you wish," Jozerah answered, removing his hand. "What is this?" the barbaric man continued, touching Cassandra's brand.

The pain was significant, and Cassandra yelled out and tried to recoil from the touch. Maltor and the strange woman walked to the other end of the table to examine the mark. Maltor also touched it, making Cassandra yell, "Stop touching it! Are you dense?"

The three walked back to stand before her. Cassandra stared at them defiantly but felt then that she had pressed her luck, and so she fell back into her trance. She was relieved to see the arcane energy and symbols dancing around the three unprotected warriors.

Maltor studied her for a bit, then let his eyes follow the rope binding her hands to the other end tied to the wall. He looked at Barktuck and back to her. He was putting together Cassandra's predicament; she could see it in his eyes.

"A brand," he said with a toothy smile.

"A what?" the woman asked.

Maltor's smile turned to one of anger, and for a moment, Cassandra thought he might lash out at the woman. But, instead, he shook his head and said, "On her hip, it is a brand."

"For what?" Jozerah asked.

"To claim ownership, as I do now," Maltor said with a smile, again grabbing a handful of her hair and bending down to smell it. Cassandra tried to jerk her hair away again, but the savage held it tight this time. "Only, the brand was performed by a weakling, a man who must tie down his woman to take her. I will therefore take his brand as my own. She is mine. Cut her down!"

The woman sliced the rope tied around Cassandra's waist with a quick strike that had Cassandra flinching and the pain in her hip flaring again because of it. The rope fell free, giving Cassandra an idea of the sharpness of the woman's axes. As Cassandra was contemplating exactly how close the strike had come to digging into her side, the wild woman went to the wall and cut the rope, making Cassandra fall to the table. It wasn't a long fall, but she would have cracked her chin hard on it if she had not managed to turn her head at the last second. Instead, she hit her cheek against the table, sending a shock wave of pain through her temple.

"Idiot!" Cassandra yelled and used her bound hands to slowly walk back into a standing position. Her hands were still bound and her ankles tied to the table, but it felt good on her aching back to stand again.

Then, the woman was beside her, her stale breath in Cassandra's face. "I am Vixa, daughter of Zorn. What is an idiot?"

"Take a bath and clean your teeth so I can refrain from retching. Once you have done that, perhaps I can explain what an idiot is. Or maybe it would be simpler to provide a mirror."

Vixa drew both axes in a flash and held them to Cassandra's throat, but Jozerah was there to grab her arms and force them down. Vixa shook him off her and stepped away, axes still in hand.

"Take your anger out on this one, Vixa," Maltor said, kicking Ronnis in the ribs hard, eliciting a groan.

Cassandra then realized for the first time that Ronnis was lying on the floor with an abrasion on his forehead and blood trickling from the wound. She could only surmise that Vixa had tried to kill him, the same way she had Barktuck, and had missed the target.

"Dress her in the old one's clothes, then kill this one. Do not take long;

when Jozerah and I reach the boats, we will leave, with or without you," Maltor continued.

Jozerah produced a large, wicked blade and sawed the ropes that bound Cassandra's hands. Cassandra noticed the pool of blood around Barktuck and his twisted, blood-covered face for the first time. He was dead, without a doubt. She looked over to see Ronnis slowly moving as if stirring from a deep sleep. She envisioned killing him once she was cut free. It would be a satisfying conclusion to their relationship.

Jozerah made quick work of her binds, and soon her hands were free. He then cut her ankle restraints. Vixa brought Barktuck's bloodied garments and threw them on the table as Cassandra rubbed the circulation back into her wrists and clenched her fists, relieving the pain in her stretched fingers.

"Put it on," Vixa said, staring coldly at her.

"Vixa!" Maltor said, stepping in front of her. "You see the brand? She belongs to me now. She follows my orders, not yours."

"A new plaything for the mighty Maltor?" Vixa spat.

Maltor's punch was quick and on target as he hit the fiery redhead in the jaw. She dropped her weapons and swayed. Jozerah was quickly behind her, keeping her from falling. He held her up so that Maltor could continue his work. He punched her in the gut hard, and she doubled over but stubbornly rose to meet Maltor's gaze. Another punch followed. The beating was brutal, and Cassandra quickly learned how vicious the people were. She eyed the dropped blades as she put on Barktuck's baggy clothing. The vestment was wet with his blood but better than freezing. She would kill Ronnis with one of the dropped weapons, then kill the two males before they beat Vixa to death.

As she finished dressing, she picked up one of the axes and focused on the vicious attack again. Vixa appeared unconscious now, blood streaming from her mouth and a large welt on her cheek. Cassandra knew she didn't have much time to assist the wild woman. Ronnis was her priority, though, so she turned, readying the axe, but Ronnis was gone! A bloody trail now remained where he once lay. Instead of human prints, however, it appeared to be the trail of a slithering snake. It led out the room's door, which was still wide open.

As her mind tried to register the scene, a firm hand gripped her wrist and squeezed. She turned to find the one they called Maltor behind her and she reflexively swung with her other hand to smack at him. She immediately knew that was a bad idea as he quickly caught her wild swing in his other strong hand. His strength was bull-like, and he promptly shook her weapon free. She barely heard it clang to the floor as she fell within herself to summon the energy around her to formulate a spell. The massive man headbutted her before she could lash at him, cracking his forehead against hers. She saw stars, and her knees buckled. All sense of magic quickly faded as the arcane symbols became cluttered and unreadable. Maltor held her up, or she would have fallen. A second headbutt followed, and her world went black.

After several uneventful days in her room, Malikai finally called for Binta to bathe one morning. He also had her clothes laundered while she soaked in the wooden tub. She only had one set of underwear and the short dress Cass had given her, and she knew something was afoot. As she bathed, she imagined the possibilities and became aroused. When Malikai came for her, he led her back to her room, wrapped only in a towel. When they arrived at her room, a collection of makeup and perfumes lined the dresser top.

"Put that on, and heavily. I will have your clothes soon enough," Malikai ordered.

Binta approached the dresser and took in the powders' and perfumes' many colors. She always used darker makeup and rarely perfume. She turned to Malikai and said, "I do not know how to use these items. These are things a whore would wear."

"Exactly." Malikai smiled, then left the room.

Binta turned back to the many vials and tins and felt intimidated. She looked at herself in the mirror and considered removing the small nose ring. She felt the small hoop in her fingers, wondering if prostitutes wore them. Finally, she decided it was her identity, so she left it. She sampled many of the items before deciding on the colors she liked the best. She painted her face heavily, as instructed, and a tingling sensation grew in her loins as she did. A few hours later, her clothes were delivered by an errand girl, nicely cleaned and folded. On top of them was her collar, also clean. She quickly dressed, adding the collar and a heavy dose of perfume. When finished, she looked herself over in the mirror. She looked pretty in the tiny dress and every bit the part of a prostitute.

She spent the next several hours waiting. She watched the sunset, and the nightlife began. She looked out her window at the many sailors coming into the inn. They advanced from the docks, from the left of her view. She could not see the ports or ships, but they had to be near because the sailors were thick. They were rather rough-looking, and she deduced that she must be in the southern part of Pelesea, near the poorest section. It made sense; Cass had plans for her, and she knew what they were. The thought excited her greatly, and she embraced her role. Binta wanted nothing more than to please Cass, to be humiliated by the vile woman. She needed to be Cass's slave more than anything.

Hours after the sun had set, Cass entered the room, Malikai at her side. Binta was lying on her bed when the two entered, and she moved to sit up quickly, wanting to appear obedient. Cass walked up to her, and Binta could see she had also made herself up. Her makeup was not nearly as thick, and her appearance was immaculate. She did not wear perfume, but her natural scent took Binta's breath away and stirred dirty thoughts inside her. Binta found her stunning. Cass bent to eye level as she hooked the small chain to Binta's leash.

"Are you ready to perform?" Cass whispered.

"Yes, mistress."

Cass tilted her head back and forth in the dull lamplight of the room, studying Binta's face. Then, finally, she wrinkled her brow and turned to Malikai. "I need more light."

Malikai made some hand gestures, and Binta's mind traveled back to her time at Victoria's school months earlier when she learned such movements. Binta had seen Greyson perform the spell many, many times. She recognized it as a light spell before bright light flooded the room.

Cass returned to studying her face and smiled. "You have applied your makeup?"

"Yes, mistress. I hope it pleases you."

Cass stood and turned to Malikai. "So, what do you think, Malikai?"

He approached and examined her face, and Binta wilted under his gaze. "She looks like a whore."

"Perfect!" Cass said with a smile. Then she leaned in close again and asked Binta, "It's showtime. Are you ready?"

"Showtime? I don't understand what you ask of me, mistress," Binta lied, her body tingling in anticipation.

"Just be yourself," Cass said soothingly, lifting Binta's chin so that she looked her in the eyes. "Just be a whore."

Binta nodded shamefully, and within a few minutes, Cass led her down the inn's hall toward the stairwell into the common area. She could hear many people talking as they approached and silverware clinking on plates. Binta grew very nervous and thought of Greyson and what he would think if he knew his love was acting in such a manner. And, of course, she thought of her dear friend Cassandra, buried just a few weeks earlier. Being submissive to Cass was her way of getting past those thoughts. She knew being an escort for the sailors would be her new life. If Greyson ever returned, she would deal with it then. But, for now, she was Binta, the prostitute, and she embraced it, although apprehensively.

When they finally appeared at the top of the stairs, Cass stopped her, and they just stood there. Many patrons crammed the place and partook of the food and drink, filling almost every table. Most were sailors, as Binta had witnessed earlier. But there were also other women there, women she could only assume were there to transact business with lonely patrons. They were sitting among the men, some on the laps of the burly sailors. They were dressed whorishly and with makeup like Binta's. They were ladies of the night, like her, she realized. However, none were as pretty as she, and none wore a more revealing outfit. Binta's heart raced as she stood there, taking in the scene. Her eyes scanned the place, picking out her competition and understanding there was little.

One woman noticed her, and stared at her and Cass, her mouth slightly agape. The man whose lap she sat upon saw her surprised look and followed her gaze. Soon his eyes were bulging at the sight as he drank in Binta. A man at another table knocked over his bottle of ale at the spectacle. He didn't react to the spilled beverage, as he, too, became enthralled with her. His friend picked up the bottle, angry at the mess at first, until his gaze shifted to the stairs, and he froze while the ale poured onto the floor. Slowly but surely, every person in the place stared at the two, and it grew silent. Once she had their attention, Cass began to walk down the stairs, her boots clicking with each step. She took her time walking down them, and Binta kept pace, knowing not to walk too fast or too slow. She felt self-conscious in the short red dress and tried unsuccessfully to pull it down to cover her underwear as they descended.

Once on the floor, Cass continued her slow walk, looking each man in the eye as they passed them, her clicking boots the only noise. Binta could not make eye contact with any of them but followed along obediently, head down. She felt their eyes, male and female, bore holes through her. She tingled.

"Gentlemen, I offer you a prize beyond your most sensual desires as you return to Pelesea. Most of you have been stuck at sea for a long time and have not seen a woman for months. Of course, you could pay one of these plain-looking whores," Cass began, holding the chin of one of the women as she passed her. The woman jerked away with a huff, but Cass continued walking around the tables, paying her no more mind.

"Or, you could pay for a premium woman such as my little pet. She is clean and submissive and very, very eager to serve. The price is five gold for half an hour and ten for three men at once for the same half-hour. Her legs are open all night, and if any of you find yourselves interested, pay Barlow at the bar, and he will give you the details of the arrangement. Anything goes. Again, she is eager to please, so do not be shy with any requests."

The room remained quiet as they circled, and Binta could feel all eyes on her. They completed their circuit around all the tables and started back up the stairwell; Binta could only imagine the view she gave everyone of her barely covered backside. Once at the top, Cass had Binta turn and face the crowd again, pausing for a final look. Then, she turned and led Binta down the hall and to her room with a smile. Her words fluttered through Binta's mind: three men at a time? The thought horrified and excited her.

By the time they reached the room and Cass opened the door, Binta heard the crowd in the dining room stir once more. Again, there was a buzz among the patrons. Cass ushered Binta into the small space to find Malikai waiting, naked and lying on the bed.

"So, how did she do?" he asked.

Cass brushed Binta's hair out of her face and said, "She was perfect; they feasted upon her with their eyes."

"Can you blame them? Look at her," Malikai said, sitting up and folding his arms over his chest.

"You are a true whore, Binta, and you have made me proud," Cass cooed, stroking Binta's cheek.

"Yes, mistress," Binta answered with a blush.

"You will earn me much gold tonight, which you will never see. You know that, don't you?"

"Yes, mistress," Binta said shamefully, looking at her feet.

"And why is that?" Cass asked.

"Because—" Binta began.

"Look at me when you answer!" Cass interrupted.

Binta slowly made eye contact and answered, "Because I like it."

"Be specific."

"Because I like serving you, mistress."

"Who does your body belong to now?" Cass asked, stepping closer.

Binta swallowed hard, trying to find a remnant of dignity in her new relationship with Cass but failing miserably. "You, my mistress," she finally answered.

"Good girl," Cass purred.

"Before the rush of strapping young men arrives, may I have the first go?" Malikai asked.

"For free?" Cass asked with a smile.

"I don't pay, my dear girl."

"Let's both partake then, like the last time," Cass countered.

"I think that is a most splendid idea," Malikai said.

He rose from the bed, and Cass took his place, handing him the leash as she did. Binta waited patiently, knowing what they would force her to do next. Her heart raced at the possibilities, but not only with Cass and Malikai. The thought of what the men in the common room would do to her had her loins aching. She wanted all of them! She would sleep with any who entered her room. She would receive nothing for giving her body, and Cass would keep all the gold. She knew that and the fact that Cass would benefit from her performance. She loved the idea and assumed the position once Cass was on the bed, her legs spread. Binta lowered her head to the bed and stuck her backside toward Malikai. She was obediently ready, and properly trained.

After Cass and Malikai warmed her up, many men came to her room that night. First was a trio of young men. Before that night, she had only been with four men in her lifetime, counting her new lover, Malikai. Never had she been with three at one time. Their stamina was a testament to their youth; she did things with those three she had never imagined doing. As they passed her around repeatedly and used her simultaneously, she thought briefly of Greyson during that first encounter. What would he think of her? The thought of him cuckolded by the dirty, unattractive men excited her even more.

Even in her heightened state of arousal, the sex became less enjoyable and more painful near the end of the night as she became overstimulated. The men didn't care and turned her this way and that to get to her and satisfy their lust. By morning, she was truly ashamed of what she had become. Over a dozen men visited her that first night as a prostitute, and she truly knew exhaustion.

As she lay in bed, trying to recover from a long night of rough sex, she thought of Cassandra and began to sob. "What have I done? Please forgive me, Cassandra. I miss you."

She cried herself to sleep as the sun rose. However, her rest was short-lived as Malikai entered when the sun was high in the sky. He took her to the bathhouse again, so she could take a much-needed bath.

Along the way, Malikai said, "You will need to clean yourself and prepare for the next night of work."

"I need some rest."

He stopped and looked at her, his visage never more severe. "You are a working whore now. This life is what you wanted, so get used to it."

Those words struck home and broke her spirit even further. He left her at the baths with a young girl who drew the water and helped her clean up. Afterward, once back in her room, she found her bed sheets cleaned and a gown laid out. Her working clothes were there, but she donned the soft garment instead, happy to wear something normal again. She slept for a while and luckily did not have to work for a few days. During that time, she rested and recovered. However, the naughty thoughts of what she had done slowly crept back into her head over those few days. She envisioned Cass counting the gold Binta had earned her pleasing the dirty sailors. Soon, she was looking forward to the next time the ships docked. She would be ready for them.

Matilda heard two girls giggle in the distance. She wandered through the grey mist, trying to pinpoint the sound. Matilda nearly lost it several times in the thick fog, but the laughter grew louder. Once she realized what direction she needed to travel to reach the girls, she could see a dull, white light from where the noise was emanating. As she closed in on the light source, the sounds grew louder, and she knew that it was not girls giggling but women. She continued to find her way, the swirling, dull mist evaporating against the whiteness. Finally, her eyes fluttered open for the first time in nearly a month.

She saw the ceiling of a room and heard the laughter loudly now. She turned to take in her surroundings, and her stiff neck barked in protest. She found herself on the floor, at the foot of a bed. She blinked away the tiredness in her eyes and looked again. She found the same scene; she was lying on the floor with no covers, as if someone had discarded her. How had she wound up there? She could not remember much at first, but as she thought about it, the image of Cassandra's spirit returned. No, not Cassandra's soul, an imposter's—Cassandra was alive! The young girl she had met at the gravesite was not Cassandra.

She sat up slowly and immediately realized she was physically depleted with little energy to move, much less sit up. Was she this near to death, she wondered? She reached up, grabbed the bed's footboard, and pulled hard to stand. She could not, but she did manage to climb to her knees and balance herself against the footboard. Without it, she would surely topple to the floor. It took her another moment to orient herself to what she saw there. On the bed, leaning against the headboard was Malikai, shirtless, with the rest of his body under the covers. Two women, one on each side of him, snuggled against him, giggling. They were under the covers, except for their heads, each lying on Malikai's chest.

Matilda saw red! The scene before her summed up exactly how well Malikai had cared for her while she wandered about the grey mists. How long had she been roaming around, trying to find her way out? Had he done anything for her besides throwing her on the floor and occupying his time with bimbos? As her anger boiled, she felt the dark powers of her demon-god surge within her. She suddenly found the energy to not only stand, but float!

She released the footboard, and instead of falling, she felt herself levitate just above it. She moved her arms to her sides and said in a deep and ominous voice, "Get out!"

Malikai and the two women all jumped at the sudden sound, one of the women shrieking in surprise. Then the bed began to shake, the bedposts banging against the wall, and Matilda repeated, "Get out!"

Both women screamed then and flung off the covers to reveal their nakedness. They hastily picked up their clothing and moved toward the door. Matilda had the door flying open and slamming against the wall with a wave of her hand. Both women ran out completely naked, their clothes in hand. Once they were out, exhaustion overcame the small priestess of Marnelphion, and she collapsed back to the floor.

Matilda felt drained and could not find the energy to lift herself again. She watched Malikai's bare feet as he walked to the door and calmly shut and locked it. Then he turned and made his way toward her. She did not even have the energy to look up at his face, so she closed her eyes. Finally, he lifted her gently from the floor and laid her on the bed. She opened her eyes and watched as he poured her a glass of water. He helped lift her head and she took a small sip. She wanted more, and so he helped her with another. Once she was satisfied, he placed the glass on the nightstand and sat on the bed.

"Welcome back, Matilda," he said.

"How long?" she managed to whisper back, her booming voice from moments before lost to her.

"A month or more."

"And you discard me to the floor?"

"I did not leave you," he said, as if that made the act appropriate.

She ignored his arrogance, expecting nothing else from the old wizard. Instead, she focused on the best news she could give. "Cassandra Rho lives," she said with a smile.

Malikai shrugged, then stood to pour himself a drink. "Do not misunderstand, Matilda; I don't care about your cause. This news does nothing for me."

"I must find her," Matilda said, struggling unsuccessfully to sit up.

"Fine, but you must build your energy before you have the strength."

"Yes, of course. I am hungry."

"I can imagine. I could help nurse you back to health, but it will cost you," Malikai said.

"Always a price with you, always a cost to pay," Matilda answered in disgust.

"That is correct. I have business elsewhere, yet I stayed in this forsaken city, waiting for you to leave your stupor. So, the way I see it, you already owe me."

Matilda knew what he was getting at and rolled her eyes, having neither the patience nor the time to humor the powerful wizard. But before responding, she felt his strong hands on her, removing her gown. "What?" she asked in surprise.

"Call to your fool husband; it has been far too long since I witnessed his humiliation," Malikai ordered, turning her over on her stomach to face the mirror.

"No!" Matilda said, summoning her strength to resist the order.

He was in her ear then, whispering a threat, and she understood he meant it. "You have run off my entertainment for the evening, and I have sat in this stinking room, waiting for you to recover. So, you will summon your husband now as a small and partial repayment of my time. Now do it."

Matilda felt his hands rubbing her, stimulating her in a way only he could. Then, finally, her resistance melted, and she focused on the mirror. What else could she do, after all? She would submit, as always, or he would leave her there to die.

"Cerus," she called.

The mirror began to smoke, and she continued calling out her husband's name until the smoke faded and an empty chair appeared. Malikai entered her then, and he felt divine.

"Call to the idiot," Malikai demanded.

She called several more times as Malikai continued his thrusting and had her nearing climax almost immediately. Cerus finally appeared through the strange mirror, staring hatefully at the scene but eventually taking a seat in the chair. As Matilda screamed in ecstasy for the next hour, he watched without moving or saying a word. Eventually, when Malikai finished with her, Matilda lay exhausted on the bed. Malikai walked over to the small table in the room and poured another drink. Then, she turned and watched the magical mirror as the image of Cerus faded, his hands wringing the arms of the chair as he swirled out of sight. Malikai only laughed at her husband's humiliation, fueling the rage within the volatile warrior.

The next several weeks were a routine for Binta. She would stay in her room, alone, aside from Malikai's daily visits, waiting for the ships to dock every five days. At that point, Cass would flaunt her to the men as she had before, then escort Binta back to her room. Shortly thereafter, her visitors would arrive for the remainder of the night. Some men were repeat customers, and after three weeks, she knew who her regulars were. Most cared nothing for her; they paid good coin to be with her and treated her as roughly as possible, emotionally detached as if punishing her for the high price.

One, however, was different. Jamison Oland, a wealthy gentleman by his looks, seemed to like her. His lovemaking was just that, honest and pure. When he visited, Binta gave herself to Jamison; it made her feel like a part of society again because it wasn't emotionless sex. She believed he truly cared for her. After their lovemaking, they would sit in her bed and chat before he left. She honestly enjoyed his company. Although she had other regulars those first three weeks of work, Jamison quickly became her favorite. He was by far the best-looking and most well-refined man of those with whom she slept.

Other than her conversations with Jamison, the only interaction she had during the long days between work was when Malikai came and escorted her to the bathhouse and brought her meals or books to read. His company was not ideal, mostly because he scared her. However, he never demanded sex from her, and she was glad. Her off days were mostly boring, as her entire existence began to revolve around the sailors coming to use her. She would look forward to it to break the monotony of the long days in between. Her work occupied her mind, and she thought of Greyson and Cassandra less and less. Serving as Cass's prostitute gave her a purpose, which she needed.

Then one early morning, after a rough night of satisfying many visitors,

Cass came to her. Binta was exhausted as she lay in bed, watching the sunrise through her window. When the door opened, Binta was half dozing, vaguely aware of the scent of her lovemaking that permeated the air. She sat with a start, covering herself with the filthy sheets, and luckily, she still wore her collar. It was the only thing she wore, and she knew better than to remove it. She hadn't seen Cass for a few weeks, so her sudden appearance startled her.

"Mistress," she whispered.

Cass walked up to her, exuding sex as she always seemed to do, and wearing the boots Binta longed to lick. Binta's arousal was immediate, regardless of how exhausted she was. Just the sight of Cass made her tingle, and Binta could not understand why, other than perhaps the milk she had consumed still affected her. Cass was the only woman she pleasured, and although her mistress never reciprocated, Binta loved it when Cass made her service her. She pretended sometimes it was Cassandra she pleased, and her heart would race. In the end, it was Cass she wanted to make happy because doing so insulted everything Binta believed in and aroused her. The relationship with Cass had become complex.

Cass attached the small leash to Binta's collar and said, "You smell like sex; this whole room smells like sex and sweat. You have worked hard, my pet."

"Yes, mistress."

"You have made me a small fortune thus far in our business endeavor, so I will not complain about your stench. As always, I'll have a bath drawn for you, and you can wash the filth of last night's activity away.

"But first, I thought I would give you a special treat for your hard work. Would you like that?"

Binta could hardly contain her excitement. Usually, when Cass spoke of a "treat," she demanded a humiliating task. That always excited Binta, but she also considered that perhaps Cass would let her out of the room and let her leave the inn altogether. Binta longed to be outside and away from the small space.

"Yes, mistress," she answered anxiously, swallowing hard.

"I thought you might. I have a special man here to use you, and I want you to let him do whatever he likes, understand?"

"Yes, mistress," Binta said, hiding her disappointment.

She was tired and sore from a busy night and had little energy left for servicing more sailors. Pleasing Cass was one thing, but she was not interested in performing for another customer. Also, realizing she would not leave her room was a great disappointment.

"He paid double for the next hour with you, and I intend to let him have at least that much time. He is very eager to see you, to use you as he wishes."

Binta thought that perhaps Jamison had returned, even though she had seen him a few hours prior. However, she never expected what happened next. The door opened, and Jabell stepped in. Cass handed the leash to him.

Binta's mouth hung open in disbelief. Jabell, the fellow student who had beaten her unconscious while Cass similarly beat Cassandra all those months ago, was in her room, holding her leash! Her ribs ached at the thought of the vile man kicking her as she lay prone on the ground. An evil smile spread across his stupid-looking face; at least that was how Cassandra would refer to him—stupid-looking. Binta's mind suddenly focused on Cassandra, and she panicked. She could not allow this evil and ignorant man to best her again, to use her sexually. Cassandra would not approve. Binta realized that she would be disappointed with how many men Binta had slept with over the last few weeks. She felt like she had betrayed Cassandra, even though her friend was gone.

"Don't permanently damage her. I need her serviceable in five days," Cass said, then left the room.

Cass locked the door behind her and Jabell pulled hard on the leash, making Binta spill onto the floor. He walked calmly to her as she gathered the sheets around her and sat on the floor against the bed.

He stood over her and said, "You and your little lesbian friend ruined me. Victoria permanently expelled me from her school, and now I work for a fishmonger, cleaning and filleting fish. Thanks to you, I'll never be a wizard." He pulled tightly on the leash, making Binta rise to her knees, then added, "What do you have to say about that?"

"She's not a lesbian," Binta said with as much conviction as possible. After all, that is what Cassandra had told her after their first kiss. She would honor Cassandra now, even if that meant suffering at the hands of Jabell.

The rage flared in Jabell's eyes, and she knew there was no stopping him. The first punch hurt, but the ones after that she barely felt as she waned in and out of consciousness. She fought off the rapist as best she could, but the beating from the enraged young man took a heavy toll. He eventually threw her on the bed and had his way with her. She was vaguely aware of the ordeal, but her head swam, dizzy from the beating, her eye swelled shut, and her busted lip throbbed. She faintly heard him calling her a whore and a lesbian, but she focused her thoughts on Cassandra, giving her the strength to see it through. Once Jabell finished the dirty deed, he beat her again, his anger far from sated. Soon the world faded away, and she slipped into darkness.

Jabell was sitting atop her, striking her still form, when Baxter and two city guards burst through the door to stop him. If they had not, Binta would probably have died that horrible morning. Her face was bruised and swollen, blood gushing from her nose and mouth. The horrific scene had Baxter back on his heels, and he considered unleashing his powerful magic on the fool, Jabell. He watched as the guards fought to restrain the struggling young man. Baxter understood he would be in trouble with Victoria if he used his magic to lash out. So, instead, he picked Binta up and removed her from that tiny room. Baxter opened a small portal in the hallway and stepped through. On the other side of that doorway, he found himself on the street outside the inn, next to the carriage that would take Binta and him to Victoria's school. Two more guards waited for him there and helped him climb inside with the unconscious girl, and soon after, the carriage sprang into action. As he looked over the badly beaten girl, he felt guilty at not having a spell powerful enough to teleport her directly to the school. He had done the best he could for her, and he hoped it was enough.

Reaching the school took quite some time since the carriage had to travel across most of the city. Once there, Baxter carried Binta to her old dorm room, and then Maina, the priestess, was summoned to heal her. As Baxter and Victoria looked on, Maina mended Binta's many wounds and washed her face. The priestess was concerned about the swelling around Binta's left eye, but the damage did not seem as bad after the healing. When Maina completed her tasks, Binta remained unconscious but seemed to rest comfortably.

Maina approached Baxter and Victoria and said, "She will survive and should be fine in a few days. Of course, she will need to rest as much as possible, but she will be all right. I hope whatever monster did this to her will pay for his crimes; she suffered a severe and vicious beating, Victoria." Maina bowed and left.

Victoria turned to Baxter and said, "I think it is time my father left Pelesea."

"I agree, but only as long as he takes that nasty Cass creature with him," Baxter replied.

"So, you finally understand my hesitance to save her from certain death?" Victoria asked.

Baxter understood that Victoria was right, and he felt ashamed for going along with Malikai's offer to heal her. However, he had been desperate to save her at the time, the pain of losing Cassandra fresh on his mind.

"Yes," he finally answered.

"Did you find her, then?"

"Yes, the informant, Mr. Oland, was very helpful in finding Binta and letting the guards know that Cass was truly behind the operation. I believe Jabell has gone mad, and Kringus will lock him away for a long time. He and Cass are both in custody and will answer to the king and queen for their actions," Baxter said.

"Are you sure Malikai resides in the same inn where you found Binta?" Victoria asked.

"I'm positive. There are guards at the ready and watching the building. He cannot come or go without us knowing."

"You don't know my father very well," Victoria sighed.

6

ᛄVIL STIRRINGS

NUENTAS FOUND HIMSELF IN THE PALACE OF THE ARCHDEMON, Nezeratu, ruler of the highest level of hell, the layer closest to the human world. There he waited obediently in the black, obsidian chair offered to him. He was a half-demon, his mother human, as was typical for half-demons. He had spent centuries in the world of humans, traveling and causing chaos as demons tend to do. He had lived in hell for the last fifty years and was now anxious to return to the world to wreak havoc again. However, he was assigned a critical mission this time, so he would have to curb his enthusiasm a bit. The prophecy had hinted at it for centuries, and as it approached, all signs pointed to Inuentas as the carrier of Slebel, a mighty sword of demon-kind. The vicious weapon was forged in hell for the sole purpose of killing demons. He embraced the prophecy and was in the palace to retrieve the weapon from Nezeratu.

He sat on the chair and could feel the souls lingering within, those not yet tortured enough and ready for eternity in the bogs. They moaned in his thoughts, and he savored the sensation. New souls were not nearly as delicious, for they still did not understand their fate. The ones trapped within the chair were old and knew all too well where they were. Inuentas could taste their despair. Once Nezeratu considered them properly brined, he would transfer them to the lower levels of hell so that they might live an eternity in the torturous bogs.

Inuentas lay his head back and swirled his tongue in his mouth as if enjoying the aftertaste of a good meal. In many ways he was, for he had absorbed some of the souls trapped in the hellish seat. He had fed on their essence just by being near the evil chair, and he had fed well. Yet, he had sat waiting a long time, which made him feel bloated with their grief.

Many braziers housing eternal flames burned through the hall, casting light on the various macabre decorations. Guillotines, gallows, and blood art decorated the walls. Most of these displays contained the remains of human bodies that once belonged to the lingering souls trapped within the palace. The walls were as black as his chair but with veins of blood running through them. The moans of the souls trapped within made him smile. Their discomfort only gave the palace more power; the more the spirits complained, the more powerful their host became.

"Fools, it is nothing more than you deserve," Inuentas whispered and chuckled.

Inuentas closed his black, pupilless eyes and savored the surroundings. He had been in the palace one other time and many centuries before, but he had never met its occupant. He lived on the top layer of hell because the evil he found there was to his liking, the chaos controlled and not unpredictable like the lower levels. This was one of the places in hell where true power resonated, and he felt honored to have been summoned by Nezeratu. His small horns, only two inches long, sprouting from his forehead, tingled with the power of the place, and his barbed and poisonous tail flicked like a cat's with anticipation. His reddish-colored skin seemed to glow against the obsidian chair. His senses heightened.

His basking was interrupted by a presence that made the hairs on his arms stand on end. The distant moaning of tortured spirits and the screams of the dead all seemed to subside. Even the souls within the chair calmed. He knew that meant Nezeratu had arrived. Inuentas sat up and swallowed nervously. He had to remain calm and show the demon lord that he was qualified to carry out the assignment.

Slowly, the presence overwhelmed him as a dark and putrid cloud formed near the chair. It grew larger as Inuentas watched, the tendrils of the shadow seeming to come straight from the walls, more specifically from those red blood-like veins coursing through them. The cloud grew to ten feet in diameter and hovered above the ground, just in front of him. It took all Inuentas's willpower not to flee the place. He was born and raised in hell and had seen many bad things in his life, but the potential power this being hinted at left no doubt that he was god-like.

"Inuentas, the Indomitable, why do you not grovel at my feet?" the cloud spoke.

Inuentas knew this was a test and understood that prostrating himself before the cloud would only show weakness.

He steeled his resolve and said, "I am here at your request, my lord. I understand you have chosen me for the most important task of delivering Slebel to the mortal world."

"And?" the cloud pressed.

"And we are not on the chaotic second layer of hell. My servitude to you is understood; I have no reason to bow before you."

There was a long pause, and the cloud held steady for many moments. Inuentas wondered if he had just facilitated his death at the hands of the demon lord. Then, eventually, the cloud spoke again, and the half-demon relaxed a bit, understanding that he had passed the test.

"I will take shape now, but not my natural form. If you saw my true self, the human blood within you would make you mad, and you would surely be a lost soul. So, instead, I will form into that which your mind can understand," the cloud said.

Inuentas watched as the cloud slowly solidified, taking the shape of an exquisite-looking human with black hair, blacker than the night, slicked back from his most handsome face. He wore an expensive silk shirt, red as blood, with a black jacket and pants. He wore rings on every finger, and completing the ensemble was a black obsidian cane topped with a gold handle. Once he formed into his new shape, Nezeratu smiled at his guest. Inuentas felt at ease with the new form and felt the power in that smile. The demon lord had changed shape, but the power was still authentic.

"Walk with me," Nezeratu ordered, then began to walk down one of the corridors.

Inuentas quickly rose and fell in line beside the demon lord, half a step behind to show respect. After all, it was the first level of hell, the one closest to the mortal world. It was the layer where the more civilized demons roamed, where thinking overruled brute force, and the lords cultivated disasters for humans instead of randomly killing them. Moreover, the inhabitants there had easier access to the world, not requiring the silly gates that the brutes of the second level relied upon, such as Marnelphion.

Nezeratu's steps clicked loudly on the floor, and Inuentas noticed the coursing red veins in the walls pumped intensely whenever they passed them. They walked silently until finally they reached an iron door. Standing beside that door was a giant demon with many human-like features. Inuentas assumed he was a half-demon as well but said nothing. The large man fell to his knees as they approached, head bowed toward the demon lord.

Nezeratu stopped and turned to Inuentas, that charming smile on his face again. "If you had bowed like this earlier, I would have made you guard one of my iron doors for the rest of your days."

Inuentas did not doubt the threat and again understood that he had narrowly avoided disaster. With a wave of Nezeratu's hand, a table sprouted from the floor, and the obsidian and red-veined material became palpable as clay. Two chairs grew forth, and the two sat. The great demon lord snapped his fingers, and a tall demon, human-like but with wings and large horns, came forth from the darkness of a side corridor. In his hand, he held a leash that fastened around the necks of two decrepit humans. The servants carried plates and utensils for the two diners. They set the table, one whimpering, nearing a breakdown.

"Don't you love the human soul in this setting, Inuentas? Before it is extracted from the body, as it struggles to understand its very doom? Take this one, for instance; it cries because it understands its rotten life's reward is an eternity of torture."

Inuentas almost felt bad for the poor creature, the human in him empathizing with it. Nezeratu nodded to the demon servant, who produced a curved blade. It was as black as the walls that the palace was comprised of, with a handle as red as blood. The whimpering human closed its eyes, knowing the intention of its wicked master. The demon ran the blade home with one quick thrust, piercing the pathetic creature in the back and slicing through its heart. It fell onto the table with a heavy thud, quite dead. The blood pooled quickly, but the table drank it just as fast. The enslaver unlocked the collar and set the damned soul free.

The hungry table soon absorbed the entire corpse, everything except the soul, which looked even more ragged than the body from which it had been exhumed. It waited for a moment, lingering and afraid to move. Finally, Nezeratu created a vortex before the pathetic thing with a wave of his hand. The soul struggled to move and escape the inevitable, but the vortex's pull would not allow it. The rift caught it and pulled it backward, stretching its shape as it did. The soul let out a pitiful scream, and Nezeratu giggled with glee. Soon the creature was gone, taken to the bowels of hell, and Nezeratu dismissed the vortex with another snap of his fingers.

"I do so love the transition. You can smell the fear, and sometimes if you are lucky, you can even hear prayers to their gods," the demon lord explained.

During the display, the lone slave finished setting the table, and the slave master produced a bottle of blood wine, placed it on the table, and bowed respectfully. He started away before Nezeratu stopped him. "Leave the dagger."

The demon turned and bowed again, producing the bloodied blade and setting it beside the wine. Inuentas watched as the parched table quickly drank up the blood from the weapon. Once the demon was out of sight, his prisoner in tow, the demon lord turned his attention to the large man guarding the iron door. "You know what I desire. Bring it to me."

The creature bowed and began turning the handle to the door. The door opened, and a smell that Inuentas could only describe as death poured from the vault. The giant creature disappeared within, and Nezeratu poured the wine for their feast. He said nothing, only sampling the liquid, then motioning for Inuentas to follow suit. He brought the drink to his lips, understanding that it could be another test. Nevertheless, he did not question the liquid and trusted the demon lord. To his relief, the wine was refreshing.

"You are a trusting soul, Inuentas."

"Only to you, my master."

Nezeratu smiled at that and finished off his glass. Inuentas did likewise. As his host poured them another drink, the sound of metal scraping stone echoed from the vault. Inuentas looked on, curious about what the creature was fetching, imagining it must be dinner, given the set table. After a few moments of listening to the growing sound, the giant demon finally became visible within the darkness, towing a large metal contraption. It appeared to be a cage to fit a human. Unfortunately, its wheels were caked with something that prohibited them from rolling correctly, hence the scratching sounds on the stone floor.

Inside the large cage was what appeared to be the remains of an angel. Its arms stretched out to the cage's sides, each held in place by barbed wire that dug deeply into the corpse's wrists. It appeared to Inuentas that the poor thing had endured many tortures before succumbing to its wounds. Its head hung limply, its chin resting on its chest. It had no eyes, which were long ago plucked from their sockets. Dried blood stained the creature's face and chest from that vicious wound. However, that was only the beginning of the many tortures the angel had endured. One hand had no fingers remaining, while the other had only one; the wings were missing, as were its legs from the knees down. Coagulated blood gelled on the floor of the cage, which seemed to be the culprit of the clogged wheels. The pathetic creature hung there, swinging, as the demon wheeled the cage before Nezeratu. The demon servant took a key and unlocked the cell, opening the door for its master.

"You see, Inuentas, this creature fought beside the New Order in the battle against Marnelphion," Nezeratu explained, taking the curved dagger from the table.

"My lord, this corpse is seven hundred years old?"

"He is older than that, I guess, and has remained my captive for a long time."

"Captive?" Inuentas asked, scrunching up his nose in confusion.

"Of course," Nezeratu said, standing and entering the cage. "You know that angels cannot starve to death, right?"

"I did not know that," Inuentas answered.

"Interesting. Then you may not know that the most delicate way to eat one is one tiny sample at a time."

The demon lord took the wicked dagger and cut a skinny slice of meat from the angel's arm. To Inuentas's shock, the creature lifted its head and jerked about, screaming in agony. The creature lived! It tried to speak, and Inuentas noticed it had no tongue. Nezeratu ignored the animated creature and took another thin slice of meat from its other arm. He exited the cage and placed one sliver of angel meat on each plate. The angel wailed for a bit but finally went limp, and its head returned to its resting spot. The demon shut and locked the door on Nezeratu's signal and then wheeled the angel back into the darkness.

Inuentas watched it go, understanding that the demon lord had feasted on the creature for nearly seven centuries, taking only tiny pieces of its flesh at a time, and probably not frequently by the looks of it. It would never die of starvation; it would never grow old. Nezeratu could eat the angel's body for many more centuries. A chill ran down his spine at the thought of it.

"Delicious," the demon lord said, slurping the morsel into his mouth and chewing slowly, savoring it.

He motioned for Inuentas to follow suit, which he did without delay. He tried to chew as instructed. He had tasted raw meat many times, and the associated blood was quite tasty, but the meat itself was terrible, almost sour. He thought that perhaps even though the angel was still alive, its soul had left long ago, making the meat putrid. He ate it happily, though, and afterward he discovered the benefits of eating raw angel meat as his strength swelled and his constitution seemed to double. Moreover, it accentuated his powers, making him more aware and formidable.

Nezeratu smiled knowingly. "It is time," he said.

He summoned another vortex beside the table and its stench left little doubt that it was a gate to the second layer of hell. Inuentas had been there once before, and the outcome was disastrous. It was the level of hell where the chaotic demons roamed, always looking for a kill. It was the layer ruled by Marnelphion.

Nezeratu stood and tapped his cane once on the floor. Inuentas watched as the cane transformed into a sword, not any sword, but the sword known as Slebel the Demon Killer. Only its blood-red hilt was visible, the blade tucked into a scabbard made of human skin. Nezeratu held it out before him, presenting it with both hands. Inuentas stood and reached for the weapon. However, when he grasped the sheath, it would not budge. The demon lord did not hold it; the blade rested on his open palms. Inuentas made eye contact with Nezeratu, confused by the spectacle. There, in the demon lord's eyes, he saw the purest evil he had ever witnessed. He could not look away.

"The angel meat will protect you from prying eyes, but only temporarily. So now, I will send you as close as possible to the flesh wall that Vasheba the demon has grown. You will find passage to the mortal world within that wall," Nezeratu explained.

"Yes, my lord."

"Be advised that you have gazed into my eyes and still live. Understand few can rightfully claim this. You know that you will see me once again if you fail me."

"Yes, I will not—" Inuentas began.

"You further understand that no one has ever looked into my eyes twice and lived to tell about it?"

Inuentas tried to find the courage to speak but simply could not. So instead, he merely nodded his understanding of the implied threat.

"Good, then off you go, and do not fail me, Inuentas, the Indomitable."

The sword came free, and Inuentas quickly strapped it on. "You will never see me again, my lord."

Nezeratu smiled and motioned toward the vortex with an outstretched arm. Inuentas nodded and stepped through.

Daro had waited in his cottage home for a sign from the goddess from the falls, the stunningly beautiful and mysterious woman. However, she never arrived, and he was tired of waiting. He could not allow her to stay in his woods without discovering the reason for her visit. It had been several weeks since their chance encounter; it had been long enough. He gathered his gear and his weapons and dressed for the cold. Winter had arrived, and the fall weather had been hateful enough.

He made his way to the falls, where he had spotted her. There was no precipitation that day, but the wind blew cold. He saw minor signs of wildlife on the way as the packed snow mainly remained undisturbed. As he neared the spot, he became nervous. If she were a true goddess, he might be precipitating his death. He had hidden away like a rabbit, so shaken was he by the mere sight of her. However, he was better than that and owed his woods the courage to investigate the intruder. It was time to step up and be the Keeper of the Woods, as he was aptly named, and to find out the truth about the visitor.

As the sound of the falls came within earshot, he realized his nervousness was getting the best of him. He wasn't worried about death; the thing that shook him so was the possibility of witnessing the woman's incredible beauty again. Did he dare look upon her god-like face once more? He stopped and pondered that thought for a moment. Yes, that would be the real test, to ignore her beauty and discover the reason for her visit to the woods. So he trudged on, telling himself that he was Daro, Keeper of the Woods.

When he was only a few hundred yards from the falls, he discovered footprints. They seemed to travel from the falls toward the western edge of the woods, precisely toward Novafontera. The prints were human, and he could tell that it would have to be a person far heavier than the small woman he had witnessed a few weeks earlier. His mind raced back to that image burned into his brain, the idea of her rising from the river, naked and stunning. He snapped out of his trance when he realized that the woman had been unarmed and would be vulnerable unless, of course, she indeed was a goddess. More precisely, she would be susceptible to whoever made the tracks.

He unsheathed both swords and hastily made his way toward the falls. He knew he could be running into a trap, but he could think of nothing but the woman's perfect face. She had haunted his dreams for the last few weeks, and he had to know who she was. If something or someone had harmed her, they would taste the bite of his weapons.

When he made the falls and the river bank where he had seen her, he found them deserted, and his heart sank. He discerned that the footprints originated from behind the falls. He approached cautiously, half-expecting to discover the mangled remains of the beautiful woman he had left there unprotected.

"Hello?" he called, but the roar of the falls drowned him out. Perhaps the mysterious woman was dead, and there was only one way to find out.

He stepped behind the falls, weapons ready, but no one was there. He looked around and understood that someone had lived there for at least a few weeks. However, it was clear that they had packed up and left. It had to be the person who made the tracks, which meant it probably was not the goddess. Either way, he intended to figure it out. He set off, following the footprints. They were only a few hours old, and he knew he would catch the person long before they reached the edge of his woods. He needed answers to this mystery.

He tracked them for nearly an hour and knew Novafontera was close. The lack of wildlife did not surprise the ranger as he approached the cursed city. Their absence was typical this close to the evil that was Novafontera.

However, the human tracks continued to lead directly toward the place, so he followed. He wondered if the Heinsvick creature had somehow made them and perhaps was not a vampire.

The city's great wall appeared before him through the canopy of leaves. The footprints remained unblemished as he exited his beloved forest and stood before that wall. He knelt and examined them once more and understood they were very fresh and heading directly to the front gate. He quickened his pace; if this were Heinsvick, he would have a word with the creature before it retreated into the fog.

He eventually turned the corner of the massive wall, and as expected, the tracks in the snow did likewise. The front gate became visible to him about one hundred yards away, and he finally saw the creator of the tracks. A man dressed in plate mail stood at the entrance, wearing a full helm, a sword strapped at his hip, and a shield on his back. The sight puzzled Daro as it was not what he expected to find. Why had this warrior traveled so far in a direct course that took him to the front gates of Novafontera? Why had he lived behind the falls for a time, and more importantly, where was the goddess he had glimpsed?

The man seemed to examine the gate as if contemplating entering the dead city. Daro decided then that this was most definitely not Heinsvick. The man could be potentially dangerous, though. The actions of this one made no sense, and it was time to find answers. Daro quickly and quietly approached from an angle that kept the warrior from seeing him through the large helm. He withdrew both blades, and when Daro was within twenty yards of the strange fellow, he stopped and said, "Did you forget your key?"

The man stopped his fumbling with the locked gate and froze in place. He slowly turned to face Daro but made no other move.

Daro kept his swords pointed toward the ground, his stance relaxed. "These gates have not opened for centuries. They are not easily going to do so now."

Still the strange man stood there, almost as if paralyzed, and did not respond. Daro did not know what to make of the fool and finally asked, "Well?"

The man did move then, slowly unstrapping his shield from his back and fitting it to his left forearm. He drew his weapon. He did not advance, but it was clear to Daro that a fight with this one was inevitable.

"Did you harm that woman at Wolf's Crest Waterfall? If you did, I could not suffer that to pass, not in my woods."

The warrior still did not respond. Daro found that to be the most frustrating thing about the unusual man. "I'll ask you kindly to drop your weapon so we can discuss this without violence," the ranger ordered.

When he made no move to comply, Daro advanced. The warrior took a defensive stance, stepping back with his right foot and bringing his shield to bear, his sword ready.

"You leave me no choice, stranger. But, trust me, if I find that you have harmed the woman at the waterfall, I will see her avenged," Daro warned, and he prepared to strike.

The warrior relaxed his posture and spoke, and though the helm muffled the words, they were unmistakably female. "It was you."

"What?" Daro asked, stepping back and relaxing his stance as well.

"At the waterfall, it was you who spied on me as I bathed in the water." The female voice rang a little louder and angrier within the helm.

"Wait, you are the woman from the falls? Please remove your mask so that I may—"

"May, what? Make fun of the way I look? Prepare yourself!" she shouted and regained her fighting stance.

"No, nothing like that! You are—"

"What? Hideous?" the warrior screamed, and she attacked with blinding speed before Daro could finish speaking.

She struck twice with her sword, swiping right to left, then quickly back the other way. Daro blocked one with his right sword and the other with his left. The blocks came easy, but he was impressed with her speed and the strength behind her strikes. She hesitated for just a moment, and he thought she would speak once more. But, instead, she struck like a snake, thrusting for his midsection. He barely got his swords before him and stepped to his right, narrowly avoiding the attack. However, the move cost him dearly as the strange female fighter used her shield to strike him on the shoulder and knock him off balance.

He stumbled backward, hitting his back hard against Novafontera's mighty wall. Daro realized the woman was no novice to fighting. She struck with an overhead chop that he dodged at the last moment. Sparks sprayed from the wall as her fine blade cut a gash in the old stone. She did not relent, slashing at him again with a growl. He blocked the attack, but the force of her swing nearly dislodged his weapon. He would not counter without knowing the woman's identity. He was fighting a losing battle and needed to disengage her. So, he did the only thing he could and rolled, letting the momentum of her attack carry him out of her sword's range.

"I concede, dear woman!" he yelled once he had regained his footing.

She stopped then and relaxed once more. Daro had seen her do that once and knew to be on his guard. She was excellent and swift. He did not relax his guard this time.

"May we talk?" he asked.

"There is nothing I have to say to you," she said coldly.

"Please, I am not your enemy."

She did not respond and did not move. Daro wanted to see her face again; her beauty had mesmerized him. The thought of glimpsing her again had his heart pounding in his chest. "Your name then?" he finally asked.

Still no response, and she did not regain her battle stance.

"Please, I am no enemy," Daro said.

After a few moments of silence, she whispered, "Sasha, the Ugly."

"What? Why, you are the most beautiful—"

"Liar!" Sasha screamed before he could finish.

Daro sheathed his swords and raised his hands. "Listen, Sasha, I am not your enemy. I stumbled upon you in the woods a few weeks ago and was overwhelmed by your beauty."

Sasha seemed to tense at those words, but Daro continued, "I found you so beautiful that I thought you might be a goddess sent here to destroy me. So, I hid in my cottage the last few weeks, so convinced was I that you were a goddess."

"I do not understand," Sasha whispered.

"It is true. Whatever people have told you, the ones who have said you are ugly are just jealous of your beauty. But, trust me, you are breathtaking. I long to see your face again." Daro stepped closer, still with his hands in the air to show he was not expecting a fight.

Sasha slowly sheathed her weapon and lowered her shield. "People have told me all my life that I am ugly. Where I come from, I look different; I am ugly in their eyes. No, not ugly, but hideous."

Daro approached her and whispered, "Where you come from, people must be blind. But I tell you honestly, you are as beautiful as a goddess. I want to look upon your fair face once more, Sasha."

He raised his hands to lift her face shield. She drew her sword in the blink of an eye and placed it at the side of his neck. He moved his hands away from her helm and said, "Trust me."

She kept the blade there. He did not dare move until she lowered her weapon. Then, once she sheathed it again, he continued his movement, grasping her face shield and slowly lifting it. His heart was pounding, and he hoped this was the same woman he had met briefly at the falls. And, to his delight, it was; there was no mistaking. He gazed upon her for many moments, and she stared back with a scowl. Even with her face scrunched up in anger, she was the most beautiful woman he had ever seen.

"Sasha the Beautiful," he whispered.

She slammed the visor down, yelling, "Do not mock me!" She then turned and walked back to the gate.

"Sasha, please, trust me."

"I have no reason to."

"I agree, but please give me a chance," he pleaded.

She did not turn back to him but continued her examination of the old gate. It was metal and rusted shut. She felt around the seams for some sign that it might open and said, "Where I come from, I have received no chances, caged like an animal because of my looks. Why should I give you a chance?"

"Sasha, I do not understand what happened to you, but I'm telling you, I don't find you ugly. Quite the contrary."

She continued to search the gate, testing it for weaknesses. After watching for a moment, Daro finally blurted out, "I know another way. I can take you there."

Sasha stopped and turned toward him before asking, "Why?"

"Why what?"

"Why would you help me?"

"Well, you don't trust me, and I figured that would be one way to prove my sincerity. Am I correct in thinking you will trust me if I show you an easier way?" She nodded slightly, and Daro was relieved to think he might have found a way to win her over.

"Good, then let's start over. I am Daro, Keeper of the Woods and friend to Sasha the Beautiful. Will you come back with me to my cottage?"

"I thought you said you would show me a way in?"

"Yes, of course, but I need supplies to enter that way, and I assure you, you do not want to enter this place at night. It is nearly dusk, and evil will soon come alive here. So come with me to my house to eat and sleep, then return here in the morning, refreshed. Tell me where you come from and why you want to enter Novafontera."

She did not move or say anything for a moment, and Daro became unconvinced that he had won her over, but after a while, she said, "Lead the way, Daro of the Woods."

They spoke little during the trek to his small home, and it was nearly dark when they arrived.

Vasheba learned of Cassandra Rho's death from the city guard she currently toyed with. After several attempts at searching for Cassandra, she decided to go to the source: a Pelesea guardsman. It was risky, and although the demoness had kidnapped and murdered almost a dozen people in the bowels of Novafontera since her arrival a few weeks ago, this one would garner the most attention from the king. She didn't care; the poisonous gas of Novafontera protected her.

The pathetic man hung upside down in the catacombs underneath the city. He was bound tight, and she lazily flicked her chains at him, the heavy barbed ones she kept wrapped around her waist. Each hit tore flesh from the terrified man and elicited painful screams. In truth, the guard was more a boy than a man, which made the torture even more rewarding for the evil creature.

Vasheba was a powerful demoness summoned by the priestess Matilda to answer questions about the Great Summoning. Matilda could not hold the raw power of Vasheba, and the demon had broken free, but not before discovering that Cassandra Rho was the key that Matilda so desperately desired. Vasheba laughed at the absurdity of it; Cassandra had died in a fire, a random accident, and now the Great Summoning was not so great after all. Her laugh sounded like death to the frightened guard, and he screamed again.

She whipped him hard with her chain to punish him for his cowardness.

Unfortunately, her strike was a little too forceful as the demoness often forgot how delicate humans were. The top half of the guard fell to the floor, followed by a stream of entrails. As the dreadful scene played out, she became distracted, sensing intruders near the gates of her home.

An instant later, she spied Daro and Sasha from within the deadly fog. She had new playthings to occupy her time; the two fools planned to enter the city. Vasheba loved games, especially when they ended with her torturing two healthy mortals and eating their souls. She watched them walk away, then turned to prepare for their return, thoughts of Cassandra now at the recesses of her mind.

Once home, Daro made up his room for Sasha to sleep, anxious to accommodate her. "I will sleep in my chair here, and you may have my bed."

She nodded as he motioned with his hand toward his room. She entered and shut the door behind her. There was a long silence before he finally heard her removing the armor. She trusted him enough to remove her protection and relax, and that mattered to him more than anything. He cleaned the kitchen and small dining area as she undressed, wanting the place to be tidy. He had never had reason to be orderly except when he stayed in the cottage at Pelesea. But he never fussed over his home as he did then. He wanted nothing more than to please and impress her.

She eventually came out, and he became overwhelmed again. Having removed the bulky armor, she wore a thin shirt and pants. The clothes accented her womanly figure, making Daro stare in disbelief. Her blond locks fell about her shoulders, and her face was as beautiful as he remembered when they first met.

She noticed his gaze and stopped. "Am I that hideous?" she asked.

"Far from it, Sasha; you are more beautiful than you realize," he said.

Her look indicated she did not believe him, but she went to the table, tentatively taking a seat. She looked up at him, and he tried to divert his gaze. Daro knew he was making her self-conscious, so he had to consciously force himself not to stare.

"Are you hungry?" he asked, trying to break the uncomfortable exchange.

"Very. My food ran out a day ago."

"Then you are in luck; I shall make us a stew," Daro said, and he gathered the ingredients.

"What is a stew?" Sasha asked.

"You've never had stew? You are in for a treat!" Daro said, quickly getting to work on the food preparation. "So, where are you from, Sasha?"

"From the falls, remember?"

"No, I mean—"

Sasha's gasp interrupted him, and he turned to see her wide-eyed, staring at a bowl of fruit on his counter. She was mesmerized by it and slowly stood. He watched as she reached the bowl and grasped an apple.

"You have these!" she said excitedly, her smile growing as large as her eyes.

"Of course. Do you want one?"

"Yes!" she said and took a bite.

Daro watched as she devoured the apple, most of the time with her eyes closed and the juices running down her chin. Her lack of manners indicated to him that she possessed no skills of etiquette.

"Do you like the apple?" he asked as she finished.

"This is what you call it? Apple?"

"Sasha, have you learned to trust me yet?" he asked.

"Yes, some."

"I have given you food, shelter, and a bed. So do you have any reason not to trust me?"

"Not yet, other than that you lie about my looks."

"Sasha, you must believe my words; I am not lying about anything, especially your looks. I don't know where you come from, but the people you knew there are wrong. Please tell me who you are and where you came from."

Sasha nodded slightly and sat back down. Daro turned to continue preparing the stew, hoping that she would warm up to him. He needed to know what she wanted in Novafontera before he helped her break into the place.

"Glacies," she whispered.

"What?"

"Glacies. It is where I am from."

"I've never heard of this place, Sasha; it must be far from here."

"I do not know. Magic sent me here, and I made the trip in a few short steps. Presin is my uncle, and Clade is my master. They sent me here."

"Master? Are you an apprentice or a prisoner?" Daro asked, stopping his food preparation and sitting at the table. He noticed her staring at the bowl, so he grabbed two more apples and handed them to her. She smiled and started scoffing them.

She answered in between bites, "They keep me in a cell. I had not seen the light of day until I came here. I had never enjoyed the snow and had never eaten an apple." She held up the fruit and nodded in appreciation.

"If you are a slave, why did they release you?"

"To retrieve Iustia, the Sword of Justice."

"And this is somewhere in Novafontera?"

"Precisely," she said, tossing one apple core and diving into the next one.

"Why did they not come themselves?" Daro asked.

"You have seen my skill with the sword, right?" she said with a slight smile.

Daro returned the smile and shook his head. He stood and began work once again on their meal. "Do you know where this sword is exactly? Do you know where to find it once we are inside?"

"We?" she asked, her eyes going wide.

"Yes, we. You didn't think I'd let you go alone?"

He did not wait for her answer, and one did not come; her gaze lowered to the table as he began cutting the vegetables.

A long while passed before she finally said, "Thank you, Daro; you are a friend to me."

He smiled and nodded, and they said no more until dinner was ready. During the meal, Sasha ate hungrily, almost like a wild animal, and Daro realized that, in many ways, she was. Whoever these people were, Presin and Clade, he knew they were not good to Sasha. They had mistreated her mentally and physically. He would make sure that never happened again. The two of them bonded quickly on that cold winter night, and when they finally turned in, Daro's dreams were vivid and wonderful.

The following day Daro awakened with the sunrise, as he usually did. He noted right away that the door to his room was open. He strolled toward it and belted on his sword as he did. He stopped outside, wanting to look in but not wanting to invade Sasha's privacy.

"Sasha?" he finally asked. No answer came, so he called to her again, a little louder, "Sasha?"

When silence greeted him again, he stepped into the doorway and looked in. The room was still relatively dark, but it appeared to him that Sasha was not there. He approached the window and opened the curtains slightly to allow the morning sun into the room. His heart skipped a beat when he saw that the bed was empty.

"Sasha!" he yelled, and he rushed toward the front door. He threw it open, immediately looking for prints in the snow. The tracks would tell him how long ago the young woman had left or if there had been a struggle. Thoughts of her uncle and other kin coming to kidnap her flooded his mind. Daro was a light sleeper. However, he had not heard anything the previous night, and if there had been a struggle, he would have. The cold wind took his breath as he began his search for tracks. It had been a cold night, and the wind made it dangerous.

It didn't take him long to find her, and his heart sank. The woman he had befriended the night before was completely naked in the snow. Her clothes lay in a pile beside her, and the snow half-covered her. She had been there a while and was probably long dead; there was no way she could have survived. What foul evil would have stripped her and left her to die, or had she been murdered before being moved to her current resting spot? How had he not heard anything during the night? Many desperate questions bombarded him.

"Sasha," he whispered as he rushed over to her.

He knelt and wiped the snow from her cold face. To his surprise, she opened her icy-blue eyes and blinked away her sleep, and Daro fell back on his rump. Sasha regained her wits and sat up, grabbing her clothes to cover her nakedness the best she could.

"What?" was all he could think of to say.

"What?" she repeated.

He stood and brushed the snow off his pants, then offered a hand to Sasha, who seemed perfectly fine. "Why are you out here? What happened?" he asked.

She took his hand but kept her other hand tightly on her clothing to keep herself covered. Daro tried not to look, but it was not an easy task as beautiful as Sasha was.

"I was just sleeping," she finally replied.

"What? It is far too cold out here; how did you survive?"

Sighing, she said, "I am carofex, attuned with the ice."

"Carofex?" Daro asked in confusion. "You are not human?"

"No. Well, not completely. My father was human."

"You are full of surprises, Sasha the carofex," Daro answered, motioning for the door.

Sasha turned and walked toward it, stopping to pick up her sword buried in the snow. Once inside, she went to Daro's room to dress as he prepared some eggs for breakfast. He called Sasha to the table once the food was ready and felt the familiar charm of her physical beauty when she sat down. Daro gave her a plate and some water, and the two ate quietly at first. He watched as she gulped down her food like a hungry animal might. Her eating manners were atrocious, and he found them charming.

"So, you slept naked in the snow?"

"Huh?" she said, looking up from her plate.

"Outside. You slept naked in the snow and the cold temperature."

"Oh, yes, of course. I love the snow. It is one of my favorite things I have found in my brief time here. Second only to apples, of course," she added with a smile.

"The cold does not harm you, then?"

"Of course not; I love the cold. Sorry to alarm you this morning, but I was warm in your bed last night. I went outside to cool down. I must have dozed off."

Daro could only shake his head and smile in amazement at his new friend. He knew little of the carofex race, especially those attuned with the ice. She was a mystery, and he could only imagine what other surprises she had for him. He was eager to learn more about her and assist with her quest. However, he could already foresee the problem of her returning the sword to her homeland, assuming they could even find it. He wanted her there with him, not thrown back into prison upon her return home.

After their meal, Daro gathered the items needed to open the drainage grate at the side of the dead city, the alternate way into the city he had hinted at before. A strong rope and a bottle of powerful acid were essential, but he knew he could not open it quickly without the strength of a horse or similar creature. He thought of the centaurs living in the easternmost part of his woods. It would take several days of travel to reach them, days that Sasha might not want to lose, and their cooperation would be tentative at best. Perhaps the acid would weaken the steel enough without the need for such brute force. He would try it, and they would find assistance if it did not work.

In truth, he did not want to enter the city and would need to inform Sasha of the undead inhabitants that called the place home. Their chances of entering the city, finding the sword, and escaping were not good. He thought about talking her out of the quest but he knew there was no stopping her. She also wouldn't wait for him to summon allies, and he would not want to risk the lives of anyone else for the evil of Novafontera anyway. So instead of trying to find a way out of the dark adventure, he embraced it for Sasha. He would stand by her, for better or worse. He had a feeling worse was on the agenda for them.

He told Sasha about the minions of Novafontera as they hiked back to the dead city. He told her of his battle with the lesser vampires and how their master lurked within the walls. In addition, he explained there could be any number of lesser vampires or other undead at Heinsvick's calling. She listened intently and took it all in, but the news did not deter her from her goal. She was going to enter the city, which meant Daro would also. By midday, they had arrived at Novafontera.

Binta sat on her comfortable bed, the light from the midday sun shining through her window. The day was cold, and the winter wind blew hard against the pane, but she felt warm and safe in her tiny dorm room. She studied her spellbook for the first time in many months, the art of magic piquing her interest again. Greyson would be disappointed that she did not maintain his church in his absence, but she knew he would forgive her if she was happy. She would attend the spring semester, and Victoria had granted her permission to spend the winter in her old dorm room, rent-free.

She smiled genuinely for the first time in a very long time, placing her book on her lap and staring out the window. She missed Cassandra tremendously, but the pain was already subsiding. Eventually, she would learn to live without her friend and soul mate. She was free from Cass's evil clutches and was safe at the school. She was ashamed of her actions but knew that whatever milk Cass had made her ingest had stirred up her twisted sexual desire to serve the vile girl. Binta knew she shouldn't blame herself, but it was hard not to. She absently rubbed her neck where she had worn her collar the last few weeks. It felt strange without it.

She looked down to the page of her spellbook where she had penned her first spell. She covered her right eye and tried to read the text. It was blurry. Even after healing from the priests, her left eye was still swollen and bruised from the beating she had suffered at the hands of Jabell. She knew that if Cassandra were still alive, she'd probably kill the young man before the king could sentence him. She smiled at the thought and vowed to be more like her friend. She would have more self-respect in the future and never fall into that trap again. A knock at the door startled her from her contemplations.

"Come in," she said.

The door opened, and a man dressed in shiny metal armor entered with a giant sword hanging from his belt. Binta's heart thumped in her chest; was she somehow in trouble? Did the king and queen find out that she enjoyed her submissive role to Cass? She closed her book and sat up straight in her bed. The man said nothing but nodded slightly and stood aside so that a tall, red-haired elf could enter. She was the most beautiful woman Binta had ever seen, and she, too, wore a small sword on her side. She wore a blue shirt and leather pants instead of armor, which perfectly accented her lithe, athletic build. Binta had never seen a true elf up close before, and the sight of her stunned her senses. Her pointed ears stuck out from her hair, and her slim facial features were far more beautiful than any human Binta had met.

"Binta Mulay, I assume?" the woman said with a smile.

"Yes, that is me," Binta squeaked, then swallowed hard.

"I am Queen Penelope Brahmore, and this is my friend, Gregory," she said with a hand extended to the man in shining armor.

With her mouth agape, Binta looked at the man. He nodded again, then turned and left the room, shutting the door behind him.

"He is only here performing his duty, but you and I do not need him, Binta," Penelope said.

Binta began to get up, moving her spellbook to the side and pulling her covers back, but the queen put a gentle hand on her arm and said, "Please, remain sitting; I do not require a formal greeting."

"I apologize, my lady. It is just that I have never met a queen before."

"And now you have, and the formalities are behind us. May I sit?" Penelope asked, bringing the desk chair next to the bed.

"Of course," Binta said with a nod, her eyes still wide in disbelief.

As soon as the queen took her seat, there was a quick rap on the door, and Gregory poked his head inside. "Lady Victoria, my queen," he said, opening the door wide and letting Victoria in.

Victoria smiled at Binta and said, "I see you have met my friend." She took a seat on the edge of the bed opposite Penelope.

"I just introduced myself," Penelope said before Binta could answer.

"I see your face is healing and almost back to its pretty form," Victoria said.

"I feel better, yes," Binta said.

"That is why I have come, Miss Mulay. The king and I are very concerned about the events centered around you and Cass Ruben on the city's far end. Will you mind answering some questions for me?" Penelope asked.

"Of course, anything."

"First, I need to know how you found yourself in this situation. You do realize that prostitution is illegal in our fair city?"

Binta lowered her head and nodded shamefully.

"We normally punish those for such crimes, but under the circumstances, we wish to be lenient," the queen explained.

"I told Kringus and Penelope about your history with Cass and Jabell and how you were probably intimidated into such lewd actions. Please correct me if I have misspoken," Victoria added.

Binta looked each in the face and swallowed hard. She was nervous in the presence of such beautiful and powerful women, but she also felt guilty. Had she been forced into service under Cass, or was that precisely what she had wanted? She figured it was a little of both but thought it better not to admit it. So instead, she lowered her gaze and nodded in agreement.

"Binta, you are not in trouble, do you understand?" Penelope asked.

Binta looked into Penelope's green eyes and saw only kindness there. She believed the queen, and she also presumed Victoria knew that she was hiding part of the truth about her service to Cass. Nevertheless, they made her feel like she could speak freely, so she smiled and nodded again.

"Good. Currently, we have Jabell and Cass in custody. Cass will probably be released but will have a hearing before the king in a few days to answer for her crimes, and my husband will pass his judgment. Despite her father's good standing in the city, I fear she will spend some time in jail.

"The young man who assaulted you will probably spend many years in jail. His most recent violent attack on you, coupled with the first when the two of you were students, is enough for Kringus to put him away for a while. Either way, you are now safe.

"The king and I would like you to stay on the palace grounds for the foreseeable future. We have a ranger friend who has a beautiful cottage near a pond within the castle gardens and in the middle of an apple orchard. It is a spectacular place to recover from physical and mental wounds."

"I don't know what to say, my queen," Binta stammered, then looked to Victoria for support.

"Do not worry, we will save your room for the spring semester, so you may attend when you are back to full health," Victoria said.

"Also, we have sent for your parents so they may stay with you until school begins," Penelope added.

"My parents?" Binta gasped.

"Yes, to help you recover from this and your loss of Cassandra. I understand the two of you were very close, is that correct?" the queen asked.

"Yes, we were very close. I miss Cassandra terribly. Why?"

"No reason. I know her death is still new, and you must think of her often."

"Yes, I do. But may I ask why we are discussing Cassandra?"

Penelope shared a glance with Victoria, and Binta understood then that something was afoot.

"Please tell me if you know something about Cassandra's death," Binta pleaded.

Penelope sighed and smiled weakly. "I know nothing that you don't already know. However, I feel Cass's friend could have some answers about what happened that horrible night at the jail."

"Malikai?"

"Yes, my father," Victoria said.

"Father?" Binta repeated.

"He is not a good person, Miss Mulay, and I need you to tell me what you know of him," Penelope added.

"I don't know much, I'm afraid. But Malikai was good to me while I worked for Cass."

"Good to you?" Penelope asked.

"Yes, he made sure I bathed and had books to read and things to do while I stayed in the room during the week."

"You mean, while you were a prisoner to Cass?" Penelope asked.

"Yes," Binta said with a nod.

"What else can you tell me about him?" the queen asked.

"Nothing, except—" The words caught in her throat, and Binta lowered her head shamefully.

"Please continue, Binta," Victoria said, patting her leg.

"I was only going to say he is an excellent lover."

Penelope and Victoria shared another glance, and Penelope asked, "What of his companion?"

"Who?"

"The woman with whom he travels. We know little of her, but he stays with a woman in the same inn where Cass held you captive. Malikai does not choose his travel companions lightly, so we hoped you knew something of her," Victoria explained.

"I never met anyone else. It was only Cass and Malikai. However, I remember they spoke briefly of another woman, but I can't recall her name," Binta said.

Penelope touched her arm gently and said, "I know it is still too soon to relive those awful events, but we appreciate you helping us." Then she rose and replaced the chair. "If you think of anything else, please let me know."

"Yes, of course."

Victoria rose then as well, the meeting obviously at its end. Penelope shook Victoria's hand and shared a smile and a knowing look. The queen turned to Binta and said, "So, how about staying with us on the palace grounds?"

"Yes. Yes, that would be wonderful!" Binta said.

"Good. I have already sent for your parents, and they will be here within a few weeks. Gregory will remain outside your door and escort you to the cottage after you collect your things. I think it is charming and I hope you do enjoy your stay. I will see that the cupboards are stocked before you arrive."

Penelope opened the door, and she and Victoria were already walking through it when Binta found her voice. "My queen?"

They both stopped, and Victoria stepped back into the room. "Yes, Miss Mulay?" Penelope said.

"Well, I was wondering, am I safe?"

Penelope and Victoria shared yet another knowing glance, and Penelope said with all seriousness, "If Malikai knows I am questioning you about him, then no."

Binta nodded meekly, and the queen smiled once more, then left with Victoria in tow. Once alone, Binta's mind raced. So, she was going to live on the castle grounds? The world was spinning out of control, and she felt her life was changing too quickly. She sat there for many moments before she could climb out of bed and pack her things.

7

VARISH

CERUS THE GREY HAD WATCHED HIS INSATIABLE WIFE, MATILDA, cuckold him with the nasty wizard Malikai many times over the last few months. He snapped the whip at his victim as he recalled the images of the lovers' embrace, and she let out another long moan, followed by sobbing. He struck her again, letting his anger play out. He had not liked the look on Malikai's smug face, staring at him through the magical mirror, wearing a smirk as he had his way with Matilda. He struck again and again and again until his victim fell limp, her back a bloody mess.

Cerus held no love for Emiline the vampire, Matilda's plaything, so it had become a familiar routine to fetch the creature after each humiliation he suffered at the hands of his wife. Each time he had whipped the vampire into unconsciousness. After the beating, the elven vampire hung limply from her chains in the circular contraption Matilda used to interrogate and torture captives. She hung there bleeding, stripped naked, and her arms and legs bound in a spread-eagled position.

Matilda had kidnapped the creature from Heinsvick, the vampire lord, with plans to keep Emiline captive and subdued in the bowels of their cavern fortress, Nesin. Cerus initially hated the idea and did not hesitate to share his feelings with his wife. So, it was only natural for him to take out his frustrations on the vampire whenever Matilda cuckolded him.

"Take her back to her hole," Cerus said, handing the whip to one of the priests of Marnelphion, who bowed, then ordered two slaves to release the creature.

He had worked up a sweat and had torn deeply into Emiline's undead flesh. The priests had assured him she would heal in her coffin, which had been the case so far. However, the beatings were more severe each time. Perhaps the damage to her back would not heal this time. Matilda would not like that, and that brought a smile to Cerus's face.

As the priest and servants dragged Emiline away, a messenger hurriedly entered the room. He was one of Cerus's men who guarded the cave entrance to Nesin. The news had to be urgent if he had left his post to come down there.

"Cerus, news from Racip!" the soldier said.

"I'm listening."

"Our spies from the port indicate that a small band of priestesses has docked there."

"Worshippers of Sinnis?"

"Of course," the man said with a wicked smile.

"How many?"

"Almost fifty, my lord."

"Tell our spy to ride back to Racip with all haste with a message for the dockmaster. He should inform him to keep the priestesses in Racip and I will collect them shortly. I will reward him accordingly."

The man bowed and said, "Yes, my lord," then turned and hurried away.

Cerus left the room quickly afterward and gathered his men. They had prepared for such an opportunity ever since the early days of their training. The hated worshippers of Sinnis were their sworn enemies, and the idea of slaughtering them gave Cerus's men great satisfaction. Cerus had partaken in a Sinnis massacre before, and he wanted nothing more than to allow his men the same pleasure. Within a few hours, one hundred hardy warriors of Gorl were riding hard toward Port Racip, with Cerus leading the way.

Merrik, the priest who had taken the whip from Cerus, examined Emiline's back. This time, the wounds were deeper as Cerus had beaten her mercilessly. He was partially to blame as he had used his priestly powers to overwhelm the creature so Cerus could transport her to the whipping contraption. Without Merrik's intervention, Emiline would be a worthy opponent for Cerus. However, with Merrik's powers to render her helpless, Cerus had taken advantage with the wicked whip. He usually wouldn't care, but Merrik followed Matilda, and she would disapprove of Cerus's actions if she knew about them. Emiline, after all, was one of her favorite possessions. So, he healed her wounds with a powerful spell, and her skin closed in many places. They would leave scars, no doubt, but they would not prove fatal.

"Not this time," Merrik whispered to himself.

He ordered the slaves to carry the unconscious vampire to the dungeons and return her to her cell. They struggled to move the unconscious creature but did as told. Soon the three stood in Emiline's large cell, the vampire lying on the floor. Her coffin was nearby, the lid removed and thrown to the side by Cerus when he had collected her for whipping a few hours earlier.

At the far side of her cell, another door led to a separate enclosure, where Kessi Rho watched the unfolding events. She was part of a group of sacrifices Cerus and Matilda had collected in recent months. Twenty young women filled the cell, all virgins and carefully tucked away to await the sacrifice.

All but Kessi huddled at the back, as they always did when one of the priests entered Emiline's cell. Merrik noticed her and stared lustfully, his eyes roaming over her. She knew this man and recognized him from a few days prior. He was the only priest she had seen in the cell for the last few weeks. He had not paid too much attention to her, but now with Emiline unconscious and not occupying his attention, he stared long and hard at her, an evil smile creeping across his face.

Kessi knew she stood out from her cellmates because her gown was torn halfway to her midriff and tied with string to hold it together. However, despite the makeshift repair, her breasts were partially visible, and the ordinarily white gown she wore, familiar to all the virgins in the cell, was stained with blood. Not fresh blood, but a faded stain that indicated the dress was in disrepair and old.

The priest found her intriguing. He took a few steps toward her as if to speak, slightly opening his mouth. Kessi did not move and did not shy away from his approach. The priest noticed her posture and stopped. He seemed to struggle with what to do next, and Kessi kept her eyes on him, fixing him with an emotionless stare. She rested her forehead on the bars and closed her eyes. When she opened them, he was on the far side of Emiline's cell, gathering the slaves. He looked back at her one last time, then pushed the two slaves into the corridor leading out of the dungeon, followed, and shut the door behind him. He fumbled with the key, obviously distracted by the stare-down he had just shared with Kessi.

Kessi breathed a little easier when he was gone. She did not want any trouble but did what she could to keep them from killing the vampire. Kessi had been in the cell for several months now, having been cast down by Matilda from a higher standing, one that Kessi could not recall. She had disappointed Matilda somehow, but she could not remember those early days in Nesin. She pulled at her torn dress, trying to cover herself. Matilda had been the one to rip it open weeks earlier, and Kessi's blood had stained her gown. The wound had been a minor one caused by one of the brutal guards striking her with his whip and gashing her finger. A minor injury, but it had bled a great deal. Matilda had not replaced the garment, and Kessi assumed it was to send her a message; she was no longer in the favor of the evil priestess, and she would wear her torn and stained dress as a reminder.

The man who had just delivered Emiline's unconscious form had stared at her nearly exposed body, and Kessi had let him. If that kept his thoughts from Emiline, then so be it. Now he was gone, and Kessi focused on the unmoving vampire on the floor in the adjacent cell. She made the priest nervous, and she did not know why. She could not even remember her name or where she came from, so she certainly couldn't understand why anyone would be afraid of her. She was glad of it and hoped it protected the vampire. She felt a kinship with Emiline for unknown reasons and did not like it when the evil men mistreated her.

"Mayla?" A voice came from behind.

Kessi turned to see Sabrina walking toward her from the shadows where the rest of Kessi's cellmates lingered. Mayla had been the name Sabrina had given her upon her arrival since she could not remember her own. Sabrina soon stood beside her, gradually followed by the others, and they all gazed into the cell where the vampire lay.

"Is she dead?" asked the youngest prisoner, a shy girl of sixteen years named Sara.

"I don't think so," Sabrina answered.

After a few moments, the gathering dispersed, and the women went to the various areas of the cell they called their own to prepare for sleep. Sabrina stayed beside Kessi and continued to take in the unconscious vampire.

Eventually, she turned to her friend and said, "You must stop being so brave."

Kessi looked at her and said, "Brave? What do you mean?"

"I mean standing at these bars. They notice you when you do that, Mayla. Did you not see the evil man in the robes look at you? I thought he would come over and kill you."

"I'm not afraid. I'll stand up to these men to protect her," Kessi answered, nodding toward the vampire.

Sabrina smiled and shook her head. "You are a stubborn one. I hope we find out who you are and your background before we—"

She stopped when she considered the dire end they all faced. They knew they were there to die, and there was no escape. "Sorry, sometimes I forget our fate, and when I remember, it is a shock all over again," Sabrina said.

Kessi smiled and nodded. She turned back toward the larger cell, not to watch over the vampire but to search her thoughts. Her mind was still a mess, and she remembered little of her former life. She knew she had a sister somewhere who played into all of it but could not remember how. She quickly became frustrated with the situation. She knew things that could help them all but could not place them. She sighed and turned away from the bars. Perhaps some sleep would help clear her mind. Her cellmates and she lived on borrowed time. They shared a pending doom and knew they would eventually die horribly at the hands of Matilda. Kessi did not know how long they had, so time was of the essence for her to figure out who she was and how she could help her friends escape the dungeons of Nesin.

Greyson and Alleah stood at the *Lady of Faith*'s starboard-side rail, looking out over the city of Racip. The ship had docked three days earlier after a sea voyage of nearly a month from Pelesea to Varish. They watched Captain Jessica conversing with the dockmaster for the third time that day. However, this time, the dockmaster had been escorted to the docks by a small contingent of men. He looked none too happy with Jessica, and although Greyson could not hear the words, he knew the conversation was getting heated. Soon, a frustrated Jessica was reboarding her ship.

She came over to the two and looked back at the dockmaster. "Honorary fellow," she said and spat over the ship's side with a glare the dockmaster's way. He then barked a few orders in response and stormed off, leaving a dozen men to guard the dock.

"I assume that did not go well?" Alleah asked.

"No, it did not."

"And now there are two ships out at sea, guarding our escape," Greyson said, looking over the boat's port side.

"So there are," Jessica said through gritted teeth. The young captain turned toward Alleah and said, "The mission is compromised."

"They know who we are? None of my sisters have been top deck and they have not revealed themselves. So, no one knows our cargo," Alleah argued.

Jessica leaned both arms against the rail and looked out over the dock. "I agree, but they are stalling, waiting for something."

"The men who destroyed Tara?" Greyson asked.

Alleah turned toward him, her beautiful face stern, her crystal-blue eyes searching his. Greyson knew she wanted a battle with the men of Gorl as much as he did. During their long trip across the ocean, they had plenty of time to discuss the events in Tara from a few months ago. They had compared notes carefully, and from what they could tell, the followers of Gorl were responsible for the raid on Greyson's home.

"Possibly," Jessica said, interrupting the two from their silent communication. "If the men of Gorl are coming, you need to disembark and be on your way."

"We will have to fight our way off the ship if we unboard against the dockmaster's orders," Greyson said.

"I do not doubt that we could do just that, but there are better ways to handle this situation," Alleah argued. She turned to the captain and asked, "So, what did the dockmaster say this time?"

"Same as the last two times: he is detaining *Lady of Faith* for five days before allowing passengers or cargo to unload. He reminds me that it will only be two more days in quarantine and asks for our patience."

"With a contingent of armed men?" Alleah asked.

Captain Jessica nodded and sighed. "He insists that the city policy is for ships sailing from Torlia to Varish to remain docked for five days before being deemed disease-free. However, something smells wrong with this. I have never docked here, that is true enough, but I have never seen a delay like this in any of the many ports I have visited."

"Someone has tipped them off," Greyson added. Both women turned to him, wearing shocked expressions.

"What?" Alleah asked.

"It is the only explanation. As you said, none of your friends have shown their faces. How would the dockmaster be suspicious of this ship? Others have docked since we arrived, and none were harassed such as we."

"I should meet with my sisters and discuss our options," Alleah said.

"Does that include me?" Greyson asked with a smile.

"Of course, you are one of us."

"I will remain top deck in case there is trouble," Jessica said.

"You are most welcome to join us," Alleah said.

Jessica shook her head and looked out to sea at the two ships anchored there. "No, I should remain up top. I do not trust this situation."

"That seems reasonable; let us know if there is trouble," Alleah said.

Jessica nodded, and then the two priests went below deck to consult with the sisters of Sinnis. Greyson knew that their next move would prove vital. Something told him they had made a mistake docking at the large port. Captain Jessica had seemed confident that they would blend in just fine in Varish, beginning with the port city of Racip. Now, she appeared nervous and second-guessing that strategy. Greyson most certainly did not feel glad to be home. Port Racip was not hospitable, and their journey to Tara would be a month's hike from there. He suddenly felt like their journey to Varish was a tremendously bad idea.

Cassandra awakened to find herself in a small, dark room that reeked of sweat and urine. She was lying on a rough bed of straw with a coarse blanket to cover up with. She was naked and drew the uncomfortable cloth around her as she sat up. She regretted the decision immediately as a sharp pain in her forehead had her grimacing and bringing a hand to her throbbing temple. She squinted her eyes against the intense pain and examined her surroundings. There were no windows and one shut door.

She let out a yelp and pulled the blanket tighter when she noticed a man in the corner, standing quietly. A small lantern was at his feet, the only light source in the dim room. The man was large, with tanned skin and muscles bulging through his thin shirt. Then the memories came flooding back: Maltor, Vixa, and another savage had inadvertently rescued her from Ronnis. This man resembled them in stature, so she knew then that they had kidnapped her.

"Where am I?" she asked between parched lips.

The man did not move and only stared at her as if she were some exotic creature. She did not appreciate how he looked her over, and her anger flared. Cassandra knew she had to be careful because she did not know where she was or how many savages there were. She focused on the magic in the air around her and was relieved to find the arcane symbols abundant in the room. Cassandra closed her eyes and called out to the ravens, but she could sense none in the area. She realized the room was gently swaying, and there was an occasional creaking of boards within the walls and floor.

"We're on a boat?"

The man stood taller and crossed his arms over his barrel-like chest.

"Fine, don't speak. And quit looking at me!"

Again, the man did not move and said nothing. Cassandra sighed and lay her head back against the wall. It made sense that she would detect no ravens if they were out at sea. Still, she had her magic, and she could seriously hurt the big man, take the lantern, and leave the stinky room. However, she did not know what was on the other side of that door. She assumed there were at least three other warriors, the ones that had taken her. She needed answers, and the large man was not cooperating. He continued to look at her, and she noticed her leg was sticking out of the blanket, almost to her thigh. The man looked at it like it was a piece of meat. She was tired of being a piece of meat.

She threw the blanket off to reveal her nakedness and stood. Her head throbbed with the effort, and she fell back against the wall. Her legs were wobbly, and the ship's movements were more noticeable when she stood. She felt nauseated, so she closed her eyes and took several steadying breaths. When she opened them, she noticed the man was staring at her and she saw red.

"What is the matter with you? Have you never seen a woman?" she said, walking on unsteady legs to the large brute.

He uncrossed his arms, and she noticed a touch of panic in his eyes. From what she had seen, these people did not respect females, and perhaps her being so bold was intimidating. She was determined to keep that edge, so she began scanning the air between them, pulling at the arcane symbols and formulating a spell that would have the man sleeping in no time. Her concentration waned as the big man picked her up with one swift movement; he was very agile for his size.

She released a surprised yelp and said, "Put me down!"

The man ignored her and threw her over his shoulder as if she were a sack of potatoes. Cassandra kicked her legs and beat the man on the back with her fists, but then the pain in her head had her second-guessing any movement. He quickly but gently put her back on the straw bed, threw her blanket to her, and walked back to his corner. He was not like the other three; he was somehow savage but gentle.

Cassandra held one hand to her head, pulled the blanket tight with the other, and lay down. She was exhausted from the ordeals she had endured in recent months and had little energy to deal with the strange man in the room. He was obviously a guard, but where were they taking her? She would be helpless until she discovered more information. She also needed the headache to subside and decided sleep was her best option. She pulled the coarse blanket around her and soon dozed off.

She awakened sometime later to discover she was in total darkness. The smell was still persistent, but the light was gone. Did that mean the man with the lantern had left her? She sat up slowly and was relieved that the pain in her head had significantly subsided. She reasoned that she had slept for a long while. She stood and again had a hard time balancing with the swaying floor. She wrapped the uncomfortable blanket around her shoulders, stretched her hands before her, and began walking to where she remembered the door.

She immediately stepped on something and squealed in fright. It was cold and fleshy. She fell back onto her bed, and her heart pounded. Was it a body? Was the silent man dead or sleeping beside her? After a long while of listening and hearing nothing but the gentle creaking of the walls, she tentatively reached a hand toward the thing she had stepped on. To her relief, it was a piece of cooked meat. She realized then how hungry she was and felt around the area.

"Yes!" she whispered excitedly as she discovered more food and, most importantly, a jug of water.

She drank thirstily, then ate her fill. She had no idea what cut of meat she was eating or what animal it came from, but it was delicious. She sat back against the wall, satisfied but still very frightened. She waited there in the dark, her thoughts wandering, trying to reason what she should do next. She was alone, and the door was unguarded, and after what seemed like an eternity, she stood and moved toward it again. Confident no one was with her, she summoned the cantrip spell she had learned so long ago in Oldorburg.

A small flame danced on her hand, providing a dim light but one strong enough to illuminate the whole of the small room. She was relieved to find she was alone. She focused on the door and made her way slowly toward it. She needed to be free of the room, but if she were on a boat, was there really anything she could do if she escaped it? She glanced at the empty plate where the delicious food had been moments before and the empty jug that once held clean water for her. They cared for her, so perhaps she should bide her time and wait until they ported. Still, the door before her was too much to resist.

"Tell me your secrets," she said to no one, and she reached for the door handle.

Before she touched it, the door swung open, and the large silent man was there. She screamed and took several steps back. He noticed her burning hand, and his eyes widened. A man pushed past him and entered the room. It was Maltor, the leader of the group and the man who had headbutted her. He stopped when he saw her hand, a small flame dancing upon her upturned palm. Then Vixa appeared behind Maltor and froze in place, petrified by the sight.

"Devil magic," Vixa whispered, staring hatefully at Cassandra.

The silent man backed out of the room. Maltor did not move, but Vixa drew her two hand axes. Maltor put an arm out toward Vixa, motioning for her to stop.

"Jak, bring the lantern," Maltor said.

The large man came back in to stand beside his leader, the lantern unhooded and bright. Cassandra could see Vixa now, and the woman's beauty struck her. She was also saddened to see the remnants of the beating she had endured at the hands of Maltor and the other warrior the day they found her. Her eyes were swollen but not fully shut, and her upper lip was gashed and bruised. Red splotches were evident on her face and neck. Regardless of the scars, Vixa was beautiful, with bright blue eyes and a head full of unkempt red hair.

All three stood silently, watching the burnless flame dance upon her hand. Cassandra shook it out and put her hands behind her back.

"What?" she asked innocently.

Maltor stepped forward, and he was more significant than she recalled. He was shirtless, and his massive chest and muscled arms made the other man, Jak, seem small. The leader's dark hair hung over his shoulders, and piercing blue eyes hinted at a rage hiding underneath the exterior. The man was intimidating, and looking at him made her headache flare again.

"That is not allowed," Maltor said, pointing to her hidden hands.

"What?" Cassandra asked, bringing her hands forth, the flame long since dispersed.

"It is weakness, and I will not tolerate it."

"It is not weakness," Cassandra said, finding her resolve.

Maltor walked up to her, and Cassandra tried to hold her ground. He stood nearly seven feet tall, which put him almost two feet taller than her.

He began to peel the blanket from her shoulders. She grabbed it, but his strength quickly forced it from her grip. He tossed it to Jak, who balled it up under his arm. Maltor then grabbed a handful of her hair as she tried covering herself with her hands.

"You do it again, and I will skin you in front of my warriors, and we will drink your weakling blood and eat your fool heart."

The look in the man's eyes left little doubt that he would do precisely that. She could only look into those dangerous eyes as he roughly held her by her hair.

"I have big plans for you, but devil magic is unacceptable. Do you understand?"

"It's not devil magic," Cassandra whispered with as much conviction as she could muster.

"Do you understand?" Maltor screamed in her face, pulling her hair tighter and almost lifting her off the ground.

"Yes!" she screamed, grabbing his arms, trying to pry the death grip from her golden locks.

He threw her onto the straw bed, and for a moment, Cassandra compared the temperaments of the two prominent men who had forcefully made her return to the straw. Jak was gentle, and Maltor was full of rage. Cassandra hugged her knees and tried to cover her nakedness.

"Give her the clothing, Vixa," Maltor said, as his eyes roamed Cassandra's body.

"No, we should kill her; she is dangerous," Vixa argued.

Maltor gave Vixa a look so profound that she looked away, produced an outfit from a sack on her side, and threw it on the straw bed.

"Put it on," Maltor demanded.

Cassandra looked at Vixa, who now kept her gaze on the floor, and she knew not to push the volatile man. She gathered the leathery clothing and found a tiny skirt and a similar top. Cassandra faintly smelled body odor wafting from the dirty material but dared not complain. She quickly put it on, and Maltor smiled.

He walked up to her once more, reached out, and retook her hair, not grabbing fistfuls like moments before, but gently taking a few strands of it and running his fingers through it. Cassandra did not understand his actions and looked to Vixa for support. The wild redhead appeared angry and perhaps jealous.

"I have plans for you. What is your name?"

"Cassandra Rho," she whispered, then swallowed hard as his eyes roamed her.

"Cassandra Rho. I like it. There are no last names in my tribe. I am

Maltor, son of Gron, and now you are Cassandra. Perhaps soon, if I deem you worthy, you will be Cassandra, queen to Maltor."

Cassandra's eyes widened, and she pulled her hair away. Those words confused and frightened her, and she had no immediate response. As her mind raced and she thought of a polite denial of his offer, Vixa screamed. Cassandra fell back against the wall, startled by the war-like cry as Maltor turned calmly to regard the enraged woman.

"What makes her worthy? She is no warrior, and she is an outsider! I could kill her with my bare hands!"

"You will not touch her," Maltor said through gritted teeth.

"She is a witch; she has devil magic. What makes her worthy?"

Maltor backhanded Vixa so hard she fell to the floor, her axes clanging after her. Jak retrieved them quickly before Vixa retaliated. There was no need, though; Maltor crushed Vixa's spirit with the hit, fresh blood pouring from the reopened wounds on her lips.

"Because she has the mark of Strenna!" Maltor yelled back.

He pulled Cassandra back to him and lifted her skirt to reveal her right hip and the snake brand Ronnis had marked her with. She had forgotten that traumatic event until then, and as she looked at the wound, she could see a distinct snake-head shape to it with two long fangs hanging from the snake's mouth. The branding was still fresh, but the pain had considerably subsided. That was until Maltor roughly rubbed a hand over it.

The pain renewed then, and Cassandra yelled out, "Ouch!"

He released her and smiled. "You are a gift from my goddess, and if Strenna allows it, you will be my bride."

"No, Maltor, I should be the one to fight for it, not her," Vixa managed to say, spitting blood onto the floor.

"No, Vixa, you are inferior, but Cassandra has potential. She is Strenna's chosen. You will do well not to forget that. Now get out."

Vixa gave Cassandra a hateful look but got up and stood before Jak. Maltor nodded to the man, and he handed over her axes. Vixa gave Cassandra one last angry glare, then left.

Maltor turned back and said, "She will not harm you now. You are under my watch and are safe. We will be home in thirty cycles of the sun. Vixa will be your instructor; she will teach you how to use a real weapon, not the devil's magic."

Cassandra was about to argue again about the devil magic not being a thing but remembered what happened the last time she tried to argue with him. So, she nodded. Maltor glanced at her brand one last time, then smiled and left.

Jak and Cassandra were alone again, and he handed her the blanket. She lay down on the straw bed and tried to find sleep once more. It was hard to come by with all that had just transpired. She knew two things: Vixa wanted her dead, and she was a natural-born witch, whether Maltor liked it or not.

The sisters of Sinnis had all agreed that they would not wait any longer for clearance from Port Racip to leave the ship. That was two days ago, and though things seemed quiet, Alleah, Greyson, and the rest sensed something unusual about the situation. They met in the hull one final time before their planned exit. The sun was going down, and only Captain Jessica remained above deck to watch the activity on the docks and monitor the two ships at sea blocking their escape.

"The time has come, and we have prayed on this long enough, sisters. Sinnis has shown us the way, and so we will take it," Alleah instructed the eager priestesses.

They all nodded their agreement, as did Greyson. He was a big part of their expedition, so they welcomed his input. His god, Plath, had given him insight into the dangers of waiting, and he wanted them to leave the ship as quickly as possible. But, to all of them, the tension only seemed to grow.

"Greyson, we have prepared one of our most sacred and powerful spells, and as discussed, we will make our escape in that fashion. However, we will not leave you behind, so I ask that you explain your strategy for escaping yourself," Alleah said.

"My dear friends," Greyson began, standing beside Alleah so everyone gathered in the hull could see him. "I have come to know and love all of you, and I expect to see this mission through and return to Pelesea at the appropriate time. So do not doubt I will be beside you when we arrive at Tara and once again when we return home."

His words lifted the morale of the nervous priestesses as Alleah touched his shoulder. He turned to regard her and saw the vast smile on her pretty face. His mind raced back through the previous months to the day he had arrived at Pelesea. Alleah had been the one to find him there, nearly dead. She had healed him, and she had nurtured him back to health. He loved her as a friend and would die for her. But he would die for all of them to honor his lost family. These women were his family now.

"Although we do not follow the same god, you have taken me in as one of your own. I have seen your rituals and have participated in some, and I attest now that your goddess, Sinnis, is right and just, and Plath is pleased with her."

All smiled, some nodded at that remark, and Greyson felt the warmth of love in the hull of that ship. He had been on an adventure with Cassandra, Binta, and Cass a few months prior, but that seemed petty to him now. Although they had shared several near-death experiences on that ill-advised trip, he had focused on his lust for Cassandra then, not the dangers it would inevitably hold. Plath had been with him those months ago, but now he could feel Plath's presence more intensely; this mission was holy and more personal to him. He meant his words; he would die for these women if need be.

They planned to use their combined powers to conjure a spell from Sinnis which would assist them in escaping the boat under cover of darkness. Unfortunately, the magic would only benefit priestesses of Sinnis, so that meant the effects would exclude Greyson.

"Although I cannot escape in the same way as all of you, Plath has a plan for me, and I will meet you at the rendezvous as agreed. So, do not fret for me, my friends, and go proudly on to Varish, and know I am right behind you."

The high priestess, Tesa, stood then and addressed him. "I think I speak for all of us. We cannot, in good faith, leave you here without knowing how you will escape the Port Racip dockmaster."

There was a murmur among the gathering, and many heads nodded at her proclamation. It touched Greyson's heart that they cared enough to ask him to elaborate.

"Please, Greyson, specifically, how will you do it?" Alleah asked beside him.

"As you await nightfall for your grand exit, I, too, await something. A storm is coming, a gift from Plath. It will not last long, but it will be devastating. So, I will use it to cover my escape."

"A storm? How can you know this?" Tesa asked.

Greyson smiled and said, "Because I have summoned it. I have prayed for it for several days, and Plath has granted me the request. I can feel it forming even now. It will strike at the exact time you make your daring move."

There was some discussion after that, but Greyson sat back down and let the conversation play out. He had given them what they had asked, and in the end, they seemed satisfied with his capabilities to escape from the ship. The hair stood on the back of his neck as the storm approached. He had never cast a spell that powerful before, and he understood it was no minor undertaking. The high priest, Berro, his father figure from Tara, had proclaimed him a prodigy of Plath at a very young age. But, for the first time since his trials, taken at the age of twelve, he believed those words. He was indeed a prodigy of Plath.

"So, we have settled our course of action. Once the moon is high in the sky, we will enact our group enchantment and become invulnerable to water. Sinnis will transform our bodies so the water passes through without impeding us, and we will no longer require oxygen for a short time. We will scale down the ship's back and drop into the sea. We will walk or swim quickly to shore, roughly fifty yards north of the boat. As you emerge from the water, the spell will automatically fade, and within moments you will become whole and ready to continue the quest," Alleah instructed.

"We will be vulnerable briefly as the spell fades?" Gina, another priestess, asked.

"Yes, there is some risk involved, but it is minimal. Plath's great storm will give us cover as we make our escape. It is a risk we must accept, and I assure you, it is minimal. Once you have your bearings, hurry north for three miles. There we will meet at the small lagoon, indicated on our map. Once gathered, we will await Greyson's arrival, then continue our quest to Tara, which is nearly two hundred miles northwest of our current location."

The storm began shortly after their meeting, just as the sun was setting. It was Greyson's conjuring, and he could feel and command it. He closed his eyes and reached out to it, letting his soul become one with the gathering clouds. It was the single most extraordinary experience in his short life, and he had never felt closer to Plath. Finally, after many moments, he opened his eyes, and Alleah was there in front of him, smiling hopefully. The other priestesses of Sinnis gathered around, and Greyson nodded. It was time.

Alleah turned and instructed her allies, "We pray, sisters, one last time for the strength to accomplish our goal; then we go top deck as planned. The time has come to take back our mission."

The priestesses bowed their heads, and Greyson gently clasped Alleah on the shoulder, motioning to her that he was heading top deck. He needed to gain a foothold on the storm; it would require his full attention. Alleah smiled and nodded, then bowed and began praying.

Greyson excitedly climbed the stairs to the deck. He focused on the storm so much that he didn't notice at first that Jessica was near the rail, appearing to whisper something into her cupped hands. Then, as his eyes adjusted to the twilight, he thought he saw something fly from her hand, appearing almost like a dragonfly.

The tiny creature flew straight for the dockmaster and his gathering men. Greyson could not be perfectly sure, but it appeared that the thing landed right on the dockmaster's upturned palm. It took him several moments for his mind to register the event before he focused back on Jessica, who briefly wore a surprised expression before turning back toward the dock as if nothing had happened.

"What was that thing?" Greyson shouted over the gathering wind.

"What are you speaking of?" Jessica shouted back.

That was when it all came together, and he understood who had compromised their mission. "Why, Jessica?" was all he could think to say.

"A woman has to make money where she can," the captain said with a shrug, then advanced on him quickly, drawing her blade.

Greyson knew he was no match for the young captain, not in close combat. But he had something she did not; he had Plath. He dove deep into himself and called to the storm. He stood there with eyes closed and his hands to his sides, palms facing Jessica. It looked like an easy kill for the lithe captain, so she swung with her scimitar. Greyson couldn't see her, but he had an idea of what she was doing and had little time to prepare for her charge.

The wind picked up substantially and suddenly, with hurricane-like strength. It lasted only a moment, and Greyson focused it on Jessica. It blew the sword from her hand and carried it far out to sea. The captain fought to remain on her feet, but the concentrated attack had her falling to the deck before the mighty wind lifted her in the air and tossed her overboard. She half fell, half dived into the water near the docks. Greyson opened his eyes, and the wind died down. He understood that the storm was his to control, the various elements capable of temporary modification as he saw fit. Lightning cracked nearby, scattering some of the men on the deck. That short strike also showed him how many enemies had gathered in the last few moments. They appeared as a mass of ants, covering the docks and making their way toward the ship, boarding planks at the ready.

The tiny magical device, simply known as a dragonfly, made its way to the dockmaster, one of the people attuned with the device, Jessica being the other. There, the tiny dragonfly wings fluttered on the silver-and-turquoise-colored item as Captain Jessica's voice floated from it.

"Dockmaster, they plan an escape at the stern, enacting a powerful enchantment to allow them invulnerability to the water. The priestesses of Sinnis plan to climb ashore about fifty yards north of the docks; they will be helpless for a few moments when they first emerge from the water. Watch for the lead light; they will use it as a beacon for those underwater. Then, use it to lure them in."

Cerus stood beside the dockmaster and listened to the message. He and his men had arrived a few hours earlier and were eager to catch their prey unaware. A smile creased his face, and he nodded to one of the captains of his army.

"Go, and capture as many as you can alive. Kill any who give you trouble. I want the leader, the one called Alleah," Cerus said.

The dockmaster turned to him and said, "According to Jessica, she is quite exquisite."

Cerus's smile doubled, and he clasped the dockmaster on the shoulder. "I will increase your reward if I have her in my grasp by the end of the attack. But, for now, rush the boat with all your men; keep the priestesses' attention away from our trap."

Cerus looked up at the dark sky just as the rain began to pour heavily. "This storm will provide excellent cover for my men. Do your job, dockmaster, and keep them focused on the docks."

Before the dockmaster could answer, Cerus was gone, running away from the docks and into the underbrush. He was rushing toward the site where the priestesses would exit the water.

"Fifty virgins," the dockmaster whispered to himself. "I better be well rewarded for this, Cerus."

He put the dragonfly in his pocket and ordered his men to charge the boat. He had to scream over the roaring wind and pouring rain. But the men charged, almost fifty strong, with the lead men carrying two docking planks. They had to make this look like the attack to cover the threat of Cerus and his men, so they would try to board the ship. Perhaps they could overwhelm the priestesses and capture them before Cerus could spring his trap. That would triple the reward, he was sure.

"Alleah! Quickly, we haven't much time!" Greyson screamed over the wind as she emerged from below deck.

"What happened?" she asked, looking for Jessica while the other priestesses crawled toward the stern, staying low and out of sight.

She stood before him now as the rain hit them almost horizontally. "Jessica alerted them to our presence. She is the traitor."

Alleah shook her head in confusion. "Why? We trusted her, and the *Lady of Faith* had often docked at Pelesea."

"I do not know, and it does not matter. Right now, we must get off the boat."

Alleah nodded and asked, "So, where is she?"

"Removed," was all that Greyson said before a rain of arrows came from the docks. He saw them at the last second and managed to summon a giant gust of wind, blowing most of them harmlessly aside. However, one stuck Alleah in the shoulder, making her scream and fall to the deck. Greyson was there in an instant.

"It's not bad," she said, sitting up with a grimace.

"Let me help."

"No!" she screamed. "It would be best if you protect the others from further attacks. Focus your efforts on the men on the docks, and I will be fine."

At that exact moment, two docking planks appeared at the lip of the boat railing. Greyson made his way quickly toward them. The wooden planks had metal tips with hooked spikes that dug into the boat, making them impossible for him to lift and toss. He looked over and saw a row of archers on the dock and many men rushing along the planks. He focused on the storm once more, calling upon its immense power. The rain poured heavily on the men climbing the planks and turned to ice, making the climb impossible. Those men unfortunate enough to be on the plank when the ice formed slid back into the men behind them, or fell into the water. Soon the planks were clear of men, with no enemy making it to the ship. Greyson took some satisfaction in that, but his joy only lasted momentarily as he witnessed the second wave of arrows wash over the deck.

As Greyson fought off the enemies on the docks, Alleah rose to expedite the evacuation of the others. She forced away the pain in her shoulder, ignoring the protruding arrow. She walked toward the stern just in time to see Gina jump overboard. She was the key to their success, as she was the most proficient swimmer. The small priestess wore no armor, so she would be vulnerable on the shore until others arrived. She carried her small mace on her hip and a thick leather sack that held her lantern. The thick satchel hid the light from enemy eyes because the light emanating from it was brighter than that of a standard lantern. Greyson had enchanted it with perpetual light, so the oil within did not burn, but the item itself glowed brightly. It would serve as the perfect beacon once Gina established a spot for the others to emerge from the water.

Their original plan had been to attach a rope to the large ship and have Gina tie the other end to a spot ashore. Then the priestesses could easily travel the same path underwater, using the rope as a guide. However, with the storm, they would have to rely on Greyson's brightly glowing beacon to guide them. Alleah didn't like taking the risk, but it was necessary. The others began to cast their water-invulnerability spells and waited for the signal. Once Gina unsheathed the lantern, they would dive in. They were all fully armored and would normally sink straight to the ocean's depths, but they trusted Sinnis to protect them from the water's deadly properties.

Alleah felt the mighty wind blow from behind her as arrows began to rain down upon the vulnerable priestesses. Greyson summoned the wind to toss most of them aside, but several found their mark. Most caused superficial wounds, but one struck deeply through a crease in the breastplate of one of the younger sisters of Sinnis. Naomi had sat up to enact her spell, but the arrow found her heart before she could complete it. She slumped to the dock as blood pooled around her. Alleah was quickly there to help, turning her over gently to her back. But unfortunately, it was too late and the young priestess lay motionless, staring blankly at the sky.

Alleah looked to the handful of nearby priestesses who had witnessed the attack and had stopped their casting. "Go!" Alleah ordered, motioning for all of them to continue with the plan.

A few others felt the bite of those arrows, but like Alleah, they shook off the pain to continue the mission—their lives depended on it. The first row of priestesses stayed low to the deck and watched for Gina's signal. The storm was vicious then, and visibility was minimal. Nevertheless, they hoped to pick up the lantern in the extreme darkness.

After the arrows fell upon his friends, Greyson saw red. His anger boiled over, and as it did, he became more connected with the storm, as if Plath were using his rage to make him powerful. He focused the storm's power on the men at the dock. Several bolts of lightning smashed into the pier where the archers stood. The strikes were swift and decisive and obliterated most of the enemies there. Those who survived felt the severe burns the lightning offered, but few were lucky enough to emerge unscathed from the attack.

Much of the dock disintegrated, and the ropes securing *Lady of Faith* were burned and frayed. The ship began to drift from the dock remnants, though few noticed it initially with the chaos enveloping the area.

Greyson knelt with Alleah, who was losing a lot of blood from the arrow in her shoulder. He felt exhausted, for controlling the powerful storm was no small feat. He could feel the power of it diminishing.

"We must remove the arrow so that I may heal you," Greyson yelled over the wind.

Alleah smiled and nodded. Resigned, she said, "Do you remember when we met?"

"Of course, you saved my life."

"You were naked from the waist down and hurt badly."

"Again, you saved me, so now I shall return the favor."

"Yes, but I want to ensure my sisters have escaped first," Alleah argued.

Greyson glanced at the stern of the boat and saw them crouched, out of view. Some looked out toward the ocean, awaiting Gina's signal, and the back half looked toward him and Alleah, very concerned with her health. He smiled at them and nodded, trying to comfort them in the stressful situation.

"They will; just have faith."

"I have nothing but faith," Alleah answered weakly.

"Well, you have me right now, and this is going to hurt," Greyson warned her.

"What is going to—" Alleah began, before Greyson broke the arrow shaft, making her cry in pain.

Alleah swooned from its intensity, and Greyson caught her and kept her from falling to the ship's deck.

"Bite this," he ordered, giving her the broken shaft.

Her eyes showed the fear that welled inside her, and Greyson decided he would do the deed quickly. As soon as she bit down on the shaft, he pulled her forward and grabbed the arrow protruding from her back. Then, in one swift motion, he yanked it free, and Alleah screamed so loud that all the sisters of Sinnis gathered at the stern could hear her over the storm.

He immediately cast a healing spell and gently laid her on the deck. He knew she would need some time to recover from that traumatic experience. He looked over at the priestesses and smiled, which they nervously returned. He glanced down at Alleah, and she was awake and smiling.

"Thank you," she whispered weakly, seemingly free of the pain.

"You bet," he said with a wink and moved toward the sisters.

As he made his way to the stern, he noticed that one of the ropes tying the ship to the docks had snapped, and the boat would be free soon. If that happened with the priestesses aboard, it would lessen their chances of escape. When he made the back of the ship, he noticed Masie, one of the less experienced priestesses.

He approached her and asked, "What is the delay? We have little time to keep waiting!"

"No signal from Gina yet," Masie replied.

He looked out to the sea where Gina was supposed to be with the lantern he had enchanted. But unfortunately, little was visible due to the storm, and the boat continued to rock. He wondered if the young woman had survived the short journey to the shore. Perhaps the storm he had summoned would be their death if she couldn't navigate the rough water.

Suddenly, a priestess in the first row yelled, "Beacon!"

All of them, including Greyson, followed her pointing finger to see the lantern shining brightly on the shore. It was much further away than expected, but it was there!

"First row, over now, the boat is detaching from the docks! So be quick, and second row, be ready!" Greyson screamed.

He needed not to have bothered, because the first row of priestesses had already cast their spell and jumped overboard before he even finished speaking. Then, the second row began casting their magic, and Greyson knew they did not need his guidance. With a smile to Masie, he left them to check on Alleah. It would be the last time he ever saw the young girl.

As planned, Gina emerged from the water and quickly removed the lantern from the leather pouch. It shone brightly, and if the young woman had been facing inland, she would have seen the warriors of Gorl surrounding the area. However, Gina focused on the boat, so her back was toward the evil men. She held the lantern high, proud of her part to guide her sisters to shore. She caught her breath and smiled at the sight of the first row of her sisters dropping into the choppy water. She would guide them on their short but treacherous journey to the shore. She dropped the lantern into the water, knowing it would shine as bright as the sun for her sisters.

A strong arm wrapped around her neck from behind her, cutting off her oxygen. Simultaneously, two men came into sight, one from her left and one from her right. The man on the right quickly yanked the lantern from her grip. The man on her left struck her in the face. She nearly blacked out from the blow and saw the man with the lantern take her spot and drop it back into the water. She tried to scream out, but the chokehold was unbreakable. The man who punched her stood before her, a wicked smile on his face. She could not make out much because of the darkness and the rain, but the smile was evident. Her mind couldn't fully register what was happening to her, but she understood enough to know they were luring her sisters into a trap. A second punch from her smiling attacker followed, and she knew no more.

Cerus smiled at the quick work his men made of the lantern-bearer. The priestesses would be no match for his men, and they would so enjoy their catch once they were herded and subdued. The men tied the unconscious woman, then returned to the shore to await the next arrival. Cerus glanced back to the bobbing ship and looked for something to indicate a leader, one that could be Alleah. According to Jessica, she inspired the trek, and he would break her, perhaps with the whip he had used so mercilessly on Emiline. A wicked smile spread across his face at the thought of it.

Tesa was among the first wave of sisters to enter the water. Unlike Gina, she and the others wore their chainmail armor, so they sank immediately. Their skin and possessions were mostly unaffected by the water due to the powerful blessing from Sinnis, but the armor still contained enough weight to make them sink a good way. Thankfully, they did not fall to the bottom, and after a short time, they began to float back toward the surface as their buoyancy adjusted to the water. Unfortunately, the water was murky, and visibility was nonexistent. Tesa panicked as she became disoriented, unaware whether she was going toward the shore or out to sea. She could not see her sisters or anything that would lead her in the right direction.

Suddenly, she saw the light as Gina submerged the magically lit lantern in the water. The power of that light was incredible, and she felt so blessed to call Greyson Kavince her friend and ally. The sudden appearance of light showed that Tesa was straying from the course and that she would have missed the land altogether and probably drowned if it were not for that powerful guiding light. She adjusted her course and moved toward it. The sensation of the spell was strange, making her efforts to move underwater a bit easier than usual, and she did not draw breath, so she did not fear the risk of drowning. She said a prayer of thanks to Sinnis as she slowly made her way toward the shore.

She looked around her as she neared the great light, and things became more visible. Mud was thick in the water, but she made out her sisters, many of them, making their way to the lantern. She understood that many more were behind her, and soon they would reunite. She picked up the pace and half-walked, half-swam toward the beacon. When she arrived at the light and breached the ocean's surface, hands were there to help her ashore. Unfortunately, her eyes had to adjust to the darkness, so she could not see who assisted her, and she only assumed it was her sisters that had arrived before her.

However, she immediately understood something was amiss as the firm grasp of those helping her was not gentle, with one of them grabbing a handful of her hair. She was in the process of reverting from her spell, so she could not speak or act quickly enough to respond to the rough treatment. She was dragged out of the water by several people, and during the brief moments it took her body to shift back to its normal consistency, she was beaten and kicked, one such attack cracking her jaw. She felt her assailants bind her hands and remove her weapon and holy symbol. She was left in the sandy mud, and as she regained her senses, she realized her doom. She watched as her sisters were thrown beside her and beaten nearly to death by strange and savage men. She tried to cry out to warn her sisters, but her broken jaw no longer worked. All she could do was cry as the realization of what was happening sank in.

And so it went for each of the mighty priestesses of Sinnis. A few moments after they exited the water, the men stripped them of their weapons and holy symbols, beat and tied them. Only Masie, the youngest who had spoken to Greyson moments before, gained her wits before being completely over-powered. She was small, so only one of the evil warriors of Gorl grabbed her, thinking she would be easy enough to handle. However, he underestimated her resolve and paid for it as he took her weapon—she instinctively brought a knee up to his crotch. He doubled over with a grunt and could not find the words to call for help. Masie surveyed the scene unfolding around her, which was chaotic and horrible. There was little light, but she understood what was happening. She ran for the woods, hoping none of the evil men would see her through the chaos.

As Masie made the tree line, she felt a moment of relief as she thought she was free, but as soon as that thought registered, a spear hit her square in the back. She fell to her knees momentarily, then face down in the mud. She could no longer move her legs but grabbed her holy symbol with her right hand and prayed to Sinnis.

The sisters had prepared a unique and powerful spell before leaving the ship's hull, temporarily allowing them to communicate with each other through their holy symbols. As she used her arms to crawl in the soft sand-like mud, she sent her thoughts of warning through her symbol. She tried to concentrate and give her sisters a chance, and she swallowed her fear when she heard footsteps approaching from behind.

Soon Cerus was there. He placed his foot on her back and yanked his spear free. Masie had never felt such pain before as the weapon tore her flesh and severed her spine. He turned her over and looked delighted to find her alive. Her hands grasped the holy symbol she wore around her neck as blood poured from her mouth and pooled around it. He jerked the item from her neck and threw it in the woods. Masie's eyes widened as he stabbed the great spear in the sand beside her head and began to undress.

Masie died soon after, but not before the evil man violated her and took her virginity. Luckily for the young priestess, she passed into the afterlife long before he hung her from a nearby tree and cut her guts out with his nasty dagger. Cerus left her hanging there with her entrails spilled upon the ground, similar to how he had murdered Greyson's family.

Greyson watched intently as the priestesses jumped overboard. He kept his head below the rail and occasionally peeked above it to monitor the activity on the dock. The men were scattered, with a few trying to pull themselves out of the cold water. The dock remains still smoked from the lightning strike, which had compromised the structure's integrity. Greyson knew that no further attacks would be coming from that side of the ship, whether from men with boarding planks or arrows.

As Masie and the last line of priestesses jumped overboard, he yelled to Alleah, "Time for you to go, now!"

The wind still roared, and the rain poured down, drowning their voices and making them sound far away.

"Help me with this," she said.

He turned to see her on her feet, recovered from the arrow wound and removing her armor pieces. He felt the storm waning and knew he would have to perform his planned strike very soon if he was going to make his escape. Just then, the final rope holding the *Lady of Faith* to the damaged docks snapped, and the ship lurched in the rough water. He fell and slid to Alleah, nearly knocking her over. However, she managed to keep her feet and continued to undress.

"What are you doing?" he asked, climbing to his feet.

"I am staying with you."

"What? Why?"

She stopped for just a moment and looked into his eyes. The undying friendship he saw there answered his question before she spoke.

"I will not leave you. You cannot swim well and will need me."

He grabbed her by the arm and said, "You should be with your sisters; I will be fine."

She jerked her arm away and replied, "I never thought that if the day came, you would argue with me if I asked you to take my clothes off."

The comment caught him off guard until he saw her genuine smile and started to work on her armor again. The ship was being pushed out to sea by the choppy water and straight toward the awaiting blockade. He could vaguely make out the crews of those ships moving ballistae into position and understood they had very little time. He glanced back to Alleah to see her wearing only her breeches and padded shirt, which she was in the process of removing. He helped her, and it took them both to remove the bulky padding.

When it was off, Alleah stood before him wearing her tight breeches and thin white shirt, part of it stained in blood. However, it did not detract from her rare beauty; the soaking rain only magnified it. Alleah's long blond hair hung in her face, and her clothes left little to the imagination, her breasts visible through the thin material. She was stunning, and she had no idea how attractive he found her. Priestesses of Sinnis didn't think in terms of sex or attractiveness. However, Greyson did, and he drank in her beauty for a few moments before moving into action.

He turned and faced the ship's port side, raising his arms toward the sky and calling upon the storm's strength, harnessing the last little bit of energy.

"Be prepared; I will summon a strike against the ships, then we will jump and swim toward your sisters," Greyson called over his shoulder.

"Oh no," he heard her say, and he turned to find her staring out toward the lantern and the gathering priestesses.

He stopped his communion with the storm and focused on his friend. "What is it?"

"There is a trap!" Alleah said, holding on to her holy symbol, receiving Masie's warning.

Alleah ran to the stern and peered out into the darkness. Greyson joined her, and they struggled to see anything in the driving rain. Finally, the lantern was visible, but it seemed a million miles away as the storm pushed the ship further out to sea. Greyson reached inside himself and summoned Plath's most extraordinary power, the ability to call and control light. He focused it on the beach, where the lantern bobbed. Suddenly, the intensity of the lantern's light bathed the area with god-like brightness. The sight broke his heart, and Alleah screamed in surprise and anguish.

The beach was crawling with men, and the sisters of Sinnis were being overwhelmed and captured. The lantern holder was not a priestess of Sinnis but one of the men luring the priestesses ashore.

"Jessica," Greyson said.

"We have to go to them!" Alleah screamed, nearing panic.

"No, Alleah!" Greyson said, grabbing her by the arm. "If you follow, you will only end up a hostage. We must escape this ship; that is your sisters' only hope."

Alleah seemed to struggle with that for a moment, and Greyson could tell she considered jumping in to help them. Greyson took her chin and turned her toward him.

"Look at me, Alleah."

She averted her eyes from the massacre on the beach and did just that momentarily, long enough for him to see the agony in them. He understood her pain, having felt the same all those months ago when Cerus and his men similarly attacked Tara. She struggled not to break his grasp and help her sisters.

"Look at me, Alleah!" he repeated, more forcefully.

She gave him her full attention then, and he explained, "You are no good to them dead, and if you jump overboard to try and save them, that is precisely what you are—dead! So come with me, and we will find a way to save them. Trust me?"

Alleah's eyes darted back and forth as she studied his face, fighting her instinct to dive into the water. Greyson could tell she did not want to leave her sisters to that awful fate. The ship lurched, and they tumbled to the deck. Something crashed into the small mast of the vessel, cracking it and toppling it over, nearly crushing them both.

Greyson helped Alleah to her feet, and after confirming she was not hurt, he inspected the damage. A ballista had directly hit the mast, and now the spear lay wedged into the deck, right at its base. Greyson looked to the sea and knew he had to invoke the storm now or never; they were out of time.

"I will cause a distraction, and we will jump off the ship on the bow side. We will then swim to shore, hopefully, under cover of the storm, then circle back to help your sisters, agreed?"

With one last glance at the lit beach, Alleah nodded. Then he was gone, facing their new attackers and raising his arms once more to call upon the powers of his god. Little magic remained in the conjured storm, but he hoped it was enough. He called to Plath, asking for the strength to funnel the energy needed to blind his enemies temporarily.

It took a few moments, and he was vaguely aware of Alleah by his side. He thought he heard her scream as a second ballista spear splashed dangerously close to the hull of their ship. He was lost in concentration and could not move if he wanted to manipulate the storm powerfully. Eventually, it came, and he unleashed the attack mercilessly on the two ships, understanding that failure to do so would mean certain death to them both.

The clouds became incredibly dark over the two enemy ships, and the rain turned to sleet, coating the decks with slick ice and making the ballista operators lose their balance. After the frosty barrage, the lightning began as multiple strikes found each ship, forking and striking masts and decks alike. More than one of the ships' hands felt the bite of those blasts and fell into the water. Others found themselves jumping overboard to avoid the lightning that bombarded the decks.

"Go, now!" Greyson ordered, pointing toward the bow of the ship.

He and Alleah ran together, hoping the barrage of lightning would distract anyone near the smoldering remains of the docks from seeing their leap. They splashed into the churning water simultaneously. Greyson struggled briefly to resurface, but Alleah guided him. Once he broke the surface and gasped for air, he appreciated how lucky he was that Alleah had stayed with him. They were much further out from the shore than he realized, and it was a long swim. Nevertheless, Alleah helped him along, and the task was more manageable after the disappearance of the conjured storm, which seemed to wink out suddenly—all sleet, rain, and lightning with it. Thunder rumbled, but the water calmed, and soon the weather was quiet.

That was when they both heard the commotion on the docks to their right. Men were running to and fro, and it seemed a chaotic scene. Greyson knew in his heart that none had witnessed their jump. They slowly made their way, with Greyson stopping several times to catch his breath and float. It took great effort for him not to sink, and Alleah helped him often.

Eventually, with Alleah's guidance, they reached the shore about one hundred yards south of Port Racip. They climbed onto the sandy embankment and made their way into the woods to find cover. They had escaped the ship, but their allies were now dead or captured, compromising their mission. They didn't say it, but both understood they were now trapped in a hostile land with no way home.

8

€XILED

QUEEN PENELOPE SHOOK HER HEAD IN DISBELIEF AS THE grieving couple exited the throne room. They had just reported their daughter, Lynna, missing and feared the worst, for they had last seen her over a month ago. She looked to Kringus, sitting beside her on his throne, distraught by the sad news. The royal couple rarely received such awful information, and Kringus always took it personally. They had granted several audiences that day, this one being the last, putting a severe damper on their moods. Pelesea was a large city, and as such, had its share of crime. Unfortunately, the south side near the docks was the worst and possibly the only place one might expect such tragic events. As of late that had not been the case, as rumors of missing persons had been reported frequently over the last few weeks, the closest being from the nearby temple. The sad news always affected the king and queen.

Penelope removed her crown, placed it in her lap, and said, "This cannot be a coincidence, Kringus."

"What are you referring to?" he asked, now intrigued.

"The fact that the jail burned down, killing Cassandra Rho, just a month ago, and now a child is missing."

Before Kringus could answer, Jespen, captain of the castle guard, reentered the throne room after showing out Lynna's parents. "My king and queen, that is the last of the grievances."

"We are done, then, Jespen?" Kringus asked, hopefully.

"No, there is still one issue that requires your judgment. A prisoner awaits your verdict," Jespen answered.

As a custom, Kringus would listen to arguments for those charged with crimes at the end of the day. After learning of Lynna, he had little patience for it, but Penelope squeezed her husband's hand and smiled, and he found his strength.

He nodded to Jespen and said, "Give us a bit."

"Yes, my lord," Jespen answered with a bow.

He turned to leave, but Kringus yelled after him, "Jespen."

He turned and said, "My king?"

"Send some men immediately to the southern docks. I want someone competent there to lead the investigation. I want Lynna found or answers for her family if she is dead. Keep the city guards on high-alert!"

Jespen bowed again, leaving the couple alone in the giant throne room. They sat in silence for many moments before Kringus spoke up. "Perhaps I should investigate the matter myself."

"I was thinking the same. Perhaps we can both go tomorrow and see what we may find."

Kringus smiled at his ever-surprising wife. She was thoughtful of the people in Pelesea, and he knew she would find an answer for the couple. Her heart was much too large to fit in her tiny frame, and he loved her for it.

"So, what are your thoughts?" he asked.

"I fear the girl is dead, my love, just like Cassandra Rho."

"And you suspect who may have committed these heinous crimes?"

"What crimes? A child is missing, and maybe a priest, and an accidental fire burned down the jail and killed Cassandra," Penelope said.

Kringus watched her face, waiting for her to show emotion. But, instead, she held a stone visage, and soon he surrendered.

"Very well! When you put it that way, it does sound too dumb to be a coincidence. Boz, then?" Kringus asked with a deep sigh.

"I suspect as much; we did not have these problems before his arrival. He left the city immediately after, and we know little about him other than he controls fire. That is a little too convenient for my liking, Kringus."

"He saved our lives, though," Kringus reminded her.

"Perhaps just to get close to you so he could commit these crimes. I knew the day he left he was hiding something; I could see it on his face. He must be the reason for the recent tragedies."

"To what end?" Kringus asked skeptically.

"Who knows with criminals? You told me the whole reason he was here was to find Cassandra. Perhaps it was to murder her? Perhaps he did just that, then left the city under our noses."

"He tried to save her, remember? He was wounded doing so."

"Yes; again, it was so convenient that he happened to be there when the jail caught fire. And he was staying on the south side of the city. So, perhaps he killed Lynna while plotting to kill Cassandra. Murderers have a hard time controlling themselves, I've heard."

"But several people have been reported missing since Boz left," Kringus argued, thinking he had made a strong point in support of Boz.

"If you are referring to the priest that went missing recently and the young city guard who did not report to his post yesterday, then yes, you are correct. However, they are not confirmed dead and are not children. They could have left the city on their own volition, quit their jobs or lost their religion. It is a big city and not every disappearance is a crime."

Kringus thought about that for a moment then said, "But Lynna's disappearance makes you uncomfortable because children don't just vanish."

"No, they don't," Penelope agreed.

Kringus sighed and said, "You are right, of course. I didn't want to believe it about Boz. He seemed so genuine."

"I know, and what happened has happened, but you know now that he is not an ally to you or anyone in this city."

Kringus sat there, letting the information sink in. Penelope squeezed his hand again to show that he was not to blame and that she supported him. He smiled and nodded to one of the guards at the door, who returned the nod and opened the door to fetch Jespen. Soon after, he entered, leading a young woman in chains and an older man who was unchained but appeared as much a prisoner as the woman. The royal couple recognized the man as Franklin Ruben, one of the wealthiest citizens of Pelesea.

Penelope sat up straight and placed the crown upon her head once more. Kringus sat stone-faced as usual when the court called upon his judgment. Of course, both knew it was the lone hearing for the day, but it was a hard one because of the delicate nature of Franklin's involvement. Anyone who knew Franklin understood Cass, his daughter, was his world. Kringus would have to be wise and his judgment perfect.

Once the three stood before the king and queen, Jespen announced the prisoner. "My king and queen, I give you Cashmere Ruben and her father, Franklin. We have detained her for breaking several laws of Pelesea, including running a brothel from Poppy's Inn, located three blocks from the southern docks. Other charges include imprisoning and abusing a civilian."

Kringus already knew the answer but asked it, following the required formality. "And what civilians have been injured by her recklessness?"

Franklin noticeably winced at the question while Cass rolled her eyes. Neither Kringus nor Penelope knew much about Cass, but both understood she experienced a near-death encounter on the adventure Cassandra Rho had dragged her on months ago. According to Victoria, she had recovered from her injuries but doing so had changed her. The girl had become reckless and mischievous and had finally injured someone.

"Miss Binta Mulay is the main victim of the crimes, Your Highness," Jespen answered.

"And Mr. Ruben has come to plead her case?" Kringus asked directly to the frazzled man.

"Your Highness, I only ask for leniency today. My daughter is a changed person as of late and knows not what she does," Franklin said.

"Father, I can speak for myself and I know exactly what I'm doing!" Cass spat.

The guards bristled at her sudden outburst, but Kringus waved them back. Jespen made a few nods to signal them silently, and the guards moved closer to Cass and became vigilant.

"You would be wise to listen to your father, Miss Ruben," Penelope piped in.

"Of course, how silly of me, my queen," Cass replied with a half-hearted curtsey.

"You will not mock the queen in my court, young lady!" Kringus roared, the veins sticking out on his neck as they did when he became angered.

Penelope held his arm to calm him as she spoke sternly to Cass. "This is not a game, Cashmere. We take this court seriously, and you will not mock my husband's judgment."

"Of course, my queen," Cass said more somberly, which brought a relieved look to her father's face. "Why don't you just tell me the charges I face so my father can pay the fine?" Cass added.

The hurt expression on Franklin's face spoke volumes to all in the room except Cass, who only seemed to be concerned with herself. Kringus paused for a moment to see how her father would respond, and when the man didn't move to discipline his daughter or react to her ignorant words, Kringus continued.

"You have broken several of our laws, Miss Ruben, and even though these are your first offenses, they are considerable."

"And they are?" she asked impatiently, seemingly bored.

Franklin glanced at Kringus then and seemed to fear the king's wrath for his daughter. But, again, he said nothing and appeared truly defeated.

With disgust, Kringus announced her crimes. "Establishing a brothel, imprisoning another person, and threatening the well-being of that person. These are severe charges, Miss Ruben."

"And who might this victim be?" Cass asked with feigned shock, looking around the room, searching for the accuser.

"You know exactly to whom we refer, young lady," Penelope added.

"No, I am at a loss, my queen. Please enlighten me."

The king and queen shared a concerned look, and then Kringus glanced at Franklin, who now made eye contact with him and appeared as if a strong breeze would knock him over. However, he only shook his head and shrugged.

"It is Binta Mulay," Kringus said flatly.

"What? That cannot be! We are business partners, that is all."

The king and queen shared a worried look once more, then Cass added, "Just ask the whore herself."

"Cashmere!" Franklin finally roared. "Watch your manners and respect the king's court. You are treading on thin ice, my daughter."

"And I am tired of this game!" she spat back at her father, then turned to Kringus and added, "Seriously, bring her in here and let her accuse me. I want to hear it from her."

"In all my years serving as king, I have never seen anyone act so brash as you are today," Kringus scolded her.

"That is because I am innocent. Bring in the so-called victim, and let us hear it from her."

Kringus understood Cass had done her research. Anyone accused of a crime in Pelesea was allowed to confront their accuser, so Kringus had Binta ready. He nodded to Jespen, who signaled the guards near a side door. They quickly disappeared through it and returned moments later with Binta. The young woman seemed timid and even a bit depressed. The guards brought her to the right of the royal couple, nearer to Kringus. He turned to address her, but her gaze was squarely on her feet.

"Miss Mulay."

Binta managed to meet his gaze and curtseyed in response. "My king," she whispered.

"Do not be intimidated; Miss Ruben cannot harm you in this room, do you understand?" Kringus asked.

"Yes, thank you," Binta responded meekly.

"I need you to tell me something, and I need you to answer honestly and fully," the king continued.

Kringus noticed out of the corner of his eye that Cass wore a smug smile on her face, and her gaze seemed to melt Binta. But, of course, anyone witnessing the display could see Cass's hold on the poor girl, which Kringus recognized.

"Yes, my lord, I understand," Binta said.

"Very well. Miss Ruben claims that prostituting yourself was not against your will. She claims she did not force you to do such an act and did not keep you against your will. Are these statements true?"

Binta glanced at Cass, who looked smug, stone-faced, and intimidating. The two young women shared a moment then, and although they spoke no words, it appeared as if Cass mentally dominated Binta in that brief exchange. After that, Binta's gaze returned to the floor.

After a few moments, Kringus prodded, "Well, Miss Mulay?"

"Yes and no, Your Highness," Binta finally said.

Kringus's brow wrinkled up, and he looked to Penelope, who only shrugged and shook her head. Then, he turned back to Binta and said, "Please explain your answer."

"Yes, she forced me to perform the acts, and she threatened me when I wanted to leave, but—"

Binta looked to Cass again, who now had a broad smile and seemed confident that things were going her way. Binta's resolve melted further, and she stared at her feet again.

"Please continue, Miss Mulay," Kringus prodded once more.

"But, no, you cannot blame her for it."

Penelope gasped at the words, and Cass let out a little laugh. Puzzled, Kringus waited for Binta to finish. She eventually found her courage with tears in her eyes.

"I liked it. All of it!" Binta blurted out and began to cry. "I was so distressed over Cassandra's death that I needed it. She is no more to blame than me."

The throne room remained quiet for a long while, the only sound being Binta's sniffles. Then, finally, Kringus nodded to the guards, who gently escorted the broken young woman away. Once she was gone, Kringus turned back to Cass, who smiled very confidently.

"So, you see, Your Highness, we are business partners. She is a whore, and I am her madam. I do the legwork and find the men with which she may fornicate. She gets what she wants, and I get paid. We didn't understand that prostitution was frowned upon in Pelesea. So, again, please enforce your fine upon me so my father may pay it, and we can all get back to our lives."

Kringus stared at her for a long while and glanced at Franklin, who stood defeated beside his daughter. Cass eventually folded her arms across her chest, the best she could while wearing the shackles, and stood impatiently waiting for Kringus to speak. Finally, with a long look toward Penelope, he announced his verdict.

"After hearing both sides of this story, I feel that the charges against you have greatly diminished."

His words made Cass unfold her arms and hold them up to Jespen so he could unlock her shackles. The guard made no move, and Cass lowered them with a frustrated sigh, waiting for Kringus to speak.

"However, your continued disregard for others has worn my patience thin. I have never met you before today, but I have known your father for years. He is a respectable citizen of Pelesea, and I would expect the same of his daughter."

Kringus turned to Franklin and said, "Sir, your daughter has not followed in your footsteps, and I hope you are as disappointed in her actions as I am."

Franklin looked at the king with tear-filled eyes and said, "This is not the daughter I had before her ill-fated trip to those mountains. Something in the adventure with that vagabond, Cassandra Rho, changed her. So, my daughter is gone, and this is all I have left."

Cass gasped and stood in shock as if someone had slapped her. Kringus did not give her time to respond to her father's heartfelt words and cut her off with his sentencing.

"I know of your history with Miss Mulay at Victoria's school, and I can see how little people mean to you after being around you briefly. You are a bad seed, Cashmere Ruben, and I want you out of my city. So, I hereby exile you from Pelesea for five years."

Cass gasped again and took a step back. She might have toppled over if Jespen wasn't there to steady her. She jerked away from his grasp and screamed, "That is not fair!"

"Silence!" Kringus screamed back, then stood to tower over the rude girl. "I'll give you time to pack your things and leave the city. Jespen will escort you home to assist you, then escort you to the gate. If I see you within the city over the next five years, I will jail you in the castle prison for twenty years."

Penelope's eyes widened at the mention of that punishment. Kringus rarely used the prison under the castle and typically reserved it for hardened criminals. He eventually took his seat as Cass stood there with her mouth agape. Kringus nodded to Jespen, who escorted her out. She grumbled the whole way and struggled against his grip, but eventually, she was gone.

"You have honored me, my king," Franklin said after his daughter had left. "Your wisdom is impeccable, and I humbly agree with your judgment."

"I hope she will return one day, Franklin, as a changed person, one that can be an upstanding citizen like her father," Kringus answered.

"Me as well, my king, me as well," Franklin answered, on the verge of tears.

Shortly after the hearing, Franklin entered his home to find two of the castle's royal guards in his foyer. Kelm, his trusted butler, was there and looked distressed. He approached Franklin and whispered, "She is upstairs packing but is in a foul mood. Another guard is with her."

Franklin nodded, looked to the two guards, and said, "Please be at ease. Kelm here will get you anything you need. I am going to say farewell to my daughter."

Neither man said anything, but one nodded his appreciation. Franklin turned and made his way quickly up the stairs. He heard the commotion before he was halfway up—it sounded like Cass was throwing one of her temper tantrums, which were commonplace of late.

"I need to speak with him; it is urgent!" she screamed.

Franklin found Jespen standing outside Cass's door on the top floor, along with the maid, Glenna. He could not see Cass, but Franklin surmised she was in her room as both were looking in, with Glenna wearing a dazed expression.

"I've told you thrice now; you may not do anything but gather your things and leave. If you do not complete the task soon, I will drag you out of the city with what possessions you have," Jespen answered.

"Master guardsman, is everything all right?" Franklin asked, peeking into the room to find clothes strewn all over the floor.

"Well, I wouldn't go that far, Mr. Ruben, but we are progressing."

"Glenna, get in here!" Cass screamed, and the maid looked to Jespen for permission. He gave her a confirming nod, and she hurried into the whirlwind of flying clothes.

"I apologize for my daughter's behavior; she is a changed person of late."

"No need to explain, Mr. Ruben; the king understands the circumstances," Jespen said with a raised hand.

Cass quickly pulled Glenna aside as the two men discussed the situation and whispered, "I need you to find Malikai."

"Who?" Glenna asked.

"Malikai, the man who saved me from certain death."

"Oh yes, I remember him. He is older with a pointy beard, correct?"

"Yes! Listen closely; tell him I will be at the front gate waiting for him. I need his assistance. Tell him the king has exiled me from the city. Therefore, it is most urgent he comes to the north gate, understand?"

"Yes, my lady, but where do I find this Malikai?"

"He is staying at Poppy's Inn near the southern docks. Ask the barkeep, and he will guide you to his room. My request is urgent, and you must go now," Cass whispered excitedly.

"But I am working here until sunset. So, I can go after that if it suits you."

"Have you not been listening!" Cass screamed louder than she intended.

The sound garnered the attention of Jespen, who entered the room and said, "Your time is nearly up, Miss Ruben."

"Father, may Glenna leave for the day? She has something she must do for me," Cass asked with a quivering voice.

"Of course, go, Glenna," Franklin reassured her.

Glenna left the room after one glance at Cass and hurried down the stairs.

"I am nearly done here; if you would be so kind as to leave me be for a few more minutes," Cass said to Jespen.

Jespen looked to Franklin, who nodded slightly, then motioned with his head toward the door. Both men left so Cass could finish her packing. Finally, she had all the needed clothes and then collected the various magical items hidden around her room. First, Cass plucked the medallion attuned to Cassandra from under her bed and gently placed it around her neck. Then she gathered the other magical trinkets she had obtained over the years, including the extra-dimensional cottage she had stolen from Cedric.

Soon, Jespen escorted her to the front door, where her father waited to say goodbye. His eyes were bloodshot, and tears streaked his face. Cass usually would have hugged him tight and even shared some tears, but her heart was changed, and those feelings eluded her. When he tried to hug her, she scoffed at him and held out her hand to stop the embrace. He looked hurt and confused, and she considered him quite pathetic.

"No, Father, not after your words that condemned me before the king."

"What? I spoke only the truth, my daughter."

"You are the reason for my exile," Cass whispered between clenched teeth.

"No, my daughter, you are."

Cass's eyes widened at the harsh words, and she considered lashing out and beating her father for his ignorance. But, instead, she looked to the three castle guards surrounding her and thought better of it.

"You are everything to me, but you are changed," Franklin said with an air of defeat. "Go and sow your wild oats. Then come back to me, the sweet little girl I once knew."

Cass stood in silence for a long time, sizing up the man she had always loved and mostly obeyed. Now, he repulsed her. He was weak and did not embrace her new identity, which had given her so much freedom. She decided then that she didn't need a father other than Malikai.

She leaned in and whispered, "She is dead. I am what is left."

Franklin fought the tears for a bit but soon began to sob, putting his head in his hands. The guards escorted Cass out of the house as Kelm tried to console her father. Cass left with a smirk on her face and with no feelings of remorse.

Later that day, long after the sun had set, Glenna finally arrived at Poppy's Inn on the far side of the city. Her loyalty to Cass was strong, having helped raise the girl since she was an infant. Cass was almost like a daughter to Glenna, and so she continued her search long after someone else might have given up. The moon was high in the sky when Glenna finally entered Poppy's warm greeting room and found shelter from the biting winter wind.

She breathed into her frozen hands, trying to thaw them, then looked around the packed room. Jovial patrons occupied most of the tables, and a warm fire blazed in the hearth.

"Have a seat at any table you can find, or at the bar if that is to your liking," a young barmaid said as she rushed by her with a serving tray full of empty glasses.

Glenna glanced over to the side of the room from which the woman had just come to find a large table full of rough-looking men, probably sailors. Most of them appeared to be inebriated or well on their way to being so. She walked the opposite way and found a seat at the bar.

The barkeep, a gristly man with an unshaven face, was frantically working to keep up with the orders of ale, both for the many tables and the crowded bar. Glenna found the last remaining stool and sat. She felt out of place as she took her seat, having no idea an inn could be that crowded at such a late hour. She waited patiently until the bartender was finally able to address her.

"So, what will it be?" he asked, wiping a glass with a towel and placing it in front of her.

Glenna wasn't sure if the glass was clean or if the man picked it up from a pile of used glasses the barmaid had just delivered.

"I am not here to drink. I am looking for someone," Glenna answered.

The man bristled at that remark. "Well, now, I do not have time for non-drinkers at my bar. If you are not going—"

"Give her some of the ale I'm drinking, Barlow," a woman seated beside Glenna interrupted.

Barlow stared at the pretty woman who now gained Glenna's attention. She was a little younger than Glenna and seemed comfortable in the wild place. She appeared innocent and pure and did not fit in with the rough crowd.

"Fine," Barlow finally answered and poured Glenna a drink, then walked off to serve other patrons at the crowded bar.

"Thank you," Glenna said.

The woman turned to her with large almond eyes and smiled. "Of course. Ignore Barlow; he gets ruder as the night wears on."

"Thanks for the advice," Glenna said, staring at her glass.

"Don't you drink?"

Glenna shook her head and smiled. "No, but I am still very thankful for your gesture."

"I am Matilda."

"Nice to meet you. I am Glenna."

"Well, you are not from around here, that is evident. So, who could you possibly be looking for?" Matilda asked.

"I was supposed to ask the barkeep, but he—"

"Forget Barlow; I know as much as he does anyway. Let me help you."

Glenna nodded, having no reason not to trust the woman. "Very well, I am looking for a wizard."

"Malikai?" Matilda asked.

"Yes! How did you know?"

"As I said, I know much about the goings-on of this place. What could you possibly want with Malikai?"

"My business is my own," Glenna said, "and I need to speak with him directly."

If Matilda was insulted, she did not show it. Instead, she smiled and downed the rest of her drink. She reached over and finished off Glenna's and then, with a smile, said, "Follow me."

Matilda stood and made her way through the crowd. Glenna jumped off her stool and followed the best she could. Many people were in the room, and Glenna had difficulty navigating through them. However, she noticed they seemed to move aside for Matilda, almost as if they were afraid of her, and Glenna tried to stay in her wake of parting customers. It wasn't easy, but she finally made the steps to the second floor and found Matilda waiting for her.

"Come, I am friends with the wizard and will take you to him," Matilda said, then turned and climbed the stairs.

Glenna followed, and soon they were at Malikai's door. Matilda did not bother knocking but entered, motioning Glenna to follow. Once inside, Glenna discovered the wizard in his bed, not sleeping but entertaining two naked women. Glenna's face turned red and she froze at the spectacle.

"What is the meaning of this, Matilda?" Malikai roared.

"This is another woman who was downstairs looking for you. I assumed she was part of the orgy."

"Never!" Glenna felt herself blurt out before she could catch herself.

"Hardly," Malikai said, staring Glenna up and down.

The sheets had partially fallen away from the wizard, and his physique was magnificent. The view of his perfectly chiseled chest and abs had Glenna swallowing hard.

"Go away, chambermaid; we occupy the room. Come in the morning, and you'll find a mess worth cleaning," Malikai answered, returning his attention to the two women.

"I beg your pardon, good wizard, but I am not here to clean," Glenna scolded.

If Malikai heard her, he did not respond, now sharing small talk with the woman to his right. His hand disappeared under the blanket, and the woman gasped, then closed her eyes and sighed. Glenna's uncomfortableness only grew as the moments passed.

Finally, she blurted out, "I have a message from Cass Ruben."

Her outburst got the wizard's attention, as he stopped playing with the woman and turned back to Glenna, which his lover did not seem to appreciate.

Malikai looked Glenna up and down again, which made her uncomfortable. She tried to step back, but Matilda blocked her path. She felt Matilda's hands on her shoulders, small delicate hands that seemed to contain the strength of a giant. Matilda pushed her toward Malikai and forcefully walked her up to the bed. Glenna became more anxious the closer she got to the man. She did not know why, but he exuded power, which scared her.

After many uncomfortable moments, Malikai asked, "Well?"

Glenna swallowed hard, then told him about Cass and her exile out the north gate. After hearing the news, Malikai seemed to be in deep contemplation. Eventually, he dismissed the two women pawing and playing with him and climbed out of bed. They both groaned and pouted, but he paid them no mind. He began to dress, and although embarrassed, Glenna had difficulty looking away. The man had the physique of someone half his age.

"Well?" Matilda asked Glenna as she continued to watch Malikai dress.

Glenna jumped and turned to face the woman, only to discover Matilda now wore a strange, almost accusing look on her face. Glenna's face immediately turned red, and she apologized. "I am sorry; I did not mean to look."

"Not that, fool! What other information do you have for us?"

Glenna looked at her, puzzled. "Information? I do not understand."

"I am leaving. I will see what my daughter is up to and return shortly," Malikai said.

Matilda pushed Glenna down on the bed, where she found Malikai's lovers kissing profoundly and caressing each other. Glenna felt very uncomfortable. Matilda was becoming more forceful than she had initially acted at the bar. And she was afraid to disobey her.

"The royal guards are watching us, so I will not leave through the front door," Malikai said.

"You mean to teleport, then," Matilda surmised.

"Of course."

Malikai waved his hand in front of him before Matilda could respond and vanished. She turned back to Glenna and asked, "Where is she?"

"Cass? At the north gate, as I said," Glenna said, shaking her head and holding her arms out.

Her actions elicited a slap from Matilda. The force of the blow was more than poor Glenna could have expected, and the woman went flying off the edge of the bed to land on her hands and knees.

"Don't play dumb with me. I know why you have truly come to us."

Glenna pulled herself up, using the bed for support. Her old joints groaned at the effort, and her entire face throbbed from the strike. The two tramps giggled at her discomfort as they huddled together. One blew her a kiss as she climbed off the floor.

Matilda grabbed her roughly by the arm. "Come with me," she ordered, dragging Glenna out the door and into the hall. She pushed Glenna against the wall and grabbed her around the throat. "I ask again; tell me where Cassandra Rho is," she hissed through clenched teeth.

"I… do not… know who that… is," Glenna grunted, trying unsuccessfully to loosen Matilda's grip.

Matilda released her, and as Glenna gasped for breath, Matilda's eyes darted back and forth, reading Glenna's face, searching for answers.

"I performed the ritual last night, and there was no doubt in the message—you would come to us with the location of Cassandra Rho."

Glenna just looked at her and shook her head, puzzled by her words. Matilda reached into a pocket and produced a key. She pulled Glenna to the next door down the hall. Matilda unlocked it and opened the door. The room was dark, the curtains drawn tight, and Glenna was shoved into it, utterly blind as her eyes tried to adjust to the darkness.

Suddenly, the room glowed in soft purple light, just enough to make out the furnishings. The light came from a small flame that now burned on Matilda's upturned palm. Glenna looked on in amazement as the flame did not burn Matilda or harm her. Matilda ignored her and led her to a chair in the corner of the room. After Glenna gained her bearings and could look around, she noticed a bed on the far side of the room, another chair near her, and a table with many bottles, beakers, and jars adorning it.

Matilda lit a tiny lantern atop the dresser and shook out the flame on her hand. Glenna could see better now, and she noticed that a man was lying on the bed, naked and tied spread-eagled to the four bedposts. Glenna let out a small shriek at the sight.

"Quiet, unless you want to join him, fool," Matilda said softly.

Glenna looked further at the man and realized a rag was tied around his head, covering his eyes, and soaked with blood. Glenna whimpered and fell back in her chair, finally realizing how dangerous the situation was.

Matilda picked up a small knife and what appeared to be tongs from the dresser top and moved toward Glenna, who began to shake with fear.

"You know the difference between you and me, Glenna?"

"What?" Glenna asked between silent sobs.

"I am powerful, and you are weak. I have dedicated my life, body, and soul to my god, and he has granted me powers you could not hope to understand."

Matilda stood before Glenna, emotionless, and explained the truth of her god to Glenna as if she were reciting a memorized poem with no feelings, just facts. Glenna trembled and sobbed, and Matilda seemed not even to notice.

"I could kill you with but a thought. If you run for the door, I will strike you down long before you reach it. If you scream, I will silence you before you even make a sound. Do you understand that what I say is true?"

Glenna looked at the wicked instruments in Matilda's hands and quickly nodded.

"Good, then you will further understand that I have ways of predicting the future, seeing things that weaklings like yourself cannot," Matilda explained, now moving toward the bed. "My god is real, unlike those that most worship. Mine is genuine and very powerful. He is coming, Glenna, and he will devour the weak, people such as yourself." Matilda looked down at the prone man, who, if alive, made no movement or sound.

"My god gave me the power for clairvoyance last night. So, you see, I knew you would come this very evening asking for Malikai." She placed the knife and tongs on the bed beside the still man. She returned to the dresser and poured a few ingredients into a glass.

"You see, my god told me this, and I know it is true because here you are," she said dramatically, waving in Glenna's direction. "What is unclear is why you have not delivered the whereabouts of Cassandra Rho as my god told me you would."

"Matilda, please, I do not know this person," Glenna sobbed.

"Shut your filthy trap, woman!"

Glenna tried to hold back the fit that boiled within her. She wanted nothing more than to roll into a fetal position, but she knew Matilda would kill her if she did. So, she lowered her head and hoped the volatile priestess would not strike her again.

Matilda added a syrupy liquid to the mix and stirred it all together. Once satisfied, she took the glass and gave it to Glenna.

"Do not spill a drop, or you will suffer mightily."

Glenna took the glass with two hands and tried to steady her nerves. The putrid smell wafting from it made her want to retch. She managed to avoid doing so, but had to concentrate not to gag.

"Bring that over here and hold it steady," Matilda demanded, returning to the bed.

Glenna followed her hesitantly. She approached the man and knew that if he was still alive, that would barely be the case. He looked malnourished, and his bones bulged through his tight skin. She could not resist looking upon his face. His mouth was ajar, showing blackened teeth, and the blood-soaked rag still clung to his face, covering his eyes.

"And so, I performed the ritual last night, and this man was good enough to donate his eyes for me to do so. That ritual revealed you to me and gave me the insight to understand you would lead me to Cassandra. That ritual did not fail, yet you have not done your part. So, we will ask our good friend, here, to help us out once more and let us borrow his tongue."

She pried the man's mouth open with one finger and reached in with the tongs to grab his tongue, stretching it out beyond his rotting teeth. Glenna could barely look as Matilda took the knife and prepared to cut the dead man's tongue out.

"You don't mind if we borrow this, do you?" Matilda asked.

To Glenna's relief, the man did not answer and, by all accounts, appeared dead. He seemed that way until Matilda began sawing on his tongue. Then he jerked and spasmed and issued a horrible wail that had Glenna nearly dropping the glass of foul liquid.

"I guess he does mind," Matilda said, but she continued her sawing until the top third of the tongue was severed.

She held it up by the tongs as Glenna fought to hold the glass steady. The man's scream quickly turned to a moan, and soon he was silent. Matilda ignored him and gently plopped the severed tongue into the liquid, where it began to boil and smoke. She grabbed the concoction from Glenna before she dropped it, then pushed her back slowly but forcefully to the chair. Soon

Glenna found herself sitting once more. The frightened woman watched as Matilda closed her eyes and whispered words under her breath while waving her hand above the morbid potion.

When Matilda opened her eyes and focused them on Glenna, the woman shrank back in her chair. The look on the priestess's face spoke volumes.

"Now drink," Matilda softly demanded.

"No, I couldn't possibly!" Glenna resisted, standing and backing into the corner of the room.

Matilda calmly followed, holding the glass in front of her. "I drank the one with the eyeballs, and now you can drink the one with the tongue."

"Why?" Glenna asked, nearing tears.

"I did so because it allowed me to witness your arrival, to predict when you would come. You will do so because you did not tell me the whereabouts of Cassandra Rho."

"But I do not know her!" Glenna argued.

A flash of anger crossed Matilda's face, but she quickly calmed and continued her instruction. "Since you lied to me, I created this to defeat your deception. Drink this, and I will know the truth from you."

Matilda approached the cornered woman and offered her the glass, which continued to smoke. The tongue was no longer visible, most of it now dissolved. Glenna swatted at the repulsive liquid, but Matilda was faster, bringing the potion in close and slapping Glenna with her left hand, knocking her back against the wall.

"If you spill any of this or refuse to drink it all, you will take his place," Matilda said, pointing to the motionless man on the bed. "Do you understand?"

Glenna held her cheek where Matilda had struck her again and slowly nodded.

"Smart old gal. Here, drink it all," Matilda ordered, offering the glass again.

Glenna slowly stood fully and took the smoking potion. Matilda looked on, and her visage indicated with no uncertain terms what would happen if Glenna failed to do precisely as ordered. So, with shaking hands, Glenna closed her eyes and drank the liquid as quickly as possible. When the remaining piece of tongue slapped against her lip, she dropped the glass and began to dry-heave.

"There, come sit down and let the liquid do its work," Matilda said, gently guiding her back to the chair.

It took several moments for Glenna to regain control of herself and sit fully in the chair. She glanced at the spilled glass to see the little bit of tongue remaining and a small pool of liquid around it.

"That's all right; you drank enough for the spell to enact fully," Matilda said with a wide smile.

Glenna could feel the liquid warming her insides, and it felt rather soothing. She visibly relaxed as her hands fell from her lap and hung limply at her sides. Her eyes glossed over, and she just stared, unblinking, into space.

Matilda smiled and pulled the other chair to sit before the catatonic woman.

"Tell me, Glenna the idiot, where is Cassandra Rho?"

There was no response for a moment, and Glenna stared straight ahead. Then, finally, her mouth moved slightly as if trying to form words.

"Take your time. Search that small mind of yours and find the answer I demand," Matilda encouraged, leaning forward in her chair, eagerly awaiting the answer.

"I… I… do not know her," Glenna answered again.

Matilda leaned back in shock, knowing her spell had worked, yet the stubborn woman still would not cooperate. She repeated her question, now bordering on desperation.

"Where is Cassandra Rho?"

Glenna's eyes watered, and large tears streamed down her cheeks as she said, "I do… not know."

Matilda stood, knocking over her chair, and gasped for air. "The spell worked," she whispered.

Her anger eventually got the best of her, and she glanced back to the knife lying on the bed. She calmly walked over and retrieved it and was soon standing in front of Glenna once more. The woman seemed not to notice and continued to stare into space.

"Thanks for nothing, you old fool," Matilda whispered.

She then plunged the knife into the woman's chest. Glenna did not react, except for the increased tears that ran down her face. That only fueled

Matilda's anger further, and the volatile priestess stabbed the poor woman a dozen more times before she left the room.

As she locked the door, she thought of Cass's modification to it. It now locked from the outside, a simple and effective change, done initially to keep Binta imprisoned and now to keep the macabre scene hidden from prying eyes. Then the simple truth dawned on her. She stopped, and her eyes widened, realizing Glenna did not know Cassandra's location after all.

"Cass knows," she whispered.

She hurriedly went to Malikai's room. She evicted his two playthings and waited as patiently as possible. Her mind was a whirlwind. Who was Cass? She had paid little mind to what Glenna had said about the girl. The king ordered her exiled, that was all Matilda could recall. She hoped Malikai would find her; she needed him to find her. Cass had to be the missing piece to the vision. Eventually, Malikai would return, and she would have her answers when he did. And soon, she would have Cassandra Rho, very, very soon.

It was early the following day, with the first signs of the sunrise, when Matilda awakened. She had stayed awake for hours, waiting for Malikai's return, but she eventually dozed off in the chair. Matilda sat up slowly, rubbing her stiff neck, when she noticed Malikai standing on the far side of the room. She could only surmise that the sound of him teleporting back into the room had awakened her. She was quick to her feet.

"Did you find her?" Matilda asked, suddenly forgetting the pain in her neck.

Malikai gave her a knowing grin but said nothing at first. Matilda stared hard at him, trying to decipher his mirth. He eventually turned and walked to his dresser to remove his cloak. Behind him stood a young woman Matilda had never seen before.

"Cass?" Matilda asked.

"Corpse? You live?" the woman said.

Matilda looked to Malikai, confused by the response.

He chuckled softly and said, "Cass, meet Matilda. Matilda, she only saw you during your catatonic fit after the spell you cast at Cassandra's grave."

Matilda's gaze drifted back to the young woman, who removed her cloak, then sat on the bed. "You were like a corpse; I thought you dead," Cass explained.

"Where is the old woman?" Malikai asked, looking around the room.

"Yes, Glenna; I wish to thank her for finding Malikai," Cass added.

"She actually *is* a corpse," Matilda said, then added, "I thought you were exiled?"

Cass glanced worriedly at Malikai, who shrugged and poured himself a drink.

"What the king doesn't know won't hurt him," Cass replied dryly.

Matilda approached the young woman, who rose from the bed, seemingly ready to defend herself if Matilda intended an altercation. She relaxed considerably when Matilda spoke.

"You know Cassandra Rho?"

"Better than that," Malikai said.

Matilda turned toward the wizard and asked, "Tell me what you know, Malikai."

"I know where to find her," Cass answered. Matilda turned back to the young woman to find her smiling widely.

"And, of course, I can take you both there," Malikai added.

"Yes, take me immediately!" Matilda said, rushing up to the old wizard and grabbing his hand tightly in hers. "I must get to her, Malikai, you know this."

"Of course, I do. Both of you want Cassandra Rho, and I can assist with that. But first, I require payment."

Matilda's shoulders slumped, and she tried to bite back her tongue. She had no time for more delays. If the girl knew Cassandra's whereabouts, she wanted to get to her immediately. Her eyes darted back and forth, trying to find a way out of Malikai's trap, but when her gaze landed on Malikai, she saw him looking smugly at Cass. He toasted his glass to her and downed his drink. Matilda looked back to Cass to see the young woman unbuttoning her blouse while biting her lower lip.

"I'll get the mirror ready," Malikai said, walking past Matilda to retrieve it from under the bed.

It seemed like a bad dream to Matilda in one way, yet also an incredible realization that Cassandra was alive and that there was a way to find her. She pondered those thoughts swirling in her head and unconsciously began unbuttoning her shirt.

The three lay tangled in the bed several hours later, the women exhausted, and Malikai resting peacefully. Cass was on one side of Malikai, resting her head on his chest and playing with his greying chest hair. Matilda lay panting on her back, staring at the ceiling. Undoubtedly, the old wizard was one of the best lovers Matilda had ever known. Her mind drifted back to the one night she and Greyson shared all those months ago. He was the only lover she had taken who was better than Malikai. A smile came to her face at the thought of it.

Then she thought of Cerus and his anger toward the young man. She would have enjoyed cuckolding the mighty warrior with Greyson. Her husband's hatred toward him would have made the sex even better for her if that was even possible. Unfortunately, the mirror had not worked the last time as Cerus did not answer its call, but the thought of him watching her with another man always aroused her and, most of the time, Cerus. What would he have done if he had witnessed Greyson through the mirror? The thought amused her immensely.

"So, why are you after Cassandra?" Cass asked, interrupting her thoughts.

Matilda looked over to see the woman staring at her, her chin resting on Malikai's chest. Her first thought was to reach over and throttle her, but she knew they had to come to an understanding. After all, if Cass wanted Cassandra, was it because she wanted to kill her as well? Most likely not, and it was a strong possibility they were friends. Whatever the reason, Matilda knew she couldn't give away the true reason for her search, not until she understood the woman a little better.

"She has caught the eye of my god, and I wish to take her to my home in Varish."

"You're from Varish?"

"Yes, Malikai and I are both from there, but as you know, traveling long distances does not deter Malikai."

"How could that fool ever catch the eye of a god?" Cass asked, appearing quite amused.

"She was born under a special moon. That makes her a bit of a goddess to the people of my religion."

"A goddess?" Cass asked with a laugh.

"In a certain way, yes."

"Well, I assure you, the Cassandra I know is no goddess."

"Tell me all about her, Cass; I need to know her," Matilda said, more urgently than she intended.

Cass sat up, and Matilda followed, neither concerned about their nakedness following their tryst with Malikai.

"There is not much to tell. Cassandra is an idiot by all accounts. She is pretentious and quite annoying," Cass explained.

"Pretentious, how?"

"She believes she is the daughter of a god. So, a self-proclaimed demigod, if you will."

"Yes, of course, and that is exactly the case," Matilda said, growing more excited with each piece of information she gleaned from Cass. The stories matched. This had to be the same Cassandra Rho.

The two women gently moved off the bed, trying not to awaken the old wizard for fear of him demanding more sex. Matilda quickly dressed and stood before Cass, who was lacing her boots up. She looked up at Matilda and stopped. Then, she slowly rose until they were face to face.

"What?" Cass asked.

"I need to know two things. First, what do you want with Cassandra, and second, is she a virgin?"

Cass seemed to find the questions amusing as she shook her head and returned to her boots. Matilda envisioned Glenna in the next room and considered preparing another truth serum for Cass, grabbing the young woman by the hair, and dragging her to the next room, when Cass finally responded.

"I want to kill her."

She said it with a calmness only a crazy, dangerous person would do. That was the first sign Matilda picked up, indicating Cass might be worth keeping alive. But, of course, she could not allow Cass to realize her goal, and she would kill the girl if she tried.

"As far as being a virgin, I'd say there is a pretty good chance," Cass continued.

"What do you mean?"

"I mean, she is a lesbian. So, I doubt she has laid with a man before. I know someone who tried, but I don't think it worked out for him. It's her loss, too, as he was quite the lover."

Cass rose and made herself and Matilda some drinks. "So, you want Cassandra alive, and I want her dead. What kind of deal can we make?"

"If you lead me to her and we capture her, I must demand she remain alive," Matilda said, and her tone left no debate.

"So, what's in it for me?"

"You lead me to her; I'll let you beat her to within an inch of her life."

Cass nodded and took a sip of her drink, considering the offer. Matilda could tell the wheels were turning in Cass's head as she was probably thinking of a counteroffer.

Matilda restated the offer and said, "For an entire year."

"What?" Cass asked, her eyes going wide.

"I will put you in charge of her care. You may torture her as you see fit but you may not kill her or take her virginity."

Cass smiled, and the look in her eye told Matilda that the offer was too good to refuse.

"You will live for one year at Nesin, my fortress, and you will live like a queen. Your only job will be to look after our special prisoner," Matilda continued.

"To Cassandra Rho," Cass said, raising her glass.

"To Cassandra Rho," Matilda repeated, and the two clanked their glasses together and drank the potent liquid down.

The drink warmed Matilda's inside almost as much as the idea of finally obtaining Cassandra. She closed her eyes and savored both. She was startled out of her trance by a loud knock on the door.

"Open up in the name of the king!" came a man's voice behind it.

Malikai had snored a few moments earlier but now sprang into action, jumping out of bed with one graceful leap. His naked form caught the eyes of both startled women, but he paid them no heed. Instead, he went straight to the door and pressed his left palm against it. Matilda could hear him softly chanting, and when his spell was complete, the energy sprang from his left hand and into the door. The transformation was sudden and instantaneous as the door grew thicker and broader, so much so that the door frame cracked and moaned in several places.

"It will hold for a short time," Malikai warned, then began to dress.

"Open up in the name of the king!" came the cry again, followed by pounding on the bulging door.

"They cannot find me within the city," Cass said.

"And so, they won't," Malikai replied, then went to a large chest and opened the lid. "You two have paid for my services. Name the place quickly if you still wish to utilize them."

Matilda and Cass watched as the seemingly old wizard lifted the heavy mirror and walked it to the chest. Matilda began to argue that the mirror would never fit into the trunk, but then she remembered who this man was. He was a powerful wizard with many toys. The mirror's end disappeared into the chest, and Malikai continued to lower it until it disappeared altogether. He did not delay and quickly began gathering other items of importance and stuffing them into his magical chest, which held much more than its dimensions seemed to allow.

"Where is Cassandra?" Matilda asked as the heavy pounding began shaking the door.

"They have a wizard," Malikai said. "The door will not hold long."

"Tell him where Cassandra is so we may be out of here!" Matilda screamed over the chaos.

"I'm trying," Cass snapped back.

When Matilda looked back at her, she saw the young woman had her eyes closed and was grasping a necklace adorned with a blue gemstone.

"What are you doing?" Matilda asked.

"Finding Cassandra."

The door split as it began to turn softer and shrink once more. The strikes were severely damaging its integrity, and it would not hold much longer. Matilda turned to Malikai, who had shut the chest lid and cast another spell. Once complete, the chest shrank to one inch in height, and the wizard picked it up and stuck it in a pocket.

He turned to Matilda and said, "We must leave at once."

"Of course, but she will not name the location!" Matilda said, waving a hand at Cass, whose eyes were still closed.

"Then I will send you somewhere safe where you may begin your search."

Matilda looked hard at the wizard, her heart suddenly beating fast. "You mean not to come with us?' she whispered.

"Our time together has passed; this is where we part ways. Now tell me your destination."

The door creaked loudly and looked like it would fall off the hinges at any moment.

"Cass!" Matilda screamed.

"Mecca-Loraine!" Cass yelled out simultaneously and opened her eyes.

Malikai gathered the two women close to him and enacted his powers. Matilda watched him as he did, knowing she would not see him again, possibly forever. It pained her more than she cared to admit. The room around her became unfocused, and the last thing she saw was Malikai's face. With a wink and a smile, it disappeared as well, and she felt herself hurtling through space and time.

When the world settled around them again Matilda and Cass found themselves just outside of the gates of a reasonably large town. Icy snow entombed the ground, and the cold wind blew off the ocean. Matilda could smell the salt air and the stench of marine life. Unfortunately, the guards had shut the gates, and the keeper did not look too enthused about letting in strangers.

"What is your business with Mecca-Loraine?" he barked.

"We seek shelter from the elements," Matilda answered, realizing then that she and Cass wore little clothing and would quickly freeze in the bitter cold.

The gatekeeper looked them up and down suspiciously. "Where have you two come from?" he asked with a growl.

"Let us in; we are freezing," Cass said.

"We are keeping the gates locked right now, missy. A barbarian raid took place a few days earlier right outside of our gates, and we fear their return."

"Do we look like barbarians?" Cass asked, lowering her arms folded across her chest to reveal her nipples through her thin shirt.

The man stared and mumbled, "No, of course not."

"Then let us in before they come back," Matilda said.

Her words seemed to snap the man out of his trance. He stepped back from the gate and nodded to an unseen gate operator, and the portcullis rose. They eventually gained entrance into the town and found lodging and extra clothing. Shortly after, they began their search for Cassandra.

9

CATACOMBS OF NOVAFONTERA

THEY HAD REACHED NOVAFONTERA TWO DAYS EARLIER AND found the storm grate open and off its hinges as if someone had opened it for them. Daro had brought heavy rope and other items he thought he would need to pry the portal open, but they were not required. He attempted to move the heavy covering, but it would have taken a dozen men or more even to lift it. However, it appeared someone, or something, had torn it free with little effort. Whatever had moved the grate was expecting them. He could only guess it was Heinsvick, the vampire lord. So, instead of entering immediately, Daro convinced Sasha to wait and watch the opening, hoping the person or creature responsible for the silent invitation would reappear. They had not, and Sasha grew bored with the wait.

"It is time to enter, Daro," she said, gathering her things from a nearby alcove where they had camped for the last two days. "I want this burden removed from my shoulders."

"Why must you do this, Sasha? I know your uncle oppresses you in your world, but here, you are free. Why return?" Daro asked.

"For my mother," Sasha said, stopping and turning his way.

Again, her appearance stunned him. How could anyone consider her ugly? Her god-like beauty had him losing his thoughts as well as his voice. He could only stare and drink her in.

"Your mother?" he finally said.

"They will not release her without the sword. Therefore, I must return for her sake."

Daro watched her pack camp, and so engrossed was he with her that he just stood there gawking.

"You're doing it again," Sasha said without looking his way.

"Oh, yes… sorry," Daro said, jumping into action to pack his gear.

He silently berated himself; he would need to be alert traveling to the undercity of Novafontera. The cursed and deadly city had not seen the light of day for nearly seven hundred years, yet they would enter it willingly. Daro couldn't deny Sasha; she was far too beautiful to reject.

"Thanks a lot," he whispered to his crotch.

Soon after, they approached the opened drainage grate on the city's eastern side. Daro lit a lantern and lowered it into the opening.

"I can see a floor; it is not far down, perhaps ten feet," he said.

"Then let us be on our way," Sasha said, sitting on the edge of the opening so her legs dangled into the darkness.

"You sure I can't persuade you to forget this quest?" Daro asked in one last desperate attempt to change her mind.

"You do not have to go, Daro. You have done enough for me, and for that, I am grateful. Stay here where it is safe."

She scooted closer to the edge and was about to jump in when Daro stopped her. "Wait," he said, putting a hand on her shoulder.

"What?" she asked, alarmed.

"I should go first."

She rolled her eyes and jumped in.

"Idiot," he whispered to himself. He took one last look around and lowered himself into the opening.

The corridor showed no signs of poisonous gas, and no creatures jumped out to attack them when they touched down. To Daro, that was a victory. He fastened the lantern to his belt, drew both swords, and led the way. Sasha followed his lead, drew her blade, and donned her shield. There was enough room for them to walk side by side down the corridor. It was a long, straight tunnel that did not deviate from its westerly direction for quite some time. The center of the tunnel floor held a groove for the water to run along. It was icy where the running water had frozen long ago. Luckily, there wasn't much runoff there because it had been too cold in recent weeks. So, other than the center of the floor, the ice was sparse and their footing unhindered.

They soon came to a spot where a doorway had been sealed up. The stones used were newer but still very old. Daro made a mental note of it. He would relay the information to the New Order when next they met, assuming he survived this expedition. Perhaps it meant something, or perhaps not. Either way, he would make as many mental notes of the place as possible. They continued walking for a long while and occasionally saw dull rays of light filtering through the ceiling from much smaller grates. The light was eerily green as the gas above diluted the light and licked at the tunnel ceiling. However, the gas never crept into the sewer system, just as it stayed within the outer city walls. Daro understood that those smaller grates led directly to the city streets and that no human had walked them for many years.

They traveled nearly an hour before they came to the first intersection, passing many of the tiny openings to the street as they did. The intersection spread out in all four directions without indicating whether one way was better than the others. Daro had no idea where they were going. The sealed-up wall was the only thing that came close to a room thus far in their journey. As they contemplated where to go, Daro discovered distinct scratches on one of the walls. He studied them and quickly discerned their meaning.

"I have found the way," he said glumly.

"What did this?" Sasha asked, raising her face shield to examine them more closely.

"Someone who wants us to go that way," he answered.

"So, it is a trap?"

"Most likely, but what are our alternatives? Perhaps this Heinsvick fellow wants to kill us, or perhaps someone is trying to help us. Either way, we have no better options."

Sasha conceded the point with a nod and lowered her visor. They continued their journey, following the markings provided by an unknown source at each intersection. There were many such areas, and the tunnels quickly became a maze. Daro was thankful they followed the markings because they could find their way out if needed. They traveled several hours that way, and dread began to overcome the ranger as they did. Sounds in the dark, sometimes the dripping of water, other times the scurrying of some unseen critter, had him on edge. He could sense it in Sasha's movement as well. The feeling was unnatural; they were no longer alone.

Inuentas had walked for several miles. Finally, he could see the fleshy wall that Vasheba had created in the mortal world. It was not prominent, yet still noticeable, standing out against the bleak landscape of the place. Many lessor demons investigated the strange creation, and Inuentas could see them scurrying around its base. As typical with that layer of hell, the distance to the wall was highly distorted, and the more he walked, the further away it seemed. Teleportation was not a skill he had mastered like many demons, so he had no choice but to continue on foot. He stepped onto a bloated body, thinking it was a black stone, typical terrain for hell, but his boot sunk into the rotting flesh.

"Curses," he whispered, lifting his foot and slinging off the decay.

He barely had time to wipe the sole of his fancy human-skin boots on the blackened grass when the next horde of demons spotted him. He had destroyed many since he had arrived on the chaotic layer of hell, and they would prove little effort for the master swordsman. They were known as bioflays and were little more than mangled souls of the damned. They rushed at him, at least twelve creatures, running on all fours, as bioflays were known to do. They looked like twisted, hairless humans but possessed razor-sharp claws and a maw full of vicious teeth. In the end, they were nothing more than sparring partners for him. He smiled as he unsheathed Slebel, feeling its hunger to feed on demon blood. He rushed to meet the assault, blade swinging to decapitate the first creature before it registered the attack.

The other creatures didn't notice and pushed the falling body out of their way to get at the intruder. Inuentas parried four attacks at one time, battling the slower creatures effortlessly. He lopped off the arm of the demon to his right, then spun to slice open the belly of the one on his left. Two more took their place as the injured fell away. It was a light workout for the skilled swordsman, and he barely breathed hard when it was over. He wiped the black blood from his blade on the grass and looked at the flesh wall, which finally seemed much closer now.

"Good," he said, starting his graceful stride toward his goal again.

However, he only took two steps before spotting the next creature and feeling the ground rumble as it approached. The sky was hazy, and he could not make it out clearly, but from the glimpse he stole, he understood it to be a garibleth, a mighty and dangerous demon. Garibleth were extremely powerful, and Inuentas was wise enough to avoid them at all costs. They stood at least twelve feet tall and had dark, red skin covering their muscled frames. Their heads were that of a child's nightmare, a flaming skull. The creature would seem dead without the glowing red dots in the eye sockets. Unfortunately, it would not be easy to dispatch, and the bat-like demons flying around were scouting for it. Those scouts were known as ceeps and were notorious for picking up their prey and flying high into the hellish sky, while a second one tore it limb from limb. They were pack hunters and were dangerous in pairs. Inuentas spotted at least four circling the sky around the garibleth. Inuentas assumed the beast knew he was there and the flying creatures were looking for him. That gave him the motivation to sprint away. Luckily, he made the wall of flesh before the garibleth saw him, although it still stomped nearby.

The fleshy wall stank of decay. Inuentas ignored the smell and searched for a weak link, tuning out the moans and muffled screams from within the macabre structure. Only a powerful demon could assemble the fleshy membrane. The wall consisted of the bodies of the mortals it had killed. Most of the time, the souls lingered within, sometimes for years, before being drawn out and tormented in the bowels of hell.

The wall was the only barrier between the two worlds, but few were powerful enough to pass through one. However, Inuentas had discovered the secret art of navigating them. He prepared a spell to protect himself from the volatile spirits within and the gooey substance that held the fleshy bits together. First, he formed an invisible magical sphere around himself that would offer protection and breathable air for a short time. Once the sphere encased him, he focused on a weakened spot in the wall and pried it open with his sword. He then forced himself in, the globe protecting him as he entered. It felt like walking against a strong water current, but eventually, he got the hang of it and found himself entirely in the membrane. It would take several hours to make the journey to the human world through the thick, fleshy wall. However, it would be worth the wait.

Daro and Sasha walked many hours within the catacombs, always finding scratches on the wall to guide them. They found several small, deserted alcoves, some containing remnants of shelving or rotted sacks; nothing indicated a weapon storage. Daro assumed a weapon storage might have the sword Sasha sought, so he kept an eye open for one. They found several more grated tunnels that burrowed deeper under the city, but neither wanted to consider those routes as options. However, the worst part of their journey was the growing uneasiness. It felt to Daro as if something was herding them and followed them. Whatever it was, he knew they were in danger, but he also understood Sasha would not be deterred from her mission.

It was Daro's mind that first began to play tricks on him. He thought he heard Grey, his wolf friend, at one point up ahead. It sounded like a whimper, as if the wolf were hurt or frightened. Daro bristled at the thought of his good friend and animal companion enduring torture by the vampire lord. He turned to Sasha to find that she was no longer beside him. It took his foggy mind a moment to sort out that information. Where had she gone? There had been no side tunnel of which he was aware.

"Sasha?" he whispered.

He turned to yell for her back the way they had come, but he heard the unmistakable whine from a dog or wolf before he could. In his mind, he knew it was Grey.

"Grey?" he asked.

The sound came from ahead, in the same direction he and Sasha had been traveling. He crept forward, his fuzzy mind quickly forgetting that Sasha was missing. He soon found a tunnel to his left, and once he brought the lantern to bear, his heart sank. The tunnel was small and continued straight for about one hundred feet before opening into what appeared to be a small room. On the far wall, he could barely make out the form of a motionless wolf lying on its side. Another whine came from the poor creature, and Daro ran into the tunnel, disregarding his safety. He soon came to the opening of the small room and there he found Grey lying in a pool of blood, a chain fastened around his neck and attached to an eyebolt in the wall.

"Grey!" he yelled and knelt beside his old friend. The wolf was alive, but barely. He looked around the small room, but nothing indicated the source of his friend's suffering.

He stroked the wolf's head and whispered, "I will get us out of here, old boy; hang in there."

As soon as the words left his mouth, there was a giant whoosh, and flames leaped up from the floor to fill the room, cutting off the exit and leaving only a tiny circle for Grey and Daro to stand. The wolf whined pathetically once more, and Daro shielded his eyes from the sudden brightness and took a step back from the immense heat. He examined Grey to see how injured the wolf was, noting the blood-soaked fur on his belly. However, Daro could not find a wound.

"What hurts you, my friend?" he whispered.

The wolf only answered with another whimper. Daro stood and looked beyond the flames to the tunnel, watching for signs of Sasha. There were none.

"Sasha!" he screamed over the roar of the flames, which continued to grow and were nearly four feet high now. "Where can she be, Grey?"

"Nearing her death, I would assume," came a voice from beyond the flames.

Daro shielded his eyes and tried to glimpse the source, but he could not make it out. "Who are you?" Daro asked, stepping to stand between Grey and the mysterious figure.

Only an outline of the man was visible beyond the flames, but the fire was too intense for Daro to focus on it.

"I am Heinsvick, the warlock," the man responded.

Daro raised his swords defensively in front of himself. "You mean Heinsvick, the vampire lord!" he screamed over the fire.

"Yes, that as well."

"Well, vampire, you may think you have won, but this fight is far from over. And if you harm Sasha, you will be sorry," Daro said through gritted teeth.

"You would do well to lose your anger, dear ranger, for I am no enemy."

"You wound my friend here and trap me with your sorcerer flames and call yourself no enemy?" Daro asked with a chuckle.

"Don't be a fool, ranger; if I wanted you dead, you would already be dead. We fight a common enemy, and I am here to offer my services."

"Where is Sasha?"

"As I have already said, approaching death's door. She will need our assistance if she is to survive."

"Why should I believe a word you have said, you undead filth?" Daro snapped back.

"Because I am here to rescue you from this trap and to fight beside you if you are wise enough to do it. Anything less will result in the death of your friend."

"Who is the common enemy that you speak of?" Daro asked, relaxing and understanding that the creature might speak the truth.

"Its name is Vasheba, and it is a powerful demon. The creature took over as the new lord of Novafontera months ago."

"A demon? That is unlikely," Daro argued.

"The times are changing, ranger. Unfortunately, this is but a foreshadowing of what is to come. And I believe your friend will be banished to hell if you disagree with this arrangement."

"Arrangement?" Daro growled.

"Yes, working together to slay the demon lord."

"We have come to find a lost sword, not to fight a demon lord and surely not to ally with a vampire," Daro said stubbornly.

The ranger tried to keep Heinsvick in sight, but the task was difficult. The flames burned hot and bright, and the best he could do was catch a glimpse of the vampire lord, who now eagerly paced on the other side of the flames. His pale complexion hinted at his state of undeath, and his red eyes nearly glowed, even in the light of the fire.

"And so, your friend is doomed, then? Not much of an ally to her, are you, ranger?"

The vampire's words dripped with venom, and Daro nearly charged through the fire to lash out at the undead creature. But, instead, he bit back his words and stayed his hand, hoping to find another way out of the obvious trap. Even if the vampire lied to him, what did he have to lose?

And if the creature was sincere with his offer to help them, how could he stubbornly refuse?

"Very well, vampire, free Grey and get me out of this trap so that we may help Sasha."

"Ahh, you do have some good sense, ranger. I wondered if you would let Sasha die because of your prejudice against my kind."

Daro let the words roll off his back and only smiled. "I have encountered your kind, and there is nothing good to say about the undead. My prejudice is well warranted."

"Very well. Trust me and take my hand," Heinsvick said, reaching into the flames with an outstretched hand.

Daro only chuckled and shook his head. "I am not a sorcerer; I cannot resist the flames," he said, sheathing his swords and glancing at Grey, who lay very still.

"There are no flames, ranger."

Daro laughed loudly and shook his head. "I am no fool, vampire. Tell me how to get Grey out of this, and I'll do it myself."

"Grey is not here but is resting comfortably in that jungle you call home. And as for you being a fool, that remains to be seen."

Daro nearly redrew his swords, wanting to lash out at the vampire. However, although arrogant, something inside him felt the creature was speaking the truth. He needed to give him the benefit of the doubt for Sasha's sake.

"Very well, Heinsvick. I'll trust you, but do not doubt I will destroy you if anything should happen to Grey or Sasha."

"I could have destroyed you long ago or left you to the demon's illusions that fill your head. Then she could come and destroy you after she finishes with your friend. But instead, I choose to help because we now share a common enemy. We must work together to defeat the new queen of Novafontera. Only our joint efforts will see this through."

Heinsvick stepped into the flames and stood unharmed in the middle of the fire, his extended hand now closer to Daro and past the wall of flames. It was unburned, and if the fire caused the vampire discomfort, he did not show it. Daro could only discern that the powerful creature had a ward against the blaze.

Heinsvick stepped through the fire then and said, "You weak-minded fool. Our time is short. Do you still not see that we are in an empty room?

There is no wolf, and there are no flames. It is a powerful spell the demoness has placed on you to hold you at bay until she slaughters your friend. In time she will come for you as well."

Daro looked at his surroundings but could not call them illusions. He looked at his hand and saw the wet blood from Grey's fur, and he keenly felt the heat from the roaring fire surrounding him. He did not believe any of it to be an illusion.

"Give me your lantern," Heinsvick said in resignation.

"What?"

"Your lantern. Give it to me, and I will show you the illusion."

Daro looked at the vampire doubtfully but knew that time was of the essence if Sasha was in trouble and battling a demon. He unfastened the small lantern from his belt and handed it over. Heinsvick immediately threw it to the ground with such force that it shattered, spraying burning oil all over Grey.

"No!" Daro screamed and dived to pat out the flames consuming his dear friend.

Instead, he found the fire burning beneath the great wolf, as if Grey were transparent. His mind raced, trying to process what he was seeing. Then Heinsvick was there, kneeling beside him. His sudden presence nearly had Daro falling over as the power the creature exuded overwhelmed his ranger senses.

"Your friend is not here; he is an illusion, simply a babysitter for the foul demoness," Heinsvick explained.

Then the vampire returned his hand to the flames and waved it around. "Again, an illusion," Heinsvick said, then put his hand in the fire from the lantern, jerking it back immediately. "And this is no illusion," he added, holding up the palm of his hand to show the bright-red burn on his pale skin.

That final act broke the spell as Daro looked around and realized he and the vampire were in a small, empty room. It was dark and cool as the fire's heat disappeared with the illusion's visual effect. Grey was gone, the prison of fire removed. The vampire was either toying with him or genuinely trying to assist Sasha and him. Daro looked in the dim light to find the vampire had extended his hand again.

"Come, we must go. It may already be too late for your friend," Heinsvick said.

Daro did not delay and took the cold hand. As soon as he did, he felt himself grow thin and fly across space. He had felt that odd sensation before and knew immediately that the vampire was teleporting him. He readied himself for what would await him at the end of that spell's journey, but nothing could have prepared him for the awful scene they found.

Sasha never noticed Daro's absence from her side as light deep in the tunnel guided her, almost calling to her. She was so focused on the strange light that she never registered that Daro's lantern no longer produced light because it was no longer beside her. Sasha quickened her pace as she grew closer, knowing that the light was a beacon for her. She knew that she would find Iustia, the ice sword, there. Her clouded mind barely registered Daro's voice calling her name, which sounded very far away. She dismissed it and carried on, having one goal in mind, Iustia, which was within her grasp. Her deceived mind did not consider the dangers of being separated from Daro.

Once close to the source, she discovered the light spilled into the tunnel from a side passage. The flicker of fire danced on the tunnel wall, the product of a large fire burning in the new tunnel. She entered the opening and found a small corridor that quickly ended in a dead end with another passageway to the left. She could not see into that second passage, but she discovered the source of the light, spying part of a brazier in the new opening from where she stood. As she studied the doorway and the brazier, it became apparent that the second passage was actually a small room.

Most importantly, the smell that emanated from that room was overbearing. It was so bad that Sasha considered discarding her helm to cover her nose. It was a disgusting odor of rotting flesh and something she could only imagine as the smell of evil. But, undeterred, Sasha advanced into the smaller tunnel that led to the room and saw a lever on the wall to her left. She felt compelled to lower it, so she did, without much thought of what it was or its consequences, her senses dulled and her mind still not understanding that Daro was gone.

There was a rumbling, and the ground shook as a large stone slab began to lower from the ceiling behind her, blocking the tunnel from which she had come. Sasha turned and watched it; she had plenty of time to run out before the slab sealed off her escape, but she felt no desire to do so. When it finally completed its descent, she turned around and made her way to the small room, where the stench grew more substantial.

She turned the corner and found several braziers, as she expected, burning within. Her mind was still foggy, but her focus was taken by the fleshy membrane that stretched out to cover the entire far side of the room. She doubled over, dry-heaving, and eventually removed her helmet, tossing it aside so she could hold one hand over her nose. The horrid-looking wall seemed like human skin pulsing with life. Large veins ran along its length, and Sasha could see the blood pumping through them. She even noticed spots on the wall that contained large, coarse hairs. She doubled over again and retched.

The episode broke the fogginess in her mind, and as Sasha collected herself, she suddenly realized she was all alone. She turned toward the sealed-off corridor and whispered, "Daro?"

There was no answer and no trace of her friend. She walked back to the lever and attempted to lift it, hoping the slab would rise. She panicked at the thought of being trapped in the small room behind her that contained the awful-smelling wall of human flesh. The lever would not budge, no matter how she tried. It would not open, and there was no turning back. She had to face the awful wall and whatever creature had created it. After collecting herself, she took a deep breath, drew her sword, and returned to the room.

The smell assaulted her again, and she put a hand to her nose. She walked right up to the abomination and studied it. The fleshy membrane seemed to pulse, and as she watched, she understood it was not throbbing, but something inside of it was moving! She took a step back and readied her sword. She thought there were people moving inside it. If she focused hard enough, she could see through the wall and the vaguely human shapes running around inside the flesh as if looking for a way out. Sometimes they would smack and claw at the membrane from within, and she could faintly hear their horrific moans. Other times, they would become entangled and bite and claw each other.

Sasha also noticed furniture in the wall, turned haphazardly, sometimes floating and sometimes resting on the floor. The wall was like a gelatinous thing that held anything that entered it. She considered using her sword to slice it open to free those caught within. But then her eye caught something else in the far reaches of the fleshy wall—a weapons rack with many polearms, bows, and swords! She knew in her heart that Iustia was there. She also knew the only way to reach it would be to enter the wall and become a prisoner.

"What is this place?" she said to herself.

The closest thing to hell you can get without actually being there, a deep, unworldly voice echoed in her head.

Sasha's eyes widened, and the hairs on her neck stood on end. She knew a creature was behind her, the same one now in her head. It took her many moments to find the courage to turn and face it—a creature she could only have imagined in her nightmares. The thing had black, leathery skin and stood twice her height. Giant bat-like wings sprouted from its back, and its hands ended in claws. Its face was deformed, with its toothy maw taking up most of it. Drool continuously dripped from the large and wicked-looking mouth. Its eyes were a beady red, and they seemed to pierce her, the intensity unnatural and evil.

However, the worst part was the wicked-looking barbed chain wrapped around its waist several times. The chain was as black as the creature's skin, and blood and gore covered the long ends that dragged on the ground.

Sasha had faced many opponents in the bowels of Iciale, most non-carofex, but she had never seen anything quite as terrifying as what stood before her then. Her knees nearly buckled with fear, but she swallowed her emotions and brought her sword and shield to the ready. She wished that Daro were still with her. She had fought him briefly when they first met, and he had eluded some of her best moves. That proved he was a good swordsman, and she desperately needed him.

Your doubts are well-founded, fool, the creature hissed in her head. *Your arrogance will be your downfall.*

The beast stood perfectly still; the only movement was the constant drool running down its chin. Sasha put aside her fear and advanced on the creature. She focused on keeping the beast out of her head, although she could feel it inside, rummaging around, reading her thoughts and memories. Sasha decided to take the initiative and attack while it played with her mind. She slashed across as she charged in, the attack perfectly placed to gash open the monster's belly.

She immediately felt herself tense up as if every muscle suddenly didn't work correctly. Her strike was true; her attack was impeccable. However, her actions slowed as if she were cutting through water, but the creature before her was unaffected. It had to be a spell the beast had conjured, yet she could not change her movement, compelled to complete the swing. At her slowed pace, it would take her several minutes to finish the attack.

You are used to getting your way, are you not? You are used to men fawning over you, caving to your desires. You are arrogant because your god-like features have made you that way, the creature said, taking two extra-long fingers and pinching Sasha's sword.

It pulled it quickly from Sasha's grasp and tossed it across the room. Sasha heard it clang to the floor, then bounce off the far wall. To her horror, she could not react or even look back. Her hands were empty, but she continued her swing as if she still possessed the sword. She could not stop her movement, and the creature was beside her then. She knew her doom and thought of her mother. She had failed her, and that broke her heart.

And now you will pay for that arrogance, the beast said, gently touching Sasha's armor with one of those wicked fingers.

Sasha could feel the touch, and although it did not hurt, she felt a ripple run the length of her armor, weakening it considerably. The creature walked around her, speaking telepathically and with those awful chains dragging on the ground behind her.

And so, I will bless you in the bowels of hell. There you will become a whore of some renown. Demon lords will hear of your beauty and come from leagues away to rape, hurt, and torture you.

"No!" Sasha yelled, somehow finding the strength to partially break the paralysis.

Her swordless strike now reached about a third of its journey. She felt compelled to continue it, even though the creature was directly behind her. She felt her armor lighten and smelled its corrosion as pieces began to fall off and turn to dust.

And now you know your doom. In moments, you will become my trophy, hell's beautiful whore.

Sasha struggled to break the slowness; her life depended on it. Her arms quivered with effort. And yet, she could do nothing as the creature raked away her padding to leave her in a thin shirt and breeches.

I also know of your plan, girl. You will not retrieve the sword, and

Marnelphion will remain safe from your murderous plotting, the voice echoed in Sasha's head.

She did not understand that last statement. Who was Marnelphion, and to what plotting was the nasty creature referring? The beast obviously did not have perfect knowledge of her desires, nor had it sorted out the real reason for her being there. It was in her head, but it had not deciphered her thoughts fully. That was a small victory, but she considered it moot as the long, filthy fingers of the beast closed around her neck.

It lifted her straight off the ground, bringing her to eye level. Then, as it choked off Sasha's air, it brought its other hand up and touched her forehead with an extended finger.

Tell me your secrets, child, the creature said.

The pain in Sasha's head was overwhelming, and she screamed out. Then, finally, the numbness of the slowing spell wore off, and she began to kick and thrash, once again able to move freely. However, that did little to comfort her as the pain in her head grew even more severe.

Tell me of the plot against Marnelphion, half-breed.

Sasha did not understand the question; the throbbing pain only made her kick more frantically. She would have screamed in denial that she knew nothing of Marnelphion, but Sasha knew it didn't matter, that the creature was already reading her thoughts. Her eyes rolled into the back of her head, and she became still, darkness overcoming her.

Yes, we know about your pathetic plot to slay Marnelphion. But I will destroy you and the sword. Now tell me where to find it. Sasha could barely hear the beast and only vaguely noticed the sudden appearance of Daro in the small hallway.

Vasheba had set the trap, and the two fools had easily entered it. Her illusions now occupied the idiot ranger, and the unique half-human specimen in her grasp would fetch much attention from the demons who roamed the human world. She would breed the woman, raising a group of attractive half-demons to cause mayhem. Vasheba would not take her to hell because with the Rho girl dead, Marnelphion wouldn't come, couldn't come. She would stay and rule Novafontera in his absence. Her beautiful new prisoner need not know the truth; the threat of taking a mortal to hell always frightened them and made their minds easier to read. Her plans were glorious, but the woman's answers puzzled the demoness.

Vasheba knew of the legends of Slebel, the mighty sword that could destroy a demon instantly. Marnelphion was no fool; he knew of Nezeratu's plot. The demon lord was Marnelphion's greatest rival and was jealous of the prophecy. He resided on the highest level of hell and had sent minions to the world with Slebel to stop Marnelphion upon his arrival. Now with Marnelphion's summoning foiled, the sword mattered little. Still, Vasheba wanted it out of circulation; if it was powerful enough to slay Marnelphion, she couldn't stand against it either.

She knew the beautiful creature she had captured was there to steal the sword. Slebel was in Novafontera. It was a mystery how it had made its way from hell to the human city, but Vasheba wanted it. She was not safe in the mortal world as long as it existed. But the surface thoughts of the woman indicated she didn't know of the legend of Slebel. Was there a different sword the beautiful creature sought? Vasheba found that unlikely but didn't dismiss the notion. She brought her finger to the woman's head once more; she would find out what she could.

Daro emerged from the dizzying effects of the teleportation spell to find a large, hideous, demon-like creature holding Sasha off the ground by her throat. Smoke wafted up from Sasha's forehead, where the beast held a long, crooked finger. Sasha made no move to defend herself, and Daro could not be sure she was alive. Although disoriented from the spell-like power of the vampire, he could not wait for the effect to pass. He ran straight toward the demon, unsheathing his swords as he did.

She towered over him, but he had the element of surprise, so he sliced hard as he ran past her. Both swords dug in deeply as he passed, and out gushed dark ichor, covering his hands and weapons.

The demon screamed in outrage and pain and dropped Sasha, who crumpled to the floor. Daro shouted her name, but she did not stir. He was almost sure she was dead, and that made him angry. He turned back toward the monster, who began twirling a nasty-looking barbed chain with a long section in each hand. He knew one hit from that awful weapon would spell certain doom. As he braced himself for battle, he vaguely smelled a horrible odor. He could not place it, but it smelled like rotting flesh. He was also aware of the strange wall that was behind him. He had noticed it when he ran past the demon but dared not turn to examine it.

"I am Vasheba, Lord of Novafontera, Eater of Dreams! How dare you strike me, fool! You will feel the bite of my chain."

Daro, usually one to taunt his opponents before destroying them, had nothing to say. The sadness enveloped him as the potential loss of Sasha took his words. He simply wanted to kill the beast; nothing else mattered. Words seemed so pointless. He would let his weapons speak for him. He was about to charge the nasty beast when a thunderous retort echoed through the small room. There was a bright flash from behind the monster, and it shrieked once again in pain. A gush of demon blood sprayed the far wall. It turned, and Daro noticed a large, smoking wound on its shoulder. Daro looked past the beast and saw the vampire; Heinsvick had joined the fight.

Vasheba turned and swung the vicious chain at Heinsvick. The vampire was wise enough to teleport next to Daro, the chain passing harmlessly through the space he had occupied moments before. Daro was already moving, sliding under the demon's legs and slashing her thighs. Vasheba howled as black, sticky blood began to pool around her. No novice to battle, her wounds only made her enraged. She summoned one of her demonic powers as Daro regained his feet and set himself for another attack. She used a powerful telekinetic ability to pick the ranger off his feet and send him flying into the fleshy wall with a jerk of her arm.

Daro turned himself so his back hit the wall, expecting to bounce off the membrane and straight back into battle. What he didn't foresee were the many hands that grabbed at him when he struck the supernatural wall. A second lightning bolt struck Vasheba in the face, making the creature howl in pain. She lashed out at Heinsvick, but her attack was blind, and he was already on the other side of the room when the chain struck the floor where he had just moved from. Chips of stone flew off the floor and showered Daro.

Daro realized with horror that the hands that grabbed and held him were pulling from the other side of the membrane and were not extensions of the wall itself. Humans were on the other side of that wall, trying to pull him through. Their pull was strong, and he struggled not to be sucked in, for he knew to do so meant certain doom. One hand grabbed him around the mouth and pulled hard, cutting off his oxygen. Two more held his arms to his sides, making it impossible for him to use his weapons. He struggled mightily not to be pulled into the other-worldly membrane. However, he was losing the fight.

Then he saw the demon focus on him. A third bolt of lightning from the vampire slammed it in the back, and he saw the spray of demon ichor splatter on the walls again. But it didn't faze Vasheba, her hate focused solely on Daro. He saw her eyes narrow, and he knew doom. The demon lashed out at him with those nasty chains. He could not move, and to remain stationary meant his death. So, he did the only thing he could—he stopped fighting, dropped his swords, and was jerked into the membrane just before the chains dug in behind him.

Inuentas had watched the spectacle unfold from the other side of the fleshy membrane. He stood within his protective sphere, just feet away from the wall that Daro had become attached to. He witnessed those hands from his side of the wall as dozens of angry souls rushed up and grabbed at him, feverishly trying to pull him in. He had also witnessed Sasha fall to the demon and felt the sword call to her as she struggled against the beast that was Vasheba. It was not Slebel, of course, the powerful artifact strapped to his hip. No, it was another sword somewhere nearby, equally powerful and dangerous.

He ignored the sentient weapon and focused on the information at hand. He had picked up on Vasheba's telepathic conversation with Sasha and was surprised to learn that the creature knew of the plot to assassinate Marnelphion. How had the demon learned of his mission?

He dared not move into the room and dispatch the wounded demon. He could easily do so, but if the creature thought the female was at the heart of the assassination, he could not reveal himself and jeopardize the mission. Instead, he stayed and watched, happy to let her take the blame. When the male was pulled fully into the wall, he knew he was as good as dead, the liquid of the membrane being extremely poisonous to mortals. Inuentas was slightly amused as the man struggled to fight the swarming souls of the damned. It was a battle the human could not hope to win. Then he faintly heard the sword call out once more to the female, and he turned to his left, seeing the weapon resting easily on a sword rack in the middle of the membrane. An idea came to him.

He moved his protective sphere toward the struggling man, and as it got closer, it began to repel the lost souls that were intent on killing him. They tried to pull their victim with them, but the magic of Inuentas was too powerful, and soon the man was entirely in the protective shell with the half-demon. Inuentas watched as the man struggled to breathe, coughing up some of the liquid that made up the membrane. His body rejected the liquid, and it was a deathly black as it clung to his chin and lips. Again, Inuentas looked on in amusement.

Daro could suddenly breathe again and sucked the delicious air into his burning lungs. He coughed up black, foul-tasting liquid that clung to his face like glue. It took him several moments to realize he was still within the evil wall. However, now he was in a protective barrier and watched as the many human-like creatures ran around that sphere, sometimes back and forth in front of him as if looking for a way to get to him once again.

After gaining his bearings, he realized he was not alone in the protective sphere. Another demon-like creature stood beside him. He was not nearly as horrifying as the one he had just battled but was more human-like. He had black, beady eyes, red skin, and a barbed tail waving menacingly over his shoulder. He also carried a large sword and donned silk clothing that looked expensive enough for royalty. Daro stood as quickly as his shaking legs let him and drew his daggers from his boots. He backed as far away from the new adversary as possible without exiting the globe.

"Who are you?" he managed to cough out.

"Obviously not an enemy," Inuentas said, holding his arms out and looking around.

Daro looked on suspiciously, but the creature did not draw his weapon or look aggressive other than that wagging tail. Then Daro saw Sasha on the other side of the flesh wall, and she stirred, slowly sitting up and rubbing her temple with one hand.

"Sasha," Daro breathed, relaxing against the strange man.

"Yes. You can save her," the creature replied with a smile.

"Again, who are you, Red?"

"I am Inuentas, the Indomitable, and I am here to save you if you are wise enough to take advantage of my good nature."

Was he first teaming with a vampire lord, then making friends with a demon? Daro did not understand the strange turn of events.

"What a weird day," he whispered.

"Your friend will die if you do not get her that sword," Inuentas said, pointing to Iustia, which rested in the sword rack.

"That is the sword she seeks?" Daro asked, lowering his daggers.

"I do not know, but the sword seeks her. It cries for her," the half-devil answered.

Daro took a step toward the edge of the protective sphere. However, he quickly understood that he would have to fight through the crowd of creatures if he exited the bubble. They swarmed to the edge of it, sensing he was close to leaving the area. Inuentas put his hand on Daro's shoulder, and the ranger brought his daggers to bear, startled at the creature's touch.

"Easy, I can help," Inuentas said, holding his hands as if to indicate he meant no harm. "Walk with me." He turned and walked toward the sword.

Daro noticed the sphere moved as Inuentas did, staying centered around him. Daro took slow steps, keeping pace and eyeing Sasha through the fleshy wall. Daro felt Sasha would not make it at the slow pace they moved.

"Can you move faster?" Daro asked.

"No. It is not easy to move through the membrane. I am moving as quickly as I can. When we reach the rack, take the sword. I will then find a crease in the flesh from which you may give your friend the weapon."

Daro glanced at the raging battle between the demon and Heinsvick and saw how vulnerable Sasha was. Sasha would die if the vampire failed to defeat or at least occupy the beast. Time was of the essence, and Inuentas was not moving quickly enough to save her. He was about to burst through Inuentas's bubble and fight to the sword when he first took note of the magnificent blade. It seemed to glow a bright white, even through the magical, protective bubble. As it came closer and more into focus, he noticed the odd shape—one like a giant icicle. From what Daro could tell, it looked to be made of pure ice. Finally, they reached it, and the sphere slowly enveloped the weapon for what seemed like an eternity until, eventually, the entire weapon rack was in the globe.

"Take it," Inuentas said, then nodded back toward Sasha.

Daro turned away from the unusual weapon to see that the demon now had Sasha around the throat, holding her limp form off the floor like a rag doll. Daro picked up the blade, which was so cold to the touch that it burned his hands.

He grimaced and yelled, "Take me to her!" through gritted teeth.

Slowly, the protective sphere began to move toward the membrane wall. Daro had never felt so anxious in all his life. He had to reach Sasha; he could not let her die.

Heinsvick witnessed the ranger being pulled into the unusual, fleshy wall just moments before the wicked chain sliced a gash into it. He could hear the moans of the poor souls trapped within as if the cut damaged their very being. To his amazement, the wound closed almost immediately with a sickly slurping sound, and within a few moments, the gash was gone, just like the ranger. He turned his attention back to the demoness, smoke still wafting from her burned face. She showed no fear of him and gave that evil smile. He focused, understanding that if he wanted his city back, he would have to take it himself.

His depleted lightning spell would no longer serve him, so he switched to another tactic and summoned a globe of energy. The magical power was the same spell that Cassandra had learned all those years ago from Ronnis's book of magic. However, Heinsvick was much more proficient in magic than Cassandra. Although her powers had grown, they did not compare to the vampire lord's. His spell engulfed his right hand with a crackling, purplish ball of deadly energy. Where Cassandra's spell could take half the face off a person, Heinsvick's could obliterate a good-sized human.

He released the ball of energy right into the opening maw of Vasheba and didn't wait to see its effect. Instead, he summoned another globe of deadly power, throwing it in right behind the first. A third and a fourth such attack followed and continued until nearly a dozen of them slammed into the demon, who now lay crumpled on the floor, a smoldering, bubbling pile of melted ooze.

Heinsvick approached, looking for that deadly chain. Oddly, he could not find it in the putrid remains. The young female trespasser, lying nearby, stirred and moaned, and he became distracted by her beauty. She was gorgeous by human standards but would easily make a goddess take notice. He had never witnessed such beauty in his entire existence and became entranced with her. If his heart still beat, it would skip one at that moment. How had he not noticed the physical perfection of that one?

The distraction cost him dearly as the whir of Vasheba's deadly chain sounded from behind. He did not have time to teleport away and barely had the opportunity to roll forward. He felt the chain's sting as it dug into his back, slicing easily through his skin and a few ribs. He grimaced at the sharp pain and came out of his roll to face the creature, only to find the other end of the vile weapon coming around for an attack.

His first instinct was to raise his right arm to block the attack. Luckily for him, he knew the devastation of that weapon and instead fell back to the ground. That kept his arm from being severed, but it did not stop the attack as the barbed chain dug through his chest, cutting through more ribs and his lungs. Somehow, his spine remained intact, but the wound was mortal, and he fell to the ground.

His vision blurred from the pain; he saw the beast standing over him, completely unharmed.

"How?" he whispered.

He then glanced at the remains that he thought were the demon. They were gone, and he then understood his folly, remembering what he had told the ranger earlier about the illusions the monster was capable of creating. He had fallen for just that; he had attacked something that wasn't even there. However, this thing that stood before him was no illusion, and neither was the weapon. He was doomed.

Vasheba had outsmarted him, and he cursed himself for not seeing the truth. Now, he waited for the killing blow, the pain in his body overwhelming his ability to summon a spell to take him away. The beast smiled wickedly, and drool splattered on the floor and his legs. As it seeped into his skin, he felt the evilness of the creature, and despair took him. He gave up and lay his head down, welcoming death.

However, it never came. A small voice that seemed very far away called out and brought him back to reality. The voice came from the woman with goddess-like beauty. Whether it was from his need to see her one last time before he perished or the fact her voice broke the hold the demon had on him, he refocused on his surroundings. The creature was no longer near him but faced the woman, who now held her sword at the ready once more. Heinsvick watched the woman's movements and knew she was a seasoned warrior. He hoped her skills would allow her to injure the demon before it killed her. There was no way to destroy it without Heinsvick and the ranger to help.

"Leave him alone, filth!" the woman screamed, even though the effort seemed to cause her head to throb, as she instinctively brought a hand up to her temple.

The beast paid Heinsvick no more mind and moved to confront the woman. He felt his blood pooling around him and dared not look at the wound to his chest. He knew the demon had destroyed him, and with most of his spells depleted, he knew he could no longer assist his new allies. The fight was over as soon as it had begun, as he heard the sword clang to the floor. He opened his weary eyes to see the demon holding the woman off the ground by the throat; the beautiful warrior kicked her legs and struggled to free herself. Vasheba brought her right hand to her newest victim, touching a long, wicked finger to her forehead. How the woman thrashed then as the demon raped her mind.

Then Heinsvick noticed something peculiar: the wall bulged near the woman and soon split open. He could vaguely hear the shrieks of the doomed souls trapped within, but the demon didn't seem to notice, now focused on devouring the beautiful woman's mind. To his amazement, a sword shaped like a giant icicle slipped through the opening in the fleshy wall. At first, Heinsvick thought he was imagining it and rubbed his eyes to verify he was not. As the sword continued to come into view, a gore-covered hand followed it.

He gingerly sat against the wall to better see the event before him. He held his wounded chest with the stump of his left arm, hoping his insides would not spill across the floor from his efforts. The old stump reminded him why he had returned to battle the demon. He thought of Emiline, and his hatred grew for Matilda. He had amputated his left hand to free himself from servitude to the nasty priestess. That old wound now meant little as his new ones would surely kill him without the healing dirt from his coffin. The demon before him had destroyed his coffin, spilling its precious contents all about the dungeon in Novafontera's castle. Hate filled him, and that hatred helped him summon the energy to continue the fight.

He called forth one of his most powerful spells that could disintegrate any substance. He pointed a shaking finger at the great demon and summoned the grey beam of light that shot toward the beast. It contacted Vasheba's arm, burning a hole, quickly cutting through its tough skin and bone. The beast dropped the woman to the ground and howled in pain. Heinsvick knew that was no illusion; the scream was real, as was the creature now turning back in his direction. As she returned on the offensive, waving her chain for a deadly strike, he saw a man emerge from the wall holding the sword. He could not be sure because black and red sludge from the membrane covered the new arrival, but it appeared to be the ranger returned from the dead and carrying the icy blade that Heinsvick sensed was extremely powerful.

Vasheba did not notice the new arrival, her attention squarely on Heinsvick now. The demon slammed the chain down for a killing blow, but Heinsvick managed to summon a shield of magical energy that thwarted the attack. Sparks flew in all directions as the weapon slammed into the invisible shield just inches from his face. The creature swung repeatedly, and Heinsvick struggled to keep the protection in place. Her rage would eventually win; he just hoped to distract the beast long enough for the beautiful female and gore-covered ranger to destroy it.

Daro stepped through the opening Inuentas created on the face of the fleshy wall. It was still an exasperatingly slow process, so he forced the sword out as quickly as possible when the opening first appeared. When Sasha, hanging limply in the demon's clutches, didn't respond to the sword's appearance, he forced himself through, ignoring the foul-smelling gore in the slight space between the opening and Inuentas's protective sphere. The creatures within the wall pulled and clawed at him in the brief distance he had to traverse, but nothing could stop him; he had to save Sasha.

By the time he made his way out of the membrane, the demon had luckily focused its attacks on the vampire again. He noticed the blood pooling around the undead creature and assumed the vampire was mortally wounded. Daro was unsure if the demon could easily kill the vampire, recalling the battle with the three lesser vampires in his woods. He had destroyed one of them, or so he thought before it had assumed a gaseous form and floated away. He shook the thoughts from his head; he could not focus on that now, and he went to Sasha, who lay motionless on the floor.

"Sasha, can you hear me?" he said, cradling her head in his arms.

Her eyes fluttered open, and she looked up at him, pupils dilated, and seemingly staring into space. She looked around to gain her bearings and brought a hand to her temple. She was grimacing from the obvious pain in her head.

"Sasha," he said once more, and she finally looked at him as if noticing him for the first time.

She sat up and moved away from him. If he had seen himself in a mirror, he would have understood her reaction as he was covered head to toe in the foul liquid of the fleshy wall. He stood and tried to help her stand, but she recoiled and found her footing.

"Sasha, it's me!" he said, holding his arms out.

She looked at him through slitted eyes as if trying to figure out who stood before her. There was slight recognition as her eyes flew open fully, and a relieved smile came to his face.

"You look horrible," she said, rubbing her temple and squinting her eyes.

Then her expression changed, and her eyes widened. Her temples suddenly no longer seemed to be a concern for her.

"Iustia," she whispered, noticing the sword in his hand.

Daro's smile disappeared, and he crunched up his brow in confusion. "No, it's me, Daro," he answered.

She stifled a laugh and pointed to the weapon.

"What?" he asked.

"Iustia," she repeated, pointing to the sword.

"Oh, this? Yes, your sword!" he exclaimed, presenting the powerful sword, hilt-first.

Rapid concussions filled the room then, startling both, and they turned to see Vasheba repeatedly flailing at the prone vampire with that wicked chain. Daro recognized the sparks that flashed before the vampire and glimpses of the magical shield that protected him from those strikes. As he looked on, he felt the sword pulled from his hand. He turned to see Sasha now grasping it, a wild look in her eyes as she held the blade up before her. He instinctively stepped back as she seemed to transform at touching the weapon.

Her skin turned a bluish color immediately, and her eyes seemed to sparkle, like how the sun reflects on water. In his mind, she seemed to become one with the sword, as if joining the two created one super force. A smile crept across her beautiful face as Daro stood there, covered in filth and his mouth agape. She turned toward the demon and ran straight for it before Daro regained his bearings. There were no words to express his awe for his most unusual new friend. He shrugged, drew his daggers, and followed.

Heinsvick was weak, too weak to maintain the protective magic that absorbed the strikes of that wicked weapon. Just as his resolve failed, the female ran swiftly toward the demon, the new icicle-like sword in hand. He watched her with great satisfaction, for he knew the bite of the weapon would significantly hurt the monster if it was comprised of ice. Sure enough, as the creature prepared for a deadly strike with its chain, the woman ran the ice sword deep into its thigh. And the beast howled like never before, the icy blade cutting through its tissue as a hot blade through butter. It severed tendons and ran through its thigh bone with that one stab, and the creature pitched to one side, landing hard on one trembling knee.

Heinsvick had a pretty good idea of what defensive tactic the demon would use, being a master at deception and illusion. He recognized the ability as it began to take shape. The teleportation spell would take the creature out of harm's way, and Heinsvick could not have that. He called upon his teleportation spell and tried a problematic maneuver that he had only successfully completed once in his long existence. He reversed the properties to teleport, manipulating the magic that gave the demon that ability. He understood the probability of doing so was minimal and knew enough of magic to know that only a true warlock, one born with the ability to manipulate magic, could hope to do so—someone like himself.

The beast blinked out of existence for just a moment but found itself in the same position that it was in before. It had worked: Heinsvick had held it in place! The stunned expression of the creature, one of pure panic, gave the vampire a sense of great satisfaction. Vasheba had destroyed the harem he had hand-selected over the centuries, and this was his way of paying her back. He relished the idea that he had just foiled the demon's escape.

"For you, my lovelies," he whispered to his dead wives.

The female warrior took advantage of the demon's apparent failed escape and slashed a deep cut across the demon's belly, opening a large gash that poured black ichor. The creature howled in pain and swung its massive chain around, desperately trying to cleave the woman in half.

That move cost the demon its right arm as the icy sword severed it at the elbow. The monster was dying, and Heinsvick knew there was a chance for them to win. He summoned all his energy, sitting up the best he could while trying to hold in his guts. He had to immobilize the beast so the beautiful warrior could finish the task. The female warrior jumped, the sword held in both hands in an overhead stab, prepared to drive home the weapon and score the kill. The demon desperately called forth its power of telekinesis, and with a wave of its remaining hand, the woman flew backward. Heinsvick cringed, understanding the beautiful woman would smash into the far wall and probably die from the impact. He could not be distracted; now was when he expected the demon to retreat.

The beast tried to teleport to safety, but Heinsvick stubbornly held her once again. The demon was on both knees, turning a hateful stare upon him. She now understood the source of her failure and focused on him. He felt the sudden pull of the demon's telekinetic power and started sliding toward the creature. The demon's strength was weak, but his depleted energy prevented him from resisting. He slid along, leaving a bloody trail like a nightmarish slug. Before the demon pulled him into her waiting grasp and, most certainly, a painful death, he saw the ranger climb over the back of the great beast, two daggers plunging as he did. They sank deeply into the demon's eyes, one in each hateful orb. A smile found its way onto the old vampire's face as his slide of doom quickly stopped.

Daro watched in horror as Sasha was thrown hard against the far wall. He knew she would have difficulty surviving the impact, and his heart raced at the thought of losing her. As Sasha had battled the beast, Daro had battled the wicked demon's mental barrage. It had assaulted him as soon as he and Sasha had charged. Somehow, it had not affected his beautiful friend, and he could only surmise that it was due to the powerful properties of the sword. However, he was not immune; the despairing thoughts the demon projected onto him took hold, and he lost interest in the battle. But with the sight of Sasha flying, the demon's hold on him broke, and he charged once more at the monster.

He watched Sasha's flight from the corner of his eye as he began his charge again. He was directly behind the demon now, and nothing would stop him as he prepared to finish off the evil monstrosity. However, what he witnessed from his peripheral vision nearly had him stopping and staring at his surprising new friend. Before crashing into the wall, she somehow contorted and faced it at the last moment. She pointed her sword, and ice shot forth in a fan, quickly covering the wall. It happened in the blink of an eye, and the ice built up around the point of impact.

There was a loud crash that sounded like a million glass bottles exploding simultaneously, filling the air with shattered glass. Daro knew it wasn't glass, but instead, it appeared to be a porous wall of thin ice that softened the blow when Sasha crashed into it. Ice fragments flew all around his friend, and she still hit the wall with a sickening thud, but he felt the ice had cushioned the impact and saved her life.

"I'm in love," was all he could mutter as he jumped onto the back of the kneeling beast. He was agile enough to climb the beast's back, using its massive wings as footholds, never using his hands as he inverted the grips of his daggers.

It tilted its head back as he climbed, and he saw the evil eyes on him for a moment. He felt the despair creep back into his mind, and that was a place he did not wish to return to. So, he did what came naturally and stabbed his daggers straight into its demonic eyes. The powerful thoughts of despair quickly dissipated as his daggers plunged deep into the soft tissue. He barely noticed the roar and the wild swing from its remaining arm because he never stopped his dive, somersaulting and rolling several times on the floor, clearing some distance between him and the deadly demon. When the roll ended, he knelt, facing the beast. He brought his daggers up in front of him, each containing a single orb—the eyes of Vasheba.

Then he heard the screams from the vile creature as it thrashed around on its back, holding its face as black liquid spewed forth from its mortal wounds. He regarded the vampire that lay motionless near him, blood pooling around him, but could not consider him more than that, not with the monster still alive. He turned to finish the task but was again taken aback by Sasha. She slowly stood from the pile of ice, blood pouring from a wound to her head.

"Sasha!" he cried, but she seemed not to hear him as if she were in a deep trance.

Her focus was solely on the demon, and when the beast slowed its thrashing and eventually propped itself up on one good arm to face its assailant, time seemed to stop. Daro did not know how powerful the demon still was and did not discount its powers even in its weakened state. But when it started to giggle, choking on its blood like a demented child, a chill ran up his spine.

"Fool, you cannot win. I will tell Marnelphion of you; his minions will hunt you the rest of your days. I assure you that your death will be slow, and you will be most sorry for your actions here today."

Sasha only stared at the creature as the demon laughed at her, taunting her. Eventually, that stare turned into a grimace, and as the blood ran down her beautiful face from a large gash on her forehead, she reached an arm out to the pile of ice she had just crashed into. Her sword, Iustia, flew from the rubble and into her waiting hand. Daro watched in amazement as the sword grew bright, Sasha calling upon its strength. He dropped his hands to his sides and stared at her as the wound on her head slowly closed, the sword's power giving her the strength to heal. Daro had never seen such power before and was at a loss. He understood he was vulnerable to an attack from the demon as he gawked at the spectacle, but he could not pull his eyes away from the magnificence Sasha had become. He turned slowly to the beast, and though it was blind, it was looking straight in Sasha's direction. Its only movement was a slight twitch in its cheek or chin as it waited for its destruction, sensing the powerful woman before it.

Sasha closed her eyes as the healing power of the sword washed over her, and she opened them when the wound was thoroughly healed. Again, Daro saw the flicker deep in those orbs as the weapon's power coursed through her. Then with a growl, she pointed the sword at the demon, and Daro thought he heard a whimper from the monster. Soon the ice fragments scattered on the floor around Sasha shot forth in the direction the sword pointed. Hundreds of glass-like ice shards, the remnants of the pile of ice that had just saved her life, flew toward the demon. They sounded like arrows to Daro and passed at about the same speed. They struck the monster so forcefully that the first few passed through it and crashed into the opposite wall. The demon made no more sound, understanding its defeat. The smaller ice slivers impaled the beast, and the larger ones ripped it apart. Within moments, the creature toppled over and began to smoke.

Eventually, the body melted into a tar-like substance, slowly seeping into the floor. Even the eyeballs at the end of Daro's daggers melted into the same goo and dropped from the blades. Daro sheathed his weapons and ran to Sasha, still in awe of the spectacle. Those shining eyes and the bluish tint to her skin truly made her appear like a goddess. She sheathed the weapon, and the traits diminished. Her beauty did not as Daro stood there gawking at her. They just stared at each other that way for many moments, Sasha a perfect specimen of female beauty, and Daro covered in blood and foul-smelling gore from the evil wall.

Finally, Daro blurted out, "Some weapon."

With a smile and a slight nod, Sasha said, "Thanks."

"Are you all right?" he asked, pointing to the place on her head where the wound used to be.

"Yeah," she said, wiping away the remnants of blood there.

Daro could tell she was as shocked over what had happened as he was, but she noticed his gawking again, he was sure. He tried to shake the spell that was Sasha, but it was not easy. So, he did the only thing he could do and turned away, breaking the power of her gaze. The tar-like substance that was only moments earlier a demon was still being slowly absorbed into the stone floor.

"Is it dead?" he asked.

Sasha walked up beside him and only snorted. He turned to her and saw a genuine smile on her beautiful face. That was all the answer Daro needed.

He was about to ask her more concerning the powers of the sword when the nasty flesh-like membrane suddenly convulsed and shivered.

They took several steps back and watched as the wall slowly bruised and turned black. It seemed to melt, just as the demon had. They held a hand to their noses as the odor of rotting flesh overwhelmed them. The two looked on in horror as the tar pulled the souls of those poor victims that formed the strange fleshy wall, taking them to hell. Their doomed screams were real and pitiful. Sasha covered her ears as the strange event unfolded. Once the screams stopped and the wall was no more, they both noticed the strange demon-like creature that had saved Daro still standing comfortably in the protective sphere where the wall once stood, amid a grand weapon storage.

Sasha began to draw her sword at the sight of him, but Daro stayed her hand with a wave. "He is an ally. He saved me and led me to your sword."

"What?" Sasha asked.

"Truly, he is not an enemy."

Inuentas waited until the entire wall was a black pool of filth on the stone floor before dismissing his sphere. Only then did he reach the pair, carefully picking his way along to avoid stepping in the fading tar. Daro noticed the boots seemed exotic and made of a strange leather, and he assumed they contained magical properties. If the smell bothered him, he did not show it, but Sasha and Daro had to concentrate not to lose their most recent meals.

He was handsome by most standards, even with his demonic traits. The only thing that did not seem inviting was the man's barbed tail, which always waved menacingly behind him. Also, the sword on his belt seemed massive and deadly. Daro would not trust the creature if he had not saved their lives.

"Inuentas, this is Sasha De'Formen," Daro said, waving a hand to his friend.

"Well, well, what a prize," Inuentas said.

He reached for her hand and gently kissed the knuckles. Daro felt a pang of jealousy but quickly shook the feeling aside. Sasha pulled her hand back just as quickly, which gave Daro great satisfaction.

"And I am Daro, Keeper of the Woods."

"Ranger," Inuentas said and shook his hand with a solid grip.

The three watched as the last of the melted wall slipped into the stone and was gone, taking the damned souls with it.

"Where did you come from?" she asked.

"It is a long story I would like to tell both of you over a meal. First, we must exit this place at once."

"I am afraid we are trapped here unless we can leave the way you came in, Daro," Sasha said, looking at him hopefully.

Daro glanced over at the dead vampire and shook his head. "That way is no longer an option," he said sadly.

"Who was he?" Sasha asked, noticing the motionless body.

"Strangely enough, a friend. We are meeting a lot of strange allies today," Daro answered, looking Inuentas's way.

"Indeed," Inuentas agreed.

"Why did you not help us?" Sasha asked the demon.

"But I did. I saved Daro so he could retrieve the sword and give it to you. Without my assistance, you would all be dead."

"You know what I mean, you stayed in your hole and watched as we battled," Sasha said, a hand reflexively going to the hilt of her sword.

"Easy, beautiful one, I am no enemy," Inuentas said, raising his hands. "However, I assure you that as powerful as your sword is, it is not the most powerful one in this room."

Sasha glanced around the room at the many weapons, obviously intrigued by his words. Daro immediately looked at the fancy sword on Inuentas's belt. When he looked back to make eye contact with the demon, Inuentas wore a knowing smile.

"There is a reason for me to stay hidden. My purpose of being here cannot be jeopardized to save the two of you. I could not let Vasheba see me, or it would compromise my mission."

"Aren't you brave?" Sasha said and began to walk toward the prone vampire. After a few steps, she stopped and added, "Also, don't call me that."

Inuentas bowed, and Sasha turned and continued to the vampire. When she was out of earshot, Inuentas said softly to Daro, "Such amazing beauty and yet so feisty. I like it."

"You have no idea," Daro whispered back, and he could feel his cheeks grow warm from the jealousy the demon's words aroused in him.

His thoughts were interrupted by Sasha's surprised shout, "He is alive!"

Daro approached the vampire, where she knelt as Inuentas casually moved in a different direction to retrieve Daro's lost swords. The vampire was a mess, with blood pouring from a nasty wound on his chest where the stub of his left hand tried to hold back the blood flow. Daro understood the severity of the wounds. Perhaps Heinsvick would turn gaseous like the lesser vampire Daro had killed, then float away and become whole once more. Secretly, he hoped that; he was fond of Heinsvick. In truth, the ranger did not know much about vampires and did not know if he had destroyed the young vampire those months ago or if she still roamed the castle above him. Either way, he expected Heinsvick to turn insubstantial at any moment.

"Ranger," Heinsvick whispered weakly.

Daro knelt to hear him. His bottom lip quivered, and Daro could tell he was in immense pain. He pitied the creature.

"I assisted you. Now I ask a favor," Heinsvick said.

"You saved us all, and I will repay you, vampire. What is it that you ask?"

"On Varish, thousands of miles from here, is the mountain fortress called—" He coughed up a large amount of blood, and the fit lasted for quite a while.

Sasha tried to quiet him and comfort the dying creature, but there was not much she could do other than gently rub his shoulder. The healing properties of her sword would only work on an ice carofex.

"It is called Nesin," he said after composing himself. "It is near to Port Racip. Find Port Racip, and you can easily find Nesin."

Heinsvick fell into another coughing fit, and more blood spilled forth.

"What is in the fortress that you so dearly want me to find?" Daro asked.

"My greatest love, my Emiline."

"A vampire?" Daro asked, his thoughts lingering on the one he had killed, hoping it wasn't somehow the same creature.

"Yes, my greatest love. She is in the hands of Matilda, priestess of Marnelphion. Matilda is evil, and you must destroy her."

Heinsvick grabbed Daro's shirt, the strength in that grip surprising the ranger. "Promise me, ranger. Promise me that you will find my Emiline and set her free."

"I will do what I can; you have my word. However, I know nothing of this Matilda and do not know the exact location of Nesin."

"I know exactly who she is and precisely where to find her," Inuentas said, walking up to join them and handing Daro his weapons. "However, we must find a way out of this place first."

Daro, shocked by the words, stood and sheathed his swords. He looked at the vampire and saw the relief that washed over him. It was his dying wish, and Daro wanted to grant it if it comforted the creature in his final moments. He took heart that the vampire trusted him to complete the task. He vowed to do everything he could to see it through.

"So be it. You have my word, Heinsvick of Novafontera. I will find Emiline and free her from the clutches of the evil priestess," Daro said.

Sasha looked up at him inquisitively, and Daro could only shrug. Then Heinsvick grabbed Sasha's hand and coughed again, the grimace on his face indicating all the pain the action was causing.

"Tell her I love her. Tell her I never stopped loving her," the dying vampire lord said.

Tears filled Sasha's eyes, and she could only nod.

He struggled to speak once more. "Grab each other's hands, and I will… save you… once again," he whispered, his voice barely audible.

"He wants us to grab hands," Sasha said with a shrug.

Daro remembered how the undead warlock had teleported him to find Sasha near death at the hands of the demon. His eyes widened at the revelation, and he whispered, "Teleportation."

"What?" Inuentas asked.

"Never mind, just grab her hand," Daro shouted, taking one each of Inuentas's and Heinsvick's hands in his own.

Inuentas shrugged and held his hand to Sasha, who looked to Daro for support. He nodded, and so she took Inuentas's hand in her own. Since Heinsvick still held her other hand, they were all connected, the chain of hands linking them together. A fleeting idea of the vampire betraying them or sending them directly to Nesin invaded Daro's thoughts, but he quickly dismissed them. The vampire lord wanted them to live and succeed because he needed Daro to fulfill his oath. The world began to spin around him as the spell took hold. Sasha and Inuentas did not become blurred, but their surroundings did, and strangely, that included Heinsvick. Again, he thought of a betrayal and hoped the vampire lord had not just delivered them into a trap.

When the world stopped spinning, and he caught his bearings, Daro found himself outside the walls of Novafontera, near the grate that he and Sasha had used to enter the catacombs. Heinsvick had saved them once more.

As he cast his final spell of centuries' worth of powerful magic and teleported the three allies safely away, Heinsvick lay back on the cold stone floor and waited for death. The last time he was in Novafontera's castle, Vasheba had thrown his casket and smashed it against the wall, spilling the healing dirt all around. Without the casket whole and the earth concentrated in one place, he would have no way to regenerate. He would turn to a gas and, without the healing powers of his dirt, would fade into nothingness.

He had lived a long time and most of that as an undead creature. He thought of his harem, and his old heart ached. He thought of all the people he had wronged as a vampire, especially the innocent ones such as Emiline. He began to sob. He would be at peace if he could hold her one last time and kiss her again. If he could take back her affliction and remove the curse of undeath, he would. He had been selfish. Only then, at the moment of his death, did he care.

He thought of Emiline as he lay there crying. Then he thought of Kessi and how he had sentenced her to death, and his heart truly broke. Then finally, deep in the bowels of Novafontera and completely alone, the great vampire warlock died.

That night, on the other side of the world, Kessi and Emiline shared the same horrific dream where someone close to them had died.

Emiline opened her eyes with a start, and her heart broke, knowing that Heinsvick had passed. She wailed into her pillow, stifling the cries so no one could hear. She felt more alone then than she ever had. No one was to look after her now that her creator was gone. She also thought she had sensed the demise of Heinsvick's many other wives. However, she was connected by blood and spirit to Heinsvick, and she knew he was gone. Now she truly belonged to the awful humans, Matilda and Cerus. Her life was forfeit.

Kessi's heart beat quickly as she tried to awaken from the awful vision. Someone had died, but her clouded mind would not reveal who. She assumed it was her sister, but she could not be sure. A horrible feeling stayed with her for the next few days, and although she told no one about the dream, she knew someone she loved was gone. She didn't know how, but the feeling was real, as was the hole left in her heart.

❦ 287 ❦

10

ÏKMA

GREYSON AND ALLEAH DISCOVERED AN INLET NEAR TO WHERE they climbed ashore. They followed it, and it eventually spilled into a river. Not daring to cast his light spell for fear of being detected, Greyson guided Alleah the best he could through the dark forest. He kept her focused on escaping the danger and discouraged her from returning to rescue her sisters in faith. It was difficult for them, each sharing the guilt of losing many friends. However, they trudged on, keeping the river to their left and using it as a guide to stay on course, to travel away from the sea, and hopefully away from danger. They did not stop until the moon was high in the sky, which made the strange woods dark and ominous. They were utterly exhausted. They tried drinking from the river, but it was too briny for consumption. They sat, each against a large tree, catching their breath and giving their tired muscles a break.

It was cold, and they were both miserable in damp clothing. Luckily, the weather in that part of the world was much milder than in Pelesea, or they would have already perished from exposure. However, they had no food, water, or supplies, and Greyson knew they were in trouble. He closed his eyes and lay his head back against the tree, exhausted.

Sleep nearly took him, however, the sound of Alleah quietly sobbing snapped him out of his stupor. She sat against a tree and held her head, crying, finally overcome with grief. Greyson gingerly made his way to her, understanding her pain and the feelings of guilt she indeed felt. He sat beside her and draped an arm over her shoulder. Alleah was one of the most beautiful women he had ever encountered and one of the few he had given up trying to seduce. Her faith in Sinnis was strong, and the goddess's worshippers were required to remain chaste. That did not stop him from fantasizing about her or stealing a peek at her perfect figure when the opportunity presented itself.

However, after all the dreams he had had in the past months about ravaging her, he genuinely felt no sexual urges at that moment as he pulled her close. She was his friend and needed him. She cried all the harder, burying her face in his chest. He held her tight as her grief played out, silent tears running down his cheeks. Neither said a word because none were needed. All their friends, people close to Alleah and sisters of her goddess, were most likely dead. Alleah cried herself out and eventually fell asleep against him. He made himself as comfortable as possible and soon followed. They slept soundly, which cost them dearly.

The sun shone brightly in the mid-morning sky when something flashed in Greyson's eyes. It was so bright that he noticed it through eyes that still hid behind their lids. That slowly brought him from a deep slumber. When he finally blinked away from the sleep, he found that he still sat against the tree, Alleah's head in his lap. His sexual desires briefly took over at the sight, but he quickly fought them away as the metallic reflection shone in his eyes again.

He squinted as it danced about his face. His heart pounded in his chest when he finally recognized the silver-and-turquoise dragonfly for what it was. The metal creature flew about them, appearing and sounding like a real dragonfly, and Greyson would have thought that was precisely the case if it didn't reflect the morning light as it moved. It was metal, just like the one Captain Jessica had used to communicate with the dockmaster. Jessica, or one of her allies, was hunting them! He had to destroy it.

He shook Alleah roughly awake, and when she finally sat up with a start, he quickly reached for a rock and stood. His back and leg muscles groaned in protest, stiff from sitting all night. He slung the stone as hard as he could, and it missed badly, crashing harmlessly into the nearby brush. That was enough for the device to fly away, back down the river in the direction they had come. Greyson watched it helplessly as it flew out of sight.

"What was that thing?" Alleah asked.

"Jessica's toy."

"What?"

"A device I saw her with before I discovered her betrayal. It looks like a dragonfly but is metal, almost like a golem," Greyson explained.

His memories raced back to the tree token that had saved his life. It was a gift from his mentor, Berro, given just before Greyson was to journey from Tara. The token had seemed useless to him at first; once activated, it would grow into a large tree. Pointless, he thought. But during his flight from Cerus, he had used it to escape. It had saved his life, and he understood the value in the tokens. The dragonfly was similarly enchanted with powerful magic. He understood then that they could not escape the pursuit if their enemies had use of the pseudo-bug. He also wondered if Cerus the Grey was behind the attack on Alleah's sisters. It made sense that the warriors of Gorl would initiate an ambush on the priestesses. If Cerus was indeed in pursuit, they were in serious trouble.

"We have to go," was all he could say.

He did not want to frighten her, but he knew a little about Cerus and imagined he would probably rape and torture Alleah to death if he had her in his clutches. Those things would pale compared to what the evil man would do to Greyson if he ever saw him again. A chill ran down his spine, and he wasted no time fleeing deeper into the woods, Alleah beside him.

"Good news?" Cerus asked impatiently.

Jessica deciphered the whirring wings of the dragonfly golem as it sat upon her open palm. Although used by the captain mostly to send secret messages, the thing could communicate on a limited basis as well. However, that communication was difficult to interpret sometimes, and she knew Cerus was not a patient man.

"Yes, it has found them," she whispered, still concentrating on deciphering the whirring.

"Them? More than one sister of Sinnis?" the savage warrior asked with a satisfied grin.

Jessica looked up and saw the twinkle in the man's eye. He desperately wanted Alleah, the group leader who sailed with Jessica across the ocean. After the extensive damage to her ship during the storm, she wanted to assist Cerus in the hunt. However, she second-guessed her actions when considering the many tortures he would exact on poor Alleah. After all, Jessica didn't have anything against Alleah or any of the other priestesses and, in truth, liked them. But this was business; it was also personal after the damage to her prized ship.

"No, I believe it to be Alleah, their leader, by far the most beautiful of the group. With her is the one man who made the journey—more of a boy. His name is Greyson."

"What did you just say?" Cerus asked, his visage suddenly very serious.

"It is Alleah, your prize, and Greyson Kavince," Jessica repeated, backing away slightly.

"Kavince?" Cerus asked, and his expression changed to one of enlightenment as if he just remembered a forgotten secret. "There are no male followers of Sinnis, dear captain."

"No, he does not worship Sinnis; he worships another god entirely."

The neck muscles bulged on the volatile warrior, and he took a step closer, his jaw tightening like a vice. "What worthless god does he worship, then?"

"I can't remember," Jessica said, becoming unnerved by the giant man.

"Is it Plath?"

"Yes, yes, that is—"

"Liar!" Cerus screamed, making Jessica step backward and trip over a tangle of roots.

He towered over her, his breathing rapid, his chest heaving with each inhale. "Tell me, Jessica, where did you find this young man?"

Afraid to say any more, yet more terrified not to tell the truth, she said, "In Pelesea, across the ocean."

Cerus stood and rubbed his chin, contemplating her words. "Where is this Pelesea?"

"It is north of Novafontera, the dead city you visited with M—"

"Silence!" Cerus screamed.

Jessica obliged and just sat on the ground, not daring to move. She watched as Cerus paced and rubbed his chin, deep in thought. His men nervously looked on, giving their leader plenty of space. Two men guarded a prisoner, one of the priestesses of Sinnis. She was a pretty woman, or at least she would be again if she survived the ordeal. They had beaten her badly, and now one eye was swollen shut, and her lip was cut and bloodied. Jessica knew her from the three-week voyage and remembered her name: Chloe. Cerus brought her along as bait. She sat on a downed tree, her bound hands in front of her. She rested there like a beaten dog, her spirit broken.

Finally, Cerus turned to Jessica and said, "Why was this man with the followers of Sinnis?"

"I… I don't remember. Greyson was an emissary of some kind, possibly from Varish."

"From Tara?" Cerus asked with an evil grin.

"That sounds correct," Jessica lied, not remembering where the man was from.

"How far away are they from us?"

"I don't know. Two miles, maybe?"

He drew his massive spear strapped on his back. "Men, our prey are close! Set off at once, double speed. Attack to injure, but stay your kill shot. They are mine; I want them alive. Follow the river!" Cerus barked.

Ten Gorl warriors ran off immediately to the west, following the river as instructed.

"Bring her to me; do not let her escape," Cerus said and nodded to the two men dragging Chloe along before turning and charging in behind the others.

Soon Jessica was alone with her tiny golem. She did not understand the interaction she had just had with Cerus, and she stood slowly and brushed the dirt from her pants. She did not understand the man's obsession with Greyson Kavince, but she sent her dragonfly off again to find the duo, then trotted up to the men pulling their prisoner along. The faster this chase ended, the better off they would all be. If they could not catch them, Jessica had a bad feeling she would be on the receiving end of Cerus's wrath.

Greyson and Alleah kept running throughout the day, understanding that to stop meant their pursuers would gain ground. Greyson knew Jessica still followed them because he would occasionally spot the shiny dragonfly flitting about. It wouldn't stay but would pass by and head back the way it had come as if reporting on their location. He had no spells to stop it and could not waste time finding a way to knock it from the sky. They needed to find a town where they could hide. However, if all the settlements of Varish were as friendly as Racip, then he wasn't sure that would be a good thing either.

The terrain started to gradually change. They had run for nearly a day and a half in a thickly wooded area with lots of wildlife; now, the trees were sparse, and there were no animals. They stopped to catch their breath, and Greyson looked around as Alleah collapsed against a tree. The trees were still big but had fewer leaves and branches, and the bark seemed darker. He had noticed batches of cattails over the last hour or so. And as he stood there, breathing heavily, his hands on his knees, he could vaguely smell something sickly, earthy, and rotting. The river was still there but did not seem to flow as quickly as it had. It was becoming slow and stagnant.

"We may have a bigger problem here than just our pursuers," Greyson said between pants.

"A swamp?" Alleah answered, having reached the same conclusion.

"Looks like it."

"Well, we can't turn back. We can change direction, maybe even cross the river here, and then travel away from it once across."

Greyson nodded, understanding that that was as good a plan as any. However, before he could respond, he heard a cry that curdled his blood. Alleah stood at once and turned toward the direction from which they had come. The cry did not sound far away, meaning their enemies were close.

"Alleah, help me!" the voice echoed. There was a sharp scream, then sobbing.

"That is Chloe. I must go to her!" Alleah said, wide-eyed.

Greyson grabbed her shoulders and said, "No, Alleah, it is a trap. They want you and are playing on your sympathy. Chloe is as good as dead, and so are you if you give in to their scheme."

Alleah looked at him, studying his face as if trying to find an answer to a most challenging dilemma. Her big blue eyes watered as she struggled to control her emotions. That was when they heard the man call out. Greyson immediately knew it was Cerus; he would never forget that voice. He couldn't see anyone yet but was confident about who was chasing them.

"Alleah Mansuell, surrender. There is nowhere for you to run. Turn yourself over to me, and I will release the others."

Alleah gasped and looked to Greyson for an answer. He shook his head and whispered, "It's a trap."

Cerus continued, "If you don't turn yourself over to me by dusk, she dies. Others will follow. Think about it, and let's end this senseless chase; there is nowhere for you to turn. I assure you Swamp Ikma is most unforgiving."

Greyson pulled Alleah behind a tree and motioned for her to peek around it. He had spotted a glimpse of a few warriors walking near the river. They wore the same armor as the men who had attacked Tara. They also carried spears, like those horrible men who killed his family. Then from the shadows of the trees came Cerus, brandishing that same crude dagger he had used to murder his family and friends. Like that horrible morning back in Tara, blood covered it.

Greyson froze and swallowed hard. His nerves got the best of him as he considered what this man was capable of. His feet wouldn't move, and he just stood and stared in disbelief and fear. Cerus was less than fifty yards away now and slowly growing closer. Greyson didn't see that; he only saw his family swaying from the apple trees again.

"Chloe," Alleah whispered, breaking him from his thoughts.

More men had appeared in the area, spread out and searching for them. Two men led Chloe, her face and arms a bloody mess. One held his hand over her mouth, and she seemed to barely have the energy to stand, much less walk.

"Alleah, we must run straight into the swamp; it is our only chance."

He grabbed her hand, turned, and ran, hoping that none of their pursuers saw them. Panic overtook him as he pulled Alleah along. He could not understand how he had fallen into the clutches of Cerus once again. He was vaguely aware that the smell worsened as they continued deeper into the bog, but his focus was on outrunning Cerus. The vegetation began to thin out, replaced slowly by black-barked trees and viny plants. The bugs also became a problem as more and more bit and stung them as they ran. By nightfall, they had to stop again, Greyson with a stitch in his side from the extensive running.

"Do you think they are still behind us?" Alleah asked.

"Yes, Cerus is relentless," Greyson answered between pants.

"They are going to kill Chloe if I don't surrender," Alleah said, nearing tears again.

Greyson grabbed her gently by the shoulders and reassured her. "Listen, I've seen what this man can do. He will not release anyone. He will kill Chloe; if you surrender, he will kill you."

"How can I take that chance, Greyson?"

"Because you trust me as your friend, right?"

She studied his face for a few moments, and even though they had run for nearly two days straight and had not bathed for longer, inappropriate images filled his head and he felt a stirring in his groin.

Her words broke his train of thought. "You are right."

He nodded and walked her briskly into the swamp and the unknown. Bugs bit him, the soft ground pulled at his boots, and he had no light source. He felt like he was heading straight into hell, and that was the lesser of the two evils he faced.

Daro, Sasha, and Inuentas packed their gear and prepared to depart for Pelesea. The three had just shared a meal at Daro's cottage and were ready to journey to the grand city. Inuentas had requested a meeting with the New Order, which Daro found strange. The demon had information concerning the events in Novafontera and possibly why a demon roamed the city before they destroyed it. Heinsvick had befriended him and Sasha to fight against the creature. If a vampire lord was concerned about the demoness, the New Order needed to hear Inuentas's tale. He decided to lead his new friends to the city and request that meeting.

Winter had a firm hold on the land, and the cold wind blew in their faces as they exited Daro's woods. Novafontera was to the southwest of their location, and all three stopped to look upon the silent but deadly place. Daro thought of Heinsvick, and he felt pity for the vampire. Ultimately,

Heinsvick wasn't such a monster after all, and Daro planned on fulfilling his promise to him. Inuentas would give him the information he needed to rescue Emiline, and he would see it through to the best of his ability.

He pulled his cloak tight to ward off the biting wind and turned to begin the journey to Pelesea. He took a few steps, Inuentas behind him, when he noticed Sasha was not following. He regarded her, standing perfectly still against the persistent wind and facing Novafontera.

"Sasha, I know the cold wind feels good to you, but to us …" Daro glanced at Inuentas, who showed no signs of being cold and only shrugged and smiled at his questioning gaze.

"Correction, to me, it is cold out here. Let's get moving while the sun is high in the sky," he continued.

Sasha turned to regard her new friends, slowly shaking her head. Daro's heart raced at the thought of her not coming with them. He had not considered that course and had focused on how grand she would find Pelesea. He walked briskly up to her.

"Sasha, you must come with us; you will love Pelesea."

His voice was near panic, and she immediately seemed to pick up on his anxiety. She smiled to calm him and said, "You are a good friend to me, Daro, Keeper of the Woods. You have assisted me in more ways than you realize. And for that, I am forever grateful."

"Then, let me introduce you to my friends; they would love to meet you."

"No, Daro, this is where we part ways."

"But why?"

The beautiful woman had affected him more than he realized, and his heart was thumping out of his chest at the mere thought of saying goodbye. It was a strange feeling to him, as he had always been a loner, but losing someone as beautiful as Sasha did not sit well. His disappointed expression spoke volumes, so she kissed him gently. Her lips were cold, and his cheek tingled from the slight peck.

"I must go and return the sword."

Daro was stunned. He was at a loss for words, trying to register the events unfolding before him.

"You are returning the sword?"

"Of course, in exchange for my mother's life."

"Sasha, don't do this alone. Come to Pelesea, and when we complete our business there, I'll come with you to confront your tormentors. Don't go back alone."

"Daro, it is not *our* business that awaits in Pelesea; it is *yours*. After I have my mother, I will return her to your world and seek you again. She will love you and want to thank you for saving her."

Sasha took his hands in hers. "For saving us both," she added and smiled.

It was the most beautiful smile he had ever seen; his friend seemed truly happy. He knew he would not convince her to follow him. In the short time he had known her, he had learned she was incredibly stubborn. He wanted to say as much, to say something that would keep her there with him, but instead, he could only look longingly into her crystal-blue eyes.

"Are you two lovebirds done? We really should get moving," Inuentas said, ending their moment.

They both turned to regard the half-demon, his arms crossed over his chest, tapping his foot impatiently. Neither responded and they could only stare at their strange new ally.

"What? The world is in trouble, and I'm the cure. We must go right away."

"So then, this is goodbye, Daro. For now, at least. Thank you," Sasha said, giving him another peck on the check.

She turned and started walking back into the woods, to the waterfalls where he had first seen her, he imagined. He watched her until she was out of sight, then, with a sigh, turned and started toward Pelesea. It would take them over a month to reach the city, and the weather would be an unkind obstacle. Although he never mentioned it to Inuentas, Daro's thoughts lingered on Sasha during that long, miserable trip. Something in his heart told him he had made a mistake letting her go. He had a bad feeling he would never see her again.

It had been three days since Greyson and Alleah had started running. They had heard more of Chloe's screams and caught glimpses of the pursuing warriors. Cerus and his men were still on the trail, and the dragonfly was the main reason, as it still appeared occasionally. They also knew that the soft ground easily left their footprints. There was no escape, and that sad reality began to take a toll on them mentally. They were both very thirsty, with no clean water for three days. Plath granted the creation of water to his older priests, and Greyson took it personally that he had not mastered that spell yet. After all, he was the prodigy of the god, and being so implied Plath would bless him with many powers. However, that wasn't the case, and the young priest completed another prayer asking his god for help.

He slowly opened his eyes, knowing his god had denied him again. The first thing he saw was the resigned look on Alleah's face. She accepted the fact that they were out of time. She smiled weakly at him as they sat panting against large, black-barked trees. She smacked at her neck, killing another of the giant mosquitos that inhabited that part of the bog. Greyson could feel one bite his arm, but he didn't even have the energy to kill it. He just let it feed, not caring at that moment.

"They are close," Alleah said weakly.

"As they have been for three days now," Greyson agreed.

"It is time for me to stop running and save Chloe."

"He said he would kill her over a day ago if you didn't surrender; we can assume she is gone. Do not make her death in vain."

"I have heard her scream today, Greyson. If not her, then another of my sisters. It is time for me to stop running."

Greyson had lost track of time and could not recall when last he had heard a scream from behind. He wanted to argue with her that it had been a while, but he wasn't sure. He was becoming delirious and in desperate need of food, and especially water. He knew she would make a stand, and he would join her, resigned to the fact they would die together. He slowly nodded his agreement. They had lost their weapons during the escape at Racip, but they still had their holy symbols, powerful necklaces of their respective gods that would allow them to cast their spells. However, he knew Cerus, and their magic would not be enough.

The dragonfly made yet another appearance, zipping over them and landing on the very tree Greyson rested against. They both looked at it with disdain, knowing that the little creature was why they never had a chance to begin with.

"I hate her," Alleah said.

"Who?" Greyson asked, thinking Alleah was as hysterical as him for thinking the magical device had a gender.

"Captain Jessica. She was in on this trap the whole time. We trusted her, and now my sisters are dead or as good as dead. I hate the woman for what she has done to us."

Greyson could only nod in agreement.

"The worst part is, we will never be able to warn Kringus and Penelope of the dangers here, of the growing threat of Gorl. They will not learn of our demise until it is too late," Alleah continued.

Greyson watched helplessly while the dragonfly buzzed over to another tree. Soon it would fly off to feed Jessica more information. He didn't care anymore. There was no longer any need to hide; the chase was over. He looked at Alleah, who was still stunning, although she was filthy and smelly. A pang of regret for not being able to bed her washed over him. He would have loved to enlighten her about the ways of sex, but alas, it was not to be, and he quickly dismissed those thoughts.

As he watched her, she began to change. He thought at first it was his imagination, and then maybe a spell she was enacting, but she looked upon him with the same confused look, so he knew she had nothing to do with it. Her skin turned dark, almost black, and soon began to look like part of the tree. Her arms melted into her body, and her legs became roots, digging into the muddy soil. He watched as her body slowly became undistinguishable from the tree as if she had never been there. He could feel the same metamorphosis occur with his body and became paralyzed as the tree absorbed him. Once the transformation was complete, he felt like he was inside the tree, looking out, but helpless.

The dragonfly flew off, beginning its journey back to Jessica, he assumed. However, the thing did something he had not seen it do before; it stopped in midair and just hung there. Its little wings beat and buzzed all about but it did not move other than to rotate slowly in the air as if caught in an invisible spiderweb. Greyson caught movement off to the side, deeper from the swamp. He thought it might be one of Cerus's men, but there were no Gorl warriors that way.

It was a man, but not one of Cerus's. He carried a staff in his hand, topped with a large purple gem that glowed and let off purplish smoke as if it burned. He stepped up confidently to the little dragonfly golem, which seemed to struggle all the greater as he approached. Greyson realized the man was holding the creature with some spell, or most likely that wonderful staff.

"Interesting," the man said, studying the struggling creature but not touching it.

After a few moments, he brought his hand up in front of him and made a fist. The dragonfly's wings beat harder, trying to free itself, but to no avail.

"Still, it is an abomination," the man added, and clenched his fist tight.

Greyson looked on in amazement as the dragonfly shattered as if the man crushed it with his hand. It fell to the ground in many pieces, and then the man turned to look straight at Greyson. He wanted to speak, ask the strange man what was happening, and let him know they did not mean harm. Sadly, he could not talk and was helpless to what the man had in mind for Alleah and him.

"The fate of you two trespassers hangs in the balance. You will either be released, be destroyed, or spend your final days as trees of the swamp. The lord of this land will speak his intentions soon enough. However, there are other interlopers I must deal with."

The strange man turned back and forth between Greyson's tree and Alleah's, waving the powerful staff as he spoke, leaving a purple trail of smoke behind.

"Oh, where are my manners? I am Breeston, Druid of Ikma, and this is Swamp Ikma, one of the most dangerous and unwelcoming places in the known world. And you are interlopers one and two," he said, turning and pointing his staff toward Greyson first, then Alleah.

Greyson could not respond, so he just listened as the man continued his introductions.

"Now, it is time for you to meet the Lord of Ikma, the most magnificent Malebak, dragon lord of the bog, judge and executioner of all who trespass here!"

The druid turned toward a large area of swampy water surrounded by cattails and dead trees. He raised his arms, the staff suddenly growing bright with purple energy. The tall grass surrounding the water began to sway, and the water bubbled.

At that exact moment, Cerus and his men appeared, and Greyson considered himself very fortunate to be trapped inside a tree. Cerus seemed not to notice him or Alleah, which was good. However, he did notice Breeston as Jessica came around him and saw the destroyed golem.

"No!" she cried, then went to the pile of metal and started picking up the crushed pieces.

Other men came then, surrounding their leader, spears at the ready. Greyson's heart broke as he saw one of them dragging along a battered and bloodied Chloe. Her face was swollen from the multiple beatings she had taken, and it looked as if the swelling around her eyes closed them. Dozens of deep gashes made by Cerus's dagger lined her arms, which Greyson surmised was why she would scream out in pain ever so often. He regretted his words from just moments ago when he told Alleah Chloe was probably already dead. She wasn't, but she couldn't be too far from it. Her arms were bound in front of her, and another rope was tied to them, with which one man led her along. She didn't put up a struggle and, in truth, probably didn't even know where she was.

"Stop! What are you doing?" Cerus barked at the druid.

Breeston paid him no mind and continued to focus on the bubbling water.

"Kill him," Cerus calmly ordered his two closest men.

They each threw their spears; both aims were true, as the missiles struck the druid in the back. However, he did not flinch as his robe seemed to deflect the attacks, pieces of bark comprising the strange garment chipping off.

Cerus motioned with a nod for the other ten men to approach the druid as he drew forth his massive spear. The men cautiously made their way to Breeston, spears at the ready. Before they had taken more than a few steps, Breeston turned to face them, lowering his arms.

"Fools," he said smugly, the water still boiling behind him.

The druid pointed his staff at a nearby tree, and the gem glowed brightly again. Then he stepped into it, disappearing altogether as if the tree had a magic door he could enter. The men stopped their approach and looked at each other in confusion. They looked back at Cerus for instructions, but he cared little for the strange man in the bark cloak, his attention solely on the churning water.

"Retreat!" he ordered.

His men stood there, not knowing what to do at first, but some saw the water becoming more and more volatile, so they soon understood their commander's order. They all started to backtrack, moving slowly toward their leader, but not nearly fast enough.

A giant black dragon burst forth from the water. It towered at least twenty feet into the air, but only its neck and head were visible, water pouring from it to splash back down into the bog. Its scales were black as night and seemed to reflect blues and whites if the light caught them a certain way. Its eyes were purple, like the druid's stone; its maw was large enough to swallow a horse and filled with razor-sharp teeth. Two large black horns curled along the side of its head, similar to the horns of a ram. It let out an angry roar and stepped with its two front legs out of the water. Cerus's men turned and ran then, knowing the dangers of delaying their retreat. Cerus watched in awe as the beast reared back to expel its deadly breath on his men.

He looked around and grabbed Jessica, who had just slowly risen from picking up the pieces of her toy. She dropped them again once the dragon roared and stood in shock as the dragon breathed. Cerus fell to the ground, pulling Jessica onto him and using her as a shield.

Greyson had never seen a dragon before, and the sight enthralled him. The tree did not seem like enough protection from the sheer power of the creature. However, he was glad to be hidden within as the magnificent dragon loosed its breath on Cerus's men. He assumed it would be fire, for all the legends he had ever heard of dragons had them using fiery breath to kill their enemies. However, it was not fire but some black, sticky substance that it breathed. It stuck to the fleeing men, and the dragon moved its head back and forth to hit all of them in a deadly wave of pure blackness. They screamed and fell to the ground as the substance seemed to eat them alive. As Greyson looked closer, he realized with horror the truth of that breath: the sticky black substance was nothing but large flies, the size of mice.

All the men writhed under the relentless biting flies as the dragon looked on confidently, waiting to see which men might need a second dose. Flies crawled on the smiling beast's teeth, and some flew around its muzzle. Greyson knew that they would both be dead if the attack had caught him or Alleah. The movements of Cerus's men began to slow as they succumbed to the insects. Only one man stood in place, the one who had led Chloe by a rope into the clearing. He was covered with the hateful flies and finally fell to his knees, then to the ground, face down and dead. Behind him stood Chloe, smacking away and squishing any flies that had passed her human shield and now bit at her. She had had the presence of mind to hide behind her captor, letting him take the brunt of the attack.

She gained the dragon's attention and would have died if not for Cerus springing up just then. He threw Jessica off him and smacked at any of the flies that remained. Jessica took a few steps away, then fell to her knees as Greyson witnessed the devastation of the breath weapon. She was dead before she fell over, and Greyson could see that her eyes were gone, presumably eaten by the large flies, and welts covered her skin. The flies flew into her mouth, eye holes, and any other place they could access and began to eat her from the inside out. It was the most horrific thing Greyson had seen in quite some time.

Cerus fought off the few insects that bit at him, and once dead, he realized he had the dragon's full attention. Chloe sensed it, too, and screamed, frozen in fear. Cerus slowly raised his hands in the air in surrender, his spear still in his right hand, contradicting his sign of peace. He tentatively took a few steps back, gauging the dragon's reaction. Faster than expected, the great black beast swept his right claw at the seasoned warrior. Cerus managed to duck at the last possible moment, but not enough to entirely dodge the attack. The dragon's claw easily cut through his armor, gashing his side. He stifled a scream as the razor-sharp claw dug in deeply. He jumped, letting it pick him up and fling him through the air. His jump helped with the propulsion, sending him far away from the beast. He landed in a roll, absorbing the impact and finding his feet quickly. He didn't even look back; he just gained his feet and fled in the opposite direction, holding his side to stem the blood flow from the vicious wound.

Malebak stretched its great neck out and breathed after Cerus, a swarm of thick insects chasing the evil Gorl warrior. Chloe whimpered but didn't move. The sound had the dragon swinging back around to regard her. Its maw was level with her face, and it could have easily swallowed her whole. Greyson expected just that as he watched. Flies buzzed around the battered woman as they flew from Malebak's mouth. Most flew off with the others, but one landed on her; it bit her arm, and blood poured from the wound. The poor girl was so frightened that she did not even try to swat it away and stood there shivering.

The mighty dragon lifted Chloe in one claw and rose straight, seeming more impressive at full height. Chloe screamed as the dragon roared. Greyson watched helplessly as it appeared the beast would pop her into its mouth like a refreshing snack.

Then the druid appeared from the tree and said, "Mighty Malebak, Lord of Ikma, I salute you on your domination of the trespassers. Your display of power is too much for simple words!"

The dragon looked at him and issued a low growl.

Breeston bowed and replied, "It is good to see you again, my old friend. Thank you for heeding my call."

The dragon grumbled and growled, sounding like the shuffling of boulders. It was evident to Greyson that it was speaking, and the druid seemed to understand its words.

"Yes, great one, you have dispatched all interlopers except for the one you have in your hand and her two friends, who the trees hold," Breeston said, motioning to the tree prisons where Greyson and Alleah resided.

"I require your wisdom in determining their fate. You may destroy them, which seems like an appropriate punishment to me; keep them forever imprisoned in the trees; or release them. Please tell me your preference so that I may see it done."

The dragon examined Chloe and grumbled something to the druid. He must have decided she would not make much of a meal, so he laid her down gently beside him.

"As you wish, my lord," Breeston said with another bow.

He turned to Chloe, who was still quivering with fear, more so now that she had received such a close look into the dragon's maw. Breeston swatted the fly that had latched on to her arm. It squished with a sickening sound. The druid wiped the remains away and grabbed her by the chin, pulling her gaze from the great dragon to his own.

"Tell me, woman, what you desire of Ikma so that I can relay that information to the lord of the swamp."

Chloe was so stricken with fright that her teeth chattered, and she reverted her gaze to Malebak and stammered something unintelligible. With a sigh, Breeston waved his staff at the tree containing Alleah, and Greyson watched in amazement as she slowly appeared again, unmolding from it. It took several moments for the transition to complete, but once it did, she then quickly ran to Chloe, wrapping her in a tight hug. Chloe went limp at the sight of Alleah and cried uncontrollably in her sister's arms.

"Chloe, I am here!" Alleah said, trying to comfort the hysterical woman.

"I'm sorry, sister; it was a trap. They—" Chloe began.

"Do not fret; I know what happened. Sit here and rest easy," Alleah said, helping the battered woman to sit on a fallen tree.

Alleah slowly rose and made eye contact with the druid, who waited impatiently for her to comfort her friend. Then, she dared to behold the massive dragon towering above her. The sight had her nearly toppling over, and she was at a loss for words.

"So, I ask again, what are your intentions in our home?"

Alleah began to stammer a reply but quickly lost her voice when the dragon swooped its head down to meet her eye to eye. Chloe whimpered beside her, and Alleah instinctively stepped in front of the battered girl, not that she could have protected her from the magnificent dragon if it had decided to attack them. Greyson could see the multitude of angry killer flies that crawled along the beast's bared teeth. He felt helpless, still trapped in the tree. There was nothing he could do, even if he were free of his prison, but he hated that he might have to helplessly watch the death of his friends.

"Luckily for you, our lord here in Ikma is very forgiving of interlopers as long as they bring gifts suitable to justify the trespass," Breeston said, standing next to the dragon's open maw with a smug look.

Alleah looked on, unable to find the words to ask forgiveness. There was such a delay in her response that Greyson was sure the dragon would eat both.

Luckily, she eventually found her words. "Mighty dragon of Ikma, we mean no harm; we were fleeing—"

"Malebak does not want excuses; he simply desires payment, foolish woman," Breeston interrupted.

"Then I offer myself as payment," Alleah said, extending her hand beside her. "I only ask that you let my friends live."

Malebak growled, the inflections of that growl varying in such a way that Greyson knew it was speaking to the druid. Breeston nodded his agreement. The dragon lifted its head slightly, and the druid stepped between Alleah and mighty Malebak.

"You understand that he could eat each of you if he so desired," Breeston explained. "Furthermore, he has offered me the honor of deciding your fate. He has a dozen meals to bloat his belly, so the desire to eat you is not quite as appealing as it could have been. Luckily, your enemies will suffice for that purpose. He will brine their bodies, and the maggots will grow large inside the corpses. After a few weeks, he will devour them, and they will be most tasty for my lord.

"So, now, the fate of you three hinges on what I decide. And a most difficult choice this is, I assure you. Though I like you more than the men who chased you, I can let you survive only at great personal sacrifice."

The druid waved his magical staff at Greyson, and he felt the tree immediately expelling him, pushing him out into the open once more. He stood on shaking legs, and the size of the towering dragon enthralled him. It seemed much more prominent outside the tree, and he felt vulnerable in the open.

"Your lives for this," Breeston explained, pointing to the great stone at the top of his staff.

Greyson came up to check on Chloe, who smiled weakly, then he stood shoulder to shoulder with Alleah, creating a protective wall in front of their injured friend.

"Dragons love treasure," Greyson whispered, catching on.

"Yes, but not like you think. Malebak eats these magical gems, which are extremely difficult for me to obtain. He will gladly take my gem in exchange for your lives if that is what I see fit."

Greyson exchanged a worried glance with Alleah, understanding the great sacrifice the druid would have to make for them to live. He owed them nothing, and it made no sense that he would give up such a prized possession. After a few tense moments of him thinking it over, a smile finally creased his face, and he held his staff up toward Malebak.

"Eat, my friend, and I will see you again soon," Breeston said.

It looked to Greyson like the magnificent beast smiled as if agreeing with the druid's choice, then gently bent down, grasped the gem between its massive teeth, and pulled. The stone sizzled and popped as Malebak pulled it loose from the tight grasp of the staff. Breeston had to pull immensely to keep the dragon from tugging the magical device from his hands. Once the gem came free, it poured forth copious amounts of purple smoke. Still holding the smoking gem in its teeth, the dragon quickly slipped back under the water and was gone.

Breeston brought the top of the staff back to observe the smoking and barren socket where the gem had been. He shrugged and said to the others, "I hope your lives are worth it."

"We thank you, Breeston," Alleah said, extending her hand.

He smiled and took it, shaking it gently.

"I am Alleah, priestess of Sinnis, and this is Chloe, my sister in the faith."

"I am Greyson, priest of Plath," Greyson added, grasping the druid's hand in a friendly and appreciative shake.

"Can your friend travel? The day grows old, and without my staff, we will become dinner to one of my neighbors if we don't get inside soon."

Alleah and Greyson went to Chloe and administered healing spells, and as the energy washed over her, they witnessed the wounds to her face and arms heal quickly. Her eyes became less swollen and her pretty face more visible. She smiled weakly and nodded her appreciation.

"She can now," Greyson said, standing once more. "I hope you have drinkable water."

"And food," Chloe added.

"Yes, yes, I do. Come along, let's get inside where it is safe. Then, I will ensure your needs are properly met."

And so the four of them traveled deeper into the mysterious bog, Ikma, leaving a dozen bodies of Gorl warriors and Captain Jessica littering the ground behind them.

Cerus knew the dangers of delaying his retreat. He could not worry about his men, although their dying screams haunted him as he ran. He could do nothing to help them, so he would have to accept the losses and try to survive. He sensed the flies behind him and had felt the woosh of dragon's breath on his heels as he had made his feet. The monster had breathed, and he witnessed what those nasty bugs could do.

Cerus was a trained veteran and god-blood pumped through his veins, but he knew he could not outrun the nightmare that the lizard had breathed forth. He could hear them buzzing behind him and felt a few land on his back and bite. He cursed his bad luck under his breath, understanding that Kavince had once again eluded him. Although he had not seen the young priest, he knew he was close to catching him. And to miss out on the prize known as Alleah was gut-wrenching. He would have had fun with her if she was as beautiful as that fool Jessica said. Now he just hoped to survive.

He spurred on, trying to run faster, but the muddy ground made it even more difficult. He was doomed unless a solution presented itself soon. A fly flew into his mouth, biting his tongue and cheek. Cerus bit down on it, squashing the vile thing. He spat it out, but two more landed on his face, biting and drawing blood. He yelled out in defiance, slapping and squishing both as he ran.

Then things went from bad to worse as a giant toad rose from a shallow bog in front of him, its mouth open, ready to swallow. Cerus's warrior instinct had him reaching for the massive spear on his back, but he stopped that natural reflex, understanding the toad was his way to survive. When the giant toad's coarse tongue wrapped around him, he did not struggle and simply let the thing swallow him whole. A few moments later, Cerus cut himself out and continued on his way. Now with the flies occupied with the toad carcass, he walked briskly back to find the river. It took him a while, but once he stumbled upon it, he followed it toward the ocean.

It took him longer than he intended to reach the shore, and when he finally made it days later, he was close to death. He had not eaten for a long while and was dehydrated; the fly bites were also infected, especially in his mouth. When he stumbled into Port Racip in a state of confusion, he was vulnerable to what hostility the people there might offer. Luckily, he was recognized and taken in for healing and rest. During the first few days of bed rest, his anger grew with his fever. His obsession with Greyson Kavince renewed, and he vowed the fool would pay with his life for the losses Cerus had suffered in Swamp Ikma.

Cerus's fever spiked, and he became delirious in the care of the dockmaster of Racip. On the occasions when he found consciousness over the next few weeks, he would scream out Greyson's name, cursing the young man who was the root of all his problems. If Greyson somehow survived Swamp Ikma, Cerus vowed to flay him alive.

Greyson, Alleah, and Chloe ate their fill and drank plenty of fresh water once they had made it to Breeston's abode, a small cottage surrounded by swampy water on three of its sides. After their meal, the three friends felt much better and, at their host's request, stayed and slept soundly. A few days later, Greyson was the first to awaken to the sun shining brightly on his face. He rose and took in his surroundings, not initially recognizing where he was. But the events that had led him to the foreign place returned, and he jumped out of bed with a start.

He found Alleah and Chloe each sound asleep in their respective rooms, and he breathed a sigh of relief. He gently shut their doors and looked for their host. He found the strange man outside the front door, sitting atop a giant mushroom, smoking a pipe, and watching a crocodile eating a large fish at the far edge of the water. Greyson walked up to him, but neither spoke for a while as Breeston puffed smoke rings into the air.

"Thank you for saving us," Greyson finally said after many moments.

"Oh, I did not save you, priest. I knew what Malebak wanted, so I obliged."

"The gem?"

"Yes. The dragon had plenty of delicious snacks littering the ground, so three more made little difference. It did not come out and tell me it wanted the gem, but I could sense it. It was happy with that decision. It has happily taken many of my valuable gems in the past," Breeston explained, then blew a rather large smoke ring into the morning sky.

"What does it do with the gems?"

"Eats them, of course."

"Why?"

"It is a delicacy to a dragon, like you or I eating an expensive steak. I do not know exactly why, but it loves them, I assure you."

"Well, whatever the reason, we appreciate you sacrificing the gem to save us."

"Is that what I did?" Breeston asked with a snort.

"That is what it looked like, yes," Greyson answered, confused at the strange man's response.

"Hmmm," was all the druid said, and he blew several more rings.

Greyson tried to decipher the meaning behind the druid's casual response but surrendered when Breeston handed him the pipe.

"I don't smoke," Greyson said, holding up a hand.

"Not yet."

"What is it?" Greyson asked tentatively.

"Ikma's finest blend of mushrooms and deep bog tobacco."

Greyson slowly took it and examined the wooden pipe, looking from it to the druid with trepidation. Breeston only looked on, not showing any emotion or offering any instructions. Greyson finally shrugged and inhaled deeply, the smoke burning his lungs and choking him. He coughed up the potent smoke and doubled over, returning the pipe to Breeston. He spent several moments coughing and spitting up phlegm.

Breeston chuckled and blew more smoke rings as Greyson suffered through his fit. "You should never inhale pipe tobacco, my friend, and indeed not as much of the Ikma special blend as you just did."

"I wish you would have told me beforehand."

"You didn't ask," Breeston said with a shrug.

Greyson shook his head and smiled. He didn't know what to think of the strange druid, but he liked him. He had taken them into his home and offered them food, water, and a nice bed. Most importantly, he had given up the power of his staff to save them. He felt he could trust the druid even in this early stage of their relationship. He then noticed the staff lying near the mushroom upon which Breeston sat. The staff's top was empty, where several tendrils curled up and once held the purple stone fed to the dragon. Greyson felt guilty about taking so much from the druid without him receiving anything in return.

"I am sorry you lost your gem; I witnessed its power, and I know the sacrifice you made for us. So, thank you," Greyson said, pointing to the staff.

Breeston regarded it and shrugged. "A replacement is already being born."

"Born?" Greyson asked curiously.

Breeston emptied his pipe on the side of the mushroom and hopped down. "Follow me," he said, moving into the small cottage. "I have something to show you."

He took Greyson to the back of the house to a large cellar door. It was wooden, seemingly made from the bark of the strange trees found in Ikma. The swampy smell was more pungent there, and when Breeston lifted the heavy door, the amplified smell of rotting leaves and swampy water filled his nose. He had to put a hand to his face to lessen the stench.

"The answer to the gem is down there."

Greyson peered down into the darkness but was unable to see. He did not want to venture below without his friends, so he said, "We are a team, the three of us. We—"

"Let them rest, the injured one especially; she can hardly travel in her condition," Breeston interjected with a wave of his hand.

Greyson looked back at the closed doors leading to his friends' rooms. They were safe and resting easily. The druid had saved them from the dragon, and Greyson had no reason not to trust him, but this didn't feel right.

"What is down there?" Greyson asked nervously.

"Gems, or at least the source of them."

"Why show me?"

"Because I can offer you your own. You will need it to find your way out of Ikma, especially if those foul men are still after you and your friends. Men like that don't give up very easily."

Greyson shook his head and said, "No, just tell me. What is the source?"

"Suit yourself, but there is no way for you to have your gem unless you go below," Breeston said, shutting the heavy door again.

"What else is down there?"

"My wife."

"Your wife?"

"Yes, and our many, many children."

"I do not understand, Breeston. You keep your wife and children below ground in a smelly cellar?"

"Careful, young priest. What you call smelly, the inhabitants of Ikma would call luxurious, including my wife and children."

"But why keep them below your home, out of sight, unless …" Greyson trailed off, discovering the reason.

He and Breeston said in unison, "They're not human."

"Her name is Xeva, and she is a sleeth."

"A sleeth?"

"Part human, part snake."

Breeston held up his hand to Greyson before he could ask. "Don't worry; she is beautiful, especially by human standards."

"How, though?"

"I know it sounds strange, and I'm not sure of the origin of the first sleeth. I can only assume the gods created them. Xeva is only one-eighth snake, so mostly human. The sleeth are a rare species, with a handful rumored to exist in the Yaddaton Desert north of here. However, I have never seen another one."

"How does she—"

"Look?" Breeston interrupted. "Human and very beautiful, I assure you. You will find her stunning if you summon the courage to visit her."

Greyson absorbed the information, still very confused at the possibility of a snake-human, but he was always interested in meeting beautiful women. After thinking it over, he said, "So what does she have to do with the gems, and what do your children look like?"

"All sleeth are both blessed and cursed, another reason I believe the gods have a hand in their existence. Xeva lays eggs like a snake once a month. Those eggs, if fertilized, will produce baby snakes. So, the first rule of Ikma: kill no snakes because they could be my offspring!

"However, occasionally, one of the eggs will hatch with a valuable gem inside. This is the blessing of Xeva because that gem will be attuned with the father's god or goddess, giving him ample power, especially for priests and other devout followers."

Greyson listened wide-eyed, understanding now the possibilities before him. If he owned a gem similar to what Breeston had used to imprison him with, he could only imagine the power that rock would give him.

"What curse?" he asked, now very curious of Breeston's strange wife.

"That you must find out for yourself!" Breeston exclaimed and clapped him on the shoulder. "Now, come with me."

"Where are we going?"

"To gather food. Your friends will be hungry once they awaken."

Greyson followed Breeston out into the swamp. He learned a lot over the next few hours: which mushrooms to pick, which lizards to catch and which ones never to touch, and even how to spot man-eating vegetation that appeared to be nothing more than harmless, flowering plants. Even though they did not discuss her again that day, Greyson's thoughts dwelled on Xeva and the possibilities she offered.

YADDATON

IT HAD BEEN A VERY LONG JOURNEY FOR CASSANDRA ACROSS THE rough sea, and the barbarians had not let her out of her tiny room until they had reached Varish. Now she stood on the bow of the large ship with Vixa, trying to let her eyes adjust to the sun she hadn't seen in nearly three weeks. She was on one of four vessels she could see as they slowly entered an inlet. No other prisoners were allowed to stand on the top deck, but Maltor had made an exception for Cassandra. Vixa stood next to her, with Jak not far away.

"We will meet the receiving party within our secret cave. From there, we will ride to Yaddaton," Vixa explained.

"Yaddaton is your home?"

"Yes, our desert home where the breeze is warm and there is no devil powder to bite at your skin."

Cassandra did not ask but could only imagine that devil powder was snow. Although she had nearly frozen to death a month ago at the remains of Farmer's Stop, she was not looking forward to the desert heat. The barbarians' tanned skin and strong body odor hinted at a not-so-enjoyable existence, especially if she was training in hand-to-hand combat. The notion seemed ridiculous, but what choice did she have? She let out a long sigh as she thought for not the first time of jumping overboard and making a swim for it. The fact that she could barely swim and that two hardy barbarian warriors were on deck watching her every move dissuaded her from doing just that. Instead, she stood and watched like a well-behaved prisoner, because that was precisely what she was, regardless of the special treatment she received.

The wide inlet eventually became a snaking river, like the one Greyson and Alleah had followed a few hundred miles south of that location a few weeks earlier. Oddly enough, the weather was reasonably warm. Cassandra knew it was the onset of winter back home, across the ocean, but she barely needed the itchy blanket because of Varish's warm weather. She would have dropped the blanket from around her shoulders if she were not dressed in a tiny loincloth and somehow even smaller top. Cassandra kept it, not just because she felt a slight bite in the air, but because of the savages that watched over her. She did not want them to stare at her nearly naked form. And so, she rode with the blanket scrunched up tight around her shoulders as the large boats gently descended the river. She saw no signs of civilization; the trees, vegetation, and wildlife were thick on both shores.

"Where are the others?" Cassandra asked Vixa.

"Others?"

"Yes, the other prisoners."

"None of your concern," was Vixa's curt response.

"How many are going to be trained like me?"

"None of your concern."

"Come, Vixa; you must answer some of my questions. I need to know my chances of succeeding in this stupid competition."

"I don't have to answer anything. You are a prisoner, and I oversee your training. You do what I say and worry about yourself, and that is all the information you need."

Vixa then turned to her fully and looked her up and down. She threw the camel-skin blanket to the ground after a brief struggle with Cassandra, who clung to it for dear life. Cassandra felt naked and could feel the eyes of the men on the deck ravaging her body. She tried to ignore them and focus solely on what Vixa would say. Vixa turned Cassandra's head to the side, then back to the other side, lifted her arms out, measured the width of her wrist, and felt her upper thighs. It was very degrading, but Cassandra tolerated it to get her answer. She wanted Vixa's evaluation. Winning the contest was her only chance to escape the savage people.

"Minimal chance," the barbarian woman finally said.

"What? Why?"

"You ask too many questions. That will get you killed or assigned to the procreation tent."

"You are my instructor. I want to make you proud. Tell me why I have so little chance, and I will try to correct my shortcomings."

Anger flashed across Vixa's face, and Cassandra thought the wild woman might strike her. Instead, she caught herself and looked at Jak over Cassandra's shoulder.

The barbarian warrior steadied herself and said, "You are small, you have no muscles on your bones, your hands are soft, you have no weapon skills, and you come from the devil's land. Most importantly, your time is short. I will train you, and Maltor will offer every chance for you to succeed, but the chances of you avoiding the procreation tent or surviving the ring are not good."

Nothing else needed to be said; it made perfect sense to Cassandra. With a snort, Vixa turned away from her and crossed her arms, taking in the scenery. Cassandra hugged her arms to her chest, still self-conscious of her skimpy outfit. She soon saw men shadowing the ships on the right shore, running through the thick vegetation. She was amazed at how quick they seemed. She could not compete with the war-mongering tribe of people. She was a witch, not a warrior.

The ships slowed, and the sails collapsed. Soon after, they veered into a small river that could barely hold them, and the men on the shore continued to shadow them. Cassandra could see more barbarians up ahead, removing what appeared to be dead trees, large rocks, and other debris on the right side of the river to reveal a cave. She picked up her uncomfortable blanket and once again wrapped it around her delicate shoulders. After Vixa's honest evaluation, she knew she could not meet Maltor's expectations.

Matilda and Cass sat at a table in The Happy Oyster, a popular tavern on the bay of Mecca-Loraine. Matilda picked over her fish sandwich, her impatience growing each day. They had been in the town for several weeks trying to find the trail that would lead to Cassandra but had seen nothing. They had discovered from an overly friendly guard that there had been two casualties during the barbarian raid, and Matilda quickly discerned that neither was Cassandra Rho. They had attended both funerals to verify that it was not her, and she was relieved to find it was an old priest and his carriage driver that had both met their demise from a barbarian axe to the forehead. The priest must have had some station in the town because of the funeral turnout.

"We cannot keep sitting in this town, waiting on your stupid necklace to work, Cass," Matilda said with an intentional edge to her voice.

"I told you, its power wanes, but I am trying," Cass snapped back.

"Give it to me then."

"No, it is mine."

"I can use my powers to possibly discern something from it that you cannot."

"Perhaps I can use *my* powers to discern something *you* cannot."

Matilda slammed her hands down on the table, jarring the plates there and gaining the attention of all the patrons in the tavern. Everyone grew quiet and stared at them for a few moments before they eventually went back to their meals and conversations.

Matilda shook her head in resignation and whispered, "She may not have even been here at all."

"Well, the last reading it gave indicated she was here, so this is all we have, Matilda."

"I know, but I have chased her across the world, just to have her slip through my fingers repeatedly. I am just frustrated."

"I understand. Remember, I want her as badly as you, and our arrangement benefits me finding her as quickly as possible."

"You plan many tortures for our little Cassandra Rho?" Matilda asked with an evil smile.

"More than you can imagine."

"Again, that works wonderfully for me, if she is not damaged permanently; I need her whole for the sacrifice. Also, after spending time with you and hearing your tales of that poor Binta creature, I cannot stress enough that her virginity must stay intact."

"Of course," Cass said.

"However, the deal we made includes your ability to find her using your necklace."

"Well, I've got us a starting point; we just need to find her smelly trail."

"So, why was she even here in this useless town?" Matilda asked for not the first time.

"As I told you, she staged her death at Pelesea and fled here somehow. It is a port town, so she came here to find passage elsewhere, most likely. But where she was heading to …"

Matilda was no longer listening but was looking over Cass's shoulder instead. The place had gone strangely quiet once more. Cass turned to see an unusual man wearing a white porcelain mask walking toward their table.

After the boats docked and the barbarians had concealed their secret cave, they led the prisoners in a single row out in the open, their arms tied in front of them. Cassandra watched as they were herded into wagons with planks of wood comprising the sides and top, with small gaps between them. The air was already hot, and Cassandra knew it would be scorching and uncomfortable in the cramped wagons. The barbarians lined up three vessels and packed as many prisoners as possible into each. All of them were female, which made sense from what she had learned of Maltor's plans. She was also the only prisoner not bound or stuffed into a wagon.

A strange animal that Vixa informed Cassandra was a camel pulled each wagon. Unfortunately, the things were smelly and not well-behaved. To make matters worse, Maltor retrieved Cassandra from Vixa's care, pulling her toward one of the larger camels. She was not thrilled by the idea of riding one of the stinky creatures, but she also knew enough of Maltor's temperament not to struggle or refuse. He led her to it, then assisted her atop it. It smelled even worse sitting upon it, and when Maltor climbed to sit behind her, she became very uncomfortable.

She did not like the savage being that close to her, especially when he took the reins and spurred their mount. He wrapped his large arms around her, and his body odor assaulted her. Again, she knew well enough to hold her tongue. As they began their trek to the barbarian homeland, Maltor's camel took the lead, with several others flanking them, followed by the wagons and more barbarians on foot. The landscape was barren there, with many reddish rocks popping up from the soil and only a few strange-looking trees and bushes scattered about. Mostly, it was just open terrain with the sun beating down on them. The harsh environment soon had Cassandra pulling the camel-hair blanket over her head for relief from the burning rays.

They traveled like that for several days. Cassandra would ride on the front of Maltor's camel each day, then sleep under Vixa's guard each night. The barbarian leader never said a word during their travel time, and Cassandra was thankful for it. Vixa had explained why such strange behavior occurred on the first night of their travels.

"You are his favorite, so you do not wear binds or travel in the wagons. He wants you as his bride, but tradition does not allow him to take a woman as a wife. Instead, she must win the title. Until then, he may not lie with you. He will ravage you once you are out of the tournament, win or fail. He is certain you will be victorious and be his queen; I have never seen him so sure of a bride before."

Cassandra thought having sex with the smelly, barbaric man seemed repulsive. She longed to be in Binta's arms, and even Greyson did not look so bad compared to the violent Maltor. Cassandra was homesick; she had lost her family and now her best friend. She wondered if she would ever see Binta, Greyson, or any of them again. She was sure they thought her dead in the fire at the jail, but it had been a ruse that only she could reveal. How she would ever get home and show Binta the truth was beyond her. She was on the other side of the ocean, far from Pelesea, she was sure. She would have to figure out a way to escape the barbarians, and that appeared to be no easy feat, noting the many guards surrounding her and Vixa as they prepared their beds.

"Would it help if I explained I am not interested?" Cassandra asked.

The rage on Vixa's face at hearing those words had Cassandra quickly preparing a spell, unsure if the wild warrior would lash out. Luckily, she regained control and moved close so the ever-watching guards could not hear.

"Do not say such stupid words, outlander! You are in a position I have dreamed of my entire life, and you speak with a fool's tongue. You are ungrateful, and you will learn our ways or die."

"Take him; I do not want him." Cassandra knew she was pushing the woman.

"He won't have me! I am unworthy in his eyes, though I would make a much better queen than you. This is the only thing he sees in you," Vixa said, pulling Cassandra's tiny skirt. She slung it down to reveal the snake brand, nearly ripping the skirt from Cassandra's hips. Vixa's breathing was hard, and she waited for Cassandra to speak.

Cassandra straightened her skirt and composed herself. She glanced over Vixa's shoulders at the nearby guards, including Jak, who was never far away. Then she saw the prisoners, still in their wagons, trying to find sleep in the cramped quarters. She could easily be among them, and Cassandra understood she had to appease Maltor to stay alive until she found a way to escape. That meant also bowing to Vixa's will. The proud warrior was assigned to teach Cassandra, and Cassandra would have to allow it, or there would be consequences. The gentle sobbing coming from the wagons had her motivated to cooperate.

"So, how many wives does Maltor have?" Cassandra finally asked, trying to sound interested.

Vixa relaxed then and said, "None."

"What? Surely I am not the first he has ever chosen as a bride. Do you mean to tell me that no others succeeded in the tournament?"

"No, none have won."

"What happened to them?"

"They are deemed unworthy, so they are assigned to the procreation tent, killed, or sold to other tribes."

Cassandra let the words sink in, understanding more and more what kind of predicament she was in and the incredible odds she faced.

"Not you, though," Vixa added quietly.

"What do you mean?"

"He has hand-selected you as his clear favorite, something he has never done before. If you fail, you will go to the procreation tent, where he will deem you his property. None of the other warriors will have you, but he will force you to give him many children. Not nearly as good as the station of a queen, but a nice life for you. You will not be killed, sold, or even used by others in the tribe. You are lucky."

Cassandra held her tongue once again at the ignorant comment. She didn't want anything to do with the foul and smelly savages but appreciated that they rescued her from Ronnis. However, that was not their primary intent, and it just happened that the leader of the murderous people was smitten with her. Cassandra was in a precarious position and knew the coming days would be an ordeal.

"Tell me of the tournament, Vixa, so that I may better understand it," Cassandra said as she lay down on her makeshift bed, which consisted of two camel-hair blankets.

The night was as cold as the day was hot in that strange part of the world, and she pulled her blankets tight. Vixa's bed was beside her, and the woman bundled herself the same way. Cassandra closed her weary eyes as the wild warrior spoke, trying to imagine the enormous task before her.

"There are five tribes of the Yaddaton Desert: the Scorpion Tribe, which consists of mostly female warriors where the females have equal rights with the males; the Vulture Tribe, where the warriors are hardy, including the muscular women; the Serpent Tribe, which is our tribe; the Culiem Tribe, which is the most wealthy and successful of the tribes; then the Sleeth Tribe, known for breeding with the sleeth of the desert. The Culiem and Sleeth Tribes usually win the tournaments."

"What are culiem and sleeth? I have never heard of these creatures."

"The culiem are desert fairies, nothing more. They are the rarest inhabitants of the great desert, and Maltor desires to catch a pair to mate. They are small, about six inches tall, and butterfly-winged. Other than that, they look human. The sleeth are snake-people who offer their tribe blessings from the gods. Their snake blood makes them elite warriors, and rumors suggest the king of that tribe is one-fourth sleeth."

"So is the Culiem Tribe part fairy?"

"No more so than the Vulture Tribe is part vulture. So, the king of each tribe will enter four hopefuls to win. Only one will outlast the others to become the queen of her respective tribe. You know what happens to the others."

Cassandra swallowed hard. The thought of spending the rest of her life in some hot tent that reeked of sex and body odor and of Binta never discovering the truth of her demise had her very nervous.

"Furthermore, each loser will be presented before the opposing king to be defiled."

"What?" Cassandra said, bolting upright. The ever-vigilant guards watching over them stood quickly and grabbed their weapons.

Vixa slowly sat up and responded, "What?"

"The loser has sex with the opposing king?"

"Yes, why?"

Cassandra snorted derisively and lay back down. The culture of the strange people was ridiculous, and the more she learned, the less she liked it.

The next day Cassandra found herself back on Maltor's camel mount, the sun beating hotter than any other day. She noticed the terrain became rockier and the dirt sandier. A mountain range loomed west of them, and the hills rolled out before them. Their course looked like it would take them around the mountains instead of through them, which Cassandra was thankful for. She could only imagine that the nights would be even colder in the mountains, and her stinky blanket would not keep her warm.

As the sun was setting on their third day of travel, Maltor spurred his stead into a gallop and veered it to the east and away from the mountains. Cassandra nearly fell, but Maltor's strong arms held her tight. She soon recovered, adjusted to the bouncing mount, and noticed four other mounted warriors from the tribe flanking them as escorts.

For the first time during their travels, Cassandra spoke. "What are you doing?"

Maltor did not respond, which made her angry. He desired her as the queen but couldn't summon the courtesy to answer her question. She was about to repeat herself and add a few choice words when she noticed their destination. It was a clump of palm trees and tall grasses in a large cluster. The scene seemed out of place, and she worried about Maltor's motivation for deviating from their course. Vixa's words rang in her head: *Maltor will not lie with you until after the tournament.* Perhaps the barbarian leader had had a change of heart or could no longer resist his urges. She craned her neck to look behind them and saw the caravan of wagons and foot soldiers continuing on its way, which concerned her even more.

Soon they were at the edge of the oasis, and she could now see birds, lizards, cacti, and other desert inhabitants. The entire place was no more significant than fifty square feet, but it included water, and the intoxicating fragrance of some unseen flower invigorated her. Maltor helped her off the camel and walked into the oasis, leaving her behind. She was about to follow when Vixa dismounted one of the camels that had flanked them and moved over to her.

"Leave him; he is checking the culiem traps," Vixa explained.

"The fairies?"

"Yes, he desires them greatly. Almost as much as he does you."

Cassandra folded her arms and said, "Yes, he cares so much for me that he doesn't even speak to me."

"He also stopped so that you may bathe."

"Just me?"

"Yes; he knows that where you come from, you would want that."

Cassandra could not deny that she greatly desired a bath, nor that her body odor had become an issue a few days earlier.

"What about the others?"

"What others?"

"The other prisoners. Do they not get to bathe as well?"

Vixa took her roughly by the arm, her grip vice-like. "Those other people do not matter. There may be a few worthy of the tournament, but most are going straight into breeding. Do not mention them again."

During the short trek, Vixa dragged Cassandra along, stumbling over small rocks or vegetation. She maintained her balance, but Vixa quickly threw her down to the ground once they arrived near a small body of water. It was no more than six feet in diameter and looked refreshing. However, Vixa was angry.

"Do not focus on anything or anyone else! The first thing I can teach you is to become selfish. Forget what you know and listen to what I say. If you cannot do this, you will surely fail," Vixa scolded her, throwing her a cake of soap. "Remove your clothes and bathe quickly. Maltor will return soon, and his mood will sour at not finding the culiem."

"Perhaps he will have caught them this time?" Cassandra asked, removing her clothing and throwing it into the water for washing.

"No, he never does. They are smart and steal the bait. Wash quickly because he will be back soon."

Cassandra dipped into the pool of water, and the temperature was incredible. She took the soap and quickly bathed, then lay back to relax. "You should join me, Vixa," she offered.

"Why?"

"To clean yourself. The water is nice," Cassandra said, thinking of how beautiful the warrior would be if she practiced better personal hygiene.

"I have already bathed this month and require none further."

Cassandra shook her head and dunked under the water momentarily to stifle a laugh. Soon Maltor returned. He stopped at the edge and looked at her lustfully, making her uncomfortable.

"It is time," he finally said, but he did not move.

"Get out," Vixa ordered Cassandra.

"No. Maltor must leave," Cassandra argued.

The volatile warrior looked briefly at Maltor, who made no expression, and she drew her axes and had them ready. Cassandra sat up, her focus on Vixa. She scanned the area for the arcane symbols and was surprised to find few, not even enough to form a basic spell. Maltor held his hand up, signaling to Vixa to put her weapons away. Cassandra noticed a lecherous smile on his face and realized she had revealed her breasts when she sat up. She covered them quickly and sank back into the water, giving Maltor a hateful expression. He laughed, turned, and left the two women alone.

"Get out!" Vixa said again forcefully.

Cassandra listened and quickly dressed. Soon they were back at the camels, and Maltor stood waiting for her with a knowing smirk. She stood by the camel, not nearly tall enough to mount it herself, and the barbarian king just stood there looking at her. She fumed at his ignorance and the rudeness of his crude behavior.

"Well?" she finally said.

"You had a bath? Are you happy?"

Her first instinct was to lash out, but she remembered her situation and knew it required delicate handling.

"Yes, it was lovely, thank you," she said with a fake smile.

There was a long pause. She could feel him staring her up and down, and she squirmed under his gaze. She finally said, "Did you catch your fairies?"

"No," Maltor said, and he grabbed her at last and helped her onto the camel.

He climbed up after her, and soon they were galloping toward the caravan. They caught up to them quickly enough and found their place at the front of the line.

"They are smart, tricky," Maltor whispered in her ear, his bad breath stronger than his body odor.

"Who?" Cassandra asked, not understanding the statement.

"The culiem. The fairies steal the bait and mock me."

"The fairies?"

"Yes, they look like miniature humans but winged and clever."

"I hope to see one someday," Cassandra said honestly. She had studied them briefly during her short time at Victoria's school. Varish was the only place to find them, and she had learned a little more about them through what Vixa and Maltor told her. As a witch, she was curious to find one.

"Heed my warning; they are dangerous," the barbarian king said.

"Oh? How so?"

"One bite from culiem will kill a human."

"They bite?"

"Yes, their mouths are filled with sharp teeth. Don't let the little devils fool you."

That was all the barbarian leader said to her for the rest of the trek home, which consisted of another day and a half of traveling. During that time, the temperature climbed, and the beating sun burned Cassandra's light skin. She covered the best she could with the blanket, but it offered little protection. Also, as scorching as the days were, the nights grew even colder, making it difficult for her to be comfortable during the day or night. By the time they reached the barbarian homeland, she was miserable.

The terrain had also slowly changed and became less rocky, with little to no vegetation other than some large cacti. Boulders still occasionally dotted the landscape, but sand eventually replaced the soil. During most of the last day of travel, the terrain consisted only of dunes. Near the end of the fourth day, they crested a particular dune to bear witness to their homeland. Maltor stopped the caravan so that Cassandra could take in the sight. From there, she could see the many tents, hundreds of them, stretching out on the sandy dunes. After a few moments, Maltor started the camel home, the newest prison in what appeared to be a long line of prisons for Cassandra.

The man in the porcelain mask walked up to Cass and Matilda's table and stood there. Matilda could tell it was a man because of the size of his hands and the style of his hair. Also, he dressed in fine men's clothing that only the wealthy could afford. The mysterious aura of the stranger, compounded with the fact he wore a mask, had Matilda very intrigued.

"May we help you?" Matilda asked.

The man pulled out a chair and sat down.

"Well, that is bold," Cass said with a smile.

"Do we know you?" Matilda asked, just as intrigued as Cass by the man's boldness.

"No, but I have been watching you since my friend's funeral. I have heard your discussions and know your desires for Cassandra Rho."

Matilda looked at Cass, who shrugged her shoulders, more intrigued by the minute.

"Well, you seem to know a lot about us. Are you going to tell us anything about yourself?" Matilda asked.

The man reached up and removed the mask, revealing a disfigured face on the right side. A hole in his cheek showed most of his teeth, and the scar ran up near his eye, which drooped slightly.

"I am Ronnis D'Breeth, former administrator of the Oldorburg Orphanage and enemy of Cassandra Rho. I want to help you find her."

Matilda stared at Cass in disbelief. Cass smiled and shrugged again, shaking her head.

"You can help us find her?"

"I believe so."

"And what is in it for you?"

"Only the satisfaction that she gets what she deserves if what you say you have planned for her comes to fruition."

"You do not want to kill her or rape her?" Matilda asked doubtfully.

"Of course I do, but she has bested me twice now, and I no longer want to do the dirty work. I will suffer no more losses at the hands of that one; she is a curse to me. However, I can help you find her. All I ask is that I get to come along and assist. Together we can track her down, I am certain."

"Did she do that to you?" Cass piped in.

"Yes, among many other things, including having my friend killed, resulting in one of the funerals the two of you attended."

"How long have you been spying on us?" Matilda asked.

"Since the day you explored the old mill house, the location of Barktuck's murder."

"We did not see you there or anywhere else in this town since we have been here," Matilda said.

"I know, that was intentional. But I know who each of you is and what your plans are for Cassandra. I want in."

"Why should we let you help? What do you have to offer?" Cass asked.

"Well, I can tell you two things: I can confirm that Cassandra was here a few weeks ago."

"I told you!" Cass said to Matilda, who nodded, sharing her excitement.

"Also, I know where she may be."

"Fine, you are in, just if you agree not to take her sexually or kill her. You may help Cass exact tortures or, just as you said, assist us in capturing her. Whatever level of involvement is fine with me. But I must be clear, and there is no negotiating on this—in the end, she is mine. In about eighteen more months, the 666th anniversary of the exiling of Marnelphion will arrive, and on that most wonderful night, I will sacrifice the virgin Cassandra Rho to my god. Can you agree to this, Ronnis D'Breeth?"

"Absolutely."

"Then tell us where she is," Matilda said eagerly.

"Very well. On the day of Barktuck's murder, I had the little witch bound and at my mercy in the old mill house."

"You did not take her virginity, did you?" Matilda asked in a near panic.

"I would have, yes, and was nearly at that point. Fortunately for you and unfortunately for me, the barbarians raided at that moment. So, as far as I can tell, the savages have her. I would guess the chances of her still being a virgin are doubtful. She might not even be alive."

Matilda was crestfallen at the information and just stared at the table and her remaining food for a moment. Finally, she said, "Where did these barbarians come from, and why did they not kill you too?"

"I have some resources that you may find quite useful, dear lady. The barbarians did try to kill me, but I escaped them," Ronnis explained, lifting his greasy hair to show the fresh scar on his forehead where the axe had struck.

"As far as where they came from and where they went, I can tell you that I followed them out of the mill house the best I could. They took Cassandra in a carriage and drove her north of Mecca-Loraine. I followed and soon found the wagon with the horses stabbed to death in a ditch. It seems they did not need the livestock or the wagon. That made me believe they were heading out to sea, so I followed their tracks for a bit, eventually leading right to a small beach. There was no sign of them, but they fled on a ship, there is no doubt.

"For the next few days, I went to the monastery where I have some carofex friends in Mecca-Loraine. I studied in their extensive library and found that the largest concentration of barbarians anywhere in the world is in the desert called Yaddaton on Varish."

"I know this place! It is only a few hundred miles north of my home," Matilda said excitedly.

"And that is probably where Cassandra Rho is if she is alive. But how do you snatch her from the midst of a horde of barbarians? This is where my line of thinking has stopped me from proceeding."

"Cerus," Matilda said.

"What is a Cerus?" Cass asked.

"Not what, who. Cerus is my husband, the greatest warrior I know. And we have a small army that would love to fight and could even stand up to a tribe of savage barbarians."

"Where is your husband?" Ronnis asked.

"In Nesin, my mountain fortress and home, located on Varish. I need to get there quickly."

"How fast can you be ready to depart?" Ronnis asked, putting the mask back on and standing up.

"Within the hour."

"Go pack your things; I will secure a passage to Varish and fetch you when ready."

"We need it to land at Port Racip if possible; Nesin is not far from there," Matilda said.

"Racip," Ronnis said with a nod, then started away.

"Wait, you do not know where we are staying," Matilda called after him.

"Yes, I do," he answered without even turning around.

Once he was gone, Cass said, "You are married but cheated with Malikai? I didn't know you had it in you."

"There are many things you don't know about me, Cass. Are you sure you want to do this? Now is the time to back out if you do not want to learn more about me and exactly how serious I am about finding Cassandra Rho."

"I wouldn't miss it for the world," Cass said, her eyes wide.

The two got up and left The Happy Oyster to gather their things. They had been in Mecca-Loraine far too long, and it was time to take the next step to move them closer to their prey. They were both very excited to have met Ronnis D'Breeth.

The barbarians led their prisoners through the main avenue between the many tents. Hundreds of barbarians lined up to watch the parade, standing just feet away. They yelled and threw things at the captive women—rocks, sticks, handfuls of sand, whatever they had available. Maltor led the procession with Cassandra beside him, which spared her the humiliating barrage. But the hate for her was just as intense; she could see it in their eyes as they judged her. They hated her and anyone who wasn't born into their tribe. She was thankful that Maltor offered her some protection from the violence, but she knew their true feelings, and as they traveled deeper into the place, that hate became more intense, like the awful smell, always the smell of the savages.

They walked down several avenues, past hundreds of tents of various sizes, made from camel skins and weathered from the sun and sand. Eventually, they came to a fork in the road where there were no tents along the right fork, only a walled structure. The wall was made of bleached wood but seemed almost like a prison to Cassandra, a lone form in the middle of the sea of tents. Maltor turned that way, guiding Cassandra with him. However, after a few steps, he turned to face the parade of new slaves. They were led slowly to the left fork, slow enough for Maltor to scrutinize them. It was almost as if he were looking for someone, or more accurately, Cassandra knew, evaluating the new stock.

Cassandra watched in disbelief as the warriors slowly ushered the slaves by. All were female and young, maybe with the oldest reaching their late twenties. Many were crying, and all were frightened. Although Cassandra could not see it, she knew their destination: the procreation tent.

Maltor signaled his men to pull out a tall, blond woman. She was slightly muscular, her skin tanned, and possibly accustomed to the outdoors and manual labor. Cassandra understood why he picked her. They pushed her into place next to Cassandra, her hands bound in front of her by a thick, coarse rope.

She smiled weakly at Cassandra, who nodded in response. After a long while, the parade of women passed, and Maltor had only selected this one woman to join Cassandra. The rest were gone, and Cassandra knew she would never see them again.

Maltor turned to Cassandra and cupped her chin in his strong hand. She did not resist as he brought her face up to look him in the eye. He did not say anything, but she knew he was telling her in no uncertain terms not to fail him. Then he turned and walked back into the mass of tents with his entourage, the crowd now cheering for their king as he passed. Vixa moved up with a couple of men to stand before Cassandra and the other woman.

"You will now enter the training compound," Vixa said, nodding toward the structure with the wooden walls. "You are the lucky ones who will fight to be our queen. Do not fail, or you will join the others, or worse."

Cassandra and the other woman exchanged a concerned look, then followed Vixa to the compound. As they approached the twelve-foot wall, Cassandra noticed warriors atop it, so she understood there must be a ledge bordering the inside of the wall for them to stand upon. Four men removed a locking bar fastened on the outside and opened the one set of heavy doors. Vixa continued the small parade, but the men escorting them did not enter and remained with the other four men at the opened gate. Inside the walled area were ten tents made like the ones they had passed along the way. They had red numbers painted on them, from one to ten, and paintings of a snake in various stages of life. The first few had eggs, tent one a whole egg, the second and third an egg cracking and breaking open. By tent five, a snake emerging from the egg decorated the camel skin. The others depicted snakes growing to adulthood, with tent ten reflecting a coiled adult snake, ready to strike. In the center of all the tents was a large, circular area for training.

Cassandra's guess concerning the ledge upon the wall was correct as she noticed it traversed the entirety of the compound. At least a dozen armed men observed them from above. Vixa led the two women to the center of the training pit and pulled out a knife. She cut the other woman's bindings as she spoke.

"This will be your home for the next three months. You will learn to fight in hand-to-hand combat."

The rope fell to the ground, and Vixa collected it; she stuffed it into a small bag she carried on her side and put away the knife. Then she drew both axes, startling Cassandra and the other recruit.

"These you will never wield. Your training will be limited to hand-to-hand combat. Even as the potential queen, you are still just females and have few rights, so you can never train with real weapons."

Cassandra could hear a couple of the men on top of the wall laugh at the remark. As Vixa spoke, other women emerged from the tents. They did not look to be prisoners but young barbarians. Their skin was tanned and their hair dark, making Cassandra and her fellow blond friend stand out and look ridiculous in their loincloths.

"These tents are ranked from one to ten, and your quarters will change depending on your performance in this pit. At the end of the training period, the four strongest warriors in tents nine and ten will participate in the tournament to become queen. For the rest of you in tents one through eight, you will return home and resume your lives. Of course, if you outsiders find yourselves in one of the lesser tents, I will escort you to the procreation tent to live out your days with your legs spread.

"Furthermore, you must learn to exist with fellow trainees during your stay here. Anything goes in the pit and your general existence when not in training. This is Breka and Lita," Vixa said, and she waved to two strong young women who stepped forward from the others.

Both appeared unfriendly to Cassandra, and she could only imagine the trouble those two could cause. Both stared hard at Cassandra and the other outsider, and Cassandra knew danger was in store for them. The barbarian trainees sorely outnumbered them, and if Vixa intended to leave them alone with the likes of Breka and Lita, they were in serious trouble.

"Through their reputation, I have granted them tent ten; it is up to the rest of you to cast them down from that spot," Vixa continued. "Of course, the two of you have tent one," she added, motioning to Cassandra and the other blond woman.

"Training begins at sun up," Vixa said, then turned and left, the doors shutting behind her.

Cassandra could hear the bar being put back into place afterward. The men on the wall immediately began whispering and pointing as if watching a battle beginning to unfold. Cassandra did not think that was far from the truth. She turned toward tent one only to find a line of angry-looking barbarian women blocking the way.

One stepped before the others and said, "I am Breka, the one who will compete for queen. My sisters of the Tribe of the Serpent know this to be true. They are here only as a formality and with the hopes that I will become injured and unable to continue. That will not happen."

She took another menacing step toward the two and said, "However, dogs like you have no chance and are here as a source of entertainment. Ultimately, you will find yourselves in the procreation tent, whoring out whatever pathetic sex you offer."

The others laughed, and Breka grabbed a strand of Cassandra's hair, studying it as if the color was bizarre to her. Cassandra knew that it was. Cassandra jerked her hair away, and in the blink of an eye, Breka punched her hard in the gut. Cassandra lost her breath and fell to her knees immediately. She could vaguely hear hoots and hollers from the men on the wall. Then Cassandra could see a set of feet standing before her. She looked up to see Breka towering over her. She then took a fistful of her hair and yanked hard, tearing more than a few hairs from her scalp. Cassandra screamed and fell to the sand, rubbing the sensitive spot.

"Which of you outsiders is Maltor's favorite?"

Cassandra knew that meant trouble, and when Breka moved over to the other woman and asked, "Is it you?" Cassandra knew she had to speak up.

The other woman shook her head nervously, and when Breka yanked out a few of her blond hairs, Cassandra said, "It is me."

"You?" Breka said with a smirk.

She walked over, bent to Cassandra's eye level, and said, "Do not think you have a chance; I will lie with Maltor by tournament end, not you. Understand?"

"He stinks, like you, so why do I care?" Cassandra responded, then jumped to her feet, where a very angry Breka met her.

She grabbed Cassandra by the throat and squeezed with incredible strength. She moved close and said, "Look, outlander, you come here with your light hair and attitude, and I will gladly beat you into submission. The only reason I don't do it now is because Maltor desires you. That protects you, but in the pit, tomorrow, you are mine. By the end of the tournament, Maltor will not want you, and I promise you, your pretty face will not be so pretty."

With that, she threw Cassandra to the ground like a rag doll, impressing Cassandra again with her sheer strength.

"These two dogs sleep outside tonight," Breka said. "Fetch me their blankets; I'll take them as a prize. If you two want them back, come and get them."

Two of the other young women ran into the first tent; they returned a moment later with two large camel-hair blankets and offered them to Breka. She took them and, with a snide look to the two outlanders, went into the tenth tent. The others slowly disbursed to their respective tents, leaving the two blond girls in the middle of the training pit.

"I'm Laryn," the tall blond said, offering Cassandra a hand.

"Cassandra," Cassandra said as Laryn pulled her to her feet.

"Well, Cassandra, I feel like we are in some kind of strange terrarium," Laryn said, looking at the many barbarians lining the walls.

"Yes, now let's get our blankets," Cassandra said, moving toward Breka's tent and gathering the symbols floating in the air to summon a potent spell.

"Wait," Laryn said, gently grabbing Cassandra's arm.

"Why?"

"Let her show her dominance; we will get our blankets back in time," Laryn said.

"We will freeze out here tonight."

"Yes, but it will only be for one night. I will earn them back tomorrow in the pit."

"You seem confident," Cassandra said, putting her hands on her hips to regard the surprising woman.

"I am."

"I know these kinds of people—not barbarians, but bullies. If you let them take, they will continue to do so," Cassandra argued.

"Trust me."

Cassandra studied her for a moment and eventually gave in with a sigh. "Fine, but we will be cold out here."

"We can share body heat," Laryn suggested.

Cassandra gave her a strange look, and after a few moments, she said for the second time in her life, "I am not a lesbian."

Laryn smiled and said, "Well, perhaps after your stay here, you will be."

They laughed, and Cassandra took a liking to the woman right away. They sat in the pit and talked until the sun went down. Cassandra told her about her family and the loss of her second mother. She told her of Binta and even Greyson and how she hoped to see them again one day. She learned that Laryn was a turnip farmer from Farmer's Stop and that Maltor and his band of savages murdered her family, which included her parents, her grandparents, and even her little brother, who was only eight years old. Maltor had murdered all the people of Laryn's small community except for the females who had reached breeding age. Cassandra felt a kinship with the newly orphaned woman, and that night when the temperature dropped, they cuddled close and shared their body heat.

The following day, Vixa kicked Cassandra and Laryn not so gently until they woke up. As they sat up and squinted in the bright morning sun, Cassandra realized the other trainees surrounded the training circle. Most wore smirks on their faces, and some even laughed at the scene. Cassandra felt she was back at the orphanage, the other orphans ridiculing her again. She hated the barbarians then, but following Laryn's lead, she swallowed her anger.

"What are you two doing in my training pit?" Vixa growled.

"We decided to sleep under the stars for our first night to take in the wonderful scenery," Cassandra lied, trying not to sound too sarcastic.

"Sleep in your tents from now on and keep out of my training pit unless we are training. If you want to act like dogs, I'll treat you as such!"

Even with Vixa's harsh words, Cassandra knew she was still the privileged one there. She also knew that Vixa could not treat her as such. Vixa wanted her to succeed and remain in Maltor's good graces. And Cassandra would try.

"Partner up," Vixa ordered.

Cassandra immediately turned to Laryn, but Breka stepped in before she could, taking Laryn by the arm and moving to an empty spot in the pit. With her new friend now paired up with the meanest woman in the compound, Cassandra was stuck with a small but muscular woman whose stench exceeded her rare beauty.

"Do any of you bathe?" Cassandra asked her as they paired up.

"I will bathe in your blood, outlander. I am Gah, resident of the third tent."

"I am Cassandra, wicked witch from the east," Cassandra answered with a smirk.

"Very funny, outlander, but I will wipe that smile off your face."

Vixa moved into the center of the pit and said, "Trainees, we will learn to fight over the next few months. Some of you have learned the basics, like how to step close, pull off balance, defend, attack, escape, and so on. So, this day will be easy for you, but for those who know none of this, you must learn quickly to keep up with the competition. To begin, we will spar so that I may judge where each of you is in your training."

"What?" Cassandra asked, turning toward Vixa. "We will fight without any instructions or training at all?"

Vixa just smirked at her and said, "Begin!"

Cassandra turned back to her opponent just in time to receive a punch in the mouth. She saw stars for a moment and felt dizziness overcome her. Cassandra fell on her backside and brought her hands to her mouth, feeling and tasting the warm blood there. All twenty women were wrestling and punching, and the men on the ledge were cheering them on. Before she had fully regained her senses, Gah yanked her to her feet by her hair.

Cassandra tried to formulate a defense and, as always, began to search for the arcane symbols to defend herself properly. However, the woman was as fast as she was vicious, and before she could put anything together for a proper spell, Gah kicked her between the legs. No one had ever hit Cassandra there before, and the impact with her pelvic bone sent waves of agony through her lower abdomen. She fell to her knees again, moving her hands from her mouth to her wounded crotch. Gah took that opportunity to pull her hair back and punched her hard in the left jaw. She saw stars and fell backward to the ground. Gah was on top of her quickly, pinning her arms down and beating her. Cassandra was the first trainee knocked out that day and would have probably been killed by the vicious Gah if Vixa hadn't intervened. The last thing she heard was the cheering from the savages on the wall.

She woke up sometime later in her tent, Laryn kneeling beside her as she lay in one of the two straw beds. Her friend applied a damp cloth to her head and a healing salve to her bruised and busted face. Laryn smiled at her when she came to. The sun was going down, so Cassandra couldn't see her face well, but she recognized the smile and knew it was genuine.

"How'd I do?" Cassandra asked.

"Not good."

The two shared a genuine laugh, but the effort hurt Cassandra's pounding head, and she subsided immediately.

"I can't do this, Laryn; I am no fighter."

"How can you tell?" Laryn joked, which had them both laughing again. "Shh, you need rest, don't over exert," Laryn said as Cassandra held her pounding head.

"How did you do?" Cassandra asked as Laryn gently applied more salve.

"Well, I got our tent back."

"And our blankets," Cassandra said, realizing one of the uncomfortable but warm blankets covered her.

"No, that one is mine; I won it back from Breka."

"You beat her?" Cassandra asked in amazement.

"Of course not, but I gave her a few good punches and earned enough of her respect to get it back."

"And mine?"

Laryn shook her head. "No, I'm sorry, but you must get that back yourself. Breka is steadfast in her ideals, and I'm afraid you'll have to earn it back."

"You are amazing, Laryn. Did they serve food at any point during the day? I am starving."

"Yes, once, at dinner time."

"Good, I am ready to eat."

"I saved you some of mine," Laryn said, bringing over a bowl of white mush.

"This is yours?"

"Yes, what is left of it. I was starving too, but I saved you as much as possible."

"Wait, where is mine?"

"Evidently, you must be able to receive your dinner, or you don't get any."

"What?"

"You must be able to walk to the gate and get your dinner when served. If not, you miss out."

"Great, so I guess I won't be eating much."

Cassandra sat up with Laryn's help. Everything hurt, and her busted lip pounded with the effort. She ate slowly, and the stuff was not very tasty but was filling. After she ate, Laryn gave her some water. According to Laryn, a bucket of water was offered to each tent at dinner time, so there was plenty of that. It was loaded with sediment but was very soothing to Cassandra's cracked lips. After she ate, Laryn completed applying the salve, and the sun was fully down by then.

"Well, sleep tight, Cassandra, and sleep well; you will need your strength," Laryn said, standing and walking toward her bed.

"Wait. Here," Cassandra said, holding the blanket up for her to take.

"No, you have it tonight; you need it more than I do."

"We'll both get cold, no matter which one is beaten more."

"What do you suggest?" Laryn asked.

Cassandra moved over, the effort causing discomfort, lifted the blanket, patted the bed beside her, and invited Laryn in.

"I am not a lesbian," Laryn said.

"Good, because neither am I," Cassandra said with a smile.

With a shrug, Laryn climbed in. They cuddled closely that night because it was frigid, and Cassandra felt like she did back when she and Binta traveled to the magical caves all those months ago in search of Cassandra's birthright. She felt close to someone at a time when she needed it. She missed Binta dearly, but Laryn was fast becoming a good friend.

The next training day resulted in a similar outcome as Cassandra did poorly but somehow remained conscious, so she earned a plate of food at the end of the training. However, the day's big news was that Laryn pinned Lita, the second-best trainee in the compound. She and Breka were the two residents of the tenth tent, and although the pin was brief, it gave Laryn a lot of unwanted attention. As Cassandra and Laryn sat in their tent eating their meal, the news of the pin was the talk of all the other trainees, which did not sit well with Lita and Breka.

Vixa focused on wrestling moves the next day and intentionally matched Cassandra with a smaller, weaker opponent. Still, she did not do well, the more petite woman quickly pinning her four out of the five times they wrestled. At the end of that third day, Vixa's disappointed look spoke volumes. Cassandra was failing miserably.

That night as she and Laryn ate, Cassandra confessed to her new friend, "I am a witch."

"A what?"

"A witch. I can use magic, like a wizard, but much better."

"Why are you telling me this?"

"I am not a warrior, Laryn, and I am surely not a barbarian queen. I don't belong here."

"Well, the training is in its early stages; you will grow stronger. You must be patient; it has only been three days."

"Come on, Laryn, you can compete with these vicious women, but not me. I'll have to use magic to get through."

"No, Cassandra, you must be careful. I heard some of the other trainees talking, and they said something about a beheading that had recently occurred in the tribe. Some old woman had been suspected and accused of witchcraft. There were rumors of her bringing a dead lizard back to life. Maltor beheaded her husband as well for good measure.

"Please promise me that if you truly can use spells, you will not do it here, not in this place," Laryn asked.

Laryn's kind words took hold of Cassandra's heart. The girl was purely good. A feeling rose from the pit of Cassandra's stomach as she watched her friend prepare for bed. Even though both were filthy and carried the sweat of three days' worth of desert heat, Cassandra did not mind Laryn's body odor. Her heart beat a little faster as she admired the beautiful woman, and she likened it to the night Binta kissed her.

Her feelings for Laryn differed from how she had felt with Binta when they shared their first kiss. That moment was special, and Cassandra had soon fallen in love with her. Although Cassandra had denied it with both Cass and now Laryn, she realized then that she liked women as much as she did men, probably more. She would not dare admit it, for fear of the bullying she would receive, not that a little bullying would have made any difference in the quality of her life the last few months!

She truly loved Binta, but this situation was different, as they were fighting for their lives. There was no future here and no opportunity to fall in love. If they had met at another place or time, Cassandra would have given herself freely to Laryn, but not here. If they were lucky, one of them would make it out alive. Most likely, they were both heading to the procreation tent.

She could not let herself get too close to her new friend, but she thought about it often and felt Laryn did as well. Cassandra never tried to get her blanket from Breka so they had to sleep close each night, and Laryn didn't seem to mind.

Later that night, as they huddled under the itchy blanket, Cassandra said, "I have refrained from using magic thus far, and I will continue to do so as long as I can. But I promise you, I can only compete in the tournament if I use my powers."

Laryn only smiled, and the two gazed into each other's eyes for a long while, Laryn even playing with Cassandra's hair. Neither spoke because no words were required at that beautiful moment. Eventually, Laryn smiled and kissed Cassandra lightly on the cheek. She then snuggled close to fend off the desert cold.

As Laryn quickly fell asleep, Cassandra held her tight and thought about her predicament. She knew to compete with those seasoned and athletic women hand-selected by the tribe, she would have to use her powers, regardless of the consequences. She fell asleep that night holding Laryn tight and thinking of ways to sneak in some magic in the coming days.

The fourth day of training produced two unexpected events. First, Vixa announced before the training that Laryn would be moved immediately to tent three due to her strong performance so far. Cassandra didn't hear them, but several other changes followed. She had not expected her friend to be taken from her that way. It shocked her and showed in her performance that day as she failed miserably against another opponent. Vixa's frustration grew, so by the end of the day, while the rest of the trainees ate, Vixa pulled Cassandra and Breka aside.

"You are the chosen one of Maltor; you are here because he wants you here, but you do not belong. Breka is the most likely one to become queen. You should not be here."

"Why are you telling me this?" Cassandra asked.

"Because Maltor asked about your progress, and your failure is my failure," the wild woman said, the anger splayed across her face. "Therefore, we will step up your training. From now on, you will compete against Breka only."

"How will that help anything?" Cassandra asked in frustration.

Vixa backhanded her hard, and she barely managed to keep her feet. She turned toward the unpredictable woman, holding her face with a hateful stare.

"You can wipe that look off your face because if you lose the next competition, no matter what it is, I will beat you to within an inch of your life."

"Name the challenge then, and I'll win it!" Cassandra screamed so loud that everyone in the compound turned to regard the trio.

Cassandra was playing with fire, she knew, but it was time to use her magic; it was time to show up the evil Breka and get her blanket back. It was time to quit taking the abuse that the barbarians specialized in dishing out. She readied her magic to lash out at Breka, Vixa, or anyone else who challenged her in the next few moments. Her patience had run out. She saw Laryn looking on and very concerned. She recalled their conversation and her request that Cassandra not use magic in Yaddaton. She nodded to her friend, letting her know as best she could that this might be goodbye.

"The challenge of the rock. It starts now, and you best not fail, you arrogant outlander."

Vixa had never called her that, making her all the angrier, not necessarily at Vixa but at the situation. She had no hope of succeeding, and Vixa was right; she should not be competing against the advanced competition in the compound. She was most disappointed because her success would boost Vixa's status in the tribe. Cassandra needed that silent alliance to hold any hope of surviving the ordeal.

Vixa gathered two rocks about the size of apples and had Cassandra and Breka stand in the middle of the training pit. All the other trainees and the men on the wall looked on anxiously. The two women stood about five feet apart, facing each other. By the look on her face, it was clear that Breka had participated in this exercise before or had at least seen it done. Either way, she wore a confident smile.

"This is not a test of strength but a test of endurance and character. If the two of you fought, all know what the outcome would be," Vixa said.

Cassandra shuffled her feet at the comment as several trainees snickered at her.

"Instead, this will see which of you has a stronger will. Each of you will hold your right hand out in front of you, palm up. I will then place the rock on your palm, and you will hold it there as long as you can, or at least longer than your opponent. You lose once your hand falls below your waist. Simple enough."

She stood before Cassandra and whispered, "And when you lose this contest, everyone will watch as I beat you."

Cassandra narrowed her eyes and chewed her lip but said nothing. She understood she was already disadvantaged, even with the simple test. Breka's confidence and Vixa's lack of it spoke volumes. They raised their hands, and Vixa placed the rocks on their palms simultaneously, then stepped back. To Cassandra's surprise, the stone weighed much more than she anticipated, and the shocked expression on her face had Breka smiling arrogantly.

Within just a few moments, Cassandra's arm was quivering with the attempt to hold her hand high, while Breka easily kept her hand at its starting position. Cassandra closed her eyes and delved into a deep meditation, trying to ignore the burn in her arm. She tried to recall a spell that could help her, but nothing in her repertoire would suffice, and nothing would be discreet.

Cassandra thought of a conversation she had with a boy at Victoria's school one day. She could not remember his name, but she liked him. He was one of the few students who spoke to her. She remembered a brief discussion between classes they shared about a spell he was learning. It was a spell of levitation, and it would be beneficial if she could recall how to cast it. She could only remember bits and pieces of the magic but understood that air density factored into it. She opened her eyes and began to search the many arcane symbols floating in the air around her to determine which ones would assist her the most with such a feat.

She had never cast such a spell, so she would have to improvise. Most importantly, she would need to do it in a way that would not garner attention. She fell into a trance as her opponent fell out of focus, replaced by the symbols that heeded her call. She manipulated them, forcing them to gather around the rock in her hand. The energy in the compound was weak, and the symbols were faint, but there was enough.

Before Cassandra could attempt to stitch the arcane symbols together for a spell, Breka let out a small scream, dropping her rock in the process. Cassandra immediately snapped out of her trance and let her rock fall to the ground. She shook her arm and rubbed the tired muscles there. All the other trainees and even Vixa stood in shock at the turn of events.

"She's a devil witch!" Breka screamed, backing out of the pit.

"What do you speak of?" Vixa demanded.

None of the others had ever seen Breka frightened, but at that moment, she indeed was. She kept backing away, mumbling that Cassandra was a devil witch. Vixa finally caught up to her and grabbed her arm, and when the young trainee did not snap out of her trance, the red-haired instructor slapped her hard across the face.

"What happened? Why did you drop the rock so early?" Vixa asked.

Breka didn't answer, so Vixa slapped her again and shook her. Breka slowly turned to regard Vixa and said, "Her eyes changed color. It was unnatural! She is a devil! She is a devil!"

Vixa turned to Cassandra, who shook her head and shrugged, pretending not to understand what Breka was talking about. She thought it an excellent opportunity to retrieve her blanket, so she approached Breka's tent. The trainees parted, giving her a wide berth, and none, not even Lita, moved to stop her. She casually walked into the tent and emerged shortly after with her blanket. She then entered her tent and hoped no one would follow, especially Vixa. No one did, and she could hear a hysterical Breka try to explain to Vixa what she saw. Luckily, no one else had seen the change, so none could confirm it. With another smack upon Breka's face, Vixa left the compound. Afterward, Cassandra could hear the guards adding the locking bar, then everything was deathly quiet. Although she was hungry, Cassandra fell asleep shortly after. She hoped as she dozed off that Laryn would come to her that night, but she never did.

The following day, Cassandra found the smaller barbarian in her tent with her, sleeping on the one bed that Cassandra and Laryn had never used. She was the weaker one Cassandra had pinned once out of five attempts a few days earlier. The small barbarian was way better than Cassandra at the combat training but still worse than anyone else there, so she now found herself in the lowest-ranking tent. Cassandra nodded to her when she rose, and the young barbarian returned the nod.

"I am not a witch," Cassandra lied.

The girl nodded again, got up, and left the tent. Cassandra rose and went to join the circle in the training pit. The others gave her some space, and all acted nervous around her. Only Laryn approached her, and Cassandra noticed how bruised her face was.

"Did this happen during training yesterday?" Cassandra asked.

Laryn smiled, always the optimist, and whispered, "No, Breka, Lita, and some others jumped me last night. I was sneaking out of the tent to cuddle with you again, but they caught and beat me."

"Why?"

"Why do you think? They are afraid now, and they know I'm the closest ally you have. They figured if they hurt me, it would also hurt you."

"I'm sorry," Cassandra said, touching Laryn's face.

The woman pulled away and said, "Be careful; this will not end here. The entire place is angry, like a nest of hornets. I fear for your safety."

"And I yours," Cassandra said as Laryn smiled weakly and moved back to her spot before tent three.

Soon Vixa arrived and walked straight up to Cassandra. Cassandra steeled her resolve and waited for the worst.

"What happened yesterday during the contest?" Vixa asked, taking her aside.

"I won."

"What did you do? Something spooked Breka."

"No, she failed and is making excuses," Cassandra lied.

"She has participated in the rock challenge before; she has always lasted a very long time, and most of the time, she wins. Yesterday's surrender makes no sense."

Cassandra only shrugged, and Vixa took out her blades and had them both at the base of Cassandra's neck before she could react. "Do not lie to me!"

"I speak the truth, Vixa. You wanted a test of our resolve and you got the result I promised you would get. It is as simple as that."

"Perhaps. Perhaps not. Either way, I am changing your partner to Lita. Breka is too afraid now, and so are most of the others. However, Lita is not, so she will substitute nicely until Breka finds her resolve again. Instead, I will pair her with Laryn."

"No, please …"

Vixa relaxed and put her blades away but only smirked at Cassandra's plea.

"She will suffer for whatever stunt you pulled, and if I find out you used that devil magic in my training pit, your fate will be decided by Maltor."

When Vixa returned to the pit, she made the adjustments, pairing up Breka with Laryn and Lita with Cassandra. Vixa then looked through the tents, taking an exceptionally long time in Cassandra's as if scouring her belongings for something illegal. It reminded Cassandra of Ronnis and the day she attacked him. Her anger boiled within, and her fists tightened at her sides.

Her thoughts were interrupted by Lita, who whispered, "Your little friend would not speak last night. She must like you to take such a beating from Breka. Today you will witness that beating firsthand. If you don't want Breka to kill her eventually, you will speak the truth, devil witch."

True to Lita's word, Breka had her way with Laryn that day, and Cassandra kept an eye on them as best she could. Laryn was a great fighter, but Breka was in a foul mood after being embarrassed, and Cassandra understood her error as Breka beat Laryn unconscious. It took Vixa a long while to step in, letting the beating go on longer than it should have. Of course, Cassandra lost badly to Lita that day, and the stronger barbarian reminded her repeatedly that she was not afraid of her and that her time was coming. Cassandra believed her as Lita threw her around like a rag doll. Somehow her victory over Breka had made things go from bad to worse.

As she sat alone in her tent that evening eating dinner, everything seemed to hurt. She had bitten her tongue during one of Lita's body slams, making eating the slop served as dinner difficult. Lita had also twisted Cassandra's arm to the point it almost broke, and she found it difficult to hold her bowl. In truth, she didn't think she could take much more physical abuse. Her thoughts lingered on Laryn, hoping she was not hurt too badly. Vixa seemed to turn on her now, so she and Laryn were in big trouble. She noticed that her new tent mate was nowhere to be found that night. She didn't think much about it and drifted off to sleep, very concerned with what the coming days held for her and her friend.

A few hours later, Cassandra was awakened by someone pulling her up by her hair and throwing the blanket off her. She screamed, but another hand was there to cover her mouth, cutting it off. She quickly realized that more than one person was assailing her. Two of the better trainees held her arms behind her back, one with her other hand clamped around her mouth. Lita stood in front of her. The large woman said nothing and punched Cassandra in the gut several times. She felt like her insides would explode with each hit, and she eventually lost her supper. The other trainees let her go then, and she lay on the ground holding her stomach and coughing up the last of her meal.

Soon Lita was behind her, pulling her to a standing position and locking her arms behind her. Her left arm ached from its abuse from earlier that day, and Cassandra cried out. Lita did not relent, and Cassandra stood on her toes, trying to relieve the pressure.

"And now it's time for you to pay for what you did to Breka," Lita whispered in her ear.

Breka appeared in the doorway of her tent, a cloth sack in her hand. Cassandra's heart beat fast, and she knew something was amiss. Lita continued the pressure on her arm, forcing her to stand on her tiptoes, and so she was unable to formulate any spell. Breka walked right up to her and backhanded her.

"I know what I saw, and you are a witch!" the vile woman said through gritted teeth. "You are not a member of the Serpent Tribe, and therefore, I will exterminate you."

She held the sack in front of Cassandra's face, waving it menacingly. To Cassandra's horror, it moved! Whatever was inside of it was alive.

"Behold, the Yaddaton Viper, the most venomous snake in the desert. Let's see if your witch powers can save you from this. Give me her arm!"

Lita released her right arm, and one of the other trainees grabbed it at the elbow, holding it out toward Breka.

"No, Breka, please!"

"Hold her still!" Breka shouted, ignoring Cassandra's pleas.

Slowly but surely, they pinned her arm so she could not move it, and Breka put the sack over it, closing it tight at the elbow.

"No, Breka, no!" Cassandra screamed as the snake bit her once, then again.

Breka smacked the snake through the sack several times, agitating it, and it bit her twice more before they removed her arm. The bites hurt tremendously, but the real pain came from the lethal poison as it coursed through her arm. Lita released her, and she immediately lost the use of her legs as the venom spread quickly through her.

Cassandra flipped over to her back and thrashed in the sand as the pain took its toll. She felt like she was on fire, and some unseen spectral hand was plucking each of her nerves. There was foam in her mouth, and it started to drip out the sides as she convulsed uncontrollably. She could barely make out Breka kneeling next to her, smiling.

"Just one bite will kill a camel. It looks like you suffered at least four. Let's see your witchcraft save you from that."

Cassandra's vision faded, but she saw Breka stand and hand the bag to a man at the tent entrance. She recognized him as one of the guards on the wall. He left immediately, and she understood he had supplied the murder weapon for Breka.

"Tuck her in," she heard Breka command the others, then felt herself pulled back to her bed.

Soon everything went black, and the world became silent. There was no more pain in her arm or fear for her life. Perhaps she had finally found an escape from the cruel world.

She awakened the next day with a massive headache. Laryn was lying beside her, and Cassandra's arm was wrapped around her friend. She didn't remember the attack from the night before right away, but when she noticed that Laryn felt very cold, she sat up with a start. Laryn's eyes were wide open, and foam leaked from her mouth. Cassandra desperately found her friend's arm and, to her horror, saw the many snake bites there. They had killed Laryn! Her thoughts were messy, and her entire body ached, especially her head. But she eventually remembered the attack and looked at her arm—four snake bites.

"How?" she asked herself, knowing she should be dead like her friend.

Then she felt the pool at her hip. She thought at first she had urinated during her death throes, but she wasn't dead. She turned to regard the collection of yellowish liquid and felt it trickling from her hip. She slowly stood and moved her hand to her hip, to the brand from Ronnis, and realized that the snake's two long fangs were oozing venom. It was rejecting the poison! Somehow, Ronnis's brand had saved her life.

She stood there wiping the brand, and more leaked out as she did. She gently wiped it off her hand and onto the blanket she and Laryn had shared on their final night together. She looked at her friend and wondered if she could have saved her. There was no hope for either of them, but now Cassandra was alone again, and that same old feeling of being abused and tortured by so many others came flooding back. Someone had taken her friend away, just like everything she cared for in her short life. Laryn was dead, and Breka was responsible. Laryn was a victim of the barbarians in more ways than one. They had murdered her family and now her as well.

"I'm sorry, my friend. May Gella receive your soul into the heavens."

She then did something she hadn't done for a very long time—she prayed. It was a prayer of hope for Laryn in the afterlife and the request she find her family there. It was also a prayer for strength, because she knew what she had to do now and hoped she would join her friend in the heavens. She stood slowly and turned to the tent opening to regard the trainees who gathered around the pit for the coming day of training.

Cassandra stepped out, and there was more than one gasp as the savages realized she wasn't dead. She saw Vixa entering the compound and knew her life was over. But she would avenge her friend before she died. As the sea of trainees parted, Breka turned to her, and her eyes grew as wide as saucers. Lita's did as well, and they all stepped quickly away from Breka, who was the target of Cassandra's scowl.

She summoned the power of her most potent spell, one of a killing ball of energy. She had used one against Ronnis long ago, which nearly killed him. She had grown powerful since then, and her spell was far more potent now. She pointed her finger at Breka, and her hand crackled with greenish energy. She let the ball of energy fly, hitting Breka in the throat. Like Cassandra the previous night, the woman fell to her back and writhed on the ground. Burned flesh assaulted Cassandra's senses, and a wicked smile engulfed her face. The other trainees scattered, and she could see Vixa running impossibly fast to interfere. She would not lose this kill like she did Ronnis.

She knelt beside Breka, pulled her to a sitting position, and said, "This is for Laryn."

She then inserted two fingers into the woman's mouth and let loose another missile. Her eyes exploded from their sockets, and there was a sickly sizzling sound as her brain fried. Smoke wafted up from the eye sockets and her mouth. Cassandra released her hair, and Breka fell to the sand with a sickening thud, dead.

Cassandra sensed Vixa behind her and turned at the last moment to find both axes, blunt side forward, swinging at her. She dodged the first, but the second connected against her forehead, sending her flying. Reality faded away, but she was satisfied; she had avenged her friend and would be freed from the barbarians once and for all.

12

A Warrior's Heart

Cassandra awakened to the sound of voices. It took her a while to gain her bearings and escape her stupor. Her head throbbed, and her body generally ached. She remembered the incident with Breka and, in a way, was disappointed Vixa hadn't killed her. That meant she was still in the barbarian tribe and would probably face torture at the hands of the savages. Either way, it would likely result in her death, so why prolong the misery? She focused more on the voices, letting them lead her out of her fogginess.

Both were male; one she recognized as Maltor, and the other sounded older. She opened her eyes finally to see she was in some strange cluster of cacti. She knew she was outdoors because she could see the sun peeking through the crowd of desert vegetation. The cacti were giant, some she estimated ten feet tall, and ranged from green to brown. Some had beautiful flowers adorning them, but they all had one common characteristic—very long needles. The plants all seemed to lean toward the center of the area, making a triangular enclosure. There was one entrance amid the plants, just big enough for one person to fit through at a time without being impaled by the needles.

She was lying in the center of the natural structure, on a stone table, her hands straight out to her sides and clamped at the wrist by a metal loop. The metal bindings held her ankles similarly. She panicked at the thought of once again being restrained and at the mercy of a tormentor. How many times in her young life had this happened? She realized she had only experienced that horrible feeling with Ronnis twice. Still, she was somehow more frightened because the savage barbarians might do things that Ronnis would not.

She looked around and saw that no one was in the enclosure with her, but she could still hear the mumbled voices and see shadows moving outside her natural prison as if several people milled about there. She lifted her head—which caused excruciating pain, especially in her forehead—to get a better look at her surroundings. There was a fire pit to her left and a small table near the stone slab on which she lay with several different tools sitting atop it. They appeared primitive, with a small hammer, a knife, and a clamp littered among other tools she could not identify. What troubled her most was that they were bloody, as was the top of the small table. The blood stains looked old but appeared to be blood, nonetheless.

She lay her injured head back down and tried to focus on the conversation. However, the mumbled voices sounded like they were further away. She gathered her thoughts and considered calling for the ravens. She wasn't sure if they existed in that part of the world, so that seemed like a terrible waste of time. Instead, she focused on the arcane symbols that always filled the air and which she could easily see if she focused on them. But, for the first time in her life, they did not come into focus well. Compared to the usual dozens, only three or four danced around her table, and even those seemed fuzzy. Her heart skipped a beat. She knew Vixa had grazed her head with the blunt end of an axe, which knocked her out, but had that hit taken away her ability to summon spells and cast them using the symbols? She focused again but had the same results. Without her spells, she was truly powerless, especially against the barbarians.

Several of the savages walked into her little prison. Maltor entered first, followed by Vixa and an older man wearing a headdress, several beaded necklaces, and gaudy rings. Like the other two, his skin was dark from a long life of baking in the desert sun. After briefly living at the temple of Gella in Pelesea, she had learned a little about religions and how they worked. The new man seemed to be a priest, judging by his garments. She focused on the holy symbol he wore around his neck: a coiled snake. She did not recognize that symbol but assumed it must be the god Strenna's, which was the god Vixa had told her about. It also made sense because Maltor thought her snake brand was from Strenna.

All three stood at her table, looking at her with great interest. She knew she was in trouble and thought it best not to speak, so she kept her mouth shut and waited. She studied their expressions: Maltor did not appear displeased, which surprised her; Vixa looked furious, which made her wonder how the unpredictable woman hadn't killed her; and the "priest" seemed impartial but very interested in the proceedings.

Maltor was the first to speak. "I should saw off your head and toss your body into the river of death for your witchcraft."

He took strands of her golden hair and rubbed it between his fingers. Again, she felt like a piece of livestock and hated it when he touched her. She knew she could not resist anything he did while shackled to the stone. So, she made no move, and he seemed lost in thought.

His eyes had a spacey glaze when he said, "However, I've decided to spare you."

"What?" Vixa screamed.

"Why else do you think she is here?" Maltor said, waving his hands at the cactus prison.

"To be tortured to death; those are our rules! The outlander must die!"

Maltor turned on her, grabbing her by the hair and slapping her hard. The priest moved back a few steps, seemingly unconcerned with Maltor's outburst, as if that kind of attack was perfectly acceptable. Cassandra would have agreed with that speculation if she had been paying attention. However, what Maltor had said had her mind elsewhere, and she tuned out the bickering. He had said "river of death," and the image took her back to the dream she had had multiple times over the last few years. The vision always started with her inside a room high on a mountain range and with Zolmex, her birthright, a rod with a blue gem adorning the top of it, within her grasp. In the dream, she eventually found herself on the shore of a river of dead bodies. Was Maltor referencing the river she had dreamed about? Had her father known these savage people would kidnap her? Was she close to finding Zolmex?

"Notel X," she whispered, remembering the words scribed onto an old scroll she had found on her adventure in Kane's cave.

She was still sorting through the questions when Maltor finally pushed Vixa away and turned back to Cassandra. His demeanor did not show any anger toward her, but instead, he wore a look one might consider love, assuming the barbarians were capable of such strong emotions. She knew then that she might not be doomed. Perhaps she'd had to go through the few days of torture at the training pit and the loss of her friend, but she felt as if Maltor had that planned all along.

"Notel X," she whispered again, trying to gain her bearings.

"I am Maltor. Wake yourself, my future queen."

Cassandra did not realize she had said the words loud enough for him to hear, and she tried to focus on her surroundings and keep her thoughts of Zolmex buried.

"She cannot win; she has proven that!" Vixa shouted.

Maltor almost turned on her again but instead ground his teeth and said, "I am going to give her the ability to succeed. She will be my queen."

"But why? She is so inferior to the others."

"She has stolen my heart," the barbarian leader said, and Vixa sighed.

He glanced at Vixa and said, "You were supposed to train her in the pits so she could win."

He turned back toward Cassandra and played with her hair once more. "Now, you will give yourself again so she can become my champion."

Vixa's eyes widened as she finally understood Maltor's intent. "You mean the essence of the warrior?"

"Exactly that."

"And I shall be that essence?" Vixa asked, puffing out her chest proudly.

"Yes, I ask this of you because you are our best female warrior."

Cassandra, with her brief knowledge of the barbarian people, did not think that they cried tears of joy or appreciation, but at that moment, she thought she saw Vixa's eyes water; Maltor's gesture had her near tears. Cassandra did not know the essence of the warrior, but it must be a great honor among the barbarian people.

Maltor looked into Cassandra's eyes and said, "You are an outlander and a witch. That is not a good combination, my potential queen. I will not tolerate devil magic in my tribe. I warned you before to refrain, and you disobeyed me. The only way I can keep you alive is to transform you. If not, my people will lose faith in me. I will not behead you, not yet. But if you push me, my queen, you'll leave me no choice.

"My second option is to remove your ability to cast your devil magic, which will be a tolerable solution for my people. If I transform you into a complete warrior, they will not fear you but will accept you."

"Maltor, please do not do this. Being a witch is part of who I am. Do not take this from me if I truly hold your heart."

She did not understand what the process of removing her magic-casting ability entailed and did not want to find out. Whatever it might be, she knew it would not be something she desired. She was proud of her abilities, and the thought of losing them had her panicked.

"There is no negotiation on this. I will not tolerate a witch amongst my people and would never allow my queen to partake in dark magics. It is a sign of weakness. You will learn better through my shaman," Maltor said, nodding his head toward the older man she had correctly identified as a priest.

The old barbarian walked up to her and grinned, showing her his yellowed teeth. "I am Grink, and I will show you the warrior's way. If you survive the process."

He ended his sentence with a wheezing laugh, and Cassandra was now very concerned with precisely what Maltor had planned for her.

"She will; she is a survivor. Think about how we discovered her and what odds she overcame in the pits. She will survive," Maltor said.

Maltor was confident, but Cassandra was not. The words from the wheezing old shaman had her very nervous about what was to come. Vixa seemed at ease, but Cassandra did not want to lose her spellcasting ability. She had fallen in love with magic at the young age of twelve. If the barbarians had a way to take that from her, it would break her heart and spirit. The fact that she could no longer find the symbols floating in the air around her made her worried the threat was real.

"Maltor, I will be your queen and fight in your tournament, but I ask you to let me do it my way. Please release me from this table and let me fight with magic. It is not a bad way, just different. Your people will grow to accept it, especially if their queen wields it. I am not a warrior; please don't try to turn me into one."

Maltor leaned closer to her, and she could see his eyes searching hers as if he was considering her plea, but he eventually said, "No."

He stood and made his way toward the door. He turned at the last moment and told Grink, "Do not kill her… if you can help it. Keep her alive through the process so that you may bask in Strenna's glory and avoid my wrath."

Grink nodded and gulped loudly, understanding it was not an idle threat. Then he turned to Vixa and said, "Prepare yourself; I will complete the purging in two moons. I will need your spirit at that time. Do not be late."

Vixa nodded and left the cluster of cacti, leaving Cassandra alone with the old shaman, afraid of what he was about to do to her. He made his way over to the table and the collection of bloodied tools that sat upon it. He took a knife and some pliers and approached an enormous cactus, one with exceptionally long needles.

"The Yaddaton cacti hold special powers, outlander. They emit an inhibitor to cancel out magic and the fools who wield it."

That made perfect sense to Cassandra. The cacti were blocking the symbols so she could not see them! She felt relief at the revelation until she thought about what the shaman was doing. His ritual must use the cacti, but how? She had to convince the crazy old shaman not to proceed with whatever he had in mind. She watched him cut the large needles from a cactus with the knife and pliers.

"I am the chosen of Strenna," she said, hoping to persuade him through his religious beliefs.

"And why would you ever say such a blasphemous thing, outlander?"

"Because it is true, which is why Maltor's heart belongs to me. Strenna sent me not to be a warrior queen but to enlighten the people of this great tribe about the ways of powerful magic. The Tribe of the Serpent will become the most powerful tribe in Yaddaton once they embrace the magic. All that starts with me. You must not remove my god-given powers to use magic, or you will displease Strenna," Cassandra lied, hoping she sounded convincing.

He brought a handful of needles to the table and laid them atop it. He picked up one that looked long and sharp and held it to Cassandra's face. Somehow his body odor was worse than any of the others, and she presumed it was because he had gone longer than the others without bathing. When he spoke, the stench of his breath nearly made her gag. She did not like the man invading her personal space.

"Careful with your foul words, outlander. You are surely no chosen of Strenna, and I can make this process as painful and miserable as I like. So, if I were you, I would shut your mouth and save it for whatever worthless god you do worship. Understand?"

Cassandra could only nod, her eyes wide at the sight of the needle. What could he possibly do to her with the needles? What kind of painful process was the shaman referring to? He smiled at her reaction and went back to his work. Cassandra closed her eyes and tried to calm herself. She could survive whatever perverted ritual this man would perform on her.

The shaman spent the rest of the day preparing his table as Cassandra looked on. He trimmed the needles to a certain length, ending with two longer and two shorter ones. Grink then mixed several raw ingredients he kept in pouches on his side. Eventually, he had created a sticky salve, which sat in a lump on the tabletop next to the needles. Then he began mixing liquids and praying over his work as he did so. Cassandra tried to observe him but could not understand what he was doing and eventually dozed off.

She awakened to an empty prison and the sun setting. Next to her now were jars of live insects and reptiles. One contained a scorpion, another a giant spider, and another a snake. The shaman was nowhere to be seen, and the temperature had significantly cooled. She hoped he would return and offer a blanket, but he did not return until the following morning, making the night in her prison most uncomfortable.

She slept little due to the cold desert air and the aching in her immobile appendages. She was shivering when Grink entered the cactus prison. His milling about awakened her from her light sleep. She immediately noticed that he wore lots of paint on his face and a different headdress, one more substantial than the day before. He gathered up what looked to be a sponge and rubbed it in the salve, wiping up a generous portion of the sticky substance.

"What are you doing?" Cassandra asked nervously.

The man did not react to her question or even bother to answer.

"May I have a drink? I am very thirsty," she tried again with a new tactic.

Again, he did not answer but went about his work, preparing his table. He eventually took the sponge and applied the salve to Cassandra's right forearm. It was very sticky and smelled horrible.

"What are you doing?"

"Applying the numbing salve," he answered without looking up.

"Numbing salve?"

"Yes, to dull the pain," he answered with a smile.

Cassandra swallowed hard, a deep panic beginning to overtake her. She could feel the primitive, sticky agent working as her forearm tingled and numbed. He finished applying the stinky ointment to her right arm, then walked around the table to her left arm. He brought the sponge to her as if he would apply it to her forearm. However, he stopped just before it made contact and stood slowly. He smiled and tossed the sponge on the table.

"No salve for that arm, as a lesson for your blasphemy yesterday, chosen one," he said with a snort.

As her right arm slowly turned numb, Grink brought a metal bracket from under the table and laid it around her head. It was circular, except for one opened end. She realized soon enough that it was a brace for her head, with the opened end fitting around her neck. The shaman adjusted it, tightening it until it fit snugly. When he finished, she could no longer move her head from side to side. Her heart raced at the thought of her binds becoming more restrictive.

Grink bent down to look her in the eye, his smile evil. "More die from the procedure than are cured."

"What are you going to do?" Cassandra asked with a quiver in her voice.

He did not answer but produced a strange-looking clamp from the table. Cassandra could no longer turn her head to see the tabletop, so he brought the clamp up to her face so she could see it. It reminded her of a miniature bear trap with an adjusting knob on the side. He giggled like a child and wagged the metal contraption before her face.

"Remember, you kill me, Maltor kills you," Cassandra said, playing the only card she could think of.

The smile melted from the shaman's face, quickly becoming a grimace. "Open that filthy mouth of yours."

Cassandra knew then that he meant the bracket for her mouth, so she did the only thing she could and tightened her lips.

"Good, I was hoping that would be your response," Grink said.

He changed his position so he stood near her head, and she could smell his stench even more. He brought his hand down and pinched her nose. She could not turn her head because of the bracket around her head, so she had no choice but to eventually open her mouth to suck in some air. When she did, Grink slammed the smaller bracket into her mouth. The metal contraption hit her teeth hard and cut her lip. She could taste her blood and the dirty metal of the unusual frame. She felt a metal plate slide atop her tongue, which protruded from the gadget. The rest of the torture device fit tightly against her lips.

The shaman held it against her mouth tightly, then turned the small adjusting knob. She could then feel the small bear-trap-like device begin to open, pressing against her teeth and making her mouth slowly open. Eventually, Grink could remove his hand as the pressure from the trap on her teeth kept it in place. He stood back and enjoyed the view when her mouth was wide open. She felt helpless and vulnerable, and the shaman's laugh promised that the next step would be unpleasant.

Grink took the salve-covered sponge and crammed it into her open mouth. The taste was horrible, and Cassandra gagged several times. It took all her willpower not to be sick. It began to numb her mouth and tongue almost immediately.

He took one of the longer cactus needles from the table and brought it up before her eyes. "And now we shall begin," he said with a wicked smile. "The needles of the cacti negate the magic powers of weaklings like you. The needles are the key. We have experimented with implanting the needles into witches who use dark magics, and it seems to eliminate their abilities. However, the process is painful and dangerous. If you wish to survive, I need you to hold perfectly still."

He took Cassandra's right arm and gently rubbed it. He bent lower, turning it to examine it the best he could with her shackled to the slab.

"What are you doing?" she tried to ask, but she could not speak with her mouth agape, so it came out mumbled and unintelligible.

"If you are asking what I am doing, the answer is simple: I am trying to find a vein to shove this needle in."

Cassandra's eyes widened, and she began pleading with the shaman, her panicking words only gibberish. Grink paid her no mind. His attention remained solely on her arm as she screamed the best she could. Then she heard him mumbling and knew he was either praying or summoning power from his god. She kept up her struggles, but she could move very little. When he punctured her arm with the needle, she screamed more.

She could feel the blood running down her arm, and the pain was intense, despite the numbing salve. He continued to chant and slide the needle into her arm, unaffected by her screams.

The pain was too much for her to bear; she cried openly. After a long while, he rose, seeming happy with his work. With a nod, he grabbed an old rag and wiped the blood from her arm, then summoned the power of his god to heal the wound, sealing the needle inside her forearm.

"Now, that wasn't so bad, was it?" he asked, leaning down and grinning at her.

She had no response, and tears rolled freely down her cheeks. Her arm throbbed; the pain was unbearable even after the healing magic had washed over the wound.

"And now, let's do the untreated arm. As I perform the procedure, please remember the blasphemous words that spewed forth from your wretched mouth."

Cassandra tried to shake her head, but the bracket kept her immobile. She tried to speak, but the clamp and numbing salve kept her from doing so. All she could do was cry, and when the second needle pierced the skin of her left arm, she screamed until her throat hurt. It wasn't easy, but she somehow remained conscious, though the pain was unbearable. Both arms throbbed and bled, and as she lay there crying, he finally removed the sponge from her mouth.

"And now your wicked little mouth," he said, holding up the smaller needles.

As Grink inserted them, one in her upper gums and one in her lower, she was glad for the numbing, foul-tasting salve. The pain was still overwhelming, but she understood what it would feel like without it. By the time the shaman had inserted all four needles, most of the day had passed. He left her there, hurting, hungry, and very thirsty. She cried for a long while as her arms and gums throbbed with pain. Eventually, sleep found her, and she slept soundly through the night, exhausted from the ordeal. Even the cold desert temperature could not stir her. She would not awaken until late the following day.

As the sun filtered into her cactus prison, she opened her eyes to find Maltor's towering form standing beside her, his arms crossed over his massive chest. The scowl on his face spoke volumes, and she knew she must look horrible. Her gums felt swollen, and her teeth and mouth hurt; the bracket was still holding her mouth open. Her arms throbbed, and she could feel the needles lodged there. A silent tear ran down her cheek, but she did not try to speak.

"It looks worse than it is, Maltor; she will be fine," Grink said, standing behind the barbarian king and wringing his hands together nervously.

Maltor turned on him, and the man wilted under his gaze. "Finish the process, and get her out of that contraption."

"Yes, my lord, of course," the shaman said, bowing repeatedly until Maltor left the cactus tangle.

Once Maltor was gone, Grink walked over to Cassandra, studied her arms, and peered inside her mouth. The grimace on his face was not reassuring. He closed his eyes and prayed to his god, releasing another wave of healing energy over her. The pain subsided, and Cassandra felt so relieved that she fell asleep.

She awakened sometime later with her left arm throbbing and the device still lodged in her aching mouth. The sun was now high in the sky, and she could glimpse it between the many cacti. She noticed then that Vixa was there, along with the shaman. She looked at her with disgust plastered on her face.

"She looks horrible. Will she survive?" she asked.

"Of course, yes, yes, of course," Grink said without much confidence. "I have implanted the needles as instructed, and now we must move to the next phase of her transformation: the enchantment of the warrior."

Vixa shook her head in doubt and moved back so the shaman could begin his preparations. He lit a fire in the fireplace, filling the small area with thick smoke and adding to the unbearable heat. He inserted several items into the fire, which popped and spat in protest. Cassandra could not see what he was doing or witness what he added to the fire, but the smell was strange and intoxicating. Soon the overwhelming heat seemed comfortable, and even her immense pain melted away as she found peace. Cassandra wavered in and out of consciousness, sleep taking her often during the preparations. On the occasions she awakened for brief periods, she would find the shaman waving a feather or a string of beads over her. Her foggy mind understood he was performing a ritual to his god.

She dozed off for an extended period. When she opened her tired eyes again, the smoke had cleared some, and the sun had sunk far into the western sky. Vixa was there beside her, and Cassandra tried to smile at her. The pain in her mouth told her that the bracket was still there and her gums were severely injured. Vixa produced a knife and held it up. Cassandra tried to shake the cobwebs from her head, but the smoke made the task impossible. She did not understand the sudden appearance of a knife.

Suddenly, the shaman came into her limited field of vision as well, on the opposite side of the table from where Vixa stood. He closed his eyes and waved a hand over Cassandra's face, mumbling a few words of prayer as Vixa looked on, holding the knife at the ready. Grink then reached into a nearby jar and pulled forth a scorpion, holding it by the tail. He moved it over Cassandra's mouth and her eyes widened and she tried desperately to move away. When it was just inches above her, he took the knife from Vixa and impaled the little creature. It squirmed and pinched at his fingers, and eventually died. The shaman let the life blood of the creature drip into Cassandra's open mouth. She gagged on the taste, but Grink was unaffected by her reaction. He performed the same ritual with a large, hairy spider and a small snake, making Cassandra drink the blood of each.

He handed the knife back to Vixa and backed away. The female warrior stepped up and held her arm over Cassandra's gaping mouth. She ran the knife across her forearm, cutting a deep gash there. Her blood began to drip onto Cassandra's face, and she maneuvered her arm so that those drops fell into Cassandra's mouth. Cassandra gagged and thrashed as the blood poured thickly down her throat to mix with the foulness she had already consumed.

When Vixa moved away, Grink poured a terrible-smelling liquid into her mouth, making her swallow the blood. She had tasted alcohol a couple of times back in Pelesea, and it tasted like a potent ale to her. It stung her throat, and after she managed to swallow everything in her mouth, he produced another small vial of greenish liquid and poured it in. That one had no taste and was quite refreshing. She relaxed briefly before the shaman chanted and waved his holy symbol over her face.

That was when she first felt the sting in her heart. It was small at first, but it grew, and her head began to throb. As the pain intensified and she began to moan and thrash, Grink's chanting became louder, and his waving hands became more exaggerated. Her heart beat faster, and the pain intensified in response to his movements. Finally, the chanting and the pain stopped when it felt like her racing heart would burst from her chest. A wave of relaxing energy washed over her from the shaman's holy symbol, and reality blurred. She drifted back into a peaceful sleep.

She awakened sometime later, and it was dark. The fire still spat out the intoxicating smoke, and Cassandra felt warm and cozy. She could not quite remember everything Grink did to her but didn't care. Her pain was gone, and she felt great. She did not feel the sharp stabbing in her swollen tongue and pus-filled gums, and her infected arms, now showing severe bruising, did not bother her. Her mind was foggy, and she couldn't focus on what was happening around her. She saw Maltor there once again, and it made her happy. She just felt very, very happy. She drifted back to sleep.

"I have completed the ceremony, and the enchantment took. Strenna has blessed her with a warrior's heart," Grink explained.

"She will fight like Vixa now?" Maltor asked.

"She has all of Vixa's skills in combat, and they will stay with her throughout the tournament."

Maltor turned to Vixa, flanked by two commanders, Jozerah and Bolin, who stood slightly behind her. She held her bandaged arm up to Maltor and smiled proudly.

Maltor turned back to Grink and said, "I want it permanent."

Vixa's smile faded, and a panicked look washed over her face. She moved to flee the structure, but Jozerah and Bolin grabbed her and held her tight.

"But there is only one way to expand the enchantment, and even so, Strenna rarely blesses those with permanent powers, even if we tried," the shaman explained.

Maltor ignored him and grabbed the knife from the table that Vixa had used to slice her arm earlier that day. He turned to the struggling Vixa as Grink looked on in disbelief.

"No, Maltor, no!" she screamed. "I have given you everything!"

"Not everything," Maltor said coldly.

He stood before her now, the knife turning in his hand as he ran his fingers through her wild hair. She had failed him too many times; the disaster with Cassandra in the pits was only one of countless disappointments. She had also been his lover over the years and had been the one in charge of training the female warriors, what few there were. She had been valuable to Maltor. Once. But now Maltor finally had a replacement for that. His beautiful and exotic queen would fill that role. She would be stronger than Vixa and would not fail him.

"Your failure to train Cassandra properly at the compound was your last. Your time has come to an end," he said, grabbing a handful of her fiery red hair.

"I have only ever tried to please you, Maltor. I—"

The knife plunged deep into her belly, cutting off her words. Maltor's commanders held her up as the blade plunged home repeatedly, Maltor's rage playing out. Vixa did not make a sound and only stared at the barbarian leader as he murdered her. Once he completed the task, he cut out her heart and looked to Grink, who nodded.

Grink knew exactly what his king wanted. He waved his holy symbol over Cassandra and began his most powerful conjuring, hopefully giving Cassandra permanent knowledge of martial combat. Grink knew that the chance for success was minimal; if he failed, he would end up in the sea of dead beside Vixa. He prayed harder than ever and felt Strenna answer his call. He felt the essence of his goddess burn powerfully within him and that energy roll over Cassandra. It was so intense that he almost stopped and wept, but to do so would ruin the prayer, so he continued as Maltor gently removed the bracket in Cassandra's mouth and brought Vixa's heart up to her lips.

Cassandra felt someone shake her gently, and she opened her eyes to find Maltor leaning over her. She smiled, and to her delight, she could. The bracket was gone, and she moved her jaw in several directions, working the stiffness from those muscles. It felt so good to be able to close her mouth again. She was so happy at that moment and pain-free. When Maltor brought the juicy apple to her parched lips, she took a large bite. She felt the juice run down her chin and fill her mouth, and it was delicious. Maltor fed her the apple, and she devoured the whole thing. It was the best piece of fruit she had ever eaten. She drifted off soon after.

She awakened sometime later, perhaps days later. All she knew was that the slumber was hard to shake, and she could only assume days had passed since her ordeal with the shaman. She was pleasantly surprised to find herself no longer strapped down to the table in the cactus outcropping. Instead, she was lying on a comfortable pile of plush pillows. She was in a large, decorative tent with two large poles, the size of ship masts, rising from the floor to hold it up. The only sign that she was still in the desert, other than the intense heat, was the sand that showed between the many decorative rugs. A large throne sat in the center, and another mound of pillows was near it, even more impressive than the ones she lay upon. There were also several chests, a mirror, a table, chairs, and other furnishings decorating the place. It was more significant than the small room she and Kessi shared in Oldorburg.

"Kessi," she whispered, and her mind returned to the last time she had seen her sister. Her thoughts also turned to her dead mother, then to Binta.

"I have to get out of here," she said, sitting on the pillow bed.

Immediately, her gums and cheeks shot red-hot shards of glass through her mouth, making her stop. She felt a similar sensation in her forearms and noticed her outfit had changed. She had been secured to the table wearing her dirty and smelly loincloth and matching top; now, she wore a silky and comfortable shirt and pants. They were very transparent, and she could see that she wore no underwear. The first thing that went through her mind was that someone had dressed her and, judging by the smell, had bathed her, as she wore the hints of strong and fragrant soap. It was not the first time someone had dressed her while she was unconscious. She vowed then to make sure it would be the last. She only hoped that Vixa had been the one to care for her while she was unconscious. She vaguely remembered the woman was with her during the ordeal in the cactus prison.

Cassandra looked at her injured arms and could easily see through the blue silky garment that they were bruised and swollen. She touched her left forearm where the cactus needle had been placed and grimaced with pain. It was very tender and sore to the touch. She felt around her mouth and discovered the same issue; her gums were extremely sensitive and hurt when she slid her tongue over them. Her hatred for Maltor and the barbarians grew as she realized the extent of the damage their careless procedure had caused.

"It looks like Maltor's plaything has stirred," came a deep voice behind her.

She turned to see two men standing guard, one in each of the far corners of the tent. One she recognized as Jak, the man on the boat who had watched over her during their journey across the sea. The other she did not recognize, but he was a giant of a man and was the one who had spoken.

"Fetch Grink and tell him the outlander stirs," he said, and Jak nodded and left.

The remaining barbarian approached her as she sat on the pile of pillows. There was nowhere to run, and she didn't want to move her arms because doing so caused excruciating pain. She figured there would be no point in moving and just sat there as the giant man bent to her eye level. She expected him to stink like all the other barbarians she had met, and he surely did not disappoint. He reached up, took some of her hair, and rolled it in his fingers, like Maltor had done before. Once more, she felt like she was being evaluated as livestock. His eyes looked her up and down, and she moved to cover herself, knowing the sheer fabric of her clothing offered no protection from his lustful gaze.

"When you fail miserably in the tournament, we will all get a turn at you in the procreation tent," he said with a wicked smile.

Cassandra gave a sarcastic smile and pulled her hair from his grasp. She wanted to offer a rebuttal, but it hurt too much to speak, so she just sat there with her fake smile. His lustful stare continued as he slowly rose. It looked to her as if he could hardly control himself and might attack her. She knew rape would be a perfectly acceptable act within the barbarian tribe, judging by the way she saw Vixa treated. He did not even consider the repercussions from Maltor if he proceeded, which made him dangerous.

However, Jak returned with the shaman before he could act on his impulse. The man backed away as Grink made his way to her, his many beads dancing about his neck as he did.

"She looks stronger now, yes?" Grink said.

Two others followed him in and appeared to Cassandra to also be shamans. They wore similar gaudy beads and holy symbols of Strenna. They nodded their agreement as Grink took her arms and studied them. He was rough and careless, and pain shot through both her forearms as he made his examination. One of the others pried open her mouth to look at her gums. The third one poked at them; the pain was more than she could take. She bit the filthy hand invading her mouth, her teeth clamping down on a finger.

The shaman hollered and smacked her hard across the face; the pain was white lightning. She fell to the pillows holding her mouth, silent tears spilling down her face. The shaman she bit turned her over and had a knife to her throat, anger splayed across his face as he sucked the blood from his finger.

"No, Bok, she is Maltor's!" Grink warned.

"The weakling outlander bit me like a rabid camel!"

"She did not kill you, so be grateful."

"She is but a female; she has no right."

"She is Maltor's chosen and has been blessed with the heart of the warrior, with the heart of Vixa," Grink said with a smirk.

Bok removed the knife, understanding the implications.

"Hold her," Grink said, motioning to the two guards.

Each took an arm, roughly at first, making Cassandra scream out in pain.

"Gently, she is still recovering," Grink explained.

The gentle giant, Jak, the guard who never spoke, understood her pain and moved his grip from her wounded forearm. The other one, whom she had just conversed with before the shamans arrived, had a vice-like grip and applied pressure to her injured arm when she struggled. He was more vicious, and she knew she would need to be careful around that one.

All three shamans closed their eyes and began to chant in unison as the two guards held Cassandra still. She struggled very little due to the amount of pain she was dealing with. After many moments, the three lay their hands on her, each of the lesser shamans gently grasping her forearms and Grink clamping a hand over her mouth. She struggled a bit at first, not understanding their intent, but when the healing energy washed over her and that awful pain subsided, she relaxed and basked in the wonderful feeling. They were healing her, trying to rid her of the infection that now festered in her wounds.

They performed their joint healing several more times, and Cassandra fully relaxed and closed her eyes. The pain washed away, but she understood it would probably be a minor reprieve. However, it felt wonderful to be pain-free, even if only for a short period.

Satisfied with their work, the shamans congratulated each other on their healing abilities and thanked Strenna for giving them such incredible powers. Something about the scene rubbed Cassandra the wrong way. The fools had healed her, and perhaps their powers had truly felt wonderful, but Grink was why she was in such pain. The stupid needle procedure had nearly killed her. Furthermore, the process could not be called a success due to the infection she now battled. She focused on the three men and called for the symbols. If she could hit Grink as hard as she had Breka, he would be dead before he hit the ground. She thought of Breka then. She had killed her; she had killed another person. Remorse ran through her mind, but for some reason, so did pride. Was she proud of her actions?

She shook the awful thought away and refocused on summoning the arcane magic like she had done many times before. To her dismay, very few of the unusual symbols came into focus. She knew they were there but were not heeding her call. The procedure in the cacti outcropping performed by the fool Grink had stolen her ability to cast spells. She might be able to do it the old-fashioned way and pen the magic into a spellbook, then commit it to memory. But where would she get a spellbook and the related ingredients for any spells? Likewise, how could she even obtain a spell in this vast land of sand and nothingness? The barbarians were responsible for taking that from her, and she looked at her wounded arms in disgust.

"We will come back tomorrow, outlander, to heal you again. The process is beginning to take, and you will eventually feel no pain from the wonderful needles that have cured you," Grink said.

Cassandra just stared hatefully at the ignorant barbarian. She wanted nothing more than to kill the fool. He had robbed her of a unique ability she had possessed for a good part of her life. She was a user of magic, a witch in every sense of the word. The idiots were trying to make her into something she wasn't: a warrior. She had failed miserably in the training compound; she had failed, that is, until she had used her magic. At that point, she had very much succeeded. At that terrible moment, she realized Grink had robbed her of a part of who she was, and the thought of killing the smelly barbarian came to the surface of her thoughts. She wished she had an axe to teach the idiot a lesson.

She shook her head to clear it, not understanding the thought that had come naturally to her. She recalled then that Vixa's preferred weapon of choice is the hand axe. She tried remembering the procedure that enhanced her abilities with the warrior's spirit. The smoke had been, at the very least, hallucinatory. Had she seen Vixa through the thick fog as the ritual began? Was she possessed of Vixa's spirit now? She needed to speak to the wild woman to find out what had happened to her during that ritual.

She felt someone playing with her hair again, bringing her attention back to the present. She turned to see the large guard squatting next to her once more. He had a hand full of hair, smelling it while never breaking eye contact. Sick of the game, she tried to pull her hair away but was not as quick as the seasoned warrior. He grabbed a fist full of her blond locks and slung her to the pillows. A jolt of pain ran through her mouth, but surprisingly, her arms ached very little from the motion.

"You lie there, outlander; Sneck will watch over you until Maltor returns," the large man said.

"Don't touch me again, Sneck," she whispered threateningly.

Again, she tried to call to the arcane symbols, but none came into focus. However, she did notice the axe that hung from Sneck's belt. She wanted it, and if she could get it, she was sure she could teach this buffoon a lesson.

He grabbed her by the hair, pulling her into a standing position. "I'm touching you, outlander. What can you do?"

"I can teach you a valuable lesson."

The man laughed and led her by her hair off the pillows. "You are a female and cannot do anything to me. Teach me a lesson? How about I teach you one right now?"

She realized that they were alone in the large tent. Jak must have escorted the shamans out. If Sneck had paid attention, he might have seen the slight smile she flashed just before he turned her around so he was behind her. He still had her by the hair, pulling her head back to rest on his chest while roughly kissing her neck. Her instincts kicked in then, but not the ones she was used to, summoning ravens or arcane energy to cast spells. The new instincts were foreign to her and yet very natural.

She first stomped on his foot and screamed as loudly as possible. Not a prolonged one, but a sharp, brief yell with the intent of startling the fool. It did just that, and she felt the grip on her hair lessen as the surprised warrior moved back a step with his injured foot. The distraction worked enough that she jerked her hair free and turned on her assailant.

Cassandra almost laughed at the startled expression on his face just before she jumped impossibly high, higher than she had ever jumped before, and hooked a leg around his neck. She moved with her momentum, swinging around his neck with ease, throwing him off balance. With all her might, she pulled with her legs and grabbed his shoulders so the off-balance warrior fell to the ground. She was up instantly, unhooking her legs and punching him in the face as she did.

She felt the satisfying crunch of his nose and hopped away before he could grab her. She stood casually, swaying from foot to foot, her hands calmly held behind her back. She smiled at the angry man as he rose to his full bulking height, towering over her. He held his bloody nose, and once he noticed the blood on his hand, he roared like a caged animal.

"There is no need to scream, fool. Simply understand that this female will teach you a lesson, and then when Maltor finds out you attacked me, well, you will be learning a much harder one, I am sure."

He issued a guttural growl, and his face became dark and menacing. Cassandra only continued to smile, appreciating her new skills and enjoying the vast world of opportunities they offered her. She thought back to the bullies at the orphanage when she was young. She could have hurt them badly with her new abilities. She thought of her altercations with Cass and knew that she would never have lost to her if she had possessed the fighting ability that now came so easily to her.

Sneck charged, just like she knew he would, the muscles in his arms corded and flexing, his eyes bloodshot and filled with rage. The blood continued to pour from his shattered nose, and she barely controlled her laughter. The dangerous situation was not amusing, and her life was very much in danger, but she knew the enraged man could not hurt her. After all, she possessed the skills of Vixa but with greater intelligence. She could outfight and outsmart him, which was evident when she brought his stolen axe from behind her back and swung it up at the last second into his groin.

There was a sickening thud, and she felt the finely sharpened blade dig in deep. Sneck stopped, and his eyes popped open wide. His large arms shook, and he stood like that for several moments. Eventually, he screamed in agony and fell over, holding his groin. Cassandra held the axe as he did, and it slid out of the deep wound. Blood covered most of the blade and began to pool around the once-proud warrior as he moaned loudly and folded himself into a fetal position, his hands grasping the mortal wound.

She held the blade up before her, blood dripping from it. She had easily lifted it from Sneck's belt when she performed the flying head scissors that had brought the giant down. How had she even accomplished such a feat? She shrugged her shoulders, unable to fathom an answer, and turned her attention back to the deadly axe. Cassandra had never used a weapon before, yet she wondered how she had made it through life without one. It was foreign in her hand, yet somehow very familiar. The strike differed from her magic; she had felt the blade slice into the man's flesh as if it were an extension of her arm. It wasn't just an attack against this fool but a direct hit to Ronnis's groin and Barktuck's. It was finally a retaliation toward Cass and the other bullies who had mistreated her over the years. It was payback for past wrongs, and she vowed then that it would not be the last.

A shout from the doorway of the tent snapped her from her thoughts. Two more guards who obviously had been standing right outside came rushing in, brandishing swords. She backpedaled and set her stance, ready to kill them, and was quite confident she could do it.

"Halt!" came a roaring voice from behind the two.

All three stopped and looked to the entrance to see Jak standing there, two axes drawn and ready, with the shamans close behind him. He pointed an axe toward Cassandra and shook his head. All eyes in the tent were on her then, awaiting her next move. She realized it might be more than she could handle, so with a smile, she reluctantly tossed the axe to the ground and put her hands up to indicate she was surrendering.

Jak moved her to the far corner of the tent and searched her for more weapons. Once he was sure she had none, he instructed the two guards to watch over her as the shamans worked on the injured Sneck. The smile never left her face as the man fought for his life. Why should she care? This was what they had wanted, a warrior to fight for queenship. In her opinion, they had just that, and it was a pleasant alternative for her to the bullying she had endured her entire life. In the simplest terms, she found it refreshing being on the opposite end of the physical abuse for once.

Jak restored her guard, finding a new warrior to take Sneck's place. The gentle giant did not punish her for the attack on Sneck and instead seemed impressed with the results of the altercation. The only change Jak made was to move her pillow bed around one of the giant tent poles. He fastened a chain to the pole, and at the end of that chain was a metal collar for Cassandra to wear. The chain was nearly twenty feet long, limiting her mobility to the immediate area around the massive pole. There was a primitive lock holding the chain to the pillar and a much smaller but equally effective one locking the collar around her neck.

No guards other than Jak would enter the radius of the chain, which she found very satisfying. She knew her newfound respect would last only until Maltor returned. Jak would not tell her where he was, so she could only wait. Although, he did make sure she had food and water, and once a week, he delivered a small tub of water for a bath. Of course, she was not allowed any privacy, so she just bathed with her clothes on, which, in the end, allowed her clothes to be washed simultaneously. The shamans visited every day at first, but as her wounds healed, they showed up less and less. Eventually, her pain diminished, and she could speak and eat normally once more. She could still feel the cactus needles in her gums and arms, but they were more uncomfortable than painful by the time the shamans finished their work. It was several weeks after that before Maltor finally returned.

He arrived one evening as she was finishing her meal. He entered the tent, along with his second in command, Jozerah. They were filthy from their travels, and Jozerah carried a sizeable circular item covered with a thick cloth. It reminded Cassandra of a birdcage, and she immediately wondered what could be under the fabric. For the first time since her attack on Sneck, she felt afraid. Seeing the barbarian leader reminded her of where she was and how brutal these people were. She had lived among them for about a month, killed one of their kind, and severely injured another. Now, with their leader back, she felt insecure.

He glared at her as he removed his belt, sword, and traveling cloak. Jozerah hung up the covered cage on a pole near the throne and, with a nod to Maltor, left. The disgusting look he gave Cassandra told her that Maltor already knew of her actions. Maltor walked over to stand before her without weapons or guards, although she saw them become vigilant when he did so.

"You've been naughty, my queen-to-be," he said as a father might lecture a child.

She stood but still had to crane her neck to look him in the eye. She tried to be brave and hold the stare, for she knew things could go badly if she displayed any weakness.

"I defended myself, nothing more."

She wanted to tell him she was not his queen and never would be. However, she held her tongue, trying to appease her potential husband. She needed him to remain obsessed with her; it was crucial to her survival.

"Poor Sneck will live but will probably never have children. That makes him an outcast amongst our people."

"He touched me."

Maltor looked at her doubtfully and bent on one knee to be closer to eye level. "I am unarmed. Will you attack me too? Do you think you can defeat me?"

"I would not attack you unless you touched me like he did," she said with cold sincerity.

"You are an outlander, a weakling user of devil magic. These are all grounds for execution, and now you have murdered and maimed my people? You make it difficult to keep you alive."

There was a long, uncomfortable silence, and he raised his filthy hand to run it down her cheek.

"If I did not desire you as a queen, I would not keep you alive. I can only give you so many chances before you force my hand. I will kill you if you do anything else."

With incredible speed, he grabbed her roughly around the neck. Her first instinct was to gouge his eyes or turn his thumbs, but she stopped and held her hands in the air. She knew not to touch him, or things would go from bad to worse.

"You are possessed now with Vixa's skills and spirit, but you are no match for me, understand."

She nodded, keeping her hands raised in surrender. Maltor's hold on her tightened, and she could no longer breathe.

"Good, because I need you to remain focused. Vixa was wild and untamed. I need you to be better. I need you to fight in the challenge circle and win and know your place when you are not within the circle. Vixa never knew her place; she was undisciplined. I need you better!"

His voice rose as he spoke so that he was screaming by the end of his lecture, and his grip had tightened so much that her face began to turn blue. She somehow kept from grabbing him, knowing that would make him angrier. He eventually threw her down upon her pillow bed, where she sucked in air and coughed for many moments. When her fit played out, she sat up and found Maltor sitting on his throne. He had uncovered the cage and stared at the tiny creature inside—a fairy! He had finally found a culiem fairy.

She was only about six inches tall, with butterfly-type wings, but appeared as a beautiful human woman otherwise. She was frightened and slinked back from Maltor's hateful stare. She reminded Cassandra of her old self, of the timid person she once was. She felt empathy for the small, beautiful creature. Maltor continued to look upon the fairy, but his mood was foul. Cassandra did not want to disturb him as she rubbed her raw neck, but she had to know something.

"You spoke of Vixa in the past tense," she said.

Maltor did not answer but only focused on the fairy.

"Why?" she prodded.

He finally turned to her with a puzzled expression. "She is no more."

"What do you mean?" Cassandra pressed, not wanting to know the answer.

"She expired, so you could be!" he yelled, standing up and approaching her again.

Cassandra's mind spun; Vixa was the closest thing she had to an ally in the tribe besides Laryn. Was she dead? Had Maltor killed her so Cassandra could take her place in the tribe? She then felt sick, realizing the fiery red-haired warrior was gone.

"How?" she whispered.

Maltor smiled arrogantly and said something that made her legs lose strength as she sat on her soft pillow bed: "You ate her heart so you could become her, both physically and in spirit."

Cassandra could not believe the words, but somehow, she knew they were true. She remembered eating the delicious apple during the ceremony but could remember little else.

"I ate an apple," she corrected.

His brow wrinkled in confusion, and he asked, "What is an apple?"

She just sat there with her mouth hanging open, trying to process the information. It was true, they had no apples in the desert, and Maltor and the others would not know what they were. She suddenly felt very ill at the realization that the juicy apple she enjoyed during the bizarre ceremony was Vixa's heart. After many moments, the nausea passed, and she lay back on her bed. By then, Maltor had a handful of advisors in the tent, and all gave her curious stares. She didn't see them, though, as she stared into space, the desert heat never seeming more suffocating than at that awful moment.

13

QUEEN'S TOURNAMENT

ATILDA, CASS, AND RONNIS ARRIVED BY SHIP AT PORT RACIP at about the same time Grink had completed the rituals on Cassandra, giving her the warrior's heart. Matilda was shocked to learn that Cerus was in the city recovering from an encounter in Swamp Ikma. She went to her husband, taken in by the dockmaster to be nursed back to health. When she arrived at the large home, she found a nervous man greeting her at the door.

"I am Matilda; Cerus is my husband."

"Yes, my lady, I know of you. I am Prelton, dockmaster of Racip," the man answered with a nervous smile, then swallowed hard.

Matilda stepped inside the man's home, and he put up no resistance, slinking out of her way. Cass and Ronnis followed, and the man grew even more nervous.

"Tell me, Prelton, why are you not at the docks?"

"The docks are closed for repairs, my lady. I—"

"Where is Cerus?"

"He rests, my lady. His wounds are still fresh," Prelton answered, wringing his hands.

Matilda turned on him quickly, understanding that her reputation had preceded her. "Ficktor, the barkeep I spoke with, informed me that Cerus has been in the city, more precisely, under your care for nearly a month. How are his wounds still fresh?"

"Please understand," Prelton answered, looking between the three new guests, "I have tried to cure him, but his wounds come from Malebak."

"What is a Malebak?"

"Not what, who."

Matilda stared hard at the man, and Cass let out a derisive snort. The man swallowed hard and added in a whisper, "The dragon of Ikma."

Matilda's eyes widened at the mention of the dragon. One of the reasons Cerus and she had chosen to build Nesin in the mountain range just north of Swamp Ikma was that the reputation of the legendary dragon would keep trespassers at bay. She had always assumed the dragon to be just that, a legend and not actual. The news of the dragon's existence had her heart racing in fear for her home and Cerus's health. He could not survive an attack from that vicious creature, assuming the stories about it were true.

"Dragons don't exist, do they?" Cass said.

"Where is he?" Matilda demanded.

"Down the hall, the last door on the left," Prelton stammered, pointing down the long hallway.

He fell back against the wall as Matilda walked swiftly down the hall. Cass followed her, paying him no mind. Matilda hesitated at the door, realizing that Ronnis lingered behind. She turned to see him before the frightened dockmaster, who was plastered against the wall, his eyes wide at the sight of Ronnis's mask.

"Boo!" Ronnis suddenly shouted, and the man let out a yelp and covered his face, slowly sliding down the wall until he was sitting.

Matilda chuckled, then entered the room. She gasped, not believing how bad Cerus looked. He lay in the bed, his head and arms the only things visible from the sheets that covered him. Bandages wrapped his entire face, save for his mouth and eyes. His arms wore similar wrappings. Splotches of blood and pus dotted the applications. The sheet covering the rest of his body displayed similar patterns of blood. His massive spear was leaning in the corner of the room, along with his armor and other belongings. She had never seen him look that bad, and she knew he was near death.

She turned to Cass and said, "Bring me that worm, Prelton," through gritted teeth.

"Matilda?" Cerus whispered through cracked lips. "Is it you?"

"Yes, my husband, I have returned," she answered, sitting on the bed next to him.

"I am dying," he whispered.

"No, my husband, you have been dying. Today, you begin living again."

Cass returned then with Prelton, who was trying to hold back his tears.

"I'm sorry, my lady! I tried to heal him; we have no proficient priests here!" he squealed.

Cass pushed him to the floor, and Matilda walked up to him, lifting his chin with her finger.

"And why did you not fetch a priest? I know the ones from Nesin would heed your call, and they could cure this."

"I... I ..."

"Silence!" Matilda screamed, then turned back to Cerus.

She summoned the most powerful healing spell she had in her repertoire. As the healing energy washed over Cerus, he let out a long sigh of relief. She cast it a second and then a third time, summoning every ounce of priestly energy Marnelphion allotted her. When she finished, she tore the sheets from the bed, revealing his bloodied legs and abdomen, his legs wrapped similarly to his arms.

"Ewww!" Cass said and held her nose, the stench of rot wafting from his body.

Matilda also had to put the back of her hand to her nose due to the stench that removing the sheets unleashed. Her husband was wasting away. She quickly went to work unwrapping him, tearing off the bandages that clung to his skin. Underneath, she found pus-filled boils and bloody lesions all over his body. Once she fully unwrapped him, she stepped back to take in the horrific sight. He was still alive and was a testament to the god-blood that coursed through his veins.

"That is your husband?" Cass said, still pinching her nose.

Matilda's nostrils flared, and the scowl on her face warned everyone in the room that retribution would be swift for Prelton. He screamed and tried to crawl out of the room, but Ronnis blocked his way. He had drawn the Black Adder and now pointed the wicked blade toward the cowering man, the poisonous weapon glistening in the daylight that seeped through the lone window.

Matilda grabbed Prelton by the collar, dragging him to the bed with supernatural strength.

"You did this!" she screamed, holding his head to get a better look at Cerus.

Prelton began to sob while holding a hand to his nose. "I am sorry, my lady, I tried everything."

"There is one thing you have not tried," she whispered and began casting another spell.

Prelton tried to flee once she released him, but Ronnis was there, and more importantly, the Black Adder was in his back, preventing him from moving. The man openly wept as Matilda cast one of her most potent spells. Her eyes turned entirely black with the essence of Marnelphion, and she stretched out a hand toward Cerus and the other toward Prelton.

"No, my lady, I am sorry. Please!" Prelton began to wail as she sucked the black death out of Cerus, through her, and into Prelton's body.

Cerus's wounds slowly faded, and Prelton began to break out with boils and lesions. He screamed at the top of his lungs and fell to the floor, curling into a fetal position. Slowly, Matilda transferred the disease from her husband to the dockmaster. Prelton's screams rang out through the neighboring blocks in the city, and the only answer to those cries of anguish was the people scrambling to change their direction to avoid walking anywhere near his home. So was the way of Port Racip.

When completed, Cerus rose, fully naked but back to health, aside from a few red splotches here and there on his skin. He strode over to his clothing and armor and put them on without saying anything.

"Impressive," Cass cooed, admiring the man's nakedness.

Matilda gave her a dirty look, and she just shrugged and smiled.

Once Cerus dressed, he grabbed his large spear and went to Matilda. He towered over her and her friends, and Cass chewed her lip in response, playing with a curl of her hair with one finger and looking longingly at Cerus.

"Where is Malikai?" he growled.

"Gone. Malikai is not your concern, my husband."

"Who are these people?" he asked with a wave of his hand to Matilda's new allies.

"Friends. I will explain. I have great news concerning the filth of Kane, and I have a reason for our army—"

"Our army?" Cerus interrupted.

"Your army," Matilda conceded, but her expression left little doubt that she was not in the mood for such pettiness.

"Continue," Cerus said with a nod.

Matilda knew she would have to be punished for her indiscretions with Malikai before Cerus forgave them. It was the routine whenever she humiliated him. It usually ended with rough sex or a few bruises. However, she had no time to play games right now. She decided then that she would probably let Cass, play with him to make up for it. She would tolerate that as long it led to Cassandra's capture.

"A great battle lies ahead of us, my husband. I will make things right by you as payment for being naughty. You may collect your reward when we arrive home," Matilda said, turning to regard Cass.

Cerus followed her gaze and caught on to her meaning. A wicked smile formed on his face, and Cass smiled back until she realized all three were looking at her.

"What?" she asked.

Ronnis sheathed his weapon and exited the room. Cerus and Matilda began to follow when Prelton croaked out a phlegm-filled cough. They turned to regard the man, who was up on his knees and trying to crawl into bed.

"Cerus, please, I took you in. I tried to help," the diseased man said, trying desperately to pull himself off the floor.

Cerus snorted and said, "You had me suffer like a leper, alone and in pain. Now you will experience what I have gone through. But thank you for taking me in; I will consider you a friend for it as long as we both live."

Cass giggled, and Cerus looked the strange but flirty girl up and down. Matilda caught the way he looked at her and let out a sigh. Cass had helped her and would continue to do so. She would let Cerus have his fun with her, but Matilda vowed that she would not let it become a habit.

The four left Prelton's home shortly after and quickly secured passage to Nesin, less than a day's travel away. Matilda promptly informed her husband of the new events concerning Cassandra Rho.

Prelton never did summon the strength to climb into the bed and died on the floor a few hours later. It would be a week before the neighbors discovered his body, the smell alerting them to his demise.

Greyson and Alleah sat outside of Breeston's small home on several dead trees that the druid had carved into chairs, watching the strange druid and Chloe as the man attended a boiling cauldron. He had finally obtained a new purple stone from his mysterious wife that lived below them, underground in catacombs partially flooded with swamp water. Greyson was curious about Breeston's wife and the possibilities she offered but had yet to summon the courage to venture down into her lair.

However, Breeston had frequented her bed recently, and she had finally produced the magical gem to make his wooden staff whole once more. Now he was showing Chloe how to mix the sticky substance that would hold the gemstone in place. His wooden staff had been recently varnished and cured and leaned against the small cottage they had all shared for the last six weeks.

"She enjoys the swamp," Greyson said, eyeing Chloe, who had fully healed from her injuries at the hands of Cerus.

"A little too much, I'm afraid," Alleah agreed with a weak smile.

"She may not want to leave when the time comes," Greyson added.

"When will the time come?" Alleah asked with a sigh.

Greyson turned to regard the large group of giant flies that buzzed around the woods just behind them. All the woods had been infected with the insects since Malebak breathed them from his gut. They did not advance too close to the cottage and gave Breeston enough room to find food and water. However, Breeston told them the dragon would dismiss the flies when it saw fit. Trying to leave before then would be unwise. Greyson didn't need to be told what would happen if they left before the flies cleared; he had witnessed the dragon's attack on Cerus and his men.

"When the flies clear, so Breeston assures us," he said with a shake of his head.

There was a long silence, and he saw from the corner of his eye that Alleah was staring into the forest. He knew she was thinking about her sisters and the significant loss their ill-advised voyage had cost them.

"When they do, where do we go?" Greyson asked.

"Chloe says that Cerus murdered my sisters in Racip. I want to find the truth of their fate. Perhaps they are all dead, but if there is a chance they are alive, I must go to them."

"We have been over this before, Alleah. We are lucky to be alive and should avoid Cerus and Racip. Trust me; I know this monster, and we cannot stand against him."

"You and Chloe should return home, and I will stay here to monitor the situation. I will find a way to free my sisters if they live. If not, I will avenge their deaths."

"No, we will not separate again. And Chloe agrees with me; we must stay together. We came to this vile land together and we will leave it together. Besides, you will need our help to free them if they are alive."

"And if they are truly dead?" Alleah asked.

Greyson took her hand and said, "Then we will help bury them."

Alleah looked at their hands, then back to Greyson, a hopeful look upon her beautiful face. Greyson noticed something there he had never seen in his friend's eyes. Was it an acceptance that their friendship was more substantial now that they had escaped death? Perhaps there was a hint of interest or love in her gaze. Either way, their hands squeezed tight as they silently gazed.

Chloe came over to retrieve more tar for Breeston, breaking the spell. She smiled at her friends, grabbed the nearby bucket of tar, and returned to the druid, discussing the staff again. Greyson and Alleah sat in silence, awkwardly considering what had transpired between them.

Finally, Alleah said, "What is your goal once we leave Ikma?"

"To find Tara, as was our original plan."

Alleah gazed into his eyes, studied them briefly, and smiled. "You are right, Greyson; once we find my sisters, we will continue to Tara."

"Only if you want. Since the disaster at Racip decimated our party, I would not begrudge you and Chloe if you sailed for Pelesea."

"Nonsense. Remember your words; we should stick together for better or worse," Alleah said with a smile.

Greyson wanted to kiss her so badly but he knew she was not allowed. He could not break the covenant she shared with her goddess. Instead, he sighed and stood, running his hands through his hair. He examined his hands afterward to find them greasier than he cared to admit.

"I could use a real bath," he said.

Without even looking his way, Alleah said, "Especially if you are to bed Breeston's wife."

"What?" Greyson asked, caught off guard by the rare sexual comment coming from his friend.

She looked at him then and smiled. "I know you want to, and your time is running out. The flies will eventually clear, and we will leave. You will lose your chance if you do not take it soon."

"May I remind you she is a snake lady, according to her husband?" Greyson said.

"And may I remind you that she can produce a stone such as that, which could hold powers beyond your imagination?" Alleah added, pointing to the gem that the druid now dunked in the boiling glue.

Alleah stood, grabbed his hands, and looked into his eyes. He immediately melted under her gaze. She was the sexiest woman he had ever met, and still, he could not touch her. Even living in cramped quarters since leaving Pelesea, he could not act on his greatest desire. And yet, when she touched him, jolts of energy shot through his groin, and her look only made him desire her even more.

She had his full attention when she finally spoke. "If she could produce a stone as powerful as the druid's, you could use it to rescue my sisters. Think of it: you could be unstoppable. We can do this together."

However, Greyson was already shaking his head, understanding her thinking was too optimistic.

"No, Alleah, your sisters are probably …"

He trailed off, not wanting to say the words, not wanting to injure his friend any more than she already was.

"What?" she asked. "Already dead?"

Again, not wanting to say the words, he nodded.

"We do not know that and surely can't give up on them."

Greyson knew that if the worshippers of Sinnis were indeed alive and in the custody of that monster, Cerus, then he could only imagine what tortures they endured. He became lost in those awful thoughts until Alleah squeezed his hands, returning him to the present.

"So, go to Xeva. See what she can do for you, for us, for Sinnis!" Alleah pleaded.

He could only smile at his friend and found her optimism contagious. "Very well. I will visit Xeva very soon."

Alleah smiled and squeezed his hands once more. Then she went over to Chloe and Breeston to watch the druid work his magic.

Greyson watched her backside as she walked away, and even though they were all filthy from the lack of fresh water, he found her irresistible.

"I always wanted to sleep with a snake," he whispered, then shook his head and joined his friends at the cauldron.

Another month crawled by for Cassandra as she adjusted to life as Maltor's captive. The days were impossibly long and tedious. Although her untoned muscles were not ready for the tournament, and she was not in top condition physically, she had time to prepare before the contest began. Each day, she exercised, moving as far away from her pillow bed as her chain allowed. She knew exercises to tone her muscles as if she had been training her whole life. So, she performed them, and she was often sore. Cassandra saw little results from her hours of meditating and exercising, but she silently thanked Vixa for the knowledge to at least pretend to be a barbarian warrior. During her meditations, she thought of Binta often and longed to see her friend again. Winter would end soon in Pelesea, and she wished she were there to see it with her friend.

Maltor wasn't in the tent much, and she was thankful for that. When he was there, he was usually talking politics with his advisors. Sometimes Cassandra would pretend to be asleep and secretly eavesdrop on those conversations. She listened carefully, trying to formulate a way out of her prison. She remembered Maltor mentioned the river of the dead, which reminded her of her vivid dreams. Would her father show her the strange burial ground and allow her to escape? If she found the river, would she find Zolmex? She did not know the answers, and none of Maltor's conversations gave her a means to escape.

During one of her spying sessions, she learned that Maltor had traded for the fairy, giving up ten pairs of snake-skin boots, a special shield, and a small caravan of camels for her. She did not discover who he had traded with, and she didn't care. However, because of its magical nature, she was interested in the culiem fairy. According to Maltor, they were highly poisonous, but he also considered them lovely decorations to adorn his tent. He would feed her little red berries, which the fairy seemed to love. He would not get too close to the cage but would play a game and toss them to her, trying to get them through the bars. Most of the time, he was surprisingly gentle with the creature, but on more than one occasion, she had witnessed him punch the cage, making it twirl and sending the fairy on a not-so-pleasant spin. His outbursts were usually the result of the creature hissing at him if he got too close to the cage. Cassandra surmised that all females of Maltor's tribe should be submissive, regardless of their race or status.

Cassandra knew from her brief studies at Victoria's School of Magic that all fairies were attuned to the world of magic. She would love to be able to study Maltor's fairy, and she thought that would be at least something he might let her do if she did become his wife. The thought repulsed her, but focusing on potential possibilities like that helped her count the days until the tournament arrived. The day was fast approaching, and Maltor became more agitated as it did. Cassandra felt as if he was feeling the pressure of trying to marry an outlander, as the barbarians called her. After all, she had killed one of their own and attacked another. She knew that if she failed, it could result in dire consequences for Maltor. His reputation as a leader would diminish with that gross lapse of judgment.

She tried to put such thoughts out of her head and focused only on preparing herself mentally and physically the best she could. She tried to call forth the arcane symbols daily, but none answered. She even tried summoning ravens a couple of times, but none came. She was sure that none lived in this harsh environment, but she hoped that perhaps other birds would come, such as the giant vultures that populated the area. When none did, she focused instead on exercises to strengthen her body. Without her spells, that was all she had, and she had to make it count.

One evening, after she had bathed and prepared for bed, with a cool breeze blowing in from a coming storm, Maltor entered the room and appeared intoxicated. The two guards who had escorted him home quickly left, and she saw Jak and the other guard become more vigilant. She assumed since Maltor was not a nice person sober, he would be a mean drunk. She was about to find out.

He lit a torch and moved over to the fairy. He stood there, gawking at his pet while it hissed at him and backed to the far side of the cage. He didn't do anything for a long while, but finally he mumbled something Cassandra could not hear and held the torch under the cage so the flame scorched the underside. The fairy immediately unfolded its wings and hovered in the small enclosure. The bottom became red-hot, and the little creature struggled to keep aloft. It barely had room in the cage to unfold its wings fully, and Cassandra knew it could not keep it up for long. Maltor did not relent and only grunted his approval at the struggling fairy. It no longer hissed at him, and Cassandra could see the frightened expression on her tiny, very human-like face.

"Maltor, why do you do this?" Cassandra asked, hoping to distract the drunken fool.

"Silence. You are not queen yet and have no right to speak," he spat at her.

She knew she had to keep prodding him to save the fairy. She would not watch her die like that. So, she continued to provoke him.

"When I am queen, I will speak, and it will be often."

He turned toward her, removing the torch from under the cage and pointing it at Cassandra. The fairy fluttered in her cell, waiting for the metal to cool but tiring quickly.

"Silence, outlander!" he cried and waved the torch menacingly.

"I will not. Where I come from, the women rule, and the men speak only when spoken to. When we are married, this is the role you'll assume."

Cassandra knew she was pushing the limits of the volatile barbarian's patience. She peered over Maltor's shoulder at the distressed fairy and knew she had to continue. The fairy watched her, silently pleading for help. The creature was intelligent enough to understand what Cassandra was doing for her. Distracted by watching the fairy, she did not realize Maltor was upon her until she felt his strong hand in her hair.

"Your rules don't apply here, my potential queen. You are very far from home."

She could smell the stench of alcohol, confirming her guess that he was intoxicated. Then she saw the torch. He had her by the hair, pulling her from the pole her leash was attached to. The chain became taut, and he held the torch at the halfway point of its length and the links began to warm, spreading toward the pole and her collar simultaneously. She knew it would soon burn her neck, and it would take a good while to cool once it became hot.

"Go ahead, break away if you can. Vixa never could. You are now Vixa, so you cannot," he taunted.

"I will be your queen, but not if you kill me."

"We leave tomorrow for the tournament. Will you be alive? Or will you join Vixa?"

Cassandra had no choice then. The chain grew slightly warm, and she knew the pain would be horrible. She saw the fairy still fluttering because the cage had not cooled enough. She had to stop him immediately. She thought about fighting him, attacking him, but being chained gave her a significant disadvantage. Also, what would he do to her if she successfully removed the torch? Attacking him would not work, so she did the only thing she knew to do.

"I will be alive. And I will win queenship, just like I won your heart."

She reached up and stroked his face gently. He recoiled from her touch briefly but then closed his eyes as she stroked it. Her other hand went to his torch hand and slowly lowered it.

"I will make you proud tomorrow. I, the outlander, will best all the potentials, and then I will become your prize. I will become your queen and learn your customs; my loins will bear children for you. It is our destiny. You knew it from the moment you saw me and the mark of Strenna on my hip. I have been hand-selected for you."

He slowly released her hair and took some of it in his fingers, rolling it as he tended to do.

"You will win tomorrow. Strenna is with you?"

"Of course, and I have the warrior's heart, remember?"

"If you fail, I will look the fool."

"There is no chance of that. I have seen it through Strenna."

"Not devil magic?" he asked, gritting his teeth.

Cassandra held up her arms, showing him her slightly bruised forearms. "No, that is now impossible."

He threw the torch to the ground, and Jak was there to put it out before it ignited the rug on which it lay. Maltor stood on wobbly legs for many moments. He then nodded at her with a grunt and stumbled over to his bed. Cassandra made eye contact with the fairy, who was still hovering in the cage, but hanging onto the cooled bars now for support. Her little eyes were wide with fear and shock, and she shivered in her small dwelling, afraid and alone.

Cassandra's collar was growing very warm, and if it grew much hotter, it would seriously burn her. She could not touch the chain, and there was no water to quench the heat. She waited for the inevitable burn. But there was a splash of cool water on her neck, and the metal cooled instantly. She turned to see that Jak had used the remnants of her bath water to douse the heated collar. She looked at him with appreciation in her eyes. He nodded and went back to his post. Soon Maltor was snoring, and Cassandra understood she had dodged a serious injury at the hands of the drunken king.

True to his word, she was finally released from her chains and led outside the next day. The sun stunned her eyes and blinded her for a bit. Maltor wore a giant headdress with many colors and had Cassandra ride on his camel again, before him as the previous time. Maltor led the caravan, followed by many warriors on camelback, the men and the livestock dressed in the tribal colors of the Serpent Tribe. The shamans, including Grink, followed Maltor and his many warriors, riding comfortably on the smelly camels. A wooden camel-pulled cage large enough to fit the other three contestants rolled behind them. After the procession, many of the tribe's people walked the journey, as was tradition. They stopped briefly at the training compound to pick up three trainees. Cassandra could only imagine the disappointed fourth trainee who would not make the trek to the coliseum. Cassandra took her place, courtesy of the king. Maltor had informed the guards only to take the top three. Cassandra was considered the highest-ranking trainee, Maltor deemed, so the fourth-place hopeful defaulted to the fifth rank and, therefore, was not invited.

Cassandra watched the top three climb into the wooden wagon. She was not surprised to see Lita, Breka's lackey, and Gah as two of the three. The other one she did not remember and did not care. She knew now that with her skills, none of those female warriors mattered; they could not beat her. Still, Lita made eye contact with her as they escorted her from the compound to the wagon. The shocked look on her face spoke volumes. She had not expected to see Cassandra again and would tell the other two soon enough. Cassandra smiled as she imagined the three riding along in the hot, wooden cage, discussing how Cassandra had made it to the tournament. Again, it did not matter because they did not matter. Cassandra just needed to focus on winning because, as she knew all along, her life depended on it.

The caravan started away, and the barbarians in the rear of the parade sang a hearty song to their god Strenna. The sun beat down on them as they rode out of the tribal lands and deeper into the desert.

"By the time the sun begins its decline in the sky, we will reach the Queen's Pit," Maltor explained.

Cassandra could only assume he meant where the tournament would occur, so she did not bother answering as Maltor continued to instruct her.

"There will be twenty contestants. In each round, random tribes will be selected, and the kings will choose which warrior will fight. There are few rules. The stronger fighter wins the round to move to the next stage. The loser will be presented to the winning king for his pleasure."

"What?" Cassandra asked in feign surprise. Vixa had already informed her of that tradition, but she wanted to tell Maltor how ignorant it truly was.

"The opposing king takes losers as playthings. They must be returned by nightfall and not permanently damaged, but those are the only rules. The last warrior standing becomes queen of her respective tribe."

"And is not raped like all those unfortunate enough to lose," Cassandra added.

"You don't like the idea of being raped, outlander?"

"No."

"Then don't lose."

Cassandra shook her head in disbelief. What kind of idiots came up with these rules? None of them gave women any rights. She thought of Vixa then and how Maltor had beaten her when they had first met. She felt sick to her stomach. She knew it was nerves mostly, but it was also because she had been responsible for Vixa's death. She pondered that for a bit as they rode.

She finally said, "And stop calling me outlander; my name is Cassandra Rho."

Maltor snorted derisively, but they did not speak for the rest of the way to the Queen's Pit.

According to what Vixa had told Cassandra about the tournament, they held the event in the middle of the desert, with the five different tribes traveling from five other regions of the grand desert to reach it. Vixa had said the place was quite interesting, and although her nerves began to get the best of her, Cassandra agreed once she saw it.

The barbarians had built a rock wall about ten feet tall surrounding the large sand-filled pit with a circumference of about fifty feet. On one side of the pit, the rock wall was absent and instead, a set of wide, stone steps led up to a balcony where five thrones sat, one for each king, facing the ring. Each throne was built at the entrance of a ten-foot by twenty-foot stone enclosure with a wooden roof. The kings had a full view of the action, while the wooden roof extended to cover the throne and provide the kings with shade. Beside each throne was a large flag symbolizing one of the tribes. Each flag marked the tribe's respective areas of the pit with their appropriate symbol: a scorpion, vulture, serpent, culiem, or sleeth. There were also small glass enclosures near each throne that looked to Cassandra to be terrariums. On the side opposite the thrones was a large dune where spectators could sit and watch the action.

As Cassandra and the other heroes of the tribe were led to the pit by Jozerah and Bolin, two of Maltor's highest-ranking warriors in his army, Maltor went in a separate direction. He did not acknowledge Cassandra or the others; he simply left them. Jozerah climbed the steps, leading Maltor's four hopefuls into the structure behind the throne with the serpent flag. Cassandra could see the folk from the Serpent Tribe, who had sung most of the way, climb the enormous dune to find seating. Barbarians from other tribes were doing the same thing, and soon, the place was full of spectators.

Cassandra and the other three potential queens for the Serpent Tribe were now standing in the shade, within the enclosure behind Maltor's throne. After ushering them in, Jozerah and Bolin took up spots at either side of the throne as guards, their backs to the potentials. A short while later, the shamans, Grink and Bok, joined them in the enclosure but sat on comfortable pillows. They both began speaking in hushed but excited tones. Cassandra watched as they prayed together as well. She knew why they were there and understood that combatants would face many injuries during the tournament. She was nervous about the possibility but confident she would not need the shamans.

She looked around the structure and found it solidly built and recently reinforced. There was nothing in the enclosure other than sand. She considered digging out or trying to pry the back of the wooden roof off and make an escape. She understood the odds of succeeding were slim, so she dismissed the thoughts immediately. The only way out was past the generals of Maltor's army. Even with her enhanced skills, she did not think she stood much chance against two of them, plus the shamans' magic. Where would she even go if she did succeed? Her only true hope of escape was to win the tournament. She had to finish first out of twenty hopefuls. Without Vixa's skills, she would have had no chance, but now she was reasonably confident she could hold her own. She decided she would meditate until the foolish event began.

She turned to walk to the back of the holding area and found the other three trainees standing in her way, shoulder to shoulder. Lita had her arms crossed over her chest, as did Gah, whose arms were thick and muscled. The third one stood there, her hands on her hips, but she did not seem so angry. The scowl on Lita's and Gah's faces spoke volumes. She had fought both women during her brief stay at the compound, and they both had thoroughly beaten her. She understood that their memories were long, but she was also confident she could dispose of them, even fighting them simultaneously if it came to it.

"You murdered Breka, outlander," Lita said through gritted teeth.

"And she murdered Laryn," Cassandra replied, walking right up to stand before them, no fear evident in her voice or actions.

"Who?" Gah asked.

"The other outlander at the compound," the third barbarian said.

"Her life meant nothing. But you killed one of us, and that will not go unpunished." Lita took another step so that the two were so close, their noses almost touched.

"And when I am queen, I will have you horse-whipped for your actions against Laryn. She was a far better warrior than either of you."

Gah then took a step to join the stare-down.

"If you two stinking idiots don't move, I will break both your necks before the tournament starts," Cassandra said.

The two turned to each other with a puzzled expression. "What is an idiot?" Lita asked.

"Exactly," was all the answer Cassandra gave. She prepared for an attack that she knew was imminent.

"Careful, rumors say she has the warrior's heart," the third trainee said, off to the side and backing further away.

"Shut up, Paisel!" Lita screamed.

A snapping sound from behind Cassandra interrupted the confrontation. Cassandra turned to see Jozerah standing there with a whip he had cracked in the air. Bolin was beside him, a similar weapon in his hand, wearing a smirk.

"Save it for the ring," Jozerah growled.

"As much as I'd like to beat all of you, it is important that you do Maltor proud today. Save your bickering for after the tournament," Bolin added.

Lita and Gah walked to the far end of the holding area, Paisel walked to another end, and Cassandra sat in the sand where she was. She closed her eyes and meditated. She listened to the growing sounds as more and more spectators arrived. She also listened intently to the whispers in the far corner. She knew Lita and Gah were talking about her, but she could not make out their words. Cassandra breathed deeply and exhaled her frustrations, deciding not to waste more time on those two. She fell into a deep trance, a warrior's calm.

Sometime later, her meditation was interrupted by an announcer, signaling the start of the tournament. She slowly opened her eyes, relaxed and ready. In front of her stood Jozerah and Bolin, backs turned to her once more, looking out into the pit. The shamans were behind the throne, similarly watching the spectacle. Lita, Gah, and Paisel were behind them, nervously pacing and fidgeting. Cassandra could see that the crowd was massive, the great dune filled, and some barbarian spectators even sat on the rock wall, legs dangling over it and into the pit. She slowly rose and walked over to stand beside Paisel, the only one in the group she did not think was a total fool.

"What is happening?" Cassandra asked her.

"The introduction of the kings."

A creature in the pit had a human torso, arms, and head, but his lower half resembled a giant snake. He held a hollowed tusk to his mouth, amplifying his voice and faced the crowd, riling them up with his words and a few waves of his hand.

"What is that?" Cassandra asked, looking at the strange announcer.

"A sleeth."

"A snake person, the same as the tribe of the sleeth?"

"Yes."

"Why do they get their own announcer? I assume he is not impartial?"

"It is the way of things; the first tribe always has privileges," Paisel answered, never taking her eye off the sleeth.

"The Sleeth Tribe is the top tribe?"

"Yes; their tribe has many sleeth mixed within their population, making them powerful foes. That is why they win these tournaments, and their king has many queens."

"They win every year?" Cassandra asked.

"Most times, yes. Their warriors are not only well trained but also have enhanced sleeth abilities. One or all of us will likely face a sleeth today," Paisel explained, then turned her head to face Cassandra and added, "Beware of them."

Cassandra nodded, then they both fell silent as the sleeth announcer introduced the kings. He used tremendous flair, making the crowd grow into a frenzy. Cassandra watched and listened but fell into that calming meditation once more. He introduced the kings one at a time, beginning with the lowest-ranking tribe.

"To start things off, we have the Tribe of the Scorpion, currently with no queens. Their masterful king and veteran of many battles is none other than King Crowsend!"

The spectators from that tribe came to life, cheering and waving their respective pennants. The supporting crowd for the lesser tribe was the smallest in attendance. Regardless, King Crowsend entered the pit waving to his people. He wore a ceremonial headdress made of scorpion tails and pincers and carried a massive sword on his back, the pommel shaped into a scorpion of gold. He ascended the massive steps and walked to his throne with a large sack. He poured the contents into the glass terrarium closest to his throne, and Cassandra could see a dozen black scorpions fall from the bag and fill most of the glass container. Warriors from his tribe quickly affixed a lid to keep them inside. The grand king then took a seat.

"The next tribe of worth is none other than the Tribe of the Vulture!" the announcer continued once Crowsend found his seat.

"This tribe currently has one queen, winning her two years ago in a deadly match against a sleeth. Please welcome King Dazor of the Vulture Tribe," the announcer said with a bit of a snarl on his face.

A mixed reaction from the crowd filled the air; boos from the Sleeth Tribe and cheers from the Vulture Tribe competed before the fighting in the pits had even begun. It took a while for the chanting to die off so the announcer could continue.

The king of the Vulture Tribe was old, slow-moving, and nearly naked. His skin was tanned a dark brown from the powerful sun, and although he appeared close to eighty years of age, his physique was very toned and muscular and he had no trouble climbing the steps. He carried a large vulture on his arm and set it upon a perch near his throne before taking a seat.

"And now, I introduce the slayer of outlanders, the master of the ocean raids, Maltor, King of the Serpent Tribe!"

Many people cheered, and Cassandra understood then the pressure the proud king faced by allowing her to enter the tournament. He was known as the killer of outlanders, yet he preferred to marry one. He was nearly naked, with his face and chest painted in green and yellow stripes and symbols, with a venomous viper wrapped around his arm, his fingers holding the head still so the deadly snake could not bite him. Jozerah and Bolin carefully helped remove the viper and place it in the terrarium once he reached the throne. Then Maltor took his seat, and the announcer continued.

"And now we have the second-ranking tribe of the Yaddaton Desert, the Culiem Tribe, led by King Boskel!"

The barbarian king made a magnificent entrance with four culiem fairies strapped to a harness wrapped around his massive chest. They fluttered about him like large butterflies. Cassandra could see that each of them, two male and two female, had their hands bound behind them and gags in their small but dangerous mouths. Cassandra reasoned that Boskel must be the one Maltor traded with to obtain his fairy.

"Boskel's tribe not only harvests the powerful and mysterious culiem fairies, but he is also the proud owner of four wives!" the announcer finished.

The large king had three culiem fairies taken away and put the fourth into a cage next to his throne. The man then took a seat, and the thunderous cheer rang on for many moments before the sleeth announcer could continue.

"And now, without further delay, please welcome the amazing lord of Yaddaton's most powerful tribe—King Brenner with the Tribe of the Sleeth!"

The crowd went wild, and all stood to witness the prominent barbarian. The man stood nearly seven feet tall and was completely naked. His heavily muscled body made Maltor look like an average man. He was the most impressive human Cassandra had ever seen, assuming he was human. She could not resist a peek at his manhood, which was substantial yet not quite as remarkable as Greyson's. The king went to the center of the pit and turned, waving to all, soaking up the cheers and the attention.

"Have you ever lain with a man?" Paisel asked.

"No," Cassandra said, shaking her head honestly.

"They say he rips his women during sex." Paisel turned to her then and swallowed hard. "You know, due to the size of his—"

Cassandra turned to her and answered honestly, "I've seen bigger."

Paisel let it go at that, and Cassandra had a hard time stifling a smile. It was true Greyson was more prominent, but she could only imagine either of them hurting her badly in an intimate encounter. Cassandra strengthened her resolve then just for that reason. She had to win to keep that possibility from becoming a reality. She fell into her meditation once more, tuning out the announcer's words.

The sleeth announcer bowed before his king and continued, "Master of wars, and slayer of dragons, King Brenner boasts the largest harem of Yaddaton with twenty-seven wives!"

The crowd roared while two giant barbarians brought a massive snake out to Brenner and wrapped it around his shoulders. He hoisted the snake and let out a war cry, and all the barbarians of the Sleeth Tribe echoed it. After what seemed like forever, the king made his way to his throne, slowly climbing the steps, dropping the snake into a large terrarium and taking a seat. It took many moments for the crowd to quiet down so the announcer could continue. He let the cheering play out for a long time, ensuring everyone in attendance knew who the most powerful tribe was.

When it finally died down, he said, "The rules are the same as always: the two combatants will fight in this pit. No weapons of any kind are allowed, and the rock wall may not be incorporated into the competition. At the discretion of the combatants, they may use their tribal animal during the fight, but it may only be used once during the entire tournament, and once used, the animal will be removed from the pit after the match.

"Also, the only way to win is by surrender. Once a warrior submits, the winner will move on to the next round, and the loser will spread her legs for the opposing king to enjoy the fruits of victory. The last one standing will become queen of her respective tribe, and the losers will return to their former positions in their tribes. If lucky and Strenna smiles upon them, they will be blessed with a child from one of these most impressive kings."

More cheering followed the proclamation, which made Cassandra sick. Females of the barbarian society had no rights, and she would never be able to live among them. She needed a way out of the madness, but first, she had to win the tournament. Failure was not an option she desired.

The announcer continued, "We also have an outlander among us today, one competing for queenship! This is the first time in the tournament's history that a king has allowed an interloper to compete."

There was a chorus of boos. Peripherally, Cassandra could see the other three women in the enclosure looking at her. She ignored them and focused on Maltor. He squirmed in his seat as the boos continued for a long while.

The announcer finally continued, "Once the outlander is defeated, which naturally will be the case—"

He was interrupted by thunderous cheers and had to stop speaking and wait for the crowd to settle down. Once subdued, he said, "She is a blond devil, a weakling that dabbles in the dark arts of the devil."

After more booing, he finished his tongue-lashing of Cassandra. "Once defeated, she will find herself in the procreation tent of the Serpent Tribe and will become a plaything for the hearty warriors of that tribe!"

The crowd stood then and cheered louder than ever. Even Jozerah and Bolin turned to regard her, smirks on their faces. Lita snorted and shook her head at Cassandra. She felt the same as always, just an outcast in a world of bullies. She didn't belong there; she didn't belong anywhere. The words to the nursery rhyme came to life in her mind: *Little Cassandra Rho, tromping through the forest, being way too loud and bringing the wolves upon us.* She shook her head and walked to the back of the enclosure; she had to remain focused. The announcer finished going over the rules.

"Each round a tribe participates in, the kings will hand-select which combatants will come forth for battle, beginning with the highest-ranking tribe. A combatant may not fight a second time until all from her tribe have fought at least once. The same is true for a third time. Also, each king has brought along two shamans to use as healing between fights at the king's discretion. Once the healing powers of their respective shamans become depleted, no more healing will be available to that tribe. Any questions, my kings?"

The kings looked at one another, eventually shaking their heads.

"Then it is time for the Queen's Tournament!"

The barbarians in attendance cheered for a long while, and when they finally settled down, the tournament began. The matchups were randomly determined by a group of barbarian warriors, one from each tribe. Cassandra wasn't sure exactly how they did it, but they settled it by rolling animal bones. The first match happened to be the Culiem Tribe versus the Serpent Tribe. Maltor rose and looked over his potential queens. All stood at attention except Cassandra, who remained deep in meditation and appeared uninterested. He waited for the Culiem Tribe to announce their warrior, a huge, muscular woman. She was as tall as most of the male barbarians of the Serpent Tribe. Maltor turned back to them after the culiem warrior entered the pit to great cheers. Jozerah and Bolin whispered in his ear as the cheering grew louder. Cassandra could make out a chant forming that only grew louder the longer Maltor delayed his pick.

"Outlander! Outlander!" they chanted repeatedly.

Cassandra closed her eyes and heard the remnants of the nursery rhyme: *So, don't go out in the woods armed only with a stick; It's better to take Cassandra Rho, the little raven witch.*

Eventually, after what seemed like forever to Cassandra, she opened her eyes just in time to see Maltor nod to Paisel. The small barbarian glanced to Lita and Gah, who nodded their support, then to Cassandra. She bowed to Maltor and rushed down the steps and into the pit. The crowd booed when they discovered it wasn't Cassandra.

The first match was between a gigantic and muscular warrior from the Culiem Tribe and the much smaller but swifter Paisel. They made their way to the inner circle drawn by the announcer in the very center of the ring. They stood facing each other, a mere five feet between them. Once the announcer had left the pit, a horn blew somewhere from the side, and the fight began.

Paisel was much smaller than her opponent and lacked muscle mass. Cassandra was curious to see how she would do because Paisel's stature resembled hers. If she could compete, then Cassandra knew she could as well, especially with Vixa's fighting skills now a part of her consciousness.

Surprisingly, Paisel used the same flying leg scissors Cassandra used to bring down Sneck a month earlier. Her opponent was surprised, and the attack was a success. However, she fell hard purposely, trying to drive Paisel into the ground. Fortunately, the sand was soft and did minor damage to the smaller warrior, but it broke the hold. The larger warrior pounced on Paisel with surprising quickness, and the warrior from the Tribe of the Serpent was quickly in trouble. The two grappled for advantage for a long while, and the larger warrior was able to punch Paisel in the ribs a few times, which eventually took its toll. Ultimately, the larger warrior was too much and finally grasped her smaller opponent securely. She lifted Paisel in the air and slammed her down over her knee, breaking more than one rib. Paisel quickly surrendered, to the cheers of many of the spectators.

The enormous warrior flexed her muscles in a pose that elicited even more cheers, planting a foot on the writhing Paisel. She then dragged the poor woman up the steps to her king, who licked his lips in anticipation. Cassandra couldn't believe the humiliating ritual, the condoned rape that was about to occur as a finale to the match. He positioned the injured Paisel on his throne and quickly disrobed. There was no shame; the crowd went wild as he took his prize. Cassandra could not watch that part and moved to the back of the enclosure once more.

After watching the first match, she had doubts about her ability to compete with the other women. After all, they were the best from each tribe, and Cassandra was not a warrior. Sure, she possessed a specific skill set now, but her body was not a fighter's body. She remembered her defeat to Cass in the schoolyard, where Cass beat her at her own game. She had failed then using her magic, which was her way. How could she ever win a fight in a contest of strength? She sat in the sand and closed her eyes, trying desperately to find her meditative trance again. She had to focus, but it was difficult with Paisel's screams in the background and the growing cheers.

Cassandra stayed in her trance for the next few matches and did not dare watch the events. However, Maltor eventually summoned her. She sensed him nearby and opened her eyes to find the large king standing before her. She did not know how much time had passed, but Lita and Gah were still there, and neither looked like they had fought.

"It is time," Maltor said. "I have an easy match for you, one you should win. I want you to advance, so this is your easiest chance. You are fighting the Tribe of the Scorpion, the weakest tribe. They base their strength on speed. Time your opponent's moves, and you can win. Remember: you have the heart of the warrior."

Cassandra wasn't listening; the crowd's chant of "Outlander!" repeatedly drowned out Maltor's words. And it was much louder than the first time. She nodded to Maltor and stepped past him and onto the top step. The sun was high, and the heat was overwhelming. The crowd cheered, understanding that they had finally received the outlander. She stood out with her fair skin and blond hair, and she could feel all eyes on her. Their stares stung her like little insects, for she knew they all hated her, even the members of the Serpent Tribe. The feeling was mutual.

She descended the long flight of steps and found the inner circle of the pit, redrawn by the announcer, and took her spot at one end. The Scorpion Tribe sent out their warrior next, a woman about Cassandra's size but with an exotic appearance. Her hair was red like Vixa's, but Cassandra's opponent kept her hair in tight braids, unlike the wild barbarian. Also, her skin was not tanned and leathery like the typical barbarians. Cassandra wondered where the woman was from, but the thought passed quickly when she made the circle. Her eyes were strange, the pupils larger than normal, and she had six fingers on each hand. Her opponent was not human!

As they set themselves to begin, Cassandra called upon those warrior instincts, wanting to take advantage and finish this strange warrior quickly. Just before the horn sounded, Cassandra noticed her opponent slightly nod toward Maltor. Cassandra turned quickly to regard the king and saw Lita slink into the shadows. Cassandra knew then that the woman was not nodding to Maltor but to Lita. With her head turned, the horn sounded.

The red-haired woman was upon her before she could snap her head back. Maltor had mentioned speed as the Scorpion Tribe's greatest asset, but she was impossibly fast. She also learned why keeping your hair braided or cut short was necessary as her opponent quickly grabbed two fistfuls of Cassandra's blond locks and tossed her to the ground. Cassandra rolled with the throw and came up, ready to fight, but the woman was not there. The breath was knocked from her as a hard kick to her back had her flying face down in the sand. Cassandra could hear the many cheers as the woman pounced on top of her, applying leg scissors and locking her right arm.

The scissors were more potent than Cassandra could believe, and it felt like her ribs would break at any moment. She managed to claw the woman with her left hand, trying to gouge her eyes, but every time she tried that move, the scissors would tighten, and she would have to stop and focus on the lock.

"And now you will suffer greatly, devil witch," her opponent whispered.

She then rearranged her hold on Cassandra's right arm so it was straight out in the sand, pinning it at the wrist. Cassandra tried to pull it free, but the scissors tightened even further when she did. Cassandra yelled out and refocused on escaping those deadly legs. They were beginning to sap her strength. Then she felt an awful pain in her forearm as the woman slammed her fist down with incredible force. The hit brought back that horrible sensation of when Grink first placed the needles in her arm.

She tried freeing her arm, but the hold was proper, and her opponent used her speed to barrage her poor forearm, each strike bringing more intense pain. She thought of that nod her opponent had shared with Lita before the match and understood Lita had somehow informed her of the needles. Cassandra screamed in pain and clawed at her opponent's face with little effect.

"Submit, outlander!" the woman yelled while continuing her barrage.

Cassandra could not lose like this, but how could she break free? She panicked and forgot all the skills she had inherited from Vixa. All she could focus on was the pain in her ribs and forearm. The cheers grew louder. However, she would not submit. The attack on her forearm continued until there was a snapping sound as the needle broke in half, two sharp ends protruding from her skin. Cassandra screamed from the awful, unbearable pain.

The woman relented her attack then and released the scissors. She stood up and raised her hands in victory as Cassandra wept, holding her injured and now bleeding arm to her chest. The fight was over; she had failed. But still, she did not submit. Perhaps the woman would kill her, which might be her only true means of escaping the barbarians. The woman pulled her up by her hair and slapped her hard several times. Cassandra could not block and could only cradle her torn arm. The hits were furious, and soon her nose was bleeding as she staggered around the pit. The cheering grew as the crowd expected the submission at any moment.

With one extra powerful slap, Cassandra fell face first to the sand and nearly lost consciousness. She managed to not black out completely, but when she fully regained her senses, the woman was on her back, pulling on her hair. She eventually ripped out a fistful of Cassandra's golden locks and stood to show the crowd. More cheers greeted the scorpion warrior. The spectators hated Cassandra, but she heard little of their reactions as she held her bleeding scalp and prayed for a quick death. Why was she even there? She could not hope to win against even the easiest of opponents.

The woman grabbed her legs and turned her over to face the blinding sun, then began to drag her by her legs over to her king. Cassandra's heart raced, for she knew what was to come next. Her opponent would not kill her, but the king would rape her. All the fiery redhead needed to do was apply pressure to Cassandra's forearm to gain the submission. All was lost, until Cassandra saw the symbols floating in the air.

The arcane symbols had returned; they were faint and weak, but they were all around her. With the needle broken, she had some spell use back. She thought quickly that she needed a spell to end this, but the symbols in their diluted state would only offer something very simple. She knew she couldn't openly use a magical attack because that would result in certain death in the middle of the wild barbarian tribes, so she had to be subtle.

Then the dragging stopped, and Cassandra found herself at the foot of the steps with the scorpion king standing on the last one. The man was as large as Maltor, though quite a bit older. He repulsed her, as did all the smelly barbarians. He licked his lips in anticipation as the redhead pulled Cassandra by the hair once more to a sitting position. She stood behind her and wrestled her right arm free. She held it tight, and Cassandra could feel the needles poke out of her skin even further and the blood pour down her arm.

"Submit!" the woman yelled, but Cassandra stubbornly refused.

Her opponent punched her forearm, tearing more of the needle free and breaking it in a second place. The pain overwhelmed Cassandra as she went limp. The woman released her and marched around her with her arms high in the sky to more cheers while Cassandra slowly moved to tuck her arm, barely conscious. When she felt her opponent dig her hand into her tender scalp again and pull her to sit up, Cassandra knew what was coming. The woman got behind her and locked her injured right arm.

"Submit, outlander!" the woman screamed for all to hear.

Cassandra recalled a simple spell she had seen Cass use against her. She had never truly learned the magic, but she had been aware of what symbols comprised it. She called them forth, hoping to enact the spell. She felt her arm pull tight, the needle tearing her skin even more, and she yelled out in pain. Her opponent eased the pressure a little when Cassandra finally spoke.

"I ..."

She applied the pressure again, trying to coax the submission. Cassandra squealed in pain and began again.

"I... hate... you!" she managed to get out.

The crowd laughed at her, cheered at the response, and her opponent laughed, then yawned. Cassandra knew her spell had taken effect. The grip loosened, and Cassandra pulled away as the smile melted from the surprised king's face. Cassandra rose on shaky legs to stand before the woman, who was not asleep but could barely keep her eyes open. She staggered, nearly ready to fall. Cassandra knew her time was limited because the spell should have put the woman out cold. She had not cast it perfectly and did not know how long the effects would last.

The crowd went silent as Cassandra eased the woman to her back. She put her arm into a similar hold she had used on Cassandra. She then applied pressure to the trapped appendage with one good arm. She did not have a lot of strength. But she did know specific holds, thanks to Vixa's knowledge. She applied tremendous pressure at the perfect angle, and her opponent moaned a little, her eyes flittering occasionally but offering no resistance. She applied more pressure and continued to pull the arm at a painful angle. Eventually, it snapped with a sickening crack. Instead of needles, bone broke through the skin of the woman's arm.

Her opponent snapped to her senses then with a blood-curdling scream. Cassandra released her, and the barbarian sat up, holding her arm, which now pointed at an unnatural angle. The woman screamed in agony as she tried to straighten her arm. As she struggled with the impossible task,

Cassandra casually walked behind her, just as the wicked woman had done to her.

She grabbed her opponent's broken arm and yelled, "Submit!"

"Submit! Submit!" the woman cried.

The stadium was silent as Cassandra grabbed the woman by one of her braids and dragged her up the steps and over to Maltor.

"Here," she said, releasing the woman at his feet, then entered the enclosure.

By the time she arrived, Maltor had removed his loincloth and was preparing to take his prize. Cassandra gave Lita a hateful look, and she and Gah backed away. She sat in the cool sand, and Grink rushed over, examining her arm.

"We must fix this," he said.

"Not without Maltor's approval," Jozerah butted in.

"She cannot fight like this," the shaman argued.

"Wait until he approves," Jozerah said, putting a hand on the coiled whip to emphasize the seriousness of his order.

Grink and Bok backed away and left Cassandra there to suffer. Eventually, Maltor finished with his prize and walked into the enclosure. The next fight was already starting, but none of the Serpent Tribe focused on it. All eyes were on Cassandra. She realized that they suspected her of witchcraft.

"You used magic?" Maltor asked.

"Of course. I told you, that is—"

A hard slap had her falling to the sand and her mouth bleeding.

"Do not do it again, or I will kill you myself! Fix the needles so she cannot work her devil magic!" Maltor yelled at Grink.

"The procedure takes too long; I cannot fix the breaks. I can only put them back in and heal the wound," Grink argued.

Maltor stepped dangerously close to the man, and the shaman shrank before his king.

"Fix her," he said and went back to his throne.

The two shamans worked on her for a long while after that as Lita and then Gah both fought. The pain was awful, and Cassandra cried out many times during that horrendous procedure. If the original implantation of the needles was terrible, the pain related to fixing them was thrice as bad. They used most of their healing on her during the procedure, which was not good for the Tribe of the Serpent.

By the time the first round was over, and only ten hopefuls remained, Gah had been defeated by a sleeth, leaving only Lita and Cassandra as the combatants for the Serpent Tribe. Maltor checked on Cassandra's arm, and after Grink explained that the wound was a significant weakness and no more healing would help it, the proud barbarian king let out a resigned sigh.

"Do not use your magic, or I will know. I will kill you. Do you understand?"

"Of course, my loving husband," Cassandra spat back.

That earned her another smack, and more blood filled her mouth.

"I am not your husband," he growled at first. But then a softer side showed on his face, and he rubbed the back of his hand over her swelling cheek and added, "But I desire that."

She recoiled from his touch, breaking the tender moment, and Maltor rose and quickly took his seat. It seemed to Cassandra that he entertained the idea of hitting her again but controlled himself enough to walk away. She swallowed hard, fearing the man and his unpredictable temper.

The second round began, and Cassandra rose to watch. She noticed then that Lita had a badly bruised face with one eye swollen shut. The shamans had not healed her wounds. Cassandra felt guilty but understood that the shamans were keeping her alive because that was what Maltor wanted. Lita did not matter to Maltor.

Bolin turned to address them. "Every tribe has two warriors left, except the Vulture Tribe, which has only one, and of course the Sleeth Tribe, which has three still. Thanks to Lita, it is not four."

Cassandra looked at the proud warrior and understood that she had defeated a member of the Sleeth Tribe. Cassandra had been beaten badly by the weakest tribe, yet Lita had won against the best. She looked down at the bloody bandage on her forearm and knew she was in trouble. She shook the thoughts away and refocused.

The first fight of the second round was between the remaining warrior from the Vulture Tribe and the Serpent Tribe. Maltor nodded to Cassandra. Her heart raced as she made her way a second time to the top of the steps. As the barbarians redrew the circle in the sand to begin the round, Maltor grabbed Cassandra's hand.

"Do not use magic, and do not lose. You have Vixa's heart, so act like it," he growled.

She did not reply and struggled to free her hand. She could tell Maltor wanted to strike her for her behavior, but he gritted his teeth and squeezed her wrist instead. She would not cave to his controlling nature; if they had been alone, he would have beat her senseless, she had no doubt. As it was, he had no choice but to release her so she could descend the stairs and enter the pit.

She put Maltor out of her mind and focused on the coming fight. The afternoon sun beat down on her even more than the morning sun had. Curiously, there were no boos or cheers as the crowd remained deathly quiet in her presence. Whether from fear or respect, they did not react to her as she entered the ring.

Her opponent came into the circle. The woman was tall and lean and stood nearly six and a half feet tall. To Cassandra's small frame, she might as well have been a giant! Also, since she was the last remaining warrior from the Vulture Tribe, Cassandra could only assume she was their best.

The match started, and Cassandra quickly gained the upper hand, easily getting the tall woman into a wrist lock. As she applied the pressure, she kicked the woman in the ribs several times, trying to weaken her resolve. But she became distracted by the symbols that beckoned her. They danced around her opponent, still weak but available.

Her distraction cost her dearly as the woman punched her in the stomach, taking her breath away. Her opponent did not have a lot of leverage, but she was strong, and the punch was effective. A second hit broke the hold and had Cassandra off balance. She didn't see her opponent's knee until it was too late. It cracked her in the face, bloodying her nose, and she fell to the sand, stunned. The woman was strong and soon had Cassandra in several different painful holds. Cassandra broke free several times using the wisdom imparted to her by Vixa, and eventually, the two combatants squared off, circling the pit, looking for an opportunity.

The match was mostly even to that point, lasting much longer than her first one. Although Cassandra had taken the worst of the punishment, she was glad to have Vixa's skills. However, she knew she did not have the stamina to fight a long match. She would need to end it soon if she hoped to succeed. Perhaps feeling the same, her opponent intensified her attacks. They grappled for control, and the match remained even until her opponent decided to play dirty, throwing sand in Cassandra's eyes after a particular roll.

Cassandra was blinded temporarily and paid the price for it as the woman landed a roundhouse kick to her jaw. The world went black, and Cassandra knew nothing for a bit. When she awakened a short while later, the vulture king's voice was close. She blinked away the darkness of unconsciousness and adjusted to the sun's blinding light. Cassandra found herself at the vulture king's throne, but did not remember the trek up the steps. She had obviously been knocked out by the kick and her opponent had carried her up the steps while Cassandra was unconscious.

"Disrobe her" was all she could make out of the old, repulsive king's gibberish.

She felt her opponent forcefully remove her top to the sound of cheering in the coliseum. She was on her feet somehow and understood that her opponent was behind her, holding her up. She felt her opponent turn her, and Cassandra could see hundreds of savages waving their banners and cheering at the sight of her naked breasts. Her vision was blurry, and she could not make out the details, but she understood what was happening. But the pain in her jaw and the throbbing of her head made it hard to focus.

Her opponent tossed her face down on the stone floor in front of the throne. She spit blood out of her mouth and tried to push herself up, but the large woman was on her back then, pressing her face onto the hot stone. She sat upon Cassandra's back and roughly pulled her hands behind her. The woman had not attacked her bandaged forearm, but she was rough with it then, causing Cassandra to cry out as the pain shot through her entire arm. She felt the woman tie her hands behind her back using her top. The woman was proficient and soon had Cassandra's arms immobile.

She flipped Cassandra over, and the sun shot new waves of pain through her aching head. Cassandra could barely keep her eyes open, so she never saw her opponent's attack. The tall woman stomped on Cassandra's midriff twice, blasting the wind from her lungs and leaving her gasping for air. Cassandra learned then why the warriors drank plenty of water but ate little food before the tournament began. Cassandra could not fight back with her arms tied and struggled to catch her breath. Her opponent removed Cassandra's loincloth and offered it to her king.

Cassandra was completely naked now and very much humiliated. The king held up her loincloth, and the spectators cheered. Her opponent returned to assault her with more stomps. She took both of Cassandra's legs and stood them up straight. She then spread them and stomped between them. More cheers erupted from the crowd, and a horrible pain shot through Cassandra's pelvic bone. She cried and tucked into a fetal position. However, her opponent was relentless and turned her back over to face the burning sun once more and put a foot on her stomach, stepping hard and eliciting a moan from her. She flexed her muscles toward the gathered mass, and the cheering became louder.

Cassandra knew she was in trouble then as the woman jerked her up by the hair and led her to her king. She kicked the back of Cassandra's legs, making her fall to her knees. She would have fallen over, but her opponent still had a handful of her hair, forcing her to remain upright.

"Your prize, my king. Please sample," the woman said, holding Cassandra steady.

The old king leaned in and flashed a wicked smile, showing only a few yellow and black teeth. He reached down and twisted Cassandra's nipples hard. He kept turning them until she screamed, and the crowd cheered again. Then King Dazor leaned further down and sucked her breast into his mouth. She could feel his tongue flick her nipple. He repeated that process to her other breast as Cassandra's opponent held her immobile.

The old king rose and said, "Finish her! The outlander tastes sweet!"

The savage spectators applauded and cheered at the request, and the woman pulled Cassandra up and walked her backward a few feet away so that she still faced the king. She pointed over Cassandra's shoulder to the giant vulture next to King Dazor and screamed, "Taya!"

The king's shocked expression spoke volumes as servants quickly untied the bird from its perch. Her opponent would use the animal to finish Cassandra, something she did not need to do in Cassandra's current state. The king knew it, and as Cassandra slowly regained her senses, she did as well.

"Take her eyes, Taya, my well-trained friend!" her opponent yelled to the bird.

She held Cassandra steady as the bird unfolded its wings. It took flight, and with one quick flap of its wings, it covered the distance between them. It turned and presented its talons, coming straight for Cassandra's face. The woman coaxed the bird on, and Cassandra remained pacified. Her only hope was to play stunned until the last moment. Her opponent presented her to the great bird but did not have a firm grip on her, thinking Cassandra was dazed. Cassandra searched her mind for a way to break the hold cleanly, but with her hands tied, the feat was difficult.

She pretended to be limp in her opponent's arms as the bird came on fast, her opponent holding her head up by her hair so the bird could tear out her eyes. Cassandra stomped on her opponent's foot at the last moment and screamed as she had against Sneck. The woman's grip lessened just a bit at Cassandra's sudden outburst. It wasn't much, but it was enough, and as the bird struck, Cassandra moved her head just enough to avoid the brunt of the attack. One talon scraped painfully down the side of her face and tore out a chunk of hair, but the other talon struck home, taking an eye from its socket.

However, it was not Cassandra's eye but her opponent's. The woman released her immediately and fell back, holding her face. The larger woman toppled down the steep steps, breaking bones along the way. She kept her hand tight around her wounded eye socket and blood soaked her hand and ran between her fingers as the giant bird sat in the middle of the pit and enjoyed its eyeball snack. Cassandra took the opportunity to sit on the top step and painfully move her bound hands over her legs so they were in front of her. She could use them then, even though they remained bound.

She stood and looked at her opponent, who was at the foot of the steps, one leg bent awkwardly. She was holding her eye and writhing in pain. Cassandra glanced at Lita and nodded, just as Cassandra's first opponent had. Cassandra approached Maltor and asked for the snake. The snake handlers acted and put the snake in a bag and handed it to Maltor.

The king held it there momentarily and asked, "Are you sure?"

"Of course," Cassandra confirmed, holding out her bound hands.

Maltor looked her naked form up and down, and the lust was evident on his face. He handed the sack over to her.

"No, Cassandra, you don't need the snake; you have her beat!" Lita yelled from inside the enclosure.

Cassandra did not turn or slow and continued her trek back to the pit where her opponent was on one knee, trying to recover.

"I will need it! Don't use it!" Lita continued to plead.

Cassandra finally made it to her opponent, who looked up at her, the grim wound now evident as she pulled a shaking hand from it. Cassandra smacked the bag a few times to rile the serpent and wasted no time emptying it on her head. The viper struck her twice on the face and slithered away. The woman dropped immediately and started convulsing. In an ironic twist, as the Tribe of the Serpent won the fight, the vulture ate the snake before it could escape.

Many cheered for her and whistled their approval as she walked naked to the old scorpion king and held out her hands. With a disgusted look, knowing that he was out of warriors and would have no queen, King Dazor tossed her loincloth to her. Cassandra walked back into her enclosure. If Jozerah had not been there with his whip, Cassandra knew that Lita would have beaten her senseless. Instead, the shamans helped untie her hands, and she dressed quickly. She had no significant wounds, though her pelvic bone and stomach ached. Maltor did not allow any healing for her this time since the shamans had precious little to give.

Lita fought soon after, and true to her word, she desperately needed the viper to win her match against a giant of a woman in the Culiem Tribe. Ultimately, her opponent beat her to within an inch of her life, and Lita was out of the tournament. That left Cassandra alone in the Serpent Tribe at the end of the second round. The final five hopefuls consisted of Cassandra, two from the Culiem Tribe, and two from the Sleeth Tribe. She would have to fight two more times. She tried to meditate some more and find peace within her while Grink rebandaged her arm and cleaned the cuts to her face caused by the vulture's talons.

In a strange rule that the barbarians had enacted, since both the Culiem and Sleeth Tribes had two remaining participants, a two-on-one was enforced, guaranteeing a victory for the tribe with two participants. In this instance, two warriors from the Sleeth Tribe fought one from the Culiem Tribe. They easily won, and the match was a formality. As usual, the culiem warrior was taken as a prize, but so was one of the sleeth warriors. The king of the Sleeth Tribe, King Brenner, made the decision of which warrior to keep to fight in the final round. The other one was not only taken by King Boskel of the Culiem Tribe but was also out of the tournament. That left one warrior in the Culiem Tribe, one in the Sleeth Tribe, and Cassandra.

Cassandra and the lone fighter from the Culiem Tribe would match up next. Whoever won would fight the last warrior in the Sleeth Tribe for queenship. The sun was beginning to set when Cassandra took the pit for the third time. Many of the gathered barbarians cheered for her. As her popularity among them grew, so did her competition. She had fought twice and barely won against the weakest tribes. To succeed, she would now have to win against the two strongest tribes. She decided then that the only way to win would be through magic. She would need to do so in a way that Maltor would not see it.

The warrior from the Culiem Tribe made her way down the steps with a fairy in tow. The tribe had not used their animal, so she brought it before the match began. This woman was like Cassandra's first opponent, built the same and with strange eyes and six fingers on each hand. After her first match, she learned that the creature, a snevol, was native to Yaddaton and was a hybrid race of the sleeth.

The snevols were super-fast and very vicious, as Cassandra had learned in her first match. She focused on the fairy, and like the fairies who had been tethered to King Boskel, it still wore a gag in its mouth. However, its hands were unbound and not attached to any harness. It fluttered around Cassandra's opponent like an agitated butterfly. It could do whatever it wanted, and Cassandra knew it would be a nuisance during the fight, but it could not bite her. Maltor said the bite was deadly, so she was glad that weapon remained neutralized.

As she waited for the horn to sound, she discovered that the arcane symbols gathered around the fairy and became clear and focused. She watched in amazement as the characters danced in the air around the tiny sprite. She remembered from her studies at Victoria's school that the little fairies were conduits of magic. That gave her an idea as she assembled a defense to counteract the speed of the snevol. She used the most concentrated symbols to cast a spell she did not know, but one Cassandra thought she could wield with a high chance of success. It was a spell to make her opponent sluggish and slow her movements. Cassandra hoped that it would make the speed of the snevol human-like. If it worked, Cassandra would have a chance, and the snevol would lose her advantage.

The horn sounded just as Cassandra inconspicuously cast the spell with a slight wave of her hand. It was an apparent success as her opponent moved much closer to human speed, and Cassandra caught her with a left jab as she tried to run behind her. The stunned woman fell to the ground, and Cassandra was there to quickly pin her. However, she immediately felt the fluttering of the butterfly wings as the fairy moved in to gouge her eyes.

Cassandra had to close her eyes tight to avoid having them raked out by the tiny, clawed fingers. Still, the fairy continued its assault even as she clenched her eyes tight. The fairy raked her eyelids, drawing blood on both, and tried desperately to open them so it could attack her eyes. Being blind did not bode well for her, and her opponent quickly broke the pin and went on the offensive. The woman was an excellent fighter, and if Cassandra had not slowed her with a spell, she imagined the match would already be over. Even at human speed, the woman would be hard to beat and nearly impossible with the help of the culiem fairy.

She decided to focus on the fairy first. She grabbed it, and it clawed her hands, but at least she could open her eyes. She opened them in time to see a sucker punch from her opponent that laid her low. Her grip on the fairy failed, and it flew away. She shook her head, trying to clear the cobwebs from the punch, and as she sat up, her opponent pushed her down and pinned her. Cassandra could do little as the woman started raining punches upon her face. She tried to buck her off, but the fairy had latched on to one of her legs and dug deep scratches into her right thigh. The snevol battered her, and she needed help.

She could not use her magic, at least not visibly, and she had no spell to attack the vicious snevol secretly. She tried to recall magic to enhance her powers. If she could find a way to give herself a little strength, even if just for a moment, she could possibly break free from the pin. Her eyes closed tight as she tried to protect herself from the punches. Her torn lip bled, and her cheeks swelled. Each hit made her see stars, and she knew her opponent would soon beat her unconscious.

She knew precisely where the fairy was because it was scratching her thigh, raking repeatedly in the same spot, causing excruciating pain. She drew the energy from within the air around the fairy and brought it into her opened wound that the creature was causing, giving her a surge of incredible power in her right leg. She used the opportunity to slam her knee hard into her opponent's back. She heard the air escape her lungs, and she went flying off her. Cassandra stood, and the fairy took flight, understanding the danger it now faced. However, it wasn't enough as Cassandra performed a perfect circle kick that caught the little creature squarely, and it dropped to the sand, either dazed or dead.

Cassandra turned to face her opponent, who was now standing but trying to catch her breath, one hand on her back. Cassandra wiped the blood from her torn eyelids, but one eye swelled shut from her beating. Still, she could see well enough to fight and knew to use her right leg as long as possible, the magic from her spell still tingling it with power. However, even then, the temporary strength faded with the fairy no longer close. As Cassandra tried to reorient herself, the snevol jumped her, surprised once again at the slowness of her actions. Cassandra saw her attack, and her leg whipped while the magic remained.

The woman went flying as ribs cracked, and one punctured her lung. Cassandra wasted no time continuing the attack, using the stomping technique her prior opponent had used before tragically losing an eye. It only took two stomps to the midriff before the woman conceded. Cassandra checked on the fairy and was glad it was still alive. She gently picked it up and brought it back to King Boskel as two men dragged the snevol to Maltor so he could claim his prize.

The king looked at her disdainfully but nodded and took the injured fairy. His tribe was now eliminated, the fact punctuated by Maltor's rape of the snevol. The gathered mass cheered loudly for Cassandra now as she walked past the spectacle of Maltor and ignored his knowing grin. She had made it to the final round, precisely as Maltor had predicted, and the gathered barbarians approved. Maltor's plan was working, making her sick.

She sat hard on the sand as the two shamans spent the rest of their healing energy to cure her wounds as much as they were able. She basked in the warmth of the healing power. She watched as they redrew the circle in the pit, and the not-so-happy sleeth announcer lit braziers around the stadium as dusk settled upon the desert. There would be one more fight. She closed her eyes and tried desperately to summon her energy and courage to complete the impossible task. Maltor did not suspect her use of magic in her last match, which gave her hope. She would use it again if she needed to against her final opponent.

Maltor came over to her as the shamans rebandaged her arm. He knelt, and his expression was serious when she eventually looked him in the eye. She knew how important this was to his reputation; he had taken an awful risk on her, and now there was a chance it could pay off. She could not believe she was still there. Cassandra felt overmatched and outfought in each bout, yet she remained. She ached all over and wasn't sure she would deliver on what Maltor desired. Looking into his eyes, she could see how much he cared for her. She wasn't sure if the savage people knew what love was, but he probably felt something close to that. She wanted to prevail, not for him, but for herself. She had come this far, and she would try to see it through.

"My queen, there is one more fight. How are your wounds?"

Cassandra held up her arm as Grink wrapped it, and the shaman made brief eye contact with the king before looking away.

"Yes, yes, very good. Strenna has healed the wounds!" Grink said nervously.

Maltor didn't even look at the man but kept his eyes locked with Cassandra's. "Your final opponent is dangerous. She is a full-blooded sleeth and very powerful."

"Great," Cassandra said, and she lay her head back against the rock wall of the enclosure.

"She is not only strong and skilled, but she has a very venomous bite. Two of her three opponents today are still struggling to survive. Beware her bite, do you understand?"

"Of course. I will try," Cassandra said, trying to relax.

Maltor stood and watched over her momentarily, then returned to his throne. The announcer gained the crowd's attention and they quieted down. Grink and Bok helped Cassandra to stand as she grimaced with pain, everything seeming to hurt. The worst was her forearm, but her lip and eye also throbbed. She could not see out of her swollen right eye. Grink's healing did little to help that nasty wound. She started toward the entrance, and her leg felt on fire. The little scratches from the fairy were deeper and more painful than she first imagined. Red lines of blood showed on her thigh from the vicious attack, and the pain there made her limp from the enclosure to stand beside Maltor.

The announcer introduced her opponent first. "And now, for our finale between Tribe Serpent and Tribe Sleeth!"

The spectators rose to cheer and remained standing. The sleeth announcer then turned to the champion of the Sleeth Tribe and raised his hand to dramatic effect.

"And now the undisputed champion of the Sleeth Tribe, a full-blooded and deadly sleeth who has obliterated all her opponents today. Let's welcome Roxin to the ring!"

The barbarians cheered, and a massive woman made her way from the sleeth enclosure, down the steps and to the middle of the pit. She was nearly seven feet tall, and her skin had a greenish hue. She had no hair on her head but had scales like a crocodile. Her eyes were snake-like, as was her tongue, which slipped out of her mouth every so often. She walked slowly, confidently and with her arms raised over her head in victory. The creature knew what outcome was in store for Cassandra.

"I have to fight that?" Cassandra asked.

She could not believe the creature's size, which towered nearly two feet over her. She also was repulsed by the fact King Brenner would take such a creature as a bride.

After the cheering died down, the announcer introduced Cassandra in a less flattering way and with less enthusiasm. "And now the challenger, an outlander from the Serpent Tribe who has somehow escaped each match without a loss. She has yet to face the Sleeth Tribe, so her task is difficult. Welcome to the ring, Cassandra Rho."

The barbarians cheered more loudly than they did for Roxin and for a longer time. Cassandra could not believe her eyes or ears as she limped down the steps, nearly falling several times. When she finally made it to the circle, the savages were cheering for her. No one had ever cheered for her. Unfortunately, all the cheering only made Roxin angry as her nostrils flared and her muscles flexed. Cassandra offered a weak smile, and the creature hissed at her.

"Great," Cassandra whispered.

"One of these fine warriors will be the queen of their respective tribe. May the best fighter win!" the announcer said, leaving the ring.

As they waited for the horn to blow, Cassandra closed her eyes and began to meditate once more, trying to ignore the pain that seemed to wrack her entire body. The horn sounded, and they rushed in. Cassandra tried her jumping leg lock since Roxin was so much taller. She wrapped one leg around her neck and tried to pull her forward, but it was like trying to pull down a deeply rooted tree. Roxin grabbed Cassandra by the arms and flipped her off her. Cassandra rolled with the throw and was back on her feet instantly. Roxin was there, quicker than Cassandra estimated for one of her size.

Roxin tried a swing with her fist, and Cassandra barely dodged it by falling backward. She was on her back and could see a large foot about to stomp on her face. She escaped at the last moment, sand splashing over her as the foot smacked the ground. Cassandra was up and ready to fight but did not have a lot of options against her giant opponent. Roxin appeared to have no weaknesses. She searched for the arcane symbols, and they faintly answered her call.

Roxin feigned another punch, and Cassandra ducked it. However, that was not the sleeth's actual attack. Instead, she kicked out with her powerful leg, straight for Cassandra's head. Cassandra saw it at the last moment and dodged most of the attack. The powerful foot clipped her and spun her to the ground. Dizziness overcame her, but she shook it off, understanding that she had to keep moving. She started to spring away, but two strong arms wrapped around her from behind. She kicked and struggled, but Roxin pinned her arms to her sides, and her kicks, though perfectly aimed for Roxin's knees, did minor damage.

Roxin squeezed in response, and Cassandra could feel her breath being forced out. She was facing the barbarian spectators and could see them cheering and waving their pennants. Cassandra could also feel the snake-like tongue on her neck, and Maltor's warning about the dangerous bite had her near panicking. Cassandra used the only weapon she had left and slammed the back of her head into the face of the sleeth. Roxin's grip loosened immediately, so Cassandra hit her again, and Roxin dropped her.

She touched the ground running and turned to see the warrior holding her nose and wobbling on her feet. Blood trickled from her hand and dripped in the sand. The creature was stunned, and Cassandra needed to move fast to finish her. She sprinted in and jumped with a flying circle kick. As she came around the spin, she saw that it had all been a ruse as a smiling Roxin met her. The sleeth caught her leg and spun her around several times before slamming her face first into the sand.

The hit knocked the wind out of Cassandra; worse, Roxin held on to her leg. The large sleeth knelt and slammed a fist into Cassandra's back. Cassandra heard a snap and immediately felt a terribly sharp pain in her side. She could only assume her rib had broken. The pain was unbearable, and the second hit in the same spot drove the broken rib into her lung. Now the pain overcame her, and Cassandra struggled to find her breath. She gasped as Roxin turned her over and placed a heavy knee on her throat. She couldn't breathe, and there was no way to remove the creature. She struggled mightily, trying to pry the woman off, but to no effect. The world started going black as she gasped for breath. All she saw was the awful smile from the sleeth as she passed out. Cassandra drifted in and out of consciousness as Roxin had her way with her.

Once Cassandra was motionless, Roxin stood over her, letting out a mighty victory roar. The barbarians cheered her on, and more than one yelled for her to disrobe her opponent. However, Roxin seemed to have something else in mind, and it did not involve disrobing Cassandra or letting her submit.

She took up Cassandra's injured arm and started unwrapping the bandages. Even the slightest movement had Cassandra moaning, but the sleeth did quick work, exposing the wound. She felt around for the needles within, and once she found them, she contorted Cassandra's arm so that they pierced through her skin once more. Cassandra fully regained consciousness and screamed. Between the pain in her arm and the stabbing pain in her chest, she truly felt like she was dying. There was no way to interrupt Roxin's play as the sleeth smacked Cassandra's forearm hard enough to break the needle in several more places. She threw Cassandra's arm down, and Cassandra slowly brought it up in front of her. To her horror, she saw five pieces sticking out of her skin. Her forearm looked like a cactus and felt like it had been stabbed in many places.

Roxin then effortlessly picked Cassandra up over her head for just a moment, bringing her down hard on her knee in a move that nearly broke her back. However, Roxin ensured Cassandra's wounded side crashed into her knee, breaking several more ribs, and Cassandra almost passed out from the pain. Roxin stood over Cassandra's limp form and again kicked her hard in the ribs. Cassandra lay motionless and closer to death than she had ever been. She felt the sleeth pull her over onto her back and lean in close. Cassandra wheezed and held her arm to her chest. She felt the sensation of blood trickling from her mouth.

She knew at that moment the vicious creature would kill her. She could not focus on the arcane symbols because of the pain and couldn't fight. She would lose and probably die in the awful pit. She thought of her mother and Kessi and of Binta and Greyson. She longed to see them but knew that was a dream she would never fulfill. A silent tear ran down her cheek as she finally realized she would lose, and the tremendous amount of pain wracking her body had her fearing to move. She closed her eyes as the beast leaned in closer.

She felt the flick of Roxin's serpent tongue on her neck a few times before she felt the bite. The teeth sank into her neck, and she could feel the venom pumping through her body. It made her sick immediately, and she moved into the fetal position for not the first time that day. Roxin raised her arms in victory, and the spectators cheered. She turned to her king, who nodded and grinned. He motioned for Roxin to bring her dying opponent to him. He would take his spoils before her body grew too cold.

Cassandra hugged her arm to her chest and felt the venom being expelled through her hip as the thick substance trickled out of her through the snake brand. She knew Roxin would think the venom paralyzed her, and she slowly formulated a plan as she lay there. Cassandra tuned out the crowd and focused on her pain. She would have to do something quickly, for the window of opportunity would close fast with her sleeth opponent.

She felt around her wounded and tender arm and determined which needle spike was the longest. She took a deep breath and pulled the needle out of her arm, and the pain was excruciating. Her moans and whimpers sounded like someone in their death throes, so Roxin paid her no mind as she walked past her and stood with her arms raised in victory toward the crowd.

Cassandra summoned her energy and stood quickly. The effort nearly made her black out, but somehow, she remained conscious. Roxin had her back to her and was slowly turning around when Cassandra started running toward the sleeth with what little strength remained in her bat-tered body. She jumped just as Roxin turned, and the sleeth dodged the human missile as Cassandra landed awkwardly in the sand behind the sleeth. However, Cassandra's true attack had succeeded and Roxin fell to her knees as Cassandra rose once more. She staggered over to stand before the sleeth, who had the needle spike sticking in her eye. Cassandra could see the tip protruding from the warrior's pupil as blood poured from the vicious wound and began to pool on the ground in front of Roxin.

Cassandra did not know how the woman remained alive but knew the wound had to be fatal. She noticed then that the entire stadium was quiet as the horde of barbarians looked on, anticipating the kill. Cassandra looked back to Roxin, and the snake woman's mouth moved as if she was trying to speak, but no words came out. Anger welled within Cassandra, a lifetime of rage at being abused, belittled, bullied, and mistreated. With every bit of energy she had left in her broken body, she punched Roxin's injured eye, driving the spike the rest of the way into the warrior's brain. The sleeth toppled over backward and died.

There was stunned silence for a long while before the barbarian spectators screamed and yelled. They chanted her name—not outlander as they had called her earlier. Now they chanted, "Rho! Rho! Rho!"

She struggled to keep her footing as the crowd cheered her, the lights of the braziers grew blurry, and the many faces of the crowd became unfocused. She was in a terrific amount of pain and near death herself. Her legs finally gave out, and she fell to the ground.

Strong arms grabbed her before she hit the sand and pulled her up. Maltor was there, and he took her into his arms. She looked up at him, her one good eye barely able to focus, but she could make out his smiling face. Now the crowd was chanting her name and Maltor's simultaneously. Cassandra ran a hand over his face and returned the smile. She had done it; she had won the tournament. She had won the most important event that the barbarians held, and so had Vixa. They had done it together.

"Let's go home, my queen," Maltor said with a smile.

Cassandra lay her head on his chest, slipping into a happy and relieved unconsciousness.

Epilogue

He New Order sat around their usual table in the castle of Pelesea. All were in attendance except the elven brothers Von and Lenore, and of course, Alleah. Von and Lenore had business in the elven city of Nessor, and Alleah was on her holy quest to Varish with Greyson. That left Kringus, Penelope, Victoria, Daro, and the recently returned Arrin. Kringus had left Arrin in Farmer's Stop, sick and in need of healing. Kringus had been forced to leave the captain of his army, his best friend, in the care of the good people of that small community. The urgency he felt to deliver Cassandra Rho's dead mother to Pelesea forced his hand. He had regretted that move ever since, but it seemed the wisest choice at that moment. When Arrin had arrived home, Kringus sent for him, and they rejoiced for most of the night, two friends catching up on recent events.

On that spring morning, the sun bathed the room, and Penelope even had a few of the windows open, letting in a marvelous warm breeze. The friends shared some small talk as always, but Kringus's eyes were drawn to Alleah's seat more and more as the conversation continued. Eventually, the small talk subsided, and all eyes were on the king, who now wore a worried expression. He focused on Alleah's chair, concerned by her long absence.

It took him a few minutes to realize everyone had stopped talking and the breakfast utensils had grown silent. He looked around the table at all the serious stares. All of them knew something important was happening in the world; they all seemed to sense it. They needed a leader, and Kringus was not only the king of Pelesea but also the leader of their magnificent group. Looking around the table at the blank stares, he couldn't help but smile. When he did, everyone slowly went back to their food. However, the conversations had permanently ceased as the friends awaited his opening remarks.

And so he began. "Friends, I am so glad you have joined Penelope and me today for breakfast. Von and Lenore are on their usual spring excursion to Nessor, and we still await Alleah's return. However, it is wonderful to see the rest of you. Especially my good friend, Arrin, whom I feared lost to us a few months ago in the despicable town of Oldorburg."

"A toast to your health, Arrin," Penelope added, lifting her goblet of juice.

"Here," Kringus agreed, lifting his goblet filled with something more potent than juice.

The friends toasted Arrin's good health, and Kringus continued, "So, we might as well start our meeting with you, good captain. What is the word from Oldorburg?"

"It is good, my king. As you and I discussed last evening, the town is now under the rule of Sheriff Max, though some would argue his comely wife Tanna may be the one running things."

There were a few chuckles around the table, and Kringus was glad for the light mood because he knew what was coming next, making the hairs on his neck stand on end.

"But there are no signs of the priests of Meshlor in Oldorburg. Max and his men have eradicated them, and the town once more lives in peace, if it ever really did before," Arrin continued.

"And you are sure that the priests are gone?" Penelope asked.

"Yes, my men and I stayed there all winter to ensure it. If it was a farce, it was a damned good one, my lady, for we ate well, rested well, and drank even better!"

All laughed at that until Kringus asked with a serious note, "What of Lord D'Breeth?"

Arrin just shook his head in honest ignorance. "We saw no sign of him, and Max could not elaborate. He feels that the man fled with the leaders of that awful church, because no one saw him again after that night we fought."

That seemed to satisfy Kringus, as he nodded and moved to the next order of business. He inched closer to the real reason for the meeting but prolonged it just a bit longer to address the absence of Alleah.

"An empty chair sits for Alleah, and I hope to see it filled again soon," he began. "She and that Greyson fellow, along with a small contingent of her sisters in faith, left our dear city nearly half a year ago in search of answers."

Everyone grew quiet, understanding that they should have returned months earlier. Something was amiss. It broke Kringus's heart because he had forbidden her to go at first but had relented when she had a small army to escort her. He had felt the party was safe with that large a group, and he trusted Greyson, even if he did ogle Penelope every time he saw her. He had a bad feeling in his stomach that he had made another grave mistake. Following his error in handling Oldorburg, this error in judgment made him feel he was slipping as king.

"No news is upsetting, but it does not mean they ran into trouble. Perhaps they are on the trail for answers," Lady Victoria added, breaking the tense silence.

Kringus smiled the most genuine smile he could muster, which was not a reasonable effort at all, and his friends saw through it, saw his pain.

"And so, we shall wait to hear her report, hopefully by the next time this group meets again," Penelope said, ending that part of the meeting. "Daro, you have news from Novafontera?" she continued.

Daro had arrived weeks earlier and disclosed the events in the cursed city's bowels to Kringus and Penelope. The queen asked him to repeat the information more concisely at the meeting. He nodded at her reference, wiped his mouth, and stood to garner everyone's attention.

"I have been beneath the city," he began.

"Of Novafontera?" Arrin asked as he and Victoria shared a surprised look.

"Yes, a few allies and myself."

"Allies?" Victoria asked.

"I'll get to that, good lady. First, I want you to know that we encountered a great evil there, a demon of no small sort. The thing nearly killed us all, and if we had not fought alongside the vampire lord, Heinsvick—"

Arrin dropped his goblet at the remark and quickly pushed his chair from the table. He watched the fine wine pour to the floor, unable to get up to stop it, his shocked expression fixed on the ranger.

"Has your near-death experience thrown your mind back into infancy, Arrin? Shall Victoria feed you the rest of your breakfast?" Daro asked.

That snapped the captain from his trance, and he grumbled something under his breath and wiped up the spilled drink with his napkin. All laughed at the comment, and even Arrin had difficulty stifling a grin.

"So, how did this happen?" Victoria asked, handing Arrin her napkin as he continued to sop up the drink.

"He was the old lord of the city, as we suspected. He bade us help him defeat the demon so he could reclaim his throne."

"So, two enemies worked together for a common goal," Penelope added.

"Yes, except …" Daro began, but he trailed off as his thoughts took him back to the catacombs of Novafontera and, more precisely, Sasha.

"Except what?" Arrin prodded.

"Except, he did not feel like an enemy. I'm not sure he ever was."

"You're serious?" Arrin added with a snort.

Daro could only nod, his expression blank. Kringus and Penelope shared a concerned glance, and Kringus stood to bring the attention to himself once more. He strolled around the table, and when he passed Arrin, he tossed his napkin for the man to use. Arrin doubled his efforts as Kringus and Victoria shared a knowing smile.

"This brings us to the most important part of this meeting. Daro brought us an emissary from Novafontera. One who seems to have many answers," Kringus said, patting Daro's shoulder as he passed him.

"Yes, he saved us all, except the vampire, who perished in the fight," Daro added.

Silence followed the grim comment, so Kringus picked back up. "The strange man has many answers, or so he says, but has not divulged any information yet."

"Where has this man been staying?" Arrin asked.

"Freely within the city proper," Penelope answered.

"Yes, I have seen him walking about," Victoria added. "He is demon-kind."

"What?" Arrin asked in shock as he finally cleaned up his spilled drink and regained his seat.

"It is true," Kringus confirmed, taking his seat as well. "And he is now willing to share the information he has longed to tell the New Order for the many weeks he has pranced around our city."

"You had him followed, didn't you?" Penelope asked accusingly.

"Of course not," Kringus said, not looking her in the eye.

Daro shook his head and smiled as he took a giant bite of food. Kringus knew the queen was right, and the ranger always seemed to enjoy it when the queen scolded Kringus in front of everyone.

Penelope kept her piercing green eyes on him until he broke, snapping his head her way and saying, "Yes, I had him followed. He is a demon; we can't have demons running free within our city!"

He then took a large gulp of his wine to distract himself from her rebuttal. He did not notice the knowing glance the queen and Victoria briefly shared.

"Pelesea is a free city, and so guests should be free to roam it until given reason otherwise," the queen said.

Kringus knew she was right but would not let the conversation continue. Instead, he motioned for a guard at the door to bring Inuentas. The man opened the door, and the half-demon came strolling in. He wore a blue silk shirt that contrasted nicely with his red skin. His black hair was parted down the middle, proudly showing off the two small black horns on his forehead. His pants were tan, and he wore a black belt with a sword attached. His barbed tail waved menacingly behind him as he walked to the table, whistling a tune. His strange black boots clicked loudly as he advanced, and all immediately noticed that the material that those shiny boots were made of seemed foreign.

When Inuentas finally made the end of the table, he took off his belt and tossed it and the sheathed sword onto it. The action had Arrin nearly drawing his blade, but Kringus waved him off. Daro continued eating his breakfast as if he had often seen this routine. They had traveled together from Novafontera and fought side by side, so the strange actions had little effect on the ranger.

"They are human skin," Inuentas said.

"What?" Kringus asked.

"The boots. I saw all of you admiring them and wanted to let you know what they are comprised of."

Kringus gritted his teeth, and Arrin watched for his reaction. Kringus knew that if he decided to act, Arrin would follow in support, as he always did.

"Beg your pardon, Your Majesty," Inuentas said with a bow. "I come from a different place, and such accessories are not unusual. Besides, they were a gift, and I had nothing to do with the deaths of those skinned."

"Enough small talk," Kringus said. "What information do you have for us?"

The demon counted with his fingers as he made eye contact with everyone at the table. After his count, he held up five fingers.

"You promised the New Order, but only five are present."

"I promised you nothing, demon," Kringus said, the muscles in his neck flexing.

Penelope put a soothing hand on her husband's forearm and said, "The missing three will be missing for a while longer. If your information is urgent, we ask that you tell us now."

Inuentas slammed both hands down on the table, jarring dishes and spilling the rest of Arrin's wine. The captain stood up and put his hand on the hilt of his weapon as Daro grabbed seconds from the platter and even refilled his goblet, not the least concerned by the strange demon.

With a broad smile, Inuentas said, "Well now, aren't you an angel straight from the heavens?" while staring at Penelope.

Victoria gasped, and Penelope seemed to blanch at the comment, but Kringus steeled his resolve and said, "Tell us the information you have, demon, or leave."

Inuentas stood once more and studied the king and queen. Kringus could tell the demon had a rebuttal but decided not to say anything. Instead, Inuentas shrugged, saying, "The times are changing, and all life in your world is in extreme danger."

No one spoke, and even Daro stopped eating for a moment and turned his head to regard the creature that had saved him back in Novafontera. They all waited for the half-demon to continue.

"The demon lord, Marnelphion, is set to return to your world."

"Impossible," Penelope gasped.

"Not only possible, my dear lady, but unavoidable. He will come if your small group cannot prevent it."

"No one can summon a demon lord as powerful as Marnelphion. The original New Order cursed him as much as he cursed Novafontera," Kringus said.

"Not true, King. On the 666th anniversary of his banishing, a wicked and mighty priestess will try to open a gate to summon him forth. She could accomplish said gate with the correct pieces in place and on that precise date."

"How do you know all of this?" Victoria asked, her eyes wide with disbelief.

"My master, a demon lord just as powerful but not as chaotic as Marnelphion, has foreseen it. It is a prophecy that none can stop."

"Except the New Order," Kringus added doubtfully, crossing his arms over his massive chest.

"Exactly!" Inuentas said, then grabbed a biscuit from one of the table platters. He added, between chewing, "It is difficult to tell if the New Order can stop the summoning. The task is tall, and the odds are against you. However, that is where I come in."

"Explain," Arrin hissed, still standing and at the ready.

If the demon realized Arrin's vigilance, he did not acknowledge it. "If the New Order fails to stop the summoning, I will destroy Marnelphion," he said with a smile, then reached for his sword and added, "With this."

He brought the red-handled sword from its sheath and held it up for all to see. The blade was serrated and made of a shiny silver metal foreign to Kringus. The only thing the king knew for sure was that the edge looked extraordinarily sharp, and just seeing it made Kringus believe only a powerful creature could wield it.

"So, when will this anniversary take place?" Kringus asked.

"In less than fifteen months," Victoria answered before Inuentas did.

The demon turned his head to regard her, food falling from his mouth as he did. After the initial shock, he nodded his agreement. "In less than fifteen months, the priestess, simply known as Lady Matilda, high priestess of Marnelphion, will attempt to open the gate."

"Is she actually that powerful?" Kringus asked doubtfully.

"Yes, she is powerful enough to perform the ceremony. But, no, she needs help."

"What kind of help?" Penelope asked.

"It must be done while the moon is high in the sky on the anniversary date. She will need to sacrifice 666 humans at that time, with the last one being the virgin child of the lich-god, Kane."

"Lich-god?" Arrin asked.

"Kane, the lich who assisted the original New Order, who ascended into godhood shortly after," Victoria said.

Inuentas cocked a thumb at the powerful wizard and said, "I like this one."

"He has a son?" Kringus asked.

"Daughter," Inuentas said with a shake of his head as he took another biscuit.

"So, we either kill this Lady Matilda or the daughter of Kane?" Kringus said.

"Exactly!" Inuentas said, more food falling from his mouth. "Your human food is tasty but with a weird consistency. You should try cartilage; it adds stability."

Arrin made a face and finally relaxed his stance. "This makes no sense, Kringus," he said with a shake of his head.

"No, it doesn't, but I believe him."

"Thank you, my king," Inuentas said with a low bow. "So, kill Matilda, kill the offspring, or my favorite option, deflower the offspring. I hear she is quite stunning."

"Where can we find this Lady Matilda?" Penelope asked.

"In Varish in her mountain fortress—at least that is where she is now."

"What do you mean, demon?" Kringus asked.

"She was here recently, under your very nose. As was the daughter of Kane."

All stopped what they were doing, even Daro, and looked on with great suspicion but much interest. Inuentas held his arms out wide and smiled so big his mouth seemed to swallow his face.

"Spit it out, demon," Kringus finally said after a few moments, slamming his fist upon the table.

"Lady Matilda was here very recently," Inuentas said.

"Barlow, the barkeep at Poppy's Inn on the south end of Pelesea, mentioned a strange woman traveling with Malikai," the queen added, speaking directly to Kringus.

Kringus nodded and added, "Yes, and the remains we found there would coincide with demonic sacrifices."

"The child of Kane is Cassandra Rho," Inuentas added.

"Matilda was here and kidnapped Cassandra?" Victoria asked, fearing that her father was involved.

"No," Inuentas said, raising a hand to stop her line of reasoning. "She was chasing Cassandra, but we do not feel she has found her."

"Boz!" Penelope exclaimed. "I knew it!"

Kringus looked at his wife and nodded his acknowledgment. They had had this conversation in private several times since Cassandra's death. Kringus had not wanted to believe that Boz had betrayed and played him for a fool, but now he accepted the fact. Boz had kidnapped Cassandra in a most remarkable scheme.

"So, Cassandra Rho is not dead?" Kringus asked.

"Far from it. Matilda chases her now."

"And the carofex, Boz?" Penelope asked.

Inuentas shrugged his shoulders and shook his head. "I do not know this creature and do not know the role he plays in all of this."

"So, what do we do?" Victoria asked, slumping back in her chair after hearing the incredible tale.

"We find Cassandra before Matilda does," Kringus answered.

Inuentas acknowledged that with a smile.

Kessi was shoved back into her cell, her hand bandaged but still bleeding. She stumbled in and nearly fell from the force as the door clanged shut behind her. She turned to see the two nervous guards start away. They were in the vampire's lair and knew what it could do, especially when harm came to Kessi or her cellmates. They exited the door on the far side of the vampire's cell, then shut and locked it quickly. Kessi leaned her head against the cool bars and looked at the coffin. It was quiet. Emiline, the vampire that looked over Kessi and the other prisoners, was in there, perhaps sleeping. Kessi sighed as the guards left. She had tried to speak with the vampire many times, but the creature seemed lost and unwilling to listen.

A warm hand on her shoulder had her smiling and turning to regard her best friend, Sabrina. She and the other virgins, nearing three dozen in number, came out of the shadows now that the guards had taken their leave. The slaves had steadily expanded the cell as the number of virgins increased. So, although the total number of prisoners had nearly tripled since Kessi had arrived, the cell was much deeper now. Each day, emaciated slaves came to the cell, usually two at a time, to chip away at the wall to expand their prison. After a few weeks, the slaves would grow weak with hunger and fatigue, and Kessi would never see them again, new slaves taking their place. And so, the cycle continued; as the population grew, so did the cell size.

"Mayla, what did they do to you?" Sabrina asked, gently taking Kessi's hand and turning it palm up.

Blood soaked her bandage so much that it dripped to the floor. Kessi looked at her hand and recalled the unusual ritual Matilda forced her to partake in. The guards had taken her to a place deep in the bowels of the cave and into an area marked heavily with the symbols of their evil god. Skulls adorned the site, and the room contained a pentagram drawn on the floor in chalk and an altar, large enough for a person to lie on.

She had felt a horrible presence in that room and suspected she had been there before. The feeling was like waking from a bad dream and trying to shake the awful images, only to realize you couldn't remember any of it. All she knew was that she could not tell Sabrina or her other cell mates about that terrible place.

Several strange-looking men wearing dark robes had laid her on the table and held her down. One of them had extended her right arm and held it tight so that her hand dangled over the edge. Matilda and another young woman, dressed in a red dress and about Kessi's age, produced a blue medallion and placed it in a small bowl under her exposed hand. Kessi had not struggled at first because she knew it was pointless. But when Matilda produced a knife and cut deeply into the palm of her hand, Kessi fought to escape. When she curled her hand into a fist on instinct, the young woman in the red dress uncurled her fingers with incredible strength and held her hand flat for Matilda to gash it.

As Kessi's screams filled the cavernous room, Matilda chanted, prayed, and manipulated Kessi's wounded hand so the blood fell into the small bowl. At one point, the younger woman even let Kessi's hand go, which Kessi instinctively drew into a fist once more. The strong woman then squeezed Kessi's balled fist, opening the wound even further and eliciting more screams from her. Matilda continued chanting, and after a few moments, the bowl smoked and a terrible stench wafted up.

When Matilda had completed her chant, the younger woman reached in and took the medallion. Kessi had expected to see it covered in blood, but instead, it had been completely dry, and the stone glowed blue with a renewed vigor. Matilda and the woman looked at each other with knowing smiles, then they ushered Kessi away. She wanted to tell Sabrina the truth but did not want to scare her or the others, so she lied.

"They tried to get information from me, but I wouldn't talk because I still can't remember anything."

"What did they ask you?" Sabrina asked.

The other girls moved around her and circled her now. Kessi could see the fear on their faces, and she knew she wasn't a good liar. She was about to tell them the truth when a voice came from Emiline's room. "Is it time to hunt, Heinsvick?"

All turned to see Emiline, the vampire, standing next to her coffin, the lid ajar. Everyone backed away from the bars and to the back of the cell. All of them, except Kessi, stared at the creature with wide eyes.

"What did you say?" Kessi asked.

Emiline seemed to glide over to her, and Kessi could hear her cell mates beckoning for her to join them. She could not, however, because her jumbled mind was unwinding, trying to recall her past.

"Is it time to feast?" Emiline asked, now standing directly on the other side of the bars.

The vampire pointed to Kessi's bandaged hand, and Kessi knew then that the smell of blood had brought her forth.

"Did you say Heinsvick?" Kessi asked.

"Yes," Emiline whispered, then her eyes filled with tears as if the mere mention of the name stabbed at her heart.

She wailed and skittered back into her coffin and closed the lid. Kessi could still hear her crying within, sobbing hysterically, and her heart broke for the creature. She felt the presence of the other women as they slowly came into her peripheral vision to stand beside her, all staring at the coffin.

"What was that about, Mayla?" Sabrina asked.

Kessi turned to her as tears trickled down her face, and her bottom lip quivered.

"What is it? Did the vampire hurt you?" Kimmie, the youngest of the group, asked.

"No. And my name is not Mayla; it is Kessi Rho. I remember who I am and why I am here. I remember everything."

The women took a few steps back to give Kessi some air, and she slowly sank to her knees. She remembered Heinsvick and the ploy to fool Matilda, which she understood with horror had failed. Cassandra was in danger!

"Cassandra," she whispered.

"What?" Sabrina asked.

Kessi looked at her, tears streaking her face, and said, "We have to get out of here."

Cassandra awakened days later, and her entire body hurt, especially her chest and right forearm. She was lying on her familiar pillow bed, again in Maltor's tent. She wore the finest silk clothes that the barbarians could muster and had been bathed. Once more, she thought of who had cleaned and dressed her. She could not recall the trip back to the Serpent Tribe, but she remembered the tournament results: she had won. She closed her eyes and considered it again: she had bested them all!

She tried to sit, and it felt like a knife stabbed her lung. She let out a small yelp and eased back onto the pillows. She closed her eyes and waited for the pain to subside. When she finally opened them, Jak was kneeling beside her.

"Fetch Grink," the large man said.

Cassandra could not see but heard a commotion by the tent entrance and knew someone had just left.

"It is good to see you, my queen," Jak said with a genuine smile.

Cassandra tried to speak but could not. She was vaguely aware of the shamans coming to see her and struggled to stay conscious. Eventually, she slipped into a deep sleep. She felt the warm waves of healing energy that the shamans summoned, which made her sleep more.

Her lungs did not hurt, and the pain in her arm was minimal. She lost track of time. When she first heard it, she wasn't sure if perhaps she had dreamed it or if it was real. When she heard it again, she opened her eyes. The sun was bright outside, and she was still on the comfortable pillow bed.

She then realized that she wore the collar again, the other end tethered to the giant support pole. She concentrated on the sound she had heard, not daring to move. She didn't want to draw attention to herself, and she didn't want to feel that stabbing sensation in her chest again.

Then she heard the sound a third time, a tiny voice pleading, *Help me!*

She blinked her eyes open and waited for the voice again. And again, it came, and she knew it was a telepathic message; no words had been spoken. She looked around the room slowly, and her eyes settled on the fairy's cage. There she was confident she found the answer to the riddle. The little fairy sat in the cage with her hands on the bars as if it were a tiny prison, which Cassandra knew it was. When Cassandra looked at her, she sat up straighter and pointed to the small door.

Please, it begged her, the tiny voice echoing in Cassandra's mind.

"The queen awakens once more!" a guard at the door said. "Fetch Maltor."

A second guard outside the tent door ran off at once. Soon Jak and a third guard stood around her. She sighed and began to sit up. To her surprise, Jak bent and helped her. The pain in her chest was faint, and sitting felt good.

"Thirsty?" Jak asked.

Cassandra nodded, and Jak motioned to a nearby bucket. One of the other guards brought a ladle of water, and she sipped from it. It felt good to her parched throat, and she smiled at her captors. Perhaps being the queen would not be so bad. The savages treated her with respect, although they still chained her like a dog.

Maltor entered then, and she gasped in shock. He, too, had bathed, and his long dark hair was in a ponytail. And instead of the usual loincloth, he wore a white shirt, a pair of blue silky pants, and sandals. In truth, she found him attractive at that moment. He rushed to her and knelt, a smile beaming on his face.

"What?" Cassandra asked, but he silenced her by gently covering her mouth.

"I have waited nearly two weeks for you to recover from the tournament, my queen. All of us have waited," he added, waving to Jak and the other guards, who nodded in agreement.

"Two weeks?" she stammered.

"Yes, you have been healing for that time, and Grink has done a fine job," he added, grabbing her arm and examining the tight bandages.

"Shall I give the word, my king?" Jak asked.

Maltor looked at her, and she noticed his affection for her in his beaming face. He opened her mouth, forcing his fingers in and running them along her tongue and gums.

She pushed him away and smacked her mouth. "Why?" she asked, spitting the taste of his fingers out.

"Yes, she is ready. Tell them!" Maltor said, then stood.

Jak ran out of the tent, and Cassandra tried to stand. Her legs were wobbly, and Maltor grabbed her, steadying her.

"Tell who what?" she asked, once standing before him.

"Why, tell the tribe you have awakened. And tell them we will wed this day!" Maltor said with a giant smile.

He leaned in close, and his smile faded into a visage of pure lust. He whispered, "I have waited far too long to have you. Tonight, I will pleasure you like no other. Tonight, you will understand the merit of your husband."

Cassandra felt ill then. She was a prisoner there and would never have the same rights as the males. How could she marry into a tribe such as Maltor's? She thought of Binta and Kessi and remembered what it was like to be free. It had been so long ago; it took her many moments to remember what a simple walk down the streets of Oldorburg felt like or how a quiet trip to the library at Victoria's School of Magic made her tingle with excitement. She even considered Baxter and how his kiss made her feel versus the violent outbursts of the savage barbarian king. She could not stay; she had won the tournament to be queen to avoid a life in the procreation tent. But now what? She had not thought that far ahead because she had not expected to win the tournament.

"I will send for you when the sun begins to set, my queen. We will have a grand ceremony, followed by much food and drink. The whole tribe will attend!" Maltor said excitedly.

He moved close to her, put a strong arm around her waist, and said, "Then we will come here, and I will take you, and you will truly become my queen."

Cassandra wanted to spit in his face but managed to smile instead. He turned and left, and she eased back to a sitting position. Jak helped her, then moved to stand in his usual spot. She had precious little time to figure things out. She did not want her first sexual encounter to be with a barbarian man who thought of her only as a queen and not as an equal. She pulled the chain around her neck slightly and knew it wouldn't budge. Even if she managed to escape somehow and obtain a weapon, she couldn't possibly fight her way out of the vast desert.

Help me, came the fairy's cry once more.

She shook her head in frustration and looked up at the cage the fairy had called home for the last few months. And there, an answer came to her. The fairy still sat in its tiny prison and brightened when Cassandra made eye contact with her.

She pointed to the cage door again, and in her mind, Cassandra heard, *I am Gophia. Please help!*

More importantly to Cassandra, she saw the plethora of arcane symbols massed around the little fairy. They were crystal clear now and concentrated around the magical being, just like they had with the fairy in the tournament. She looked at her tightly wrapped forearm and understood she had taken a great deal of the needle from that arm in her last attack against Roxin. She quickly formulated a plan and nodded to Gophia, a smile forming on her face. She knew exactly how she would escape the barbarians.

About the Author

A fan of fantasy and science fiction from a young age, Phillip Martin dreamed about writing stories. He's used that desire to run roleplaying games and even develop them. His roleplaying stories have created countless adventures and worlds for the benefit of his closest friends. Finally, some of his vivid imaginings have been immortalized in print for others to enjoy. Phillip lives in Christiansburg, Virginia, and can be found at www.cassandra-rho.com.